ALASKA SPARK

BLAZING HEARTS WILDFIRE SERIES BOOK ONE

LOLO PAIGE

If you're resilient with love, we'll have no regrets!

Lo Lo Paige

Alaska Spark
Blazing Hearts Wildfire Series Book One

Copyright © 2020 by LoLo Paige
First published by LoLo Paige 2020
ISBN: 978-0-578-67685-2
Library of Congress Cataloging-in-Publication Data
TX0008881278

This is a work of fiction. Though based on actual events in a real setting, it is an imaginary story that never happened the way it is written. The author has taken artistic license with some details regarding locations and some wildland firefighting activities for the story to proceed smoothly. Every attempt has been made to make the rest as accurate as possible. Any resemblance to actual persons, living or dead, is entirely coincidental.

Designations used by companies to distinguish their products are often claimed as trademarks. All brand names and product names used in this book or on its cover are trade names, service marks, trademarks and registered trademarks of their respective owners. The publishers and the book are not associated with any product or vendor mentioned in this book. None of the companies referenced within the book have endorsed the book.

Front Cover Design by Sylvia Frost www.sfrostcovers.com
Editing by Three Point Author Services
www.threepointauthorservices.com
Proofread by Kelsea Koths, Kaitlin Nerlfi, and Margie Faraday
Promotional smokejumper photos courtesy of Buck Nelson, Fairbanks, Alaska
www.bucktrack.com
Promotional photos courtesy of Bobbi Doss, Hells Gate Fire Dept., Star Valley, Arizona

Contact publisher and author at
www.lolopaige.com

Dedicated to the memory of all wildland firefighters who have paid the ultimate sacrifice and to those who continue to risk their lives to protect people, property, and natural resources from the destructive force of fire in North America and overseas.

For my family and friends, living and non-living,
who encouraged me to be a writer and helped me to keep writing when I wanted to give up.
Thank You.

Cousin Donna, lover of romance: This one's for you.
I'm so sorry I didn't finish this in time.

FIRE LINE

Left it all behind
    like a fire out of control.
    Our love burned us to the ground
    from the wild fire in my soul.

Love tore us apart;
    burned out, can't ignite that spark.
    I can't take it when you're gone.
    I can't take it when you're home.

My barren heart is
    no place to shelter a dove.
    All that's left of the fire line
    is a hint of what was love.

– S. R. Cyres, 2020
    Anchorage, Alaska

*I*n her three years as a wildland firefighter, Tara Waters had not seen a firenado incinerate a house like a nuclear-powered blast.

Until today.

She prayed she never would again.

It wasn't her job to question whether the hand of God had hurled an apocalyptic firebrand, or whether the devil's finger had whirled stormy air into a fire vortex, inhaling oxygen and exhaling acrid smoke. Her job was to fight the damn fire. The storm fueled it with seventy mile-per-hour winds and spit lightning into the forest like a dragon drunk with power.

Tara stood two blocks from the main road leading into a subdivision near the southern edge of Butte, Montana. She squinted at the flames engulfing the one-story home. Dry stands of lodgepole pine and Douglas fir trees lured the hungry flames. The sound of crackling branches and popping needles echoed as sweet-smelling pine, honeysuckle, and sagebrush blended into the sharp reek of burning timber.

She spotted movement on the front porch of the burning house. Her spine numbed.

An elderly man with a walker stumbled down the porch steps. *No!* He didn't have a snowball's chance in hell to outrun the charging flames blitzing through crown after crown of towering trees.

"Dammit, someone didn't evacuate! Where's the city fire department?" Tara shot a distressed glance at the only road leading into this neighborhood, then back at her boss, Jim Dolan.

Jim barked into his hand-held radio. "Missoula crew needs backup and fast. We can't hold it away from the houses. We'll lose the entire subdivision if we don't get an engine in here now!"

A deep voice on his radio responded back.

Jim's expression mirrored the dread clutching Tara's chest. "They'll get an engine here when they can free one up."

"There's no time! We have to get him *now*." She lowered her goggles over her eyes. Flop sweat dripped down the lenses. Tara had never left anyone helpless and wasn't about to start now.

"I'll get him. I can do it." She took off and sprinted toward the man. *Legs, don't fail me now.*

"Tara, not enough time!" her boss yelled. "Get the hell back here. I'm ordering you!"

Resin snapped and tree trunks burst as if dynamited. Pine needles glowed red and crackled. Brown smoke spun to black, as flames rushed at the besieged homeowner.

Intense heat bit through Tara's flame-resistant, Nomex shirt and pants, scorching her chest and legs. She floundered through tumbleweed, tripping on rocks, and weaving around torched lodgepole pine. She tugged her orange neckerchief over her nose, willing herself to reach this man.

She pushed harder, faster. Fifty yards left, almost there... twenty-five... *I've got this.*

Smoke billowed and she lost sight of him. She skidded to a halt, her eyes piercing the smoke, frantically searching. When the smoke thinned, she caught a glimpse of him collapsed on the ground. He raised an outstretched arm. *He sees me!*

A sudden wind gust lunged a wall of flame forward, pitching fireballs bigger than anything she'd ever seen. Flames danced in front of the porch and the imperiled man disappeared inside a blanket of orange. If he screamed, Tara couldn't hear it. The fire robbed the air of sound except for its own tornadic roar. A scream lodged in her throat, searing it.

Somewhere, a nearby car gas tank exploded, causing her heart to stutter. She stumbled backward and hit the ground.

Tara choked back nausea as revulsion gripped her. Her body numbed despite the unforgiving heat. She could not will herself to stand. Her muscles wouldn't work. Paralyzed, she sat on the ground, glued to the unburnt green, transfixed by smoke and flame.

"Get out of there!" yelled a nearby voice as something slammed against her. Strong arms locked around her abdomen, lifting her and dragging her back.

She struggled for a grip on the moment, trying to free herself from the vise grip. "Let go!"

"Wait till the flame front passes," a deep voice pressed.

Internal hysteria seized her, and her breathing became sporadic and ragged. "I couldn't get him—"

"Nothing you could do," said the gruff voice. The arms restricting her released. A firefighter stepped around her and rested gloved hands on her shoulders. His once yellow shirt was sooty with grime, matching hers.

"Look at me."

She locked onto the taller firefighter's big blue eyes, an oasis in the orange and red chaos.

"I can't—can't breathe..." She couldn't inhale without coughing. Her mouth tasted like cinders and her stomach's contents still wanted out. She hated her confusion, her lack of control.

The man lifted Tara's filthy goggles onto her hardhat. He

placed a firm hand under her arm to support her. "Look at me. Inhale...exhale...you're going to be okay."

She focused on the gritty face looking down at hers. "Shouldn't have stopped me," she croaked, planting her boots apart for stability.

"You were in danger. I had to get you out."

"He was a dad...a grandpa..." she choked out, erupting into a coughing fit. The image of the man engulfed by flame had etched itself inside her head. She wanted to run screaming across the burnt black to erase it... *because you never run into the green. You could die.*

She almost had.

"He wasn't yours to save."

"Who are you, God? I can take care of myself." She gritted her teeth and stepped back.

The stranger let go of her shoulders and opened a water canteen, holding it out to her. "Take a sip."

"Thanks." She gulped greedily, then splashed water on her face. Her heart still knocked from the turbo injection of adrenaline. "Sorry about the God comment," she mumbled.

He gave her a dimpled smile. "No worries. You could have died with the homeowner. What's your name?"

"Tara." It came out angry and she didn't care. She swayed, then steadied herself. She raised her hands in front of her and squeezed her eyes closed. "Give me a minute. Where's the— where are we?" *Don't lose it. Not here, not now.*

"In the black. Out of harm's way." He pushed his goggles up onto his hardhat, revealing white circles around the pools of blue. Ash and grit streaked his neck and clung to the stubble on his rugged face.

He snapped his fingers. "Tara, look at me. You're safe. You'll be okay."

"But *he* isn't." She could hold back the tears, but not the tremor in her voice.

"You did what you could. Compartmentalize. Focus on the job." His deep baritone offered her a lifeline. It steadied her.

"Working on it." She eyed the flames moving away from them, her breathing still ragged.

He fixed his gaze on her and held it there. "Slow your breath. You'll hyperventilate."

She saw empathy in his eyes. "Okay, dammit. I *am*." She sucked in smoke-tainted air and blew it out, battling for normalcy. There was nothing normal about seeing a person burn to death and failing to prevent it.

Jim made his way to them and peered at Tara. "You okay?"

"Yes." *No.* She was still trying to figure how the fire reached the old man before she did. That was not supposed to happen.

Jim nodded at the firefighter. "O'Connor, thanks for helping out."

O'Connor smiled at Tara's boss. "Hey, Jim. Came around a building and saw her close to the flames." He motioned at her. "She's dazed, but okay."

Jim spat on the ground. "She tried to get a homeowner out. Did you see him?"

"No, just saw her on the ground in front of the flames. She seemed to be in shock," said O'Connor.

Tara snapped her brows together. "Hello, don't talk about me like I'm not here."

"Sorry, I'm explaining to your crew boss—"

"I can explain it myself, thanks." She forced a quick smile at O'Connor.

Jim shot her a look and shifted his long-handled Pulaski Axe to extend his hand to the firefighter. "Appreciate your helping out."

O'Connor shook it. "No worries. Glad I was close enough to help. I'm sure you've heard this hellcat's running and we've lost containment. The Incident Commander ordered crews to retreat. He'll hit her hard from the air."

Tara sized up his confident, easy manner. He'd brought calm to her storm. She was thankful, but couldn't form the words.

"Caught it on the radio. We're moving out now." Jim looked from O'Connor to Tara.

"I need to find my smokejumper crew," said O'Connor. "Don't envy you having to do an AAR for the line of duty death of the homeowner."

"Yeah, I've done After Action Reviews. They aren't fun, but necessary for lessons learned," replied Jim.

"Our jump crew will be meeting with McGuire shortly," said O'Connor. "I'll inform him about the fatality unless you want to since a member of your crew was involved."

Jim's gray mustache became a straight line. "I'll do it."

Tara gave O'Connor a double take at the mention of her ex-fiancé, Travis McGuire, a smokejumper and the incident commander for this fire. So, O'Connor was a smokejumper. Of course he knew Travis.

"Smokejumpers are the superheroes of wildfire," said Tara with a wry smile. "I've always thought part of your standard issue should be red capes with an "S" on your jump suits."

O'Connor's face softened into another dimpled smile. "You're back in action now." He hoisted a chainsaw to his shoulder as if it were made of aluminum foil.

"I was never out of the action." She squinted up at him.

Few bested her at five feet, eleven inches. Despite the dirt and soot streaking his face, she noted a blue-eyed, movie star charm, accentuated by a lot of bright, white teeth.

O'Connor stared at her a moment. "I'm glad you're all right. Remember your ten standard firefighting orders." He turned to her boss. "Good to see you Jim." He tugged his hardhat with thumb and forefinger as he strode off across the black.

"I'll do that," she hollered to his retreating backside. She rolled her eyes at his subtle reminder of the ten command-ments of wildland firefighting she could recite forward and backward. She was well aware of the one she'd violated, attempting to save a life: *Base all actions on current and expected behavior of the fire.*

"Hey, O'Connor, wait a minute." Jim glanced at Tara before trotting after O'Connor for a private conversation. He gesticulated as he spoke, the way he always did, then pointed in her direction.

O'Connor looked back at her, nodding. Jim patted his shoulder and O'Connor lifted a hand to her and vanished into the smoke.

"What did you say to him?" She hadn't screwed up deciding to go after the trapped homeowner. She screwed up by not being fast enough.

"I thanked him for helping you." Jim shot her a grim look. He took off his hard hat, revealing a tousled crop of silver. "Still okay? I know it's a bummer." Jim was stuck in a time warp from the 1970s, reminding Tara of her father.

She gave him a mechanical nod. She was anything but okay.

"I told you to fall back. You went anyway." His steely gray eyes pierced her.

"A life was at stake——"

"*Two* lives were at stake, dammit!" shouted Jim, slamming his hard hat to the ground. He stared at it a moment, his mouth in a straight line. "We'll talk later," he muttered. He bent to pick up his hat and stomped off.

"Missoula Crew, retreat to the safety zone," Jim called out, leading the crew at a fast clip. Everyone fell into single file, following him through the burnt black.

Shit. Jim was pissed. Tara blinked back the pressure building behind her eyes. *No crying in firefighting,* Dad always said. And by God she wouldn't. She wasn't weak.

Unfortunately, Tara knew the drill. Jim would place her on administrative leave, routine protocol for a line of duty death. She could be terminated for ignoring a direct order, despite the fact she'd risked her life to save another. Not only had she failed, she had landed in deep shit for trying.

She would do it again in a heartbeat.

🔥

*T*ara breathed relief when the crew reached the safety zone, a mile away on a hilltop road, where their vehicles were parked. A panoramic view of the fire stretched out before them. Unable to halt the destruction at the city's edge, the twenty firefighters surveyed the four-story flames. The pristine, blue-green forest south of the city was now a sullied, smoking disaster. No one spoke. They stood with clenched jaws, surveying the battle they'd lost.

"Dammit!" Tara's vision of the old man's outstretched arm flooded into her psyche. Nausea pushed up. Her hand flew to her mouth as she willed her stomach contents to stay put.

Jim approached and offered her his canteen. "Have a sip. The fire devil was a freak event. It happens. You didn't have time to get him out. It wasn't your fault." His brusque tone seemed apologetic, but still sliced her.

The water cooled her parched throat and dribbled down her chin as she gulped. She wiped the droplets away with the back of her gloved hand. "I had to try, Jim."

"I know you did."

"How do you know the smokejumper who pulled me back?"

"Ryan O'Connor, a friend of mine. I met him on a fire in Alaska." Jim spat on the ground again. "He was doing recon for the incident commander when he saw your situation. Good thing he happened by." Jim cleared his throat, shaking his head.

Her situation. So, this is how it would be labeled. She shouldn't have had a situation. The homeowner should have evacuated. She shouldn't have had to run into the fire. The smokejumper shouldn't have had to drag her back out. Her thoughts muddied and she was too weary to sort them.

Jim backed up to address the Missoula crew. "Everyone load up and head back to camp."

Tara's good friend and crewmate, Katy, put an arm around her waist as they walked toward a transport van. "Wish I had a mirror. You look like a friggin' zebra. Those auburn locks are singed." Katy tugged a frayed tendril that escaped from Tara's yellow hardhat.

"And you reek like burnt toast." Tara gave her a half smile. She appreciated her friend's attempt to lift her spirits.

"I'm sorry about what happened back there. Glad someone was close enough to help. You okay?" asked Katy.

"Define okay." Tara shook her head. "I hate this job sometimes. Hell's fury gorged on another victim. Fire doesn't know the difference between trees, homes, or humans. It only robs. It only takes." She stared at a dead tree stump, wanting to punch it. "What good are we if we can't protect people? You don't forget a death like that. Ever."

"Don't beat yourself up. No point going down that road," said Katy.

Too late. She'd already gone down Guilt Street and hung a right on Failure Avenue.

Jim sunk into the driver's seat and keyed his radio. "McGuire, this is Dolan. Missoula crew has fallen back to our safety zone. Recommend hitting Roosevelt Subdivision hard with mud drops. Air attack, do you copy?"

The air tanker pilot replied. "Incoming drop in two minutes."

"Copy that," radioed McGuire, sounding relieved.

The low rumble of her ex-fiancé's voice gut punched Tara. She'd be married to Travis McGuire right now if he would have been faithful. His voice used to ping cupid arrows to her heart.

Now, it made her want to level her drip torch and douse him with flame.

"Missoula crew clear for air drops. I'll report back at zero seven hundred." Jim let go of the talk button. "Thank God for Bendix King radios," he mumbled.

McGuire's voice came back. "Weather's calmed. We expect containment tonight."

"Good deal. Catch you on the upside. Dolan clear." Jim thrust his radio back in its holster on his waist belt. He glanced back at Tara in the rear seat.

She avoided eye contact. She'd gone against his orders and the homeowner died anyway. A shitty day by any standard; and she knew it was about to get worse.

Her stomach twisted, dreading which way the veritable Pulaski would fall.

The crew arrived at their permitted encampment on an alfalfa field, which led to rolling woodlands untainted by fire. The sun slipped below the timbered Rockies, shedding light on a scarlet sky.

Tara tugged her tent from its bag and shook it out, spreading it over freshly cut alfalfa. She inhaled the sweet aroma that cleansed her lungs after ingesting smoke all day.

Jim moseyed over and spoke in muted tones. "Listen...sorry I came down on you so hard."

"Not saving the homeowner wasn't in the cards." She grimaced and swallowed. The dull ache in her chest became sharp pangs.

"You did what you thought you had to. But you went against my orders." His jaw twitched.

She straightened and her muscles tensed. "I've never had a

habit of not following orders. Please give me the benefit of the doubt."

"Here's the thing. I've been thinking you need a break...to help you move on." His stare bored into her soul. "You and I both know why you ran into that fire to save him."

She stiffened, irritated that he knew her so well. "I *have* moved on."

He shifted his weight where he stood. "The agency will advise administrative leave and counseling after the line of duty death today. Lord knows a reprimand or suspension won't do a damn bit of good for you."

She shook her head. "Sorry you think that I messed up, Jim. But the way I see it is I had no choice." She stared at wispy layers of leftover smoke hovering over the Rockies.

"Off the record, I understand. But I think you should take the admin leave."

"No. I need to keep working." She waited for Jim to look at her.

Instead he bent to break off a single blade of grass. He fiddled with it as he spoke. "Figured you'd say that. I'll make a deal with you. I won't make a federal case of you ignoring my directive and I'll agree to you staying on the job if you agree to get counseling. But not here."

"Then where?"

"Alaska has requested resources. Fires are ramping up in the Interior."

She gulped. "Oh, come on. Don't ship me to a miserable outback for trying to save a life—"

"—and nearly losing your own." His jaw jerked harder. "You thought saving someone would make up for not saving your dad."

His words carved a hole in her chest. She fought to control the quiver in her voice. "Not fair."

"Hear me out, Tara. Alaska can use your skills. You're

trained and disciplined. Change will do you good. A different place helps after losing a loved one. I'm doing you a solid here."

Her voice rose. "Alaska? You can't be serious. Let me stay to get on the Lolo Interagency Hotshot crew. I already meet their fitness requirements. But I can't do it from five thousand miles away." She waved her hand in a northerly direction.

"Twenty-five hundred miles, give or take," he corrected. "Look, I've known you since you were in diapers, when me and your dad worked on the Lolo Hotshots. Saving the world won't bring him back. I promised him I'd watch out for you." He stared at her a long moment. "I don't break promises."

"Is this the boss talking or the family friend talking?"

"Both."

"I take it I don't have a choice." She fought the pressure behind her eyes as her world crashed and burned yet again. Leaving won't get her any closer to working with the Lolo hotshots.

"Speaking as your boss, no. I'm reassigning you to the BLM Alaska Fire Service for a sixty-day detail."

The sky and trees twisted as her vision blurred. "AFS? The Bureau of Land Management? You can't be serious."

"As a family friend, I hope you accept this reassignment. And as your boss, you'd be well advised to take it. I'll Skype you into the After-Action Review meeting from Fairbanks. That shouldn't be a problem." He removed his hardhat and rubbed his forehead.

"Come on, Jim. Get me on the Lolo Hotshots instead," pleaded Tara.

Jim raised his hands, seeming to placate her. "Sometimes life smacks us on the head with signs. Today you had one. I hope you pay attention. It's hard to heal from a line of duty death on top of a family loss. I'll arrange for you to get counseling up there."

"I'll arrange it myself," she muttered, turning away. She'd be damned if he'd see her cry.

"Make sure you do. I'm demob'ing you from the Copper Peak Fire as of zero seven hundred tomorrow morning. Go home and pack. Alaska Fire Service is top notch. You'll be in capable hands."

"Please don't demobilize me." She emphasized each word, hoping he'd cave.

He hesitated and let out a tired sigh. "Your flight leaves for Fairbanks at zero nine hundred, day after tomorrow." he called over his shoulder. His boots crunched on the gravel road as he walked back to the men's encampment.

"Bloody damn hell," she muttered, her heart thudding.

The moon vanished behind the drifting haze as night settled in, leaving her in the dark. Today was a freaking sign? Of *what*? Fighting fire in Alaska wasn't at all what she wanted. Jim knew what her career goals were. How could he do this?

Her friend Katy sauntered over. "What was that all about?"

"Jim reassigned me to freaking bum-screw Alaska." She spit the words like bullets. "He thinks I need a change. Did I seem like I lost my shit today?" Tara had proven herself a competent firefighter on the Missoula crew. But now she wasn't so sure.

"I thought you held it together, considering. Can he reassign you if you don't want to go?"

"He just did. As of zero nine hundred the day after tomorrow, I'm out of here."

"Alaska. The last wild place. A friend in dispatch said a load of calendar-worthy Alaskan smokejumpers worked this fire. And I do mean *calendar* worthy, Tara." She laughed.

Tara flashed back to the one she met today. *Nope. Forget it.*

"You know how I feel about smokejumpers, after Travis. Dad warned me about dating them, but I didn't listen. Then again, he didn't want me working in fire. Didn't listen to that either." She huffed out air.

"Travis was a douche, but not all of them are. The one who helped you today sounds like an okay guy."

13

Something stabbed Tara's chest. "I wasn't nice to him. I was pissed and embarrassed he had to help me. It's awful seeing someone die. And I just sat on the ground like an idiot..." She choked on her words.

Katy hugged her. "You did the best you could. Go to Alaska, take lots of bug dope, and don't get eaten by a Griz when you go pee." She ambled to her tent and grinned at Tara. "Because as we all know, that's when the bears show up." She laughed again.

"Right. See you in a couple months, Katy." She crawled inside her tent, her head pounding.

She coaxed her down filled sleeping bag from the nylon sack, shook it, and let it settle on the tent floor. Sitting on her bag, she tugged off her boots and socks. Her back muscles tingled, and her joints ached. She wished for someone with strong thumbs to knead her sore shoulders. The strong hands that had gripped her after today's nightmare would do the trick. Thank God the Alaskan smokejumper showed up. If their paths ever cross again, she'll remember to thank him for helping her.

Her insides knotted at the way she had treated Ryan O'Connor after saving the day. She shouldn't be cynical about smokejumpers. They trained hard and worked harder. But after Travis' chronic disloyalties, she'd sworn off every blasted one.

She chuckled at the one good thing about going to the Great Alone, as poet Robert Service had referred to Alaska—she could distance herself from Travis. His voice on the radio today had ignited fresh pain. She berated herself for her weakness—she was powerless to extinguish the ache in her heart. At least she wouldn't hear his voice from the middle of the godforsaken tundra.

"Alaska. Oh God..." she groaned, squeezing the bridge of her nose with thumb and forefinger. All she wanted was to belong, to have family again. When Dad and Jim worked on the Lolo Hotshots—the Delta Force of firefighting—everyone celebrated holidays and birthdays together, like a close-knit family.

How could she get on the hotshots from middle-of-nowhere Alaska?

This wouldn't help her move on from losing Dad. Failing him would haunt her the rest of her life no matter where she went. Working in a desolate wilderness wouldn't help on that score.

Two thoughts plagued her as she drifted to sleep. Never again would anyone on her watch die in a fire.

And never again would she fall for another smokejumper.

I always get burned.

CHAPTER 2

*T*he Boeing 737 swung side to side and bucked upward. From his middle seat in the exit row, Ryan O'Connor repositioned his baseball cap and glanced around his seatmate to peer out the window at orange air and red sun. Yep, fire season had officially kicked in. Even after seeing spectacular country in the Lower Forty-eight fighting fire, he always appreciated coming home to the Alaska Smokejumper Base in Fairbanks.

The flight between Anchorage and Fairbanks wasn't usually this rough. It must be a strong thunderstorm. While others figuratively peeled their stomachs off the overhead panels, Ryan stayed relaxed. He'd grown accustomed to planes bouncing in wind-driven wildfires as he had prepared to jump out of them.

He first noticed the tall redhead in the airport lounge in Missoula and he'd lucked out getting the seat next to hers. The leggy, blue-jeaned beauty kept her face toward the window. But there was nothing to see but smoky, orange sky.

A scent wafted from her. Eucalyptus. Smelled good, compared to the smoke he'd inhaled jumping the nasty blaze outside of Butte. Eucalyptus reminded him of his native state of

California. He loved the aroma, but it was one of the worst tree fuels to fight in a wildfire.

The jet dropped. One hand flew to her chest and the other grabbed his thigh. *Hot damn.*

"Sorry. Not a fan of turbulence." She yanked her hand from his leg as if she'd touched a hot stove. Blushing, her head pressed back against the seat.

He knew that voice.

"No worries," he said, wheels spinning. "This airline hasn't left a plane up here yet." He longed for more turbulence. Maybe she'd land in his lap next time.

Then it hit him like a planeload of retardant. *This was the fire-fighter he'd pulled back from the flame front in Montana.*

The one Jim Dolan had asked him to watch out for, as a favor. Jim hadn't said much other than he was reassigning her to AFS on a sixty-day detail due to 'some personal shit.' And he'd also mentioned something about making sure she got counseling. With all the chaos that day, Ryan amazed himself for even remembering their ten-second conversation.

He'd been hiking to join his Fairbanks crew when he came upon the terror-stricken firefighter sitting in the path of a running flame front. His EMT brain recognized her paralysis as trauma and he'd had less than a nanosecond to get her out of there. He'd dropped his gear to run and grab the woman from behind and drag her into the burnt black, away from the flames. *Tara. She said her name was Tara.*

This presented an awkwardness he hadn't banked on. He flipped open his instructor training manual and pretended to read. He needed time to figure a way to finesse the situation.

So far she appeared oblivious of who he was. If she recognized him, she didn't let on. He'd been covered with ash and grime, same as her.

He snuck a quick peek, but long enough to notice the graceful lines of her neck. Should he introduce himself as the guy who'd prevented her from certain death? No, too cheesy and egotistical. No firefighter cared to admit having to be rescued. He'd think on it. First, he needed rest. He closed his manual, shoved it under the seat in front of him, and covered his face with his baseball cap. Dozing on a bumpy flight was not a problem; he could sleep on jagged rocks wrapped in razor wire in a hurricane.

The steady drone of the plane settled him into comfortable bliss. He burrowed deep into softness. Suddenly, Zombie, his jump boss, tapped him awake. He yelped in surprise, forcing his eyelids open. Only Zombie wasn't the culprit tapping his thigh... his gorgeous seat mate was. He removed the baseball cap and lifted his head from her shoulder.

"Sorry, didn't mean to..." he mumbled, smoothing his hair back as heat flooded his face.

She chuckled. "You must have needed a nap."

He pressed his forearms on the armrests to sit up straight. "Sleep is a rare commodity this time of year."

"Tell me about it."

The plane crabbed left and jerked right, causing his knee to bump hers.

She flinched, then stiffened. "Flying isn't my favorite."

"Alaska Airlines pilots are the best. You're safe. You'll be okay."

Her head swiveled to him. "What did you say?"

He stared at the intense, green jewels he remembered from the first time he'd looked into them. He waited for her to figure it out.

It took a moment before she lit up. "You're the one. The smokejumper from Alaska. You said the same thing to me." Her expression changed to quizzical.

Time to come clean. He grinned. "Yeah, I'm the one. What did I say exactly?" He hadn't a clue. He was discombobulated by her lovely face. *Stop staring at her, moron.*

"Yes. That I'd be safe and okay." She drew back, eyes wide with discovery. "You're Jim Dolan's friend. Why didn't you say something?"

"I didn't want to put you on the spot." He kept smiling and shrugging like an idiot.

"So, you're the Alaskan smokejumper who helped me."

"Ryan O'Connor. And you're Tara Waters, right? Pleased to meet you again." He extended a hand.

Her gaze dropped to his callused hand. She accepted it with a puzzled expression. "I told you my first name on the fire, but how do you know my last name?"

He groped his brain for a quick explanation. "Uh, your... your crew boss mentioned it."

She cocked a brow. "What did Jim tell you about me?"

The jet touched down hard at Fairbanks International Airport and she pulled her hand away. *Whew, saved by the landing.* As the wheels pressed the runway, the engines amped and drag pulled him against his seat. He leaned forward to look out the window. Scrawny black spruce and a grazing moose whizzed by.

The long-bodied plane lurched to a halt and passengers heaved forward in unison, then thudded back against their seats. The pilots cut the engines, turned off the seatbelt sign, and people spilled into the aisle, collecting their booty from overhead bins.

"Sorry I didn't recognize you earlier." Tara leaned back, staring at Ryan, as if he had just parachuted into his seat. "And here we are, sitting right next to each other."

"Yeah," he chuckled. "What were the chances?" *Who cares?* He loved life's little flukes.

Ryan unbuckled his seatbelt and continued smiling like a doofus. She was gorgeous. *Don't ask how I know your last name.* Jim had warned him that she wasn't to know he'd asked Ryan to watch out for her. He'd almost blown it.

"Uh, how are you doing after the…after the Montana fire?" he asked, aiming for casual.

"Not bad. Just the usual night terrors, curled up in a fetal position." Her unblinking green gaze fixed on him.

"Yeah. That sucks." He knew all too well how much it sucked and wished he didn't.

She gave him a partial smile. "I'm kidding. I'm doing okay."

"Sorry I intervened, but…" He stopped, letting his words dangle. He didn't want to make her feel worse.

Her toe tapped the floor. "Don't worry. You did what you had to. I would have done the same." She looked away from him.

"If you want to talk about it sometime…" he trailed off. *Dammit.*

"Thanks, but I'm good." She said it in a way that he knew to back off.

He couldn't help himself. "The agency advises counseling after a line of duty death. I can hook you up with some names. But just so you know, I'm a good listener." *Shit.* He'd waded in too deep, judging by the furrows in her forehead.

"I'll keep that in mind." She flicked a glance at him with a hint of a smile.

"Sounds good." What a beauty. Green eyes like Alaskan birch leaves and dark, red hair the color of manzanita bark in California chaparral. He compared everything to trees.

A dull ache throbbed Ryan's knees when he stood to deplane. He shook out each leg. Hiking steep terrain had done a number on him. He wasn't twenty anymore and had piled on another decade. When he retrieved his fire pack from the overhead bin, he spotted a similar one. "This pack must be yours."

She nodded.

"Here you go." As he plucked her seasoned pack from the bin, he noticed its frayed corners and a faded U.S. Forest Service patch on the front. Dark smudges lined the weave of the fabric. He inhaled the familiar smell of smoke as he lowered it to her.

"Thanks." She gave him a quick smile and took it.

He hoisted his daypack to his shoulder and his neck pinched. Couldn't wait to lie down. A deep tissue massage sounded good right now. "Heading to AFS?"

"Alaska Fire Service. Yes, I am."

"Follow me to the limo."

Her mouth hung open and she gawked at him. "Seriously?"

"Poor man's limo. The white box van variety." His eyes drifted to her full lips and he glanced away.

"Oh, right. Thanks." She lifted her muscular, long limbed frame from the seat.

She looked terrific in jeans. Far cry from grimy Nomex. Feminine, strong, and fit. He'd sensed her strength while holding on to her in the Montana fire. She was only a head shorter than his six-four. A mass of shiny, dark red hair was knotted at the back of her head.

He motioned her to go ahead of him, inhaling eucalyptus as he followed behind her. *I had my hands on this woman.* Granted, not in a desirable way, but the fresh thought stirred his insides.

Once inside the terminal he fell into step beside her. "First time in Fairbanks?"

"Yes, but wish I could have seen the mountains as we flew in."

"The smoke comes and goes. It'll clear eventually." He took out his cell phone and tapped a text. His phone chimed a notification. "AFS runs shuttles between Fort Wainwright and the airport during fire season. Mel is on his way. He's our shuttle guy."

Ryan led her toward baggage claim, and he noted her sidelong glances as she walked alongside him.

"Are you originally from Alaska?" she asked.

"Nope. California transplant."

"Forest Service?"

"No, BLM. Fire is organized differently here. We have six state and federal agencies under one coordination unit."

"How's Alaska's fire situation?" She pulled out her cell and powered it on.

He checked the updated situation report on his phone. "Forty-nine thousand lightning strikes in the last four days. It's only the first of June, so it will be an action-packed fire season."

Her chin dropped. "No way. That seems excessive."

"Alaska's a big place." He stopped walking and held his phone out to her.

"Incredible." Her phone vibrated and she pulled it from her back pocket.

His eyes darted sideways to her phone screen, catching a text from someone named Katy:

Howz Alaska? Any hot guyz up there?

Hot guys? Is she in the market for one? He blinked and resumed walking, forcing his eyes straight ahead.

Smokejumpers rarely had time for anything but fire during a busy season. He'd do what Jim Dolan asked—keep an eye on Tara Waters this week in his training class and hook her up with counseling. After that, he'd be back on jump status, fighting fire.

As they reached baggage claim and waited for the conveyor belt to move, he knew one thing for certain.

His training class was about to become a whole lot more interesting.

CHAPTER 3

$\mathcal{T}$ara didn't have an opinion about Alaska. The smoke was so thick flying in, she had missed out on the dazzling scenery everyone raved about. And that turbulent flight...her friends had always razzed her about her fear of flying because she would rather face a wall of flame than stuff herself in a metal tube hurtling through the air.

But O'Connor was spot on. The plane had landed safely.

She stood next to him at baggage claim, pretending to study her phone. She'd shared a flight to Fairbanks with the person who'd dragged her insubordinate ass away from the Copper Peak Fire. The freakiness of being on the same flight *and* sitting next to him nuked her brain.

No words could describe it. Mortified. No, embarrassed. Worse. Humiliated for failing to save a life and not self-rescuing. She was grateful he'd helped her, but she wanted him to know she wasn't helpless. She'd worked hard to build her reputation in fire and didn't want to be thought of as weak.

She felt compelled to explain. "Listen, the reason I—"

An obnoxious buzzer cut her off and rubber flaps separated at the baggage opening, spitting bags onto the serpentine conveyor belt. O'Connor obviously hadn't heard her as he moved to claim his pack.

Bad timing. She'd explain later. As she waited for her pack to appear, her phone notified her of another text from Katy:

Saw Travis at Beer & Billiards after Copper Peak. Told him you were fighting fire in Alaska. He said you'll like it up there.

Tara texted back:

Tell McGuire smokejumpers in Alaska are HOT, on and off the fire and I've already met one. Make him think I've moved on. Don't say why I'm reassigned here.

The conveyor delivered her pack and she lifted it to her shoulder, shoving aside her annoyance at Katy's mention of her ex.

O'Connor grabbed his pack and lifted his baseball cap, revealing sun tinged, brown hair. Combing his medium-length locks back repeatedly with his fingers, he looked to be taming an outgrown cut.

"Our ride is here." He motioned to the doors leading out to ground transportation.

She was ogling him and her skin heated. From the moment she had recognized him, she was knocked back. This was how he normally looked? A feast for the eyes. Angular, tanned face; muscled and taller than most. The standard unisex garb of hardhat, blackened yellows, and green Nomex pants, plus layers of grime and sweat made everyone look alike on the fireline. What a difference a shower made.

The doors swung open and a warm, smoky breeze blew tendrils from Tara's face. Her hair stunk less from smoke, after several shampoos and rubbing in a few drops of eucalyptus essential oil. The stuff seemed to work.

O'Connor called out to a short, cowboy-skinny guy with a

long gray mullet, topped with a Linsey Helicopters baseball cap. "Melbourne, my man, good to see you."

Mel stood grinning next to the white box van with an open rear door. "Dances-With-Smoke, how was the Lower Forty-eight?" He high-fived O'Connor and rolled his toothpick to the other side of his mustache.

"Still burning. Zombie ordered me back for refresher training." Ryan let Mel toss his packs in the van.

"Bosses. Can't live with 'em…" Mel grinned. "…can't stand 'em. Where's your jump crew?"

"They took a later flight. I found this stray instead." He flashed a smile at Tara that warmed her as she stood next to the van, a pack slung on each shoulder.

Mel straightened and motioned at Tara's pack. "Forest Service brat?"

"Sure am." Tara eyed the BLM logo on the driver's side door, a blue and green triangle of a tranquil mountain scene with a stream running through it. Strange not to see the familiar yellow and green Forest Service conifer logo.

"This is Tara Waters from the Lolo Forest in Missoula," said O'Connor.

"Pleased to meet you. I'm Melbourne Faraday. Call me Mel. Here, I'll toss these in for you." He eased her large fire pack from her shoulder and held out his hand for her day pack.

"I can do it." She preferred handling her own gear. But he'd helped O'Connor with his, so she wouldn't make it a big deal.

Mel heaved both of Tara's packs in, then repositioned his cap the way guys did by default when they couldn't figure what else to do with themselves.

"Thanks."

"He likes to do it. Makes him feel useful." O'Connor grinned, sliding on a pair of Ray Bans. He ran fingers slow and smooth along the bows of the frame, fitting them behind his ears, finishing with a flourish by tapping the bridge. She'd seen guys toss sunglasses on countless times, but it amused her at the methodical way this one did.

O'Connor opened the front passenger door. "Want to ride shotgun?"

She waved him to the front and climbed into the back seat. "Thanks, O'Connor, but I'll be a backseat driver."

"Ah, control freak. Call me Ryan." He hopped in and closed the door, then turned to look at her. "Noticed you weren't crazy about flying. At least our plane didn't fall on someone's house."

"Since you mentioned it, I did see a lady in black riding a broom outside my window." A corner of her mouth turned up, but her eyelids insisted on lockdown for the night.

"Why were you sent here while Montana's burning?" Mel pointed his aviator shades at the rearview as he accelerated onto the highway.

Tara snapped her lids open. "Um, well I…" She didn't think to rehearse her soundbite for being reassigned here.

Ryan tilted his head back and casually interjected. "You're on a temporary detail assignment, right?"

She appreciated him tossing her a slow pitch. "Uh-huh. Temporary detail assignment."

Score another point for Ryan. Not only was he kind and considerate, but he seemed to have a unique sensibility, knowing what she'd been through. She remembered his calm voice and denim eyes when hell became reality that day on the fire.

"Welcome to never-ending daylight," said Mel. "Helps to have a sleep mask."

"Thanks, I'll keep that in mind." She didn't need one at the moment, her eyelids were heavy enough.

Mel fiddled with the radio tuner, settling for *Jump*, by Eddie Van Halen. "O'Connor, they're playing your song."

"No jumping this week. Maybe next." Ryan folded his arms and leaned back.

Tara opened her eyes as Mel drove past several buildings to a far corner of the military base. The van rolled to a stop at the first of three two-story, rectangular gray buildings, framed in the indigo twilight.

"Home sweet home, ladies and gents." Mel smiled at the rearview mirror and idled the engine.

She cranked the door handle and stepped out. The sweet scent of cut grass filled her nostrils and a wave of loneliness swept over her. She let out a long, slow breath. *Here I am, Alaska.* She may as well be on Mars with Mark Watney.

Ryan was already at the rear of the van unloading their packs. He lifted hers and held it out to her.

Her heart ticked up as she took it. As Katy would say, *this guy's indicator arrow is well within the charm zone on the smoking hot firefighter meter.* After Tara had broken her engagement, she'd defaulted back to Dad's advice not to date smokejumpers. She was in Alaska to fight fire, prove her mettle, and go home to join the Lolo Hotshot Crew; not crush on another smokejumper.

On the plane, she'd been surprisingly relaxed when Ryan fell asleep on her shoulder. She'd waited ten, twenty minutes—okay half an hour before waking him. But that was before she recognized him and wanted to crawl under her seat.

Ryan slammed the rear door and hollered at the open driver's window. "Later, Mel. Thanks."

"You bet." Mel drove off and they retrieved their gear.

Ryan led the way up a few concrete steps. "Here's the barracks. You'll be mixed in with emergency and hotshot crews, and a smattering of visiting smokejumpers."

She hoisted her weighty packs. "Thought jumpers all stayed in separate quarters."

"Mostly, but not always. Depends how many are here."

"Right." Great, smokejumpers stay here. She'd steer clear. But at least this guy didn't flirt, which she appreciated. It annoyed her when guys hit on her at work. Refreshing to meet a guy who maintained professionalism.

She raised her chin at him. "I appreciated you not saying the real reason why I'm here." She wanted to say more, but she was physically and emotionally drained.

Ryan smiled. "I don't judge. Why you're here is your business. Since you are, I hope you enjoy it."

His words warmed her. "Thanks." She walked inside to the main lobby and he followed.

An older, platinum blonde stood behind a small counter, furiously scribbling on a yellow legal pad.

"Hey, Rosie, how's my favorite barracks manager?" Ryan boomed out a greeting.

Rosie beamed at him. "How's my favorite firefighter? Your being back home has certainly brightened my evening." She gave him a cat-eyed look, and for a minute Tara thought she might throw her arms around him.

He pointed his thumb at her. "This is Tara, a fire eater fresh from Montana."

"Welcome to Alaska." Rosie smiled as she placed some forms on a clipboard.

"Rosie will fix you up. If you need anything, holler. See you later." He sprang up the stairs as if he weren't carrying two heavy packs.

"Nice meeting you, Dances-With-Smoke," Tara called after him, watching his splendid backside longer than she intended.

He signaled a wave before disappearing to the second floor.

"Pretty, isn't he?" Rosie's voice had a dreamy texture as she stared after him.

Tara gave her an odd look. The woman could be his grandmother.

Rosie's tone snapped to den mother mode. "Don't get attached, he's always gone. And you'd have to get in line after all the other women. Sign here." She pushed a pen and clipboard across the green-speckled Formica. "You'll bunk here during training and between fire assignments. Room 265, second floor.

Men on the left, women on the right. And no hanky-panky. We frown on cross-pollination. After all, this is a government facility." Rosie peered above her skinny glasses, dead serious.

Tara swallowed a laugh. "Don't worry, I don't plan to pollinate. I'm here to fight fire." She stifled a yawn. Sleep. She wanted sleep.

"Good. Keep your eyes on the flames and not the other pretty scenery and you'll do fine. Breakfast in the mess hall starting zero five hundred. Training is in the AFS building on the other end. Here's a map." Rosie handed it to her along with her room key.

"Thanks, appreciate it." Tara hoisted her packs and trudged to the second floor. She found her room in the long, darkened hallway and unlocked it.

The paneled door swung open, revealing a dark-haired woman dozing in a twin bed. Another twin bed hugged a white wall, with neatly folded sheets and blankets on the mattress. An oscillating fan hummed, circulating air around the small room.

Tara gently closed the door. Though a tan shade covered the window, Alaska's all-night twilight lit the room enough to move around. She riffled through her pack for toothpaste and toothbrush and squeezed into the tiny bathroom. Too tired to plait her long hair into a single braid, she left it in a messy bun.

Tiptoeing to her bunk, she tripped on a book, splayed on dark linoleum. She squinted at the title: *Vixens of Lust*. Glancing at the softly snoring, blanketed lump, she figured this woman should be fun, judging by her reading choice.

She pulled out her phone to set her alarm. *Dang it, dead battery.* Too tired to search for an outlet, she'll hear her bunkmate get up in the morning. She made the bed and flopped down, drifting off, dreaming of orange skies and blue-eyed, denim-clad firefighters; smoke-dancing and weaving around her.

And Dad. She always dreamed about Dad—reaching out in the flames.

CHAPTER 4

*R*yan stood at the front of the training room, clipboard in hand, intent on not gawping at the out-of-breath, copper-haired woman framed in the double doorway. Sure enough, Tara Waters had landed in his Fire Refresher Training class.

Yessiree, there is a God.

He delighted in her obvious surprise to find he was her training instructor. Her chest rose and fell like a tide under a steroid moon. Usually latecomers bothered him, but not now, as he watched her blow wild red strands from her face.

"Welcome. Take a seat," he said casually.

"Sorry I'm late," she mumbled to the largely male room of sixty trainees. She beelined for a seat in a corner. Subtle stares followed her as she plunked down and slid her daypack to the floor. Her waist-long hair sprawled around her green Lolo Forest T-shirt like a spidery cape.

Gunnar Alexanderson, Ryan's jump partner and co-instructor, cleared his throat and eyeballed him a hot woman alert. No female escaped Gunnar's scrutiny. And judging from the ogles of the other males in the room, Tara didn't escape theirs either. Ryan knew where that could wind up.

His big-brother protective instinct kicked in. He motioned with his clipboard. "Empty seat up front."

"I'm good here, thanks," said Tara with a definitive nod.

"Suit yourself."

He moved to the front of the room. "Good morning. I'm Ryan O'Connor, your Fire Refresher Training instructor for the week." He gestured at the brawny, blonde skyscraper standing next to him. "This is Gunnar Alexanderson, my co-conspirator. He'll give you an introduction while I pass these around."

Ryan moved through the room, distributing the *Alaska Handy Dandy Firefighting Field Guides*. He held one out to Tara. "Easier to stay awake in the front."

She took it with a double take. "Handy Dandy? Catchy title." Her gaze settled on his chest.

He tucked his chin and looked down at his tee, with *Alaska Smokejumpers* and a parachute splayed across his chest.

Vivid pools of green strayed to his, with a slight furrow between her brows. "And you're also the training instructor."

He couldn't tell whether she was surprised or annoyed.

"Five bonus points." A corner of his mouth went up and he strode back to the front.

When he turned, Tara was on her way to the seat he'd suggested.

"You're right. Easier to stay awake up here," she stage-whispered.

"Sure." He feigned indifference, but it took considerable effort. When he'd agreed to keep an eye on Tara for Jim Dolan, he hadn't counted on her being a raving beauty under all that soot and grime. He remembered those emerald eyes and how she had risked her life to save another. His neck hairs prickled as she moved closer.

She slid into a chair next to the dark-haired woman Gunnar had already described to Ryan as the "Southern Beauty."

Ryan leaned on the side of a desk, fixing his observation anywhere but on the redhead in his proximity.

As Gunnar swaggered to center stage, Ryan resisted smirking. After years of working together, he was used to Gunnar dipping into his reservoir of charm with his unmistakable, Norwegian accent.

"Good morning," said Gunnar, flashing his signature grin at the roomful of trainees. "Some of you are from the Lower Forty-eight states, and others are seasoned AFS firefighters returning for another season. While you've all had basic fire training, AFS requires a one-week refresher specific to Alaska's unique conditions…"

Gunnar lectured for an hour. When he finished, Ryan lifted off the table and moved to the center. "My firefighting expertise is from incident commanding and jumping a fair amount of fires. Fire behavior and terrain up here differ from the Lower Forty-eight. Alaska is the largest, least populated state with a thousand ways to kill you if you aren't careful. She's a ruthless beauty and unforgiving if you make mistakes. One thing to remember when fighting fire in Alaska: Expect the unexpected. Firefighting up here is not for the faint-hearted."

As Ryan continued, he avoided looking at Tara. But the harder he tried not to, the more he noticed the tilt of her head and how she cupped her chin. She had an unblinking hold on him. When he did look her way, she'd snap her gaze down to her notebook.

"Everything you need to know about wildland firefighting in Alaska is in your Handy Dandy. Make sure you read it cover to cover." Ryan finished his lecture and glanced at his watch. "Time for lunch."

"Be back at one sharp," Gunnar called out, as people rose and filed out.

When the room emptied, Ryan tossed his clipboard on a table and sat, blowing out air.

"S'matter, Ryno?" jabbed Gunnar, hands on hips. "This gig too much for you? Should I tell Zombie you're wimping out?"

"Having a tough time concentrating," admitted Ryan.

"You're enthralled by the stunning beauties in this year's trainee harvest. Could prove difficult for your rule of not dating co-workers."

Ryan straightened. "Enthralled. That's a big word for you. Did that hurt?"

"My mastery of English is better than the average American's." Gunnar scratched his nose with his little finger.

"Don't bullshit a bullshitter. Your proficiency in English is only to impress and seduce American women." Ryan gave him a dour look.

Gunnar had no rules about dating coworkers—mostly because he never stuck with anyone long enough to cause any hassles. He attracted women like magnetic North, especially when they learned he'd been an Olympic downhill skier for Norway *and* a smokejumper in Alaska.

"There's an old Norwegian saying—if it works, don't fuck with it," said Gunnar.

"Hate to break it to you, but Americans came up with that one."

"And Norskes perfected it. Let's go eat."

Ryan cocked a brow. "Go ahead, be there in a few." His attention was elsewhere. *On her.*

"Okay. I'll eat your share." Gunnar shot him a look and left for lunch.

He sat back and folded his arms on his chest. *Remember my unwritten rule: Never get involved with women at work.* When he'd dated a firefighter on his California crew and their relationship had gone south, crew morale went south right along with it, as people chose sides. Infighting had spread like a runaway fire.

But Tara Waters? He liked her dry wit and there was no denying her beauty. Something else excited him yet made him apprehensive—her fearlessness. A double-edged sword that often proved hazardous for firefighters. It had nearly killed Tara on the Copper Peak Fire. He knew all too well how snap decisions on a dangerous fire could get firefighters killed.

Tara's competence and integrity were a breath of fresh air. He wanted to know her better. He wouldn't be working with her after this week's training. She'd be assigned to a crew, and he'd be back on Zombie's jump list.

Smokejumpers trained to be procedural and take charge. *I need to devise an Incident Action Plan to date Tara. Same as I do when I incident command a fire.*

"I will IAP the shit out of this," he said to himself. Proud of his idea, he grabbed his trusty clipboard, flipped a page on his tablet and set to work:

Incident Action Plan (IAP)

1. Objective: Date Tara Waters.

2. Strategy: After training ends, ask Tara out. Otherwise, I may not see her the rest of fire season.

3. Immediate Priorities: Training firefighters new to Alaska. Keep an eye on Tara Waters this first week as Jim Dolan requested.

4. Organize Resources: After training, she'll be with an emergency fire-fighting crew and I'll be jumping fire and no longer working together.

5. Coordinate Activity: A) Follow unwritten rule, do nothing B) Bend my rule, ask her for a future date. C) Screw it, date her now.

6. Ensure Safety: The usual protection (if I get that far).

7. Risks/Stakes: A) Pushing thirty-one. B) May be a one-time opportunity.

Formulating a plan for his dating strategy appeased him. He leaned back with pursed lips and assessed his options, tapping his pen on the tablet. Option 5-B seemed doable and could work as a moralistic compromise.

He tore the sheet off the tablet, folded it into his pocket, and headed for the mess hall, where he still had time to wolf down a sandwich and a few pints of milk.

And if he couldn't measure up to Tara's standards, he'd implement Plan B:

Fly by the seat of his Nomex.

CHAPTER 5

*T*ara's stomach gurgled, informing her she was more than ready for lunch. She hadn't eaten since yesterday, on the plane. Yawning, she followed everyone out of the building.

The brunette she'd been sitting next to crooked a scarlet, polished finger at her. "Walk to lunch with me," she politely demanded in a Southern drawl.

Tara smiled at her. "Sounds good. I'm Tara Waters."

"I know. I'm Angela Divina. Tickled to pieces." She held out a manicured hand and Tara shook it.

On her way out the door, Tara stopped and squinted at a Forest Service job announcement for the Lolo Hotshot Crew, posted on a bulletin board. She was tempted to yank it off, but instead made a face at it and followed Angela out the door.

Angela waited for her to catch up. "Is your name Tara because you're Irish or because your mother's favorite author was Margaret Mitchell?"

"My mother was into Celtic mythology. She used to tell me Tara was a place where kings met, and people sang about heroes. What about you? Is Angela Divina Southern-Italian?"

"Southern-Sicilian." Angela kicked a small rock, skittering it along the asphalt.

"Ah. So, if I piss you off, you'll have me whacked?" Tara brushed her fingertips across her throat in a *Godfather* imitation.

Angela stroked her chin with the back of her fingers. "Nothing personal, just business. And I'm Southern, so I'd be polite about it."

As the two women laughed and chatted on their way to the mess hall, Tara observed the impressive layout of the Alaska Fire Service. The smokejumper base was a modest one-story building with a light blue roof and ALASKA SMOKEJUMPERS, written in large, white letters along the ridge of the rooftop. They breezed past a large tan building, the AFS Fire Cache Warehouse. The tarmac behind the buildings led to air taxiways and runways connecting the rest of the Army base.

"Sorry I didn't wake you this morning. Wasn't sure you'd be in refresher training." Angela's soft Southern lilt sounded like she was fielding questions in a beauty pageant.

"No worries. Sorry if I woke you last night." Tara couldn't help wondering what this perfectly coiffed, manicured beauty was doing in firefighting.

"Oh hon, I sleep like the dead. Rosie mentioned you're from Montana. I asked her about you. Hope you don't mind."

"I don't mind. It's reassuring to know your bunkmate isn't a serial killer." She turned toward Angela and grinned. "I'm from the Lolo Forest, Missoula. You?"

"North Carolina. A friend lured me up here, bragging about the hot guys in Alaska." Angela shoved her hands in her pants pockets.

Tara laughed. "Well, are they?"

Angela leaned her flawlessly made-up face toward her. "Sweetie pie, if I have to tell you, I reckon we need to talk."

"Oh, trust me, I'm an expert on hot guys in wildland firefighting." Tara watched a helicopter hovering to land across the tarmac. "What did you do before this?"

"Beach lifeguard at Duck, an island off North Carolina. Got tired of fending off drunks and pulling snotty-nosed brats out of the ocean." Her voice was melodic and relaxed.

"You're a long way from home."

"My biological alarm jingled, so reckoned it was time to do something about it." Angela dipped her chin and smiled at a group of guys trooping past. One turned around to flirt with Angela and his buddy jabbed him.

Tara chuckled. "What are you, an old lady of twenty? And you chose to dangle your hook from the Alaska firefighting pier?"

"I'm a teensy bit older than twenty, hon," Angela lifted a brow and giggled. "So, what do you think of our taller-than-life instructors so far? That Ryan is a mouth waterer. And the Norwegian has sumptuous, wolf-like peepers."

"Wolf-like?" Tara laughed, watching a small plane take off on a nearby runway. "They certainly have altitude, that's for sure. At least six-three. Six-four is the max allowed for smokejumpers. They both know their stuff. Then again, they're smokejumpers." She said it as if she tasted something bad.

"You say it as if it were a plague."

"It is for me. I've sworn off that segment of the male population. Long story."

"Aren't they all? Nothing leaves my vault once it goes in. My personal code." Angela gave her a reassuring grin.

"Okay. Here's the condensed version. My ex-fiancé is a Missoula smokejumper, a Zulie. While we were engaged, he hooked up with a female jumper in McCall, Idaho, a dispatcher in West Yellowstone, and a hotshot firefighter in Bozeman."

"Your fiancé four-timed you?" Angela's eyes grew big. "Love triangles are bad enough, but yours sounds like a wreck-tangle."

Tara snorted. "Before Travis, there was another jumper. Two months in, I bumped into his wife at a party. You might say I'm gun shy when it comes to smokejumpers. They're off my to do list."

Angela swung toward her. "You shouldn't assume every smokejumper is that way. These Alaskan ones are nice."

"Dating people from work never ends well." Tara shook her head. "Fire and romance don't mix. Most relationships wind up in flames. Pun intended."

"Sometimes a girl just wants a little heat with her fire." Angela's coy expression reminded Tara of a smug cat with a mouse tail dangling from its mouth.

She thought of her ex sleeping around. "If you troll for romance at work, be careful of being burned. People lose their jobs *and* hearts when things go south. I've seen it a dozen times. I'd rather have everyone's respect than get laid."

Angela let out a dreamy sigh. "We'll see what the fire season brings."

Tara squinted at hazy shadows of mountains in the distance. "Hey, the smoke is clearing. Still haven't seen Denali though."

"Oh hon, when Denali is out, you'll know it. She's a woman who rules the roost, plays hard to get, and shows up when you least expect her." Angela moved ahead, swaying her hips in her olive-green fire pants. She pushed the mess hall door open.

"I'm starving." Tara followed her shapely bunkmate up the center aisle separating two sections of tables and benches. Her much shorter bunkmate possessed a self-assured composure Tara liked.

Tara chose a spinach salad and a tunafish sandwich, while Angela loaded her plate with a cheeseburger and fries. They sat down and chatted in between bites with Angela punctuating Tara's story tidbits with melodious giggles. Tara was relieved to get along so well with her bunkmate.

After lunch, the women left the mess hall and Tara waved Angela to go ahead without her. "I have to make a call." She pulled out her cell and tapped Jim Dolan's number. While waiting for him to answer, she scanned the horizon for the elusive Denali. Still playing hard to get.

"Hello?"

"Hi Jim, it's Tara."

"Hey, how's Alaska?"

Tara took a breath. "Saw a job announcement for a slot on the Lolo Hotshot Crew." She steeled herself to keep an even tone. "Can you please recommend me for this position? I'll email my application."

A sigh on the other end. "You just got up there."

"It feels wrong being here. Why are you so reluctant to help me?"

After a moment of silence, he said, "I am helping you. This is the best thing for you right now. Aren't they treating you well up there?"

"They're treating me fine."

"Open your mind and open your heart. Give it a chance. We'll talk in a few weeks. Bye, Tara." He ended the call.

"No!" Tara glared at the phone in her hand. The best thing? Give it a chance? *It's my life! I call my own shots. I decide what is good for me.*

She jammed the cell in her pocket. People stared as they moved past.

Thanks for abandoning me, Dad. And screw you, Travis, for breaking my heart. She had lost her family and her sense of belonging. She wanted them back. Instead, she was left with an aching loneliness she despised.

She fought tears on her way back to class and lifted her chin in defiance. No more tears will she waste on Travis. Not a single one.

The afternoon passed quickly, and when training ended for the day, Tara hurried to the barracks to put on her running gear. She always felt better after a hard run. Didn't matter where; as long as she pushed herself hard. She ran so long she missed dinner. Spent, she trudged back to her room, showered, and fell into bed.

Tomorrow *had* to be better.

&

"*T*ara, wake up!"

Her eyelids flickered open. She rolled onto her back and blinked in the twilight.

Angela propped herself up on an elbow. "You were screaming. Scared the shit out of me."

Tara rested her forearm over her face. "Sorry."

"What were you dreaming about?"

Tara sighed. "My dad."

"I'm sure he's fine." Angela's lacy, sleep mask hugged her forehead like safety goggles.

"He's...actually, he's no longer on the planet."

"Oh my God." Angela groped for the lamp switch and light filled the room. "I'm so sorry."

"It's okay, almost been a year." Tara rubbed her eyes and watched mosquitoes party on the ceiling.

"It's never okay to lose your daddy. If you want to talk about it, I don't mind." Angela reached for her water bottle and sipped.

Tara rubbed her arm. "No point in reliving it."

"Hon, if I lost my daddy in the last year, I'd need to unload." Angela tugged her skimpy night shirt higher on her plentiful chest.

"Not fun to talk about." Tara fingered the faded, orange bandana around her neck. She had fused into a pathetic glop of grief, guilt, and anger for so long it felt like her new normal.

Angela nodded at her. "Maybe you should take off your neckerchief. You might choke in your sleep."

"Oh, I never take this off. It was Dad's. Mom gave it to him for good luck and he wore it on every fire. Now it's my good luck charm. It protects me."

Angela looked at her a moment, then rose to refill her water bottle from the tiny bathroom faucet. She returned and plopped on her bunk. "Tell me about your daddy."

Tara pushed herself up to sit. She plucked her own water bottle from the nightstand between their bunks. She stared at it, unblinking, and picked at the label. The familiar heaviness twisted her chest and her head ached along with it.

"He worked as a city firefighter after fighting fire with the Lolo Interagency Hotshots for thirteen years. He also taught fire science at the University of Montana, where he met my mom. When she died—"

"Oh, you unfortunate thing. You're an orphan." Angela gave her a sympathetic look.

"I was in eighth grade when she got ovarian cancer. Before she died, she made my dad promise to quit the hotshot crew to work for the city. So he'd be close to home." She peeled the label from the bottle and rolled the sticky pieces into balls between her thumb and forefinger.

"I lived with Dad in a log home up Pattee Canyon, outside of Missoula. Last year, there was a late-night storm and lightning hit the trees next to the house. Dad always meant to cut those stupid trees. How ironic is that?" She sipped her water. "Here we were, fire-fighters, preaching to others about defensible space around homes. One of us should have cut the damn trees." Tara shook her head.

Angela stayed still, listening.

Tara pressed her fingers to her temples, head pounding. "On Travis's birthday, we got a hotel room because he lived in shared quarters at the Missoula Smokejumper Base. I wanted to give him a...you know..." She glanced at Angela and raised her brows. "A special birthday present before we got married."

Angela gave her a knowing look. "I totally get that."

"Jim called my cell at four in the morning. He said there was a fire and to have Travis drive me to Jim's house. Told me not to go home. I left Travis at the hotel and drove home." She shook her head. "Should have listened to Jim."

Angela blew out air and sat on the edge of Tara's bed.

Tara took a deep breath. "The neighbors tried to get Dad out, but the fire torched the second story first." She paused to calm herself. "The fire burned so hot, they only found bone fragments. He just—disappeared."

"Not your fault. How would you have known?" Angela said softly, placing her hand on Tara's.

"I should have been home. I could have gotten him out. He'd be alive right now." Grief still cleaved her heart.

Angela squeezed Tara's shoulder. "Don't do that to yourself. All guilt does is make you feel useless."

"When you lose your parents, you're stuck in that moment of desertion. I quit firefighting and stayed with a friend until I could get my ducks lined up. Jim Dolan was Dad's best friend and I badgered him to hire me back on the Missoula fire crew. Like father, like daughter, as Jim always says."

Angela seemed incredulous. "Shoot, girl! You need to go be a lawyer or a baby panda bear trainer. Anything but a firefighter. Why torture yourself?"

"It's complicated."

"Usually is." Angela handed Tara her water. "Tell me about your dream."

"It's always the same. Dad and I run toward each other, but I can never get to him. When Dad was a Lolo Hotshot, everyone on the crew celebrated birthdays and Christmases together. When he died, it all faded away. I want my family back. And I want to make it right for not saving him."

"Maybe your daddy wasn't yours to save. I'm sorry, but your desire to be your father's legacy reeks of self-sacrifice."

Blood left Tara's face and she gawped at Angela as if she'd oozed from a wall.

Angela pulled her head back. "Why are you looking at me like that?"

"Ryan said the same thing on the Copper Peak Fire." The hairs on Tara's neck prickled.

"You knew him before you came up here?"

"Sort of. I tried to evacuate a homeowner, but I wasn't fast enough. For some ungodly reason, I couldn't move. Next thing I knew O'Connor dragged me back. Then by some weird fluke, we were seatmates on the flight up here." It still blew her away to think of it.

Angela raised her brows. "Has it ever occurred to you that you were meant to be here?"

Tara gave her a dour look. "I can't imagine why."

"I believe everything happens for a reason. Each of us has a unique purpose. Mine is to find the sexiest guy imaginable, marry him, and make beautiful babies."

"Sounds more like a goal." Tara gave her wry smile.

"There's a reason why Ryan helped you on that fire. And that you wound up sitting next to him on the plane. Not to mention he became your training instructor." Angela stood and moved to her bed. She fluffed her pillow. "If you ask me, it's good, old-fashioned destiny."

Tara snorted. "No. Just coincidence." She thought of Jim Dolan's comment about signs.

Angela yawned, her drawl in overdrive. "Time for shuteye. Morning comes early up here." She crawled into bed and pulled up the covers.

"Morning is all night up here. So bizarre." Tara yawned.

"Go to sleep, Montana. Dream about unicorns farting rainbows." Angela turned off the lamp.

"It's hard for me to talk about things, but I feel I can trust you. Thanks."

"Not a problem. Now get some sleep."

"Good night." Tara tugged the bandana over her eyes and rolled to her side. She rubbed the faded neckerchief with her fingertips.

If she had only stayed home the night of the house fire. Dad died and she lived, only because she planned to have sex with her fiancé for his thirty-second birthday. And he cheated on her anyway. Rack up an A-plus for failure.

As she listened to the soothing hum of the fan, a lone tear slid from under her bandana and made a slow journey across her cheek.

CHAPTER 6

"There's an exam at the end of class today on the U.S. Forest Service, *Ten Standard Firefighting Orders and Eighteen Watch-out Situations,*" announced Ryan on the second day of training. "If you don't know them, you'd better start memorizing."

A groan circulated the room.

Ryan raised his clipboard. "Hey, these are agency requirements, not mine. Know these, they'll save your life. Next we'll cover mop-up." He lectured about the importance of mopping up fires to make sure hot spots were out and emphasized the dangers of slipping into smoldering ash pits and squirrel caches, known to injure firefighters.

His voice grew raspy and he glimpsed his watch. "Time for a break. Be back in fifteen."

As people rose and shuffled out the door, Ryan took a can of Coke from his day pack and snapped it open.

Gunnar sauntered over. "Hey. Are we still on for flying into Denali Park tomorrow after class?"

Ryan slurped. "Yep. I called Reeves and reserved the Cessna."

"I'll pay for the fuel since you're doing this for me." Gunnar plucked the Coke from Ryan's hand, took a healthy drink, and burped. "Don't worry. I've had all my shots." He handed it back.

Ryan studied it and grimaced. "Thanks for leaving me your swill."

🔥

*T*ara and Angela ambled toward the break room. Caffeine was in order. People filed in for their beverage of choice and wandered out again.

"Can you recite your *Ten Standard Firefighting Orders and Eighteen Watch-out Situations*?" A fit, petite woman with short, blonde hair strolled in, hands in pockets. "Liz Harrington, Reno." She extended a hand.

Tara shook it. "Pleased to meet you. Tara Waters."

"I need a Coke to stay awake." Angela yawned, feeding coins into a pop machine. "I loathe exams. Wish I could get out of taking it." She smiled at two guys seated at a nearby table.

"Women wriggle out of requirements all the time," said the bald guy with a Bronx accent. He sounded out of place this far north.

"Yeah, they always expect preferential treatment," said the guy next to him.

Tara took in the dark-haired guy with the goatee. He wasn't bad looking, but the way he fixed his amber eyes on her made her uneasy. She shifted her gaze to the older-looking bald guy. "Don't believe we've met."

"Nick Rego." He rolled a toothpick around with his tongue. His rolled-up shirt sleeves revealed prominent Marine tattoos encircling his forearms.

Tara turned to the dark-haired guy with the goatee and pleasant smile. "And you are?"

His glinting eyes roved her top to bottom. "Mike Hudson."

Something about him bugged her. She focused on Rego. "So,

Rego and Hudson, seriously?" Tara smiled while stirring her coffee.

"Yeah. Seriously." Rego gave her an unblinking stare. "Scientific fact. Women aren't built for the stamina or endurance to fight fire." He swept a brown-eyed gaze over Tara, then surveyed Liz.

Liz folded her arms. "What rock have you guys been living under for the last fifty years?"

Tara had been down this road. "Care to cite your scientific reference? FYI, I pull my weight on every fire I work. I can certainly handle a fitness test of walking three miles with a forty-five-pound pack under qualifying time."

"Good for you." Rego sported a mouth full of straight teeth.

"Fitness tests aren't a problem for us," interjected Angela. She lifted her chin, looking down at the men.

Rego turned his attention to the curvaceous brunette. "We'll see day after tomorrow in the pack test." He leaned his chair back on two legs. "Won't we?"

"You think we can't hack it?" Tara looked him in the eye.

"Didn't say that," said Rego. "Just said women aren't built for the stamina or endurance to fight fire. Where I come from, women are protected. They aren't the protectors."

Tara finished her coffee and flipped the cup expertly into the trash. "Where I come from women do the protecting as much as, if not more than, men. What do you think a single mom does, or any woman with kids? So, Harvey Weinstein, we've moved on from patronizing women in the workplace."

Rego lifted dark, bushy eyebrows. "I'm not patronizing anyone. How many people have *you* saved in a fire?"

Tara froze. *Why would he ask that? Did someone tell him about her? Did Ryan?*

Angela sensed Tara's hesitation and swooped in. "Okay, how many have *you* saved?"

Rego narrowed his eyes. "My fair share, honey, believe me."

"I'm not your honey, sugar. Ya'll are aware you can be fired for sexist comments." Angela poured on the Southern and bobbled her head like a cobra.

"Not a sexist comment, Miss Scarlett. Just fact." Rego failed miserably at a Southern accent. "And you'd have to prove it."

Liz whipped out her phone, tapped video record, and pointed it at him. "Care to elaborate?"

Ryan's tall frame suddenly filled the doorway. "Is there a problem here?"

His abrupt presence jarred Tara. "Nothing I haven't run into before. Excuse me." She gave Ryan a fake smile and brushed past him on her way out the door.

"Asshats," Liz tossed over her shoulder as she and Angela followed her out.

"Well. Those two were inspirational, don't you think?" Tara smirked as the three women strolled to the training room.

Angela snorted. "Weren't they though? That unibrow was a wilderness growing on that bald guy's face."

"Yeah and the goatee guy was an interesting specimen," said Liz dryly.

"Something about him creeped me out," said Tara. "I've met chainsaws with more personality. Anyway, we'll prove both of them wrong at our fitness test later this week."

In Tara's experience, guys like Rego and Hudson were a minor annoyance in the overall scheme of things, and she wouldn't waste energy on them. But Rego's comments made her wonder if Ryan had mentioned something to him about helping her in the Copper Peak Fire.

Tara wondered what Ryan said to Rego and Hudson after they left. She didn't need a white knight to rescue her. Ryan already helped her once and she appreciated it, but it would stop there. *I'll fight my own battles, thank you very much. I'm a firefighter, not a damsel in distress.*

She'll make sure Ryan gets that message. Loud and clear.

🔥

*R*yan waited until everyone cleared the break room except Rego and Hudson. Rego was solid in stature with a sassy reputation, but he was a good firefighter. Ryan knew him from previous fire seasons as a rugged outdoorsman who called it as he saw it. Still no excuse for inappropriate comments. Hudson was an unknown entity. Ryan hadn't worked with him.

He crumpled his Coke can with one hand and tossed it in the recycle box. "What was that about, gentlemen?"

"Don't know what you mean." Rego worked his toothpick with a neutral expression.

So, they're going to do this. Ryan stared hard at Hudson, then Rego. While he exuded calm, he envisioned turning them inside out and stuffing them inside a grizzly bear den. "Shouldn't have to tell you boys. Nix the inappropriate comments or it'll cost you your jobs."

"We didn't say anything inappropriate. Just plain fact."

"Gentlemen, I'm not here to argue. You've been warned. Are we copacetic?" Ryan smiled and left the room. He didn't have time for this bullshit.

"Don't have a clue what you're talking about," Hudson called after him.

"Losers," he muttered, strolling the long hall to the training room. Can't fix stupid. But he could sure get it fired. Men and women walked a constant tightrope in the wildland firefighting profession. Sadly, he hadn't been surprised when a few gender-based incidents in the Lower Forty-eight had gone viral and wound up in Congressional hearings.

That afternoon, Ryan directed the trainees to practice deploying aluminum fire shelters, an exercise he called shake-n-bake drills. He set up a large fan to simulate strong, fire-driven winds. Each person donned work gloves to shake out the wind-blown shelters, then flopped to the ground on their stomach, pulling the shelter over their body. They held it down with their hands and feet. If they didn't do it under twenty seconds, they'd practice until they did. Ryan had no mercy; their speed could make a difference between life and death.

Back in the training room after the drills, Ryan made announcements for the next morning. "Report here at 7 a.m. for fitness tests. Wear footwear you train in, comfortable clothing, and bring your packs. We'll weigh them before the test to make sure you carry forty-five pounds. If you don't, we'll have extra weights available. Don't be late." He flicked his eyes at Tara.

Next, Gunnar passed out the exams. Tara was first to finish and dropped her test on the table next to Ryan. "Do you have a moment after class? I'd like to talk to you."

"Sure." He tried not to sound eager.

She returned to her seat and busied herself with *Coming into the Country*, by John McPhee. One of his favorite books about Alaska. *She's scoring points with me.*

As Ryan waited for the room to empty, he straightened the exams into an even pile. He was curious why Tara wanted to talk to him, then smiled to himself because he didn't care why. He tucked his clipboard under the stack of exams and patiently waited for the room to clear.

CHAPTER 7

*T*ara had noticed Ryan glancing in her direction as he lectured during class. She didn't view it as flirtatious. More like he was sensitive to the fact they had shared a rather intense moment while working on a fire. Since he'll be evaluating her performance and competency to fight fire in Alaska, it was important to her that she set the record straight.

She waited for the training room to empty. First things first. "I haven't properly thanked you for helping me on the Copper Peak Fire." She paused. "You said if I needed to talk—"

Ryan raised a finger. "Hold on a minute." He strode to the back of the room and closed the double doors, then dragged a chair to the table across from her. He arranged himself on it. "I'm a good listener. And I keep confidences."

She tried not to gape at the well-defined physique, highlighted by his navy-blue T-shirt. She admired his passion in class when he talked about fire. He obviously ate, breathed, and lived firefighting. And she liked the respectful way he treated firefighters.

"I want you to know what happened before you showed up —" she stopped to control the tremor in her voice.

He leaned forward, resting his corded forearms on the table. "You don't have to justify anything to me."

She looked at him directly. "It's important that you know. Have you told anyone you helped me? Like Rego, maybe?"

His eyes grew big. "Hell no. No one in Alaska knows anything about that. I provided a statement to the Forest Service After Action Review team in Missoula before I left, but that's it. Why do you think I would tell Rego?"

Tara tore her gaze away from his and looked down at her lap. "He asked how many I'd saved on fires. I thought he somehow knew."

"I don't discuss things like that. Don't pay attention to Rego. He's always running his mouth off." He gave her a wry smile. "Your secret is safe with me."

She believed him. "Can I tell you something? Yesterday after class, I Skyped into the After-Action Review with the Forest Service in Missoula. I didn't cast blame on anyone but myself for misjudging fire behavior and thinking I could outrun it."

He nodded. "I've participated in AARs before. They aren't fun, but it's important to analyze the situation for lessons learned, to prevent it from happening again."

She appreciated his understanding. It made her words come easier. "I told them yesterday, that when we fight fire where homes and wildlands meet, we trust others to get people out in mandatory evacuations. I'm not pointing fingers, but somehow the ball got dropped in making sure everyone was evacuated." Her voice caught and she hesitated. *Be careful. Don't want your instructor thinking you can't hold it together.*

He shifted in his chair but stayed quiet and listened.

She leaned back and folded her arms. "In California, those hellacious Santa Ana winds cause fast-moving fires. On a bad fire last year in Santa Clarita, we were directed to go house-to-house to make sure everyone got out. Law enforcement was shorthanded."

"Santa Ana wind fires are terrifyingly fast. I've worked several."

Tara glanced at him. "Have you ever seen a fire devil? Weather people call them firenadoes."

He nodded. "Once. In California."

"On the Montana fire, it was like a dragon had breathed flame on that house and blew it up. I saw the guy with a walker and knew he couldn't get out on his own. Jim warned I couldn't get him in time. God, I couldn't just stand there and do nothing." She shook her head. "I won track meets in high school and college. I thought I could pull it off." The pressure was building behind her eyes.

Despite her pooling tears, she somehow trusted him with her raw underbelly. "I'm not a weak person."

"That's the last thing I'd think about you." He pulled a red bandana from his pants pocket and slid it across the table. "Being able to talk about it is a sign of strength, not weakness."

The gentle way he said it drew her gaze to his empathetic one. "I was so shocked when the fire…took him. I couldn't move —couldn't move anything." A renegade tear fell. She grabbed the bandana and swiped it away. "Thanks for pulling me back. Sorry I was a jerk. I was mortified you had to help me."

"Don't be. Anyone would have reacted the same. You'd have gotten yourself out. All I did was speed things up." He gave her a sympathetic smile. "Did Jim advise you to get counseling for the line of duty death?"

Tara swallowed. "Yes. But I didn't want to go on admin leave, so he suggested I come up here for a change of scenery. I'll do my time and return to Missoula to work on the Lolo Hotshot crew."

"You make it sound like working in Alaska is a prison sentence. Seriously, reconsider counseling. Your agency will pay for it."

Was it his sincere concern or his easy charm causing her breath to catch? "I'm working things out on my own."

"It helps to work through what you've experienced with a professional."

"I'll think about it." It came out snottier than she meant it to. "I mean, I'll consider it. Thanks."

An awkward silence fell between them. He stared at her a long moment. "Well, you know what's best for you."

She leaned back in her chair and stared at the bandana she rolled in her hands. "I want you to know something. I don't normally need rescuing. I'm not helpless." She looked up at him.

"Never thought of you that way. Quite the contrary. If you were a guy, I would have done the same. Sometimes people need help, that's all. Even firefighters." He gave her a close-mouthed smile and moved to the white board where he picked up an eraser and rubbed away his class notes.

Tara tried not to notice his biceps flex and unflex as he erased his wildfire scenarios from class. When she realized she was ogling, she jerked herself to action and found another eraser.

"One other thing," she added as she helped him erase. "I can handle chauvinist douches, like today in the break room."

He paused and gave her a sidelong glance. "As an instructor, I have the responsibility to stop offensive comments. Teasing or serious. Zero tolerance."

She hated wiping away his beautiful handwriting. "You galloped in on your white steed to slay the dragons and thank you for that, by the way." She turned to him, holding the eraser. "But I can slay my own dragons."

He stopped to look at her. "I have absolutely no doubt that you can."

"So, how much did you hear anyway?"

"You had me at Harvey Weinstein." He slanted a grin at her.

She laughed and looked into his eyes. "You liked that?"

No one on the planet has eyes this blue. He must be wearing tinted contacts.

"Like I said…I don't let people get away with offensive remarks."

"Good to hear you say that." She watched for any nuance that would belie his comment. His credibility as her training instructor depended on how well he supported women firefighters. "Guys with sexist attitudes do it to get a rise out of us, so long as they can get away with it."

"True." He finished cleaning the white board and turned to her. "I have to point something out. Rego and Hudson laid the fly on the water and you bit the hook."

She shrugged. "They questioned my ability to do the job, so I called them on it."

"I'm not condoning what they said. Just saying they baited you."

His vibe rippled her insides and her breathing shallowed. To distance herself, she wandered to the wall map while her heart vaulted an imaginary pommel horse. She slid her forefinger to Kwigillingok, on the Bering Sea coast in southwest Alaska.

She spoke to the map. "I don't care what motivates people to make ignorant comments. I won't let them get away with it." She turned to see him leaning against the white board scrutinizing her. Heat crawled up her neck.

"This agency doesn't tolerate gender bias and harassment. But they can't do anything unless it's reported. Want to file a complaint against Rego and Hudson?" He set down the eraser and swiped his hands.

"Why? Because they have old-fashioned beliefs that women should be protected and aren't built to fight fire? I told them to stop their comments. Most people do when you call them on it. That's been my experience anyway."

She suddenly felt self-conscious and turned to the map, sliding her finger along the boundary of Denali National Park.

She aimed for a casual tone. "So where did you go after I saw you on the Copper Peak Fire?"

"Met up with my jump squad while air attack did their thing. Tanker pilots were the real heroes. Their mud drops bought us time to get a saw-line around the head and contain it. We had a good incident commander."

"Travis McGuire." She was amazed how easy her ex's name rolled off her tongue.

"Right, McGuire. One of the Zulie jumpers. You know him?"

"Uh-huh. I know him." No way would she say how. How bizarre that he mentioned her former fiancé. Could any of these coincidences get any weirder?

A thought struck her. "How do you know my crew boss, Jim Dolan?"

She swore he gave her a deer-in-the-headlights expression.

"I met him several years ago on a fire in Alaska's Interior."

"What did he say about me that day on the Copper Peak Fire?"

"He thanked me for helping you. That's all." He flicked his eyes at the wall clock.

She glanced at her watch. "Oh, sorry to keep you. I have to go anyway, to catch dinner before mess hall closes."

"Wait, I'll go with you." He gathered the exams and set them on his clipboard.

"If I walk with you to dinner, people will say I'm hitting on the training instructor," she teased. Being new here, she wanted to establish she wasn't about that.

"You care what people say?"

"I like to keep things professional." Saying it matter-of-factly aided her resolve.

"So do I." He locked his gaze on her. "In Alaska, people are pretty chill."

She scrambled for an even keel. "I'm sure they are."

Ryan stood and tucked the exams under his arm. "Okay, let's go."

The way he said it sounded casual and intimate, as if he'd known her all her life. She felt easier with him than she'd expected. They left the training room and exited the building.

As they strolled toward the mess hall, Tara found herself dragging their pace. A group of guys sauntered past, dipping their heads at Ryan, eyes fixed on Tara.

"How long have you been jumping in Alaska? What did you do before?"

"This is my fifth season. Worked on the Mendocino Hotshot crew in California and did some heli-rappelling. Thought I'd jump out of planes instead of dangling below helos, so I applied to Redding Smokejumper Base. Got my degree at Humboldt and transferred up here."

"Impressive resumé."

He angled toward her. "It's a living, right?"

She admired his controlled calm for someone with such a perilous job. "Let me guess—you're addicted to the insane adrenaline rush of jumping out of a perfectly good airplane to tame a raging inferno. You travel to beautiful, exotic lands and have seen indescribable rainbows and sunsets. You experience what the average person doesn't, and millions will never see." She gave him a triumphant smile.

"Something tells me you're familiar with smokejumping." He smiled back, displaying dimpled cheeks and nice teeth. *What the heck kind of dental plan does he have?*

"I worked at the Missoula Smokejumper Base a few years back—plus I know people who work there." No way would she say how she'd almost married into it.

"Love the job, especially up here. You're right. I've seen beauty I can't describe. I'm no writer or poet, that's for sure."

"You graduated, so you must have done *some* writing. What's your degree?"

"Fire science and natural resources. You?"

"Master's in fire science from University of Montana." She reached the entrance of the mess hall.

"Ha! We're two of a kind. You know, Alaska is even more spectacular from the air. I could show you sometime—" Ryan's phone interrupted with *Ring of Fire*. "Hey, hang on a sec." He covered the phone to talk to Tara. "Go on in and I'll count to ten, so you won't be walking in with your training instructor." He moved away, smiling into his phone.

Was it a girlfriend? She pulled the door open, inhaling grilled food. The door slammed behind her and she hurried to the food line. She loaded her tray with a pork chop, rice, and steamed broccoli before setting it on a table and sliding onto the bench seat.

She sawed at her pork chop, keeping one eye on the door. A pony-tailed woman wiped off her table and another swished a mop on the linoleum, causing her to shovel in the rest of her dinner. When she left the mess hall, Ryan was nowhere in sight. Who'd caused him to miss dinner? Smokejumpers never missed a meal.

Had she heard him correctly? He'd show her Alaska from the air. Oh crap, not more flying. Of all the fires in all the forests in all the states, Ryan had jumped into hers. And he'd earned her quiet stamp of approval for instructor credibility.

But don't get attracted.

She would not allow herself to get sucked in again. While Ryan made her insides a little gooey, she would firmly plant him in her WFBNM—Work Friend but Nothing More category. No more smokejumper entanglements. Dad had warned her before the first one.

And of course, she didn't listen.

CHAPTER 8

*R*yan entered the Jump Shack, the heartbeat of the Alaska Smokejumper Base. He wandered past the taller section where parachutes hung gracefully from the ceiling, then passed the Ready Room where jumpers stored gear and suited up to jump fires.

His stomach growled. Dad called just as he'd summoned the nerve to invite Tara to go flying. By the time he'd explained the IRS required minimum distribution to his dad for the hundredth time, the mess hall had closed. So much for getting to know Tara over dinner.

He stopped off in the small break room to scope out leftovers in the fridge. He rescued a smashed ham and cheese sandwich bunched up in a corner. Scowling at it, he heard whistling in The Loft, the long rectangular room where jumpers repaired chutes and other firefighting equipment. He entered and tossed his clipboard and exams on a wall counter.

"About time you dragged your sorry ass in here." Gunnar bent over a long chute table, inspecting lines and harnesses under a bright hanging light. "You're not getting out of rigging chutes just because you have tests to grade."

"Okay, slacker, then help me." Ryan bit into the mutilated ham and cheese.

"Ryno, you're better at that stuff than me."

"Yeah, right." He flopped into a worn, out-of-place armchair.

During morning roll call his first year, three Ryans were on the Alaska jump list. Ryan O. soon became Ryno. After he'd commanded a few fires, jumpers christened him 'The Charging Ryno' for his fearless, unrelenting approach to fighting fire.

"Long day?" Gunnar eyeballed a chute seam.

"Aren't they all?"

"Depends." Gunnar grinned. "On the company one keeps."

"Meaning?"

"Observed a certain redhead waiting to talk to you after class."

Ryan waved away his comment. "She had questions."

"Uh-huh, whatever you say. Tomorrow's syllabus is on my laptop." Gunnar motioned at the wall counter.

"What a stand-up guy. I take it back. You aren't a slacker." Ryan grabbed a parachute and unfolded it on a long, narrow table.

Gunnar smoothed out folds on the table. "Have you figured out crew assignments?"

Ryan straightened and yawned. "I've assigned everyone but Rego and Hudson. Still deciding which crew to stick them on."

Gunnar smirked. "I know where I'd like to stick them."

"Wish they'd wash out, but they won't."

"Waters sure won't."

Ryan cracked a smile at his jump partner's finesse at scoping out female firefighters each season. "No, she's quite...fit." He eyed his friend. "Planning to hit on her?"

"Maybe." Gunnar gave him an impish grin as he assembled more chutes.

"Don't waste your time. She's here on a temporary detail but plans to get on the Lolo Hotshots, in case you have a bead on her." He'd be damned if Gunnar would ask her out first.

"She's in the wrong state. Shouldn't she be in Montana?"

Ryan hesitated. He wouldn't out Tara. "She's going back, so don't get your hopes up. You know how hard it is to have meaningful relationships during fire season. A minute here, an evening there—and that's if you're lucky."

"Since when have you been interested in a meaningful relationship? Your last firefighter girlfriend turned out to be a porn actress."

Ryan thought of his ex, Amber, a firefighter on his Mendocino Hotshot crew. Last he heard she had indeed quit firefighting to make adult films. "She left firefighting to work naked. All I could figure was it paid more and wasn't as physically demanding."

Gunnar grinned. "That's debatable. I've always thought firefighters made the best girlfriends. They're strong, built well, and you don't have to explain how dangerous your job is."

"Sounds like dating a truck. I no longer date people I work with. Remember the woman I dated on our California crew?"

"She dumped you because she preferred women. She was only passing time with you."

"Thanks for the ego boost, asshole." Ryan made a face.

"So, date one you won't be working with. You won't be working with the three standouts in our training class after this week."

"Standouts?"

Gunnar gave him his you're-a-dumbass look. "Liz Harrington, Angela Divina and Miss Waters. I happen to know Liz dances at a strip club in the off season. 'Blaze' is her stage name. A nod to her other job, I'm thinking."

Ryan narrowed his eyes. "Wow, you're a regular search engine of information. How'd you come by that info?" Gunnar seemed to have an inside pipeline with fire people in every western state.

"My buddies on the Black Mountain Hotshots in Carson City. They go to Reno for her shows because one of them dates her. He says she's a good dancer, knows her way around a pole."

"Well, up here she's a firefighter." Ryan scrunched his face. "Think it's best to remember that."

"Then there's the lovely Miss Divina. I go weak in the knees for Southern belles. And on that note, it's time to hit the hay so I can fantasize." Gunnar yawned, scratching his chest.

"Wait until after training." Ryan recalled the first day when Angela had unbuttoned the first few buttons on her fire shirt. Until then, he'd never thought of yellow Nomex as sexy. Even so, Angela held no interest for him.

"I know you. You won't be able to stick to your rule of not dating trainees."

"I'm offended by your lack of faith." Ryan helped Gunnar lay out the chutes to hang in the Loft the next morning.

"Not to change the subject, but what time are we flying to Denali tomorrow?" asked Gunnar.

"Be behind the barracks by half past three. Mel will drive us to the airport. I'm releasing class early so people can prepare for fitness tests Thursday." Ryan pointed at him. "Bring a jacket and don't forget your camera."

"Yes, Grandpa. Anything else?"

"Thanks for getting us ready for tomorrow. You don't suck so bad."

"All right, but you're still ugly." Gunnar thumbed his nose and made his exit.

Ryan opened a drawer in the jump desk and lifted his tatum, the paper-sized metal container where he stored paperwork. He referred to it as his portable office. Unclipping the tablet from his well-worn clipboard, he inserted it in the tatum, and snapped it shut. Remembering the stack of exams, he grabbed them and headed out.

He approached the Ops office on the other end of the Ready Room, where his boss, Larry DiPrete hunched over piles of paper and folders. One thing about firefighting, thought Ryan. No shortage of paperwork.

"Later, Zom—I mean Larry," Ryan corrected himself as he headed out.

Smokejumpers dubbed Larry DiPrete with the name Zombie because he never slept. Ever. Zombie wore a perpetual bug-eyed expression. His gray cowlick and one pant leg always tucked in his boot gave him a disheveled appearance. Precious few got away with calling him Zombie. Ryan wasn't one. It appeared he hadn't yet earned the privilege.

"Get them people trained up. I need your ass back here," Zombie's voice rumbled after him.

"Working on it," muttered Ryan, pushing the door open. It slammed shut behind him.

He strolled toward the barracks as the sun lingered on Chena Ridge. Shadowy spruce emerged from the dissipating smoke haze at the edge of the base. High above, sockeye-colored clouds transformed the sky into a lava flow. Denali appeared, keeping watch over all of it.

He loved Alaska. She always surprised him with a new face.

Tara drifted into his mind as he took in the saturated sky. He sensed an underlying strength in her he admired. Her anxiety about flying presented a perfect opportunity to put his action plan to work. Technically, he wouldn't be breaking his unwritten rule of not dating co-workers with Gunnar along.

It would not be a date. And he could get to know her better.

He entered the barracks and plodded up the stairs to the second floor. He rounded a corner in the dark hallway as a pair of green eyes came at him.

"Oh gosh, excuse me." Tara stumbled backward after crashing into him at a fast clip, toothbrush in hand.

He backed up, welcoming the view of her skimpy tank top and shorts. And those legs—*shit, those legs.* He mumbled something but hadn't a clue what.

"I was looking for another bathroom. Our room faucets don't work." She talked fast, hair dangling around her. Even in the twilight, he noted her flushed cheeks.

"This is the men's wing," he choked out, clearing his throat. It took every ounce of fortitude not to stare at her breasts spilling out of the tank top.

"I'm still figuring out the lay of the land. Should have used my phone GPS." She sounded way too cheerful. "Um, that was a joke." She waved her toothbrush.

"Uh, yeah, phone GPS. Right." He laughed, bobbing his head like a damn chicken.

"Did I hurt you? Smacked you pretty hard." She gave him a once-over, then parked her gaze on his face.

He smoothed a palm down his chest. "Don't think so. Everything seems intact." His eyes drifted down, horrified to see a bulge down south.

"Don't want to injure the training instructor," she laughed, as she tugged up her tank top to cover cleavage.

Oh, no, don't do that.

The action increased below his belt buckle. His plane had lifted off; nothing he could do about it. *Abort, abort, get to my room. Now.*

"Ladies' bathroom is at the other end." He pointed. When she turned in that direction, he about faced and hastily retreated. "See you in class," he tossed over his shoulder.

"Okay, sorry. Good night," she stage-whispered after him.

"Uh-huh good night." He jammed his key in the lock and snatched one last peek at those amazing legs. He all but pushed the door off its hinges to get it open. *She's sorry? I'm not.* He ducked inside, slammed the door, and leaned against it.

Holy shit. Had her beautiful chest touched his? He wasn't sure. How was he not sure? Guys remember those things. Dazed, he flopped on his bed, lifting his long legs onto the mattress, his size thirteens dangling off the end. His clipboard fell to the floor.

He closed his eyes and replayed the vision of a scantily clad Tara Waters. His heart thudded. Great. Now when he'd invite her to go flying tomorrow, she'll think he's hitting on her because he'd seen her half-dressed. No, half-naked. *How the hell am I supposed to resist this woman until I no longer work with her?*

He dropped a hand to the floor, groping for his clipboard. Lifting it, he reviewed his action plan, then tossed it on his nightstand. He watched mosquitoes bounce along the ceiling. Timing. It's always the damn timing.

You're a smokejumper, for cripes' sake—you jump from airplanes to fight raging infernos. You'll figure it out.

He fell into a deep sleep, grinning like the Cheshire Cat and delighting in visions of naked, green-eyed goddesses brandishing auburn fire.

CHAPTER 9

*T*ara woke early, refreshed, and energized. She planned to squeeze in a run and go to the weight room before class.

When she stepped outside, the sun was already high. This far north the sun stayed up all night like a Vegas gambler. What an odd place, she thought. Dressed in black Capris and a tank top, she tucked in her ear buds, and powered on her mp3 player. Portugal The Man, playing *Feel It Still*; her favorite tune to ramp up her run. The music freed her mind to wander.

She did some stretches and hit the road, her feet keeping time to the song. She jogged east toward the Chena River and turned left, entering the six-lane running track. The early morning warmth pleasantly surprised her as she sipped her water bottle. Several runners dotted the rubberized track.

An eagle pair caught updrafts, circled above the river, commanding air. She envied their fearless ability to fly. Ever since Dad died, flying had become an issue. She wasn't sure why and didn't want to overthink it.

She loved running early in the morning when everything smelled fresh and new. Birds chirped louder and the dew-kissed, subarctic grass sparkled like glitter. The smoke had cleared, and the clean air felt heavenly to her lungs. Near the river, a moose munched willow.

An image of a startled Ryan after last night's collision made her smile. Traipsing the hall in search of a bathroom in skimpy PJ's wasn't one of her smarter choices, but no one had room in a fire pack for a bathrobe.

Tara felt a swoosh on her left—someone zoomed past, flipping her thick braid over her shoulder. Ryan O'Connor, going full tilt. He raised an arm and waved, leaving her behind like a laggard.

She assessed his receding backside. Nodding approval, she doubled down and sped up. He sprinted fast—but running was *her* deal. Didn't take long to catch him. She pulled the buds from her ears and let them dangle.

He slowed to a jog; a red bandana tied around sun-tinted hair. He'd tucked some behind his ears and she liked how the tiny flips poked out under his lobes. His sleeveless tee revealed muscle true to what she'd envisaged after hours of studying him in class.

"Morning." He grinned, a bounce to his step. Way too hyper for this early.

Tara figured there ought to be a law against it. "Are you always this depressed in the morning?"

"Generally, yeah."

Wow, those dimples. A competitive mood grabbed her. "So, are you up for a race? One lap and finish here." She tapped her toe where they stood.

"Think you can take me?"

"Caught you just now, didn't I?"

"Wait a minute. Let's catch our breath." He studied his watch, then glanced up. "Ready go." He shot off like the roadrunner being chased by Wile E. Coyote.

"Hey, that wasn't a full minute!" she protested, tearing after him.

They pounded around the track as if escaping a charging moose. She knew how hard smokejumpers worked out; she used to race Travis. Annoyed at herself for thinking of her ex, she sped up near the end of their lap. Once alongside Ryan, she pushed hard to keep up. He lunged ahead a few yards before the finish.

He circled back to her, his chest heaving and his shoulders glistening. "Not bad."

"You jumped the start." Puffing hard, she bent, hands on thighs. Her lungs ached.

"Yesterday you mentioned winning track meets." He wiped his forehead with a short towel around his neck.

"I won a few races. But mostly worked out with my dad. He was a hot-shotter."

"Firefighting runs in your family, I take it. Hotshots are animals when it comes to workouts." Ryan paused to catch his breath.

"So are smokejumpers." She shook out her arms, checking him out from behind her shades, hating that this vision was turning her on. "And that makes you an animal."

His brows lifted above his sunglasses. "You're talking about workouts, right?"

"What else would I be referring to?" She stretched her calves, knowing full well the gamut of things 'animal' could imply.

"Not touching that one," he chortled, pressing an arm across his chest to stretch it.

He pointed at a hill on the other side of the river. "If you hike up there you can see Denali. There's a footbridge across the river. Want to check it out?"

"Do we have time?"

"The way you cover ground, yeah." He took off running toward the river and she followed.

He slowed at the footbridge. "As I was saying last night…" He paused.

She waited for a wisecrack about wandering the halls in her skivvies.

"I can help with your aviophobia."

"My what?"

"Fear of flying. On the flight up here, you said you hated flying."

"You remembered that?"

"You grabbed my leg."

"Oh, right. Forgot about that," she lied, her face heating. She recalled the firmness of his thigh muscle. "You fell asleep on my shoulder, so we're even."

"Hm, right. I did." He gave her a broad grin. "Normally I don't sleep on the shoulders of strangers."

Had she known then he'd be her training instructor, she would have concealed her unease about flying. Firefighters were not in the habit of voicing fears. About anything.

She turned to him with hands on her hips. "Hating to fly doesn't equate to a fear of flying. Technically speaking."

"Same thing."

"No, it isn't. You can hate something without fearing it—just as you can fear something without hating it. I fear grizzlies, but I don't hate them. And I don't fear flying."

He nodded slowly. "Interesting logic. Never thought of it like that."

"Thanks for your keep-calm-and-fly chat on the flight to Fairbanks. You seem relaxed on planes."

"When I'm not jumping from them, I fly them. Got my private pilot's license a few years ago. One of the reasons I transferred to the Alaska Smokejumper Base."

They crossed the bridge running side-by-side, their feet tapping the wood. He led her up a gentle slope that opened to a treeless mountain plateau.

He stopped and Tara nearly bumped into him as she gaped

at a monolith jutting into the air like a skyscraper. "Is that Denali?" She pulled off her sunglasses.

"Affirmative." He stood next to her, breathing hard.

Warmth flushed through her. Caused by Denali or Ryan? She wasn't sure. Maybe both. "Now that's a mountain. Looks like a giant snow cone." She took in the white majesty, dappled with vertical, jagged shadows.

"I can fly you up close and personal since you've assured me you don't have aviophobia." He slid his gaze from Denali to her. "You'd see what the average person never gets the chance to. I'd even throw in a glacier landing."

Her eyes widened. "You land on glaciers? How does that work?"

"The plane I fly has wheeled skis. I can take you to where time stands still. Are you up for it?"

His words hung in the air as she stared at Denali, processing his question. Should she go? She couldn't wimp out, no matter how terrified she was of flying in a plane that could fall out of the sky into a narrow chasm of blue ice and be lost forever. *Don't let him know you're scared.*

"When are you going?"

"Today after class. I promised Gunnar I'd fly him into Denali Park. Only takes a few hours."

"Today?" She gulped. Flying up to America's tallest peak in a small plane? It'd be scary enough in a big plane, let alone a small one. This was insane.

He checked his watch. "We'd better go. I'll jog back with you, unless you're worried people will think you're hitting on the training instructor."

"Yeah, right," she snorted, attempting to prove she thought nothing of the sort.

They jogged steadily and slowed their pace as they approached the barracks.

71

Ryan turned to her and she saw her reflection in his shades. "What do you say, want to go?"

She looked at him a long moment. "I'll think about it."

"Is that a solid maybe? People who have flown with me say I'm a damn good pilot. Even Gunnar says so." Ryan pulled the towel from around his neck and wiped his face.

How could wiping sweat be sexy and how was she not supposed to notice? She dropped her gaze to her watch. "Everyone says that when they're back on the ground in one piece." If Gunnar went along, she'd be one of the guys like on a fire crew. She was good with it.

"No worries. I'm Mister Safety." He'd thrown down the gauntlet.

Not that she was apprehensive going alone with Ryan, but the thought did flutter her insides.

Who wouldn't want an up close and personal tour of the tallest peak in North America? She wanted to go but didn't want to freak out doing it. Ryan was a stickler for safety, so who better to go with? *They'll land on a glacier!* How many can say they've done that?

"Told you, I'm not afraid. What time?" She stared at him, duck-paddling about where she could lay fast hands on some Xanax.

"I'm ending class early so people can prepare for tomorrow's pack test. Be at the back door of the barracks at half past three. Mel will shuttle us."

"Okay." Heart clamoring, she wondered if she was more terrified to fly or more thrilled at his invitation.

"Bring your camera with lots of juice." He reached the door to the barracks and held it open.

"Thanks." She clambered up the steps and grinned at him as she bolted for her room.

Angela roused as Tara burst into their room, peeling off her damp, sweaty clothes and tossing them on her bed. Was she foolish for agreeing to this? Despite her trepidation about flying, windmills spun in her chest.

"Good morning," called Tara, stepping into the shower.

"Mornin' sunshine. Do we have water this morning?" Angela rubbed her eyes.

Tara turned the handle and tested the spray. "We sure do." She smiled, letting water massage her as she unraveled her thick braid.

She may be anxious about flying, but after all…she was still an adrenaline junkie at heart.

*R*yan appreciated that Gunnar had planned an action-packed day for training. Since the weather was decent, they moved the class out to the lawn, pausing their talks for loud planes and helicopters. Ryan ran the trainees through their paces with on-the-spot Shake-N-Bake drills to deploy fire shelters.

During lunch, Ryan confirmed his reservation with Caribou Aviation to rent the Cessna Skyplane 182; the same plane he'd learned to fly and had flown several times into the Alaska Range. He looked forward to being in the air again.

He ended class early, hearing no complaints. The corner of his eye caught Tara hurrying to the barracks, and he brightened. He ticked off an inventory of the gear he'll take as he headed to the barracks, with one eye on Denali, daring her to weather in. He'd be disappointed if clouds filled in the mountain passes and they'd have to turn around. He wasn't certified for IFR—Instrument Flight Rules, relying only on instruments to guide him between the mountains if they weathered in.

Once in his room, Ryan changed into a dark North Face pullover, cargo pants, and his Caribou Aviation baseball cap. He grabbed his leather flight jacket and tossed aviator shades in a day pack, with water, snacks, and other safety gear.

A knock at the door. He swung it open to Gunnar, looking guilty. "Bro, can we go another day? Can't today."

"You're canceling on me? Geez, Gunns, the plane is only available today. Next week we'll be jumping fire."

"My cousins are in town on a Princess tour. They're leaving for Anchorage tomorrow. Sorry for the short notice." He gave Ryan an apologetic smile.

Ryan shrugged. "Well okay, but now I can't take you till after fire season."

"Still going today?"

Delight replaced disappointment, but he hid it from his jump partner. "Yep, need the flight hours." He debated telling Gunnar he'd invited another passenger. Nah. Let him think he'd be lonesome as hell.

"Sorry bro." Gunnar backed out the door. "Have a good flight."

"I'll try." Grinning to himself, Ryan grabbed his gear and headed behind the barracks, where Mel and Tara stood talking next to the box van. As he approached her, he assessed. Jeans, athletic shoes, and a T-shirt were not enough for winter conditions.

"Better grab a warm jacket and hiking boots if you have them. It's ninety-two degrees here, but where we're going, it's sixty degrees cooler. Think January."

Tara studied his leather jacket and heavy boots. Her eyes grew big. "Sixty degrees? Hold on a minute." She scooted back into the barracks.

Ryan tossed his day pack on the back seat of the van before hauling himself in beside it. "Tara can ride up front."

"How did you talk her into flying with you when you just met her?" Mel leaned against the driver's side door and repositioned his baseball cap. He pulled out his Copenhagen and grimaced at the empty can. Sighing, he tucked it under the worn circle in the pocket of his jeans.

"I'm naturally charming, I guess."

Mel snapped his head up. "Don't give me that aw shucks bullshit. You smokejumpers are all about procedure."

Ryan thought of his Incident Action Plan to date Tara. He knew Mel was dead right about that as he watched Tara skip down the steps to the van. He could watch her all day. And he had. *Control yourself. Keep it professional.*

She peeked in the open passenger door. "Where's Gunnar?"

"He canceled. His cousins are in town." Ryan gauged her reaction.

"Oh, too bad. Geez." She seemed genuinely disappointed. Maybe she'd agreed to go because Gunnar was going. She gave him a polite smile. "Okay if I ride shotgun?"

"It's all yours." Ryan looked forward to spending time with her but hoped it wasn't obvious.

"Thanks." She slipped into the passenger seat and slammed the door. Mel turned the ignition and pulled the van onto the road leading out of Fort Wainwright.

"O'Connor, being the gentleman that he is, gave up his traditional front perch for you. Beauty before age." Mel gave her a sidelong glance.

"So, now I'm a gentleman. Not what you said last week. And I'm offended by your age slam." Ryan flicked his thumb and forefinger at the back of Mel's head. He liked giving his buddy a hard time.

Mel aimed his eyes at the rearview and Ryan thumbed his nose at him.

Tara twisted to grin at Ryan. "So, you're an old man, huh?"

What a gorgeous smile. He wanted to kiss it. "Technically, I'm only—"

"He hit his third decade," interrupted Mel.

"Thanks for ratting me out," grimaced Ryan. "Mel rolled

into a much higher number last month. He tried to keep it a secret, but we have ways of finding things out."

Mel jabbed his thumb toward the back seat. "This joker and the other knob-heads flew a '*Melbourne Faraday is 40*' banner behind a Cessna all over Fairbanks. Hid my age for years until that little stunt."

"You should lay off the Botox, Mel. And let's not discuss what you did for my thirtieth…" Ryan trailed off, catching himself. Melbourne had hired girls to dance at Ryan's birthday party at a jumper's house in Fairbanks. Cops showed up when neighbors complained people were skydiving from the roof onto a big army fuel bladder filled with water. Friends of Seth Boone, former Navy SEALS.

Tara didn't need this information.

"What did you do for his thirtieth?" she asked Mel.

Ryan held his breath. *Be a good man, Mel.*

"We uh… gave him a surprise party," said Mel like he wasn't guilty of anything. "And he was surprised."

Ryan changed the subject. "Talkeetna Air has been flying in and out of Denali all day. Reported light clouds and calm winds."

He couldn't wait to show Tara his most favorite place on earth.

CHAPTER 10

*T*ara had been in Alaska three days and here she was about to fly around North America's tallest mountain. All day her chest and stomach had felt like a volcano about to blow, and it worsened on the drive to the airport.

Sixty degrees cooler in Denali. She could fake a migraine. She let out a long sigh. *I'm a firefighter, not a chicken shit.*

Mel pulled the van up to a single-story building, Caribou Aviation, across from Fairbanks International Airport. Mel and Ryan hopped out.

Tara hesitated and took a deep breath. She slowly climbed out with her day pack and hung shyly back as Ryan approached the building. *Too late to back out now.*

A stout, graying man came from around the building and extended a chubby hand. "O'Connor, good to see you."

Ryan shook his hand with both of his. "Reeves, thanks for loaning me the Cessna on short notice."

"Glad she was available. She's all ready to go." Reeves nodded at the red and white, single engine aircraft, gleaming on the tarmac.

"She's a beauty." Mel handed Ryan's day pack and leather coat to him. He flicked his eyes to Reeves. "Still for sale?"

"Anything's for sale at the right price. O'Connor's been workin' me for a deal," chuckled Reeves, crow's feet framing the slits of his eyes.

"Got to jump fires, earn that hazard pay." Ryan glanced at Tara.

She raised brows in understanding, knowing the value of hazard pay in bumping up their paychecks. She glanced at the handsome aircraft that would undoubtedly cost a ginormous amount of hazard pay.

Ryan motioned to her. "Reeves, this is Tara Waters. First trip to Denali."

Reeve's eyes crinkled and his grin widened. "Matt Reeves, Caribou Aviation."

"Good to meet you," she said.

"Hope Denali shows. Should be a romantic trip if she does. Have a great flight, you two." Reeves gave Tara a polite nod.

"Thanks Matt," Ryan called after Reeves as he ducked inside his office.

He assumed she was Ryan's girlfriend. Her cheeks warmed and she shot a look at Ryan. To her relief he hadn't noticed she went red in the face. He appeared oblivious to the romance comment.

"Leaving you to it," called Mel, folding himself in the van. "Gotta get my bird ready for morning. Radio your ETA when you're ten minutes out and I'll be here." He pointed at Tara. "You're in for an experience. It'll blow your mind."

She smiled back at him. "I'm sure it will. Thanks, Mel." The thought of her jouncing in this small plane twisted her insides. *Why did I agree to this?*

"Catch you later, Mel. Thanks." Ryan turned to her, slinging his day pack to his shoulder. "Ready?"

She nodded, strolling alongside him. "You've made offers? A plane like this must be expensive."

"It's a chunk of change for sure."

She felt like an intruder to this intimate side of Ryan's life. She hardly knew him. He was different from his fire instructor persona; more relaxed and animated. He was very much in charge and seemed as passionate about flying as he was about firefighting. She admired his confidence.

He slid his fingers along the sleek fuselage, peering under it and checking whatever else pilots did before they flew. "She's a beauty. But I need time to raise the cash." He straightened, gazing off in the direction they'd be flying.

She could tell he loved this plane. "What are your plans once you buy it?"

"Start a flightseeing business. Fly tourists and climbers in and out of Denali."

"So, you want to stay in Alaska."

"That's the plan." He opened the cargo bay near the tail and loaded their gear.

Gee, too bad, she stopped herself from saying. This is the last place she'd want to settle down. She'd heard repeatedly Alaska had a million ways to kill you every ten minutes. And how the odds were good, but the goods were odd, when it came to the dating population. Ryan was indeed an exception to that worn out cliche.

"Going to build a log home with caribou jumping your white picket fence?"

"Already have one. Minus the fence, but with moose." He pulled a small personal locator beacon from his pants pocket, pressed a few buttons, and shoved it back in his pocket. *Reassuring to know if this plane goes down, someone will find us.*

"A log cabin? I'm still surprised seeing houses instead of igloos. Before this, the furthest north I'd ever been was the Calgary Stampede."

He laughed. "Now there's a rocking time. After a fire in Alberta a few years back, we partied at the stampede with the Zulies."

Smokejumpers were a bonded brotherhood and most of them knew each other across the western states. Had Ryan and Travis partied together? The thought made her cringe. *Some things I'm better without knowing.*

"Where's your cabin?" asked Tara.

"North of Fairbanks. A jumper made me a deal. He raved about the sweeping views and riverfront access. Bought it sight unseen."

"Why would you buy property you've never seen?"

"He texted photos. I like to fly fish, so it was a no brainer. He was motivated to sell—got a girl pregnant and needed cash. I lowballed him to the point I felt guilty."

"That's great. Not the guilty part, I mean the part where you got a good deal."

"Lucked out on that one." Ryan's passion for the last frontier was evident. He closed the cargo door and twisted the handle.

"Let's get airborne."

"Alrighty." She forced a smile to mask the terror knocking around in her gut.

"First, part one of the Ryan O'Connor no fear program." He reached in the pilot's seat and handed her a clipboard. "This is my pre-flight checklist."

She smiled, amused he was never without a clipboard. Too jittery to read anything, she gave it a once over and handed it back. "Looks good."

"I'm all about safety and prevention. Just like firefighting." He removed his sunglasses and they dangled on his chest. Tossing the clipboard on his seat, he rested his hand on the fuselage. "What scares you about flying?"

"I don't know. A mechanical failure or severe weather conditions, I suppose."

His sapphire gaze steadied on her. "But what scares you?"

Her pulse picked up. "I don't want to fall…" She exhaled and glanced toward Denali. "I don't want to fall out of the sky." What she almost said was, *I don't want to fall for you.*

"You know how safety conscious I am. I nag all of you constantly in training."

His words calmed her some but didn't rid her anxiety about being in the air.

"We fear what we can't control. Do you trust me?" He angled his head, smiling.

Travis had asked her the same thing when she heard about his cheating, except he'd twisted it into the negative accusation of *don't you trust me?*

She looked straight at Ryan and her skin tingled. "Yes. I trust you."

His face softened. "Good. The mind is a powerful thing. Think of what makes you happy."

She stared at him, tongue-tied. What makes her happy? *I've lost those things.*

"On second thought." He jerked his head toward the Cessna. "Let's get in the plane."

She breathed relief after being put on the spot. "Unicorns farting rainbows. Lying on a beach somewhere."

"There you go." Ryan grinned and opened the passenger door. "Climb aboard."

She stepped up and hoisted herself into the cushioned seat. He closed the door and secured it.

She watched his easy gait as he rounded the nose to the pilot side. A slight breeze teased his hair when he opened the door and tossed his leather jacket in the back seat.

Her heart pulsed like a petrified rabbit at the thought of liftoff. She prayed she wouldn't barf in this beautiful, expensive plane. She slipped a hand to her stomach.

What had she gotten herself into?

CHAPTER 11

ara scrutinized the six colorful monitors stretching across the flight panel while Ryan ran his pre-flight checks. She clasped her seat belt and tried to slow her breathing.

He offered her a black and dark-green headset with an adjustable mic. "Put this on and think happy thoughts."

She eased on the headset and her hands trembled as she tried to tighten it. "Someone had a huge head."

Ryan's mouth twitched as he leaned in to help her. "How's that?"

Her eyes narrowed. "Are you laughing at me?"

"Wouldn't dream of it." He replaced his sunglasses with aviator shades, adjusted his headset, and positioned his mic. "Hear me okay?"

His even baritone streamed into her head and she liked him there.

"Yes," she said, positioning her mic.

Ryan looked regal in that pilot seat, with his aviator shades and headset. She boomeranged between his heat and her dread of zooming through the air in a fiberglass tube with only a flimsy stick to hold it up. But her trepidation soon overtook all thoughts of attraction to the pilot. She swallowed hard.

"I'm required to follow certain protocols flying into Denali. I filed a flight plan with the Talkeetna Flight Service Station." He showed her a topographic map of Denali Park and slid a little finger along the route. "We'll follow the Parks Highway, then head northwest along The Great Gorge over Ruth Glacier. We'll land in the Ruth Amphitheatre. Sound good?"

"Yep." It was all Greek to her. She tensed. "What do you want me to do?"

"Enjoy the scenery. Take photos." He flipped switches on the instrument panel with a self-assured cadence she found comforting.

"I'll point out the landmarks." His smooth, rich voice floated in. "Copy?"

She forced a close-mouthed smile. "Copy."

"Weather reports say calm winds. But Denali's weather can change in an Anchorage minute. If that happens, we'll turn around." He placed one hand on the control wheel and the other on the throttle. "Got your camera ready?"

Tara raised the digital Nikon with her sweaty palm, her hand shaking. As the solitary propeller spun into a whirring fan, her heart knocked. She visualized it bursting free of her chest and splatting on the windshield. *I've watched too many sci-fi movies.*

"Prepare for takeoff." Ryan mimicked a commercial pilot's tone, but sheer terror prevented her from cracking a smile as her innards turned inside out.

He taxied the plane to the end of the runway and made a slow turn. The engine powered up for rollout and the plane gained speed. The ground fell away. Braided river channels and buildings scattered across the valley bottom.

Tara took in the rolling hills and streams leading from Fairbanks into the wilds of the Interior. The endless landscape displayed contrasting shades of velvety, green forest and gray, glacial-scoured rivers winding through faraway valleys. Yup, Alaska was a show-off, all right.

She let out a long breath after the effortless takeoff as they floated higher.

Ryan ascended to cruising altitude and powered back the engine to a smooth, steady hum. Once she became accustomed to the sparkling waters and endless black spruce moving below her, she calmed. She caught his occasional glance. His surety and relaxed manner slowed her pulse and settled her nerves.

The late, afternoon skies had cleared, leaving few scattered clouds. Her breath caught as the majestic, blue-and-white Alaska Range rose into view.

Ryan banked the Cessna to the left, heading south. "Alaska has thirty-nine mountain ranges and seventeen of the twenty highest peaks in the U.S. You've heard the cliché that everything's bigger in Texas, right? It's five times that up here. Pisses off Texas." He gave her a lopsided grin.

She acknowledged with a smile and peered down to see how tree spires would look like a bed of upside-down nails to a smokejumper. "I don't know how you jump into this stuff."

"Very carefully." He lifted his water bottle and took a sip. "Help me out. Watch for planes and helicopters. Lots of air traffic this time of year."

"I'm all over it." Scanning airspace made her feel useful. No aircraft would pose danger on her watch, by God.

Hills morphed to mountains separated by glinting rivers. The timberline reached as high as it dared. Slate-gray granite formed saw-toothed spikes, ready to spear even a Cessna. Endless, snow-capped mountains rolled all the way to the horizon line.

"This is unbelievable. Will we circle Denali?"

He scanned his airspace. "No, but you'll be close to her when we land on Ruth Glacier."

"These peaks are massive," she breathed, thankful for Ryan's piloting ability so she could take in the grandeur. The plane didn't bounce, though it dipped and rose now and again. She liked how he operated the controls, confident and relaxed.

They flew over white, rugged peaks, where cerulean ice cascaded down, forming U-shaped valleys. Then as if by magic the mighty Denali made her grand entrance. Tara found it hard to believe that land could rise this high from the earth. The immensity and majesty of this mountain overwhelmed her, and sudden tears blurred her vision. She took a deep breath to force back the powerful emotion of seeing Denali so close for the first time. She blinked back the tears and turned to see Ryan smiling at her.

He must have been reading her. "That's how I felt when I saw her for the first time." He banked the plane to the right. "We're over Ruth Glacier. She's thirty-five miles long."

"It's breathtaking." Tara thought the glacier looked like the world's biggest, craziest toboggan run. Ribbons of snow, ice, and rock, flanked each side as if landscaped by design.

"Talkeetna Mountain Traffic, Cessna T84, destination Ruth Glacier, five thousand feet," radioed Ryan.

"Cessna T84, stay on Talkeetna traffic 123.65 frequency, listen for aircraft entering from Moose's Tooth," came the rapid reply of a woman's voice.

"Copy that, fifteen minutes from glacier landing on Ruth Amphitheater. Cessna T84, clear."

"Mountain Traffic, clear."

Ryan pointed. "We're entering The Great Gorge at thirty-two hundred feet."

"This is incredible," she murmured. Buttressed on either side by solid granite cliffs, The Great Gorge reminded her of a stairway to heaven; each proud landform outdoing the last, a grand entrance leading to Queen Denali.

Ryan tracked the aircraft to the right and pointed to a towering metallic-looking cliff on the western side of the Gorge. "The Moose's Tooth. These are foothills. Denali is a system of mountains with lesser peaks all vying to be champ of the Alaska Range."

"And you said you didn't have a way with words." She stared ahead, smiling into her mic.

He raised a brow. "I can turn a phrase now and then. Time to land. You ready?"

"Uh-huh." She tensed. How can he land without plummeting them into a crevasse? Her body became rigid as she braced for descent and landing.

Ryan throttled back. The Cessna floated down, and the wheeled skis touched, bounced, touched, bounced. Once down, the plane jiggled through uneven snow.

She folded her arms firmly against her chest to stop the girls from jiggling. Her hair shook loose from its bun and landed on her shoulders as Ryan brought the plane to a halt and cut the engine. The propeller slowed and became still. Sudden quiet.

Tara's relief welled into joy at landing safely on terra firma. "Nice job, Captain O'Connor."

"Welcome to Denali. Grab your jacket and camera and stay close." He pulled on his leather jacket and opened his door.

"Okay." She pulled on her North Face, then tugged the pins from her collapsed bun, letting her hair fall to her waist. She'd fix it later. Grabbing her camera, she stepped from the plane into a winter wonderland topped by a brilliant, azure sky.

They stood in front of the nose, taking in the magnitude of mountain and rock reaching skyward. The clouds drifted apart, revealing the mighty mountain.

"Get photos of Denali while you can. She's making a rare appearance." Ryan held out his hand. "Better yet, give me your camera. He took several photos of her with Denali in the background, then handed back her camera. "So, what do you think?"

She spread her arms, turning in a circle. "It's fantastic."

"No, your flight. How was it?"

"Tremendous. You're a good pilot. No, a damn good pilot. I can say this now that I'm back on the ground." She meant it.

His face broadened to a grin and he shoved his hands in his pants pockets. "Technically, no, you're on ancient ice. But good, mission accomplished."

A K2 Aviation plane landed and pulled up next to the Cessna. "O'Connor!" yelled the bushy-haired pilot, exiting the aircraft. "Fancy meeting you here. Shouldn't you be jumping out of these things about now?" He gestured at the Cessna as he strode toward them.

"Curly, my man. Fine day for flying." Ryan extended a hand.

Curly shook it and turned to Tara. "You couldn't find better company than this guy? Curly Thomas, K2 Aviation. I shuttle climbers in and out of Denali."

"Hi, I'm Tara. Stuck my thumb out and he gave me a ride," she teased back.

"You have good taste, O'Connor." Curly pointed at her camera. "I'll take a photo of you two, if you like."

Her eyes darted at Ryan to gauge his reaction.

"Sure. Get us with the plane and Denali in the background." Ryan motioned for her to stand next to him.

She moved closer but kept some distance, like a shy high schooler posing for prom.

"Come on, look like you're enjoying this." Curly fiddled with her camera. "O'Connor, put your arm around her."

Ryan hesitated. For once, she sensed that he wasn't calm and relaxed. She decided to help him out, so she slipped an arm around his waist and smiled. "It's okay, go ahead." *No harm, right?*

Once Ryan had the green light, he snaked an arm around her shoulder and squeezed. She inhaled the scent of his coat leather and a warm current zapped her. Here she was, standing on a glacier next to one of the best-looking guys in Alaska, alongside the tallest mountain in North America.

Curly aimed the camera. "Come on, O'Connor, plant one on

her. You're on a frigging glacier for chrissakes. Doesn't get more romantic than this."

Tara gave a jittery laugh. What's the deal with these aviation guys and their romance comments?

"Well, Waters, should I plant one on you?" Ryan's baby blues searched hers, asking permission.

She drew a short breath. Time stopped. Her heart became a rapid-fire, symphonic bass-drum, thundering her pulse at least up to two-hundred fifty.

"Hello? Tara, you in there? If you don't want to..."

She laughed. An unseen force strong-armed her to nod permission.

Ryan leaned sideways and pressed his lips to her laughing mouth for all of seven seconds. Maybe eight. She tasted mint and her heart imploded.

He lifted away like it was a touch-and-go landing and straightened.

Curly peered at the images. "Nice photos." He walked to Tara and returned her camera. "You two look good together."

"Thanks." Staring straight ahead, she stood frozen, like the glacier, licking her lips and tasting mint. *Did that really happen?*

"See you after fire season, O'Connor. Nice meeting you, Tara." Curly's voice faded as he walked back to his plane to help his clients unload the last of their mountain climbing equipment.

"Thanks, Curly, have a good one," Ryan hollered after him. He didn't seem in a rush to let go of her shoulder.

"Good to meet you." She waved a mechanical goodbye, at a loss for what to do or say now.

They stood still as stones watching Curly's wheeled skis lift from the glacier. The K2 plane engine drowned out all sound until it rose and banked right. The wing caught the sun's reflection as the plane gained altitude and grew small in the forever sky. The three climbers had taken off on cross-country skis toward their base camp, a good distance away.

"You know," said Ryan, dropping his arm from her shoulder. "I can do better."

She thought he meant taking off from the glacier. "So how do you plan to—"

"Like this." His arms pulled her close as he swooped in for another landing. He brushed his lips over hers, then lifted off and touched down again to explore her upper lip. He slid his lips to her lower one.

Holy cripes, he sure knew how to kiss! The smell of ice and mountain air and the scent of his leather jacket spun her heart into a fireball, despite her best effort into talking herself out of him. Heat seared through her veins and every cell in her body ignited. *Can I melt on a glacier? Why, yes, it seems I can...*

He slid his tongue along her lips. She parted them shyly and kissed him back. His tongue slipped into her mouth, slow and easy, giving and taking; she welcomed it with her own.

A low moan vibrated her throat and she squeezed the leather on his shoulders. She felt his body tense and she sensed him forcing himself to stop.

He gradually broke the kiss and eased his mouth away from hers. "I think that was a game changer."

She still had hold of him. "Is that what you call it?"

They stared at each other, while Tara's head swam.

Ryan rocked a little, as if willing himself to let go. He took a few steps backward with the back of his hand to his mouth. "Shouldn't have done that."

She scrambled for logic. "Well, Curly told you to."

"Not the second time." Ryan stared at her as if they'd done something terribly wrong. For such an always-in-control guy, he was clearly rattled.

His being thrown off stride amused her, but she sensed the sudden awkwardness between them. *Change the subject.* "How do you know Curly?"

"My Talkeetna flight instructor. He taught me glacier landings." Ryan fiddled with the zipper on his jacket.

"You're good at glacier landings. And other things." Heat crept up her face as she secretly gave him an outstanding performance rating on kissing technique. A game changer?

What an understatement.

"I'm sorry. We have to work together. We can't let that get in the way of—"

"I know. Don't worry about it." But *she* would worry about it, even though she knew the drill. *Oh shit.* Her no smokejumpers rule had gone up in flames on a glacier. "We got caught up in the moment. Curly thought we were…you know, already hooked up." She moved her hand in fast circles.

"I broke my rule of not dating trainees." He rubbed the back of his neck.

"But theoretically this wasn't a date. Gunnar was supposed to go." She gave him a shy grin. "Besides, I didn't exactly push you away."

He smiled. "No. You didn't."

How do we get back to normal after opening Pandora's box? She looked him in the eye. "We can pretend it didn't happen…so we don't mess up our working together."

"Good idea. Let's just, let's just…" He trailed off with a red face and cleared his throat. "We'd better get going. It's two hours back to Fairbanks." He seemed flustered.

She let out a nervous laugh. "Sure. What happens on the glacier stays on the glacier…right?" She flashed him a grin.

He chuckled. "Right."

Tara turned and walked to the Cessna, her boots sinking in sun-softened snow. She opened the door and hauled herself in. *Pretend The Kiss never happened? Yeah, right. Who am I kidding?*

Ryan closed her door and secured it.

She watched him circle the plane for his pre-flight inspection, hating herself for wanting him to kiss her again. Logic screamed no. Her reckless heart shouted yes! Well, *he* started it. What *was* that anyway?

Deep down, she knew. He had ignited her spark. If it combusts into a full-fledged, roaring inferno, she'll be a goner; doomed to repeat the past with yet another smokejumper. *Holy hell.*

Ryan settled into the pilot seat and fastened his seat belt. "Everything okay?"

She put on her headset and gave him a thumbs up, trying not to look like a lovesick puppy.

He studied his pre-flight checklist and slipped into pilot mode. His voice streamed into her ears. "Ready?" He said it softly, pulling her gaze to him as he smoothly flipped switches.

"All systems go." She fake-smiled at the windshield as her insides turned to goo.

Ryan throttled the plane up to speed. As the Cessna rose from the glacier, Tara glimpsed Denali flirting with wispy clouds. He banked to follow The Great Gorge out of the park, staying to the right near the east granite wall. The landscape appeared different on the way out, a reversal of scale. He ascended the aircraft, allowing for a bird's-eye view of the braided glacial streams splaying in every direction through the valley like shimmering, silver ribbons.

Tara peeked at the images on her camera and marveled at their carefree expressions; Ryan's dimples, amplified by sunlight, his arm resting on her shoulder, as if they'd been together a long time.

He was noticeably quiet on the flight back, and she wasn't sure whether that was good or bad. She wondered what he was thinking but hesitated to ask.

Leaving the park behind them, Ryan banked left and pointed the Cessna north to Fairbanks. The steady engine hum lulled her into relaxation.

Ryan's voice streamed into her headphones. "Denali, on your

LOLO PAIGE

left." He leaned back, so she could see around him out his side window.

She took in Denali's alpenglow, a neon cotton candy. The mountain was dazzling, but what caught her eye was the luminescence that backlit Ryan, like a Greek god. Her breath hitched.

She aimed her sunglasses out the window, but her gaze was one hundred per cent on him.

He turned to her and smiled in that certain way he had, dissolving her like sugar in hot tea. "Beautiful, isn't it?"

And just like that, he'd completely disarmed her. Was it elation that made her tingle all over or something else? Something she didn't want to feel but was powerless to stop...a surge of raw heat that seized her heart and melted it into a drippy goo that oozed down to her core—injecting her with delicious thoughts of what she could do to him. Or what he could do to her. *Stop it, idiot. Don't do this to yourself!*

Overcome by the sentiment she was powerless to name, all she could manage was to nod at him with an idiotic smile and mumble. "Yes. It's beautiful."

And she wasn't referring to Denali.

🔥

*M*el waited in the van while Tara and Ryan put the Cessna to bed in its hangar. Ryan climbed in front and Tara sat in back. It was the same as her first night in Alaska, except for one minor detail; the guy riding shotgun had become her kryptonite. His kiss had lurched her off balance. She didn't know what to think or how to feel. *He's my flipping training instructor!*

Mel dropped them off and as Ryan followed her to the barracks, there was an awkward, intimate silence between them. When they hit the second floor, they faced each other in the dark hallway.

The tension was palpable. Tara spoke first. "Ryan, I—"

"Let this simmer, okay? We need to finish training. I shouldn't have done that." He shook his head.

Her heart plummeted and despite her own suggestion they pretended The Kiss never happened. "I just wanted to thank you for today." She said it fast, knowing where this was headed.

Nowhere.

"Oh, right. Sorry. Got ahead of myself." He fiddled with his room key, flipping it between his fingers.

She swore he blushed.

"I appreciate you inviting me to go. I'll return the favor sometime." She couldn't help hoping so.

"You don't owe me any favors. I enjoyed your company." He looked down at his feet and slid his gaze to her. "Well...fitness tests in the morning. We'd better get some rest."

"Okay. Good night." She partially turned, then faced him again. "Ryan, today was incredible. And you're a damn good pilot." And she meant it.

"Thanks. I appreciate that. Good night, Tara." His footsteps echoed along the men's hallway and as she walked to her room, she heard him open the door and close it.

She paused, her hand on the doorknob. *He may have kissed me today, but I can't let him into my heart.* Nothing like being on a diet and someone offering you a donut.

Or a hot fudge sundae.

CHAPTER 12

*a*t 5:05 a.m. Ryan sprang out of bed with boundless energy. He went for a run, showered, and ate, all the while thinking about yesterday's flight. *With her.* What an enjoyable day. The weather had cooperated, and the plane behaved as he knew it would. Once they had lifted off, Tara seemed more at ease. He liked to think he was the reason.

He had done everything he could to make Tara feel comfortable without causing her more anxiety. Like holding a nut out to a squirrel—no sudden moves or he'd scare her away. While he'd managed to ignore Reeve's romantic flight comment, he'd blown it when Curly suggested kissing her. Not one of his brighter moments. But she seemed to have sensed his awkwardness afterward when she said, "What happens on the glacier stays on the glacier."

Then he went and fucked it up by kissing her a second time. *She's a trainee, for chrissakes.* He turned it over a thousand ways from Sunday, but always with the same conclusion.

I want to kiss her again.

What he'd liked about yesterday was getting outside of fire world, and Tara seeing him as someone other than an instructor or a smokejumper. No fire hierarchy on the plane, just the two of them in Alaska's endless, blue sky.

He would be working with her two more days. After that, it was anyone's guess if he'd see her again before fire season ended. Tara was a rare jewel and he may not find another gem like her.

He opened the door to the AFS building and took the stairs two at a time to the second floor. Back to work. Focus and keep it real. Busy day ahead. He squared his shoulders.

Ryan entered the training room and right away zeroed in on Tara. The sight of her shiny, red hair delighted him, but he must treat her like everyone else. A twinge of guilt hit recalling the day before. *Put it out of your brain. You have a job to do.*

He moved to the front of the class with his clipboard. "Good morning, everyone. Listen up—as you know, we have pack tests this morning. After lunch, we'll post the crew lists. Two buses are waiting outside to take us to the running track. Ready? Let's go!"

Ryan motioned everyone out the double doors. Gunnar tossed him a stopwatch and they followed everyone out to the buses.

*A*ngela swung into the seat next to Tara near the front of the bus. "Hey, you."

"Ready for your fitness test?" Tara asked.

Angela sipped coffee from a Styrofoam cup. "Ready, yes. Do I want to do it? No. Didn't get much sleep."

"Haven't talked to you since yesterday in class." Tara watched people board the bus.

Angela leaned sideways. "Where were you?"

Tara whispered. "I went flying with Ryan into Denali Park."

"What, like hang-gliding?" Angela practically yelled, choking on her coffee.

Several faces glanced back at them.

Tara laughed and put a finger to her lips. "Shh—don't want the whole bus to know. Ryan is a small plane pilot. He invited me to go flying. Gunnar was supposed to go but canceled."

Angela's eyes bugged. "Wow! So, it was just the two of you— wait a minute, aren't you afraid of flying?"

"That's why he invited me. To help me with my fear of flying." As soon as the words left her mouth, she knew her reason sounded lame.

"Right. A possum doesn't play dead and I have a bridge to nowhere to sell you." Angela smirked.

"We landed on a freaking glacier! It was incredible." Tara gestured with her hands, still astounded at her magical experience of flying close to Denali Mountain. "There's just no words."

"Wow, a glacier. Is that all?"

"Is what all?" Tara knew good and well what Angela wanted to know.

"Thought maybe you'd ravish each other, seeing as how neither of you can take your eyes off the other."

"Ravish? Give me a break." Tara pulled back as her face heated. "No! No ravishing. I'm here to fight fire, not for booty call. It was just a plane ride." If Tara were a certain wooden puppet, her nose would be poking the person sitting in front of her.

Angela gave her a knowing look and leaned in close to Tara's ear. "Hon, I've seen how he looks at you. From what I can tell you have Prince Charming syndrome because he rescued you."

Tara sputtered. "I do not!" She'll go to hell for lying. Change the subject, turn the tables. "So, where were *you* last night? You were gone when I came in."

"Hanging out with Colorado." Angela flashed her pearly whites at a brown-eyed, dark bearded guy who entered the bus.

His fire shirt hung open, exposing his Rocky Mountain Hotshots tee, with rolled-up sleeves revealing tatted flames encircling his bulging forearms. He winked and raised his coffee in greeting to Angela, before sinking into a seat three rows behind them.

The door closed and the bus lurched forward.

Tara leaned over and whispered. "You're playing with fire. If word gets around, you'll be reputed as only being here to meet men. Just saying…"

She trailed off as a red flag waved in her brain. *Who am I to talk? I went flying with our fire training instructor and we kissed on a glacier.* Ryan helped her with—aviophonics—or whatever the heck he called it, because she'd be flying to wildfires all around Alaska.

It's my rationale and I'm sticking to it.

"I told you, that's why I'm here. Hello," murmured Angela, teeth gnawing her coffee straw. "Hey, I'm not judging."

The bus stopped next to the running track. Tara and Angela poured off the bus with the rest of the firefighters. A second bus pulled up and more streamed out.

"Hoo-ee," said Angela. "It's hotter than a moose's butt in a pepper patch."

Tara chuckled and adjusted her sunglasses. "For this early in the morning, it sure is."

Angela positioned herself to casually observe the Chena Hotshots as they filed off the bus. Her sultry cat-eat-canary grin twitched the corners of her mouth.

Gunnar strolled up. "Ready to get your packs weighed?"

"You bet," purred Angela, as she and Tara followed him to a hanging scale, supported by a tall tripod.

Tara gave Gunnar her pack and he weighed it. "Forty-five, you're good to go." He handed it back to her.

"Thanks." She couldn't wait to see what her new personal best was for her pack test.

Gunnar weighed Angela's. "Thirty-five, add ten pounds. Here's a ten-pounder." He lifted her pack off the scale and set it on the ground, handing the weight to her.

"Thank you, kind sir," she simpered, her lilt on full throttle.

"You're welcome. You Southerners are so polite." Gunnar displayed a toothy grin.

Angela gave him a coy smile. "I've heard the same about Norwegians."

Tara jabbed her with an elbow.

"Ow!" Angela shot her a killer look.

Rego showed up with his pack. "Think you girls can handle this?" He leered at Tara as she threaded her long ponytail braid through the back of her Missoula Ranger District baseball cap.

"Don't worry, we're fixin' to kick some serious tush." Angela tilted her head to the side and smiled sweetly.

"Is that so, Scarlett? Well don't hurt yourself, you hear?" Rego winked and ambled off with Hudson.

"Oh, I won't, sugar," mumbled Angela. And if looks could truly kill, Rego would be dead in a heartbeat.

Angela pursed her lips. "He doesn't know squat about women. The other one is so dumb he thinks the Arctic Circle is a racetrack." She adjusted her black visor to shade her face, letting her dark hair cascade down her back. Then she eased on a pair of Oakleys, as if preparing to sun at the beach.

Tara worked hard to keep a straight face. She got a kick out of her bunkmate's talent for putdowns. "Where's your pack?"

Angela spun around. "Oops, I left it by the scale." She hurried over to retrieve it.

Tara noticed Rego and Hudson standing next to Angela's pack as she bent to pick it up. Hudson shot Tara a winning smile. "Good luck," he called over to her, staring at her intently as Angela walked back to her.

Hudson's gaze made her uneasy. She gave him a polite nod and turned her back to him.

"This feels heavier than a bag of wet gators," grunted Angela, as she adjusted the weight on her back. "Staying up late last night was not a good decision."

Tara bent to stretch her hamstrings. "Not with a fitness test today."

"Don't worry. I'm in decent shape." Angela flexed her toned bicep.

Tara spotted Ryan in his yellow fire shirt, talking to a group of test monitors. *Wow.* Some guys rocked the Nomex, and Ryan was definitely one of them. Yesterday's image of him flying the plane while bathed in Denali's alpenglow inserted itself in her brain. She blew out air and angled for a better view as he helped testers adjust their pack weights and offered them water bottles. He clearly knew how to set people at ease. She admired that about him.

"You're smiling at him," breathed Angela in Tara's ear.

"Who?" Tara's defensiveness popped out before she could lasso it.

"Don't give me that. You know who." Angela aimed her shades in Ryan's direction. "Look at him charm the crowd. He could talk a squirrel off a nut truck."

Tara burst out laughing. "You're killing me, Divina."

Ryan called for the group's attention. "Okay, people. Today's pack test will test your muscle strength and aerobic endurance—the things that could make the difference between life and death on a fire."

What a commanding presence. Tara chuckled, recalling his freaked-out expression when they'd crashed in the hallway the other night. A total opposite of his work demeanor.

Tara and Angela positioned themselves behind the start line.

"Everyone ready?" Ryan called out. "If you need water, we'll provide it. Monitors will call out your time. Twelve laps under forty-five minutes. First group to the starting point."

"Hey, Waters, Divina." Liz Harrington appeared on the other side of her. "Ready for this barbaric shitshow?" She flashed them a toothy grin.

"Yes ma'am. Okay, ladies, let's kick it." Tara waited for the go signal and braced to start.

Angela shifted her pack. "My head is killing me." Her eyelids drooped and even her makeup didn't hide the tired lines on her face.

"Five, four, three, two, begin." Ryan clicked his stopwatch and scribbled on his clipboard.

The herd took off at a brisk pace. The three women stayed even with each other as several flamingo-legged people breezed past. Liz and Tara pulled ahead. As they approached the first mile mark, Tara heard coughing a short distance behind her. She slowed and glanced back at Angela, who had stopped with coughing spasms.

Tara fell back and put a hand on her shoulder. "Angie, are you okay?"

"Sipped water...down wrong pipe." Angela coughed so hard she bent over, her shades falling to the ground.

Tara picked them up.

"Go on, I'll be fine," gasped Angela, snatching her sunglasses and putting them back on.

"You sure?" asked Tara.

"Go! Now! I'm fine." Angela's coughing lessened, but she seemed fatigued.

Tara resumed her power walk stride, glancing over her shoulder at her friend.

"One mile," called out a monitor with a stopwatch, noting numbers and scribbling on a clipboard. Tara pushed hard. Sweat formed at her hairline. She peered back to see Angela stumbling. Something was wrong.

Should she go back? She slowed, trying to decide. What's more important, helping a friend or doing my own test? Tara stopped and went back to help.

"Shoot, I can do this—I've done it before," Angela puffed toward Tara. "Go on."

"No. I'll help you." She grabbed hold of Angela, helping her along.

"Twelve minutes," hollered a monitor, noting their numbers on his clipboard.

They weren't going to make it with twenty-two minutes left.

"I can't—I feel dizzy—" Angela stopped, panting.

Gunnar rode up on a bike and stopped. "What's wrong?"

"Angela is feeling lightheaded." Tara helped her friend off the track to the grass.

Angela pressed fingertips to her temples. "I feel awful as all get out...I..." she trailed off and her knees buckled.

Gunnar threw down his bike and caught her before she hit the ground.

"Let's get this weight off your back." Gunnar unbuckled the straps and helped Angela out of her pack.

"Thanks. That feels better," mumbled Angela, wiping her forehead.

"Man, this feels heavy." Gunnar lifted Angela's pack and peeked inside. He pulled out two ten-pound weights. "I gave you one weight. There's two in here."

"What? How can there be two?" panted Angela, staring at him in alarm.

Gunnar seemed puzzled. "No wonder you had a tough time."

"How could that have happened?" Tara helped her friend to sit on the grass.

Ryan jogged up. "What's going on?"

"Angela couldn't finish. Her pack was over-weighted," said Tara.

Ryan gave her an odd look and squatted next to Angela. "Let's check your heart rate." He pressed fingers on the side of her neck, checking his watch. "How do you feel?"

"Like grim death. Everything's spinning."

"Your pulse is erratic." Ryan offered her his water bottle.

"Drink this. Slowly." He nodded at Gunnar. "Take her to the med clinic." He keyed his radio. "Need a golf-cart at the one-mile mark."

A voice on the radio acknowledged.

Angela's doe-eyes watered. "I can do this. Let me try it again."

Tara turned to Ryan. "She can test again, right? This wasn't her fault."

"First we have to get her to the med clinic." He extended an arm to Gunnar. "Let me see her pack."

Gunnar handed it over. "I only gave her one ten-pound weight. There's two in here."

Ryan lifted it. "It does feel heavier than forty-five. I'll weigh it to be sure."

The golf cart pulled up. "Come on, I'll take you." Gunnar helped Angela into the back seat and hopped in next to her.

"You'll be all right, Angela," Tara called after her as the cart drove off.

Tara and Ryan stood next to the track, watching the last of the testers cross the finish line.

He turned to her. "That was generous of you to stop and help."

"I couldn't just leave her there." She gazed off in the direction of the disappearing golf cart.

"Tara."

She snapped her gaze to him. "Yeah?" She wished her heart wasn't palpitating. Were they going to keep ignoring The Kiss? Obviously, they had to at work. She wanted to talk to him privately after work, but he always seemed busy.

"You need to resume your test, either from here or start with the next group. Your choice." Ryan was good at acting like nothing had happened between them.

She couldn't figure him out. He might be one of those guys who drifted from woman to woman without emotional attachment. She'd seen her share. But he'd kissed her like his plane was going down. And she'd kissed him back like she'd been in it. That had to mean *something*.

"I'll start with the next group." She lifted her pack to her shoulders and stepped around him.

"Wait a second," Ryan called after her.

She stopped and turned. "Yes?"

He waved her toward him. "I'll carry your pack. Give it here."

"You have Angela's. I can carry my own pack to the start line."

He slung Angela's pack over one shoulder like it contained balsa wood. "I'm not saying you aren't strong enough. But it wouldn't hurt for you to have the same equal advantage the second time around."

"Thanks, but I'm not concerned." She headed to the start line. *Geez, guys and their protective instincts.* She couldn't help but smile at Ryan's polite offer, despite his ignoring yesterday's heat on the glacier.

"Wait."

She turned around again. "What is it?" Maybe he'll talk about yesterday. *Yeah right. My hair will turn gray in a rocker before that happens.*

He hesitated. "Never mind. Go on ahead."

"Okay." Things had become officially awkward. She adjusted the weight on her back and continued to the start, keenly aware Ryan followed a short distance behind. Why couldn't she have met him off the job somewhere, like in the Top Hat bar in Missoula or on a ski trip to Bridger?

"Pace yourself, people. Good luck." Ryan strolled over to join a group of test monitors.

Tara reached the start point and a wild impulse struck her. She glanced around to see if anyone paid attention. Satisfied no one was, she eyed the pile of weights near the scale. Plucking two ten-pound weights from a stack, she tossed them in her pack. She hoisted the heavy pack to her shoulders and secured it.

It was a risky, over-achiever move, and had everything to do with proving herself. She knew how hard it would be to come in under forty-five minutes with sixty-five pounds, but she'd done it before under an hour. Completing her test under forty-five minutes should not be a problem.

Besides, Rego's assertion that women couldn't hack it irritated her more than she let on. *I'll show these Alaskans how we do things down south.*

🔥

*a*ll Ryan had tried to do was help Tara so she'd be fresh to retake her fitness test. She offered help to others but couldn't seem to accept it herself. He couldn't afford to show favoritism or any attraction; not in this testosterone-saturated environment. He shouldn't have kissed her yesterday. He kicked himself for the millionth time. *What a total dork move.*

He weighed Angela's pack. Fifty-five pounds. Had she added a ten-pound weight by accident or had someone else done it? No one would deliberately do that, would they? He shook the idea from his head.

The second group poised at the start line. "Five, four, three, two, begin." Ryan hollered, clicking his stopwatch. Tara strode forward with a steady, brisk pace and disappeared into the middle of the pack. The monitors would take it from here. He settled in to wait.

Before long, the first group of hotshot crews approached the finish, as expected. Someone pulled ahead of the group. He did a double take—Tara Waters had beat them all to the finish line.

"Thirty-eight and thirty," shouted a monitor, clicking his stopwatch. "Good job."

"Thirty-nine," the monitor called out to the first of the

hotshots, thirty seconds behind Tara.

Ryan watched other finishers but secretly focused on Tara. Thank God for polarized sunglasses.

Drenched in sweat, she walked off the track to remove her pack.

Intuitively, he lurched to help her and remembered where it got him the last time he'd offered. She may not need physical help, but he understood the importance of supporting her capabilities on the job. Especially after the line of duty death she had experienced on the Montana fire. He knew all too well how important that was.

Tara undid the straps and let her pack slide from her shoulders to the grass. She bent, hands braced on her knees, panting hard. Her hair fell in a loose, messy knot to one shoulder.

He tried not to stare as she lifted her water bottle and sucked down half, then poured the rest on her head. Water streamed down her flushed cheeks, saturating her already drenched T-shirt.

Holy shit. Watching her swallow in a wet T-shirt caused a hot tidal wave to slosh over him, a sensation he couldn't afford to indulge in right now. He blew out air, drumming fingertips on his thigh. *Keep the professional neutrality pasted on out here. Don't gape at her, idiot.*

He turned away to monitor other testers, but an invisible force took hold of his head and rotated it back in her direction.

Grinning ear to ear, Tara lifted her pack and passed it to Reed Cameron, the weigh-in monitor, who had taken over for Gunnar.

Reed hung it on the scale and high-fived her.

She took two weights from her pack and dropped them on the ground. She sighted Ryan and flashed him a euphoric smile with a celebratory thumbs-up, obviously pleased with herself.

He responded with a thumbs-up. *Yes. I am very much impressed. Remember my job.*

Ryan collected the finish times from test monitors and flipped through them: Tara Waters, thirty-eight minutes, thirty seconds. By the time he freed himself from the group, she'd grabbed her pack and joined the rest of the finishers waiting for a bus ride back to AFS.

🔥

ara would have skipped to the trainees clustered on the lawn, but her body felt like lead and every muscle ached. But she was ecstatic with her time and curious what the fastest times were overall. She proved to herself she could do it and enjoyed showing off her capability to a certain smokejumper.

Reed Cameron had been impressed. "You should be on a hotshot crew," he'd said after weighing her pack.

While waiting for the buses to arrive, several of the hotshot crew members clustered around, congratulating Tara. She stood tall, relishing her accomplishment. She couldn't have done it without Dad pushing her to hike all those steep forest slopes around Missoula, while carrying heavy weight in her day pack.

After the congratulations ended, she wandered over to sit on the grass.

Liz was the first one to her. "You smoked that track like a chipmunk on speed. How the hell did you do that?"

"Guess how many pounds. Go ahead, guess," gushed Tara. She could barely contain herself. "Sixty-five."

"You're insane! You could have killed yourself. Why did you do that?"

"To see if I could."

"What did the instructors say? Have you told them?"

"Not yet." She couldn't wipe the silly grin off her face. Her gaze shifted to Ryan, standing at the finish line talking to the test monitors and her blood raced through her veins.

*R*yan made his way to Reed Cameron, who was busy dismantling the scale and gathering equipment.

"Hey Reed, the woman you were talking to—the redhead? What was her post-test weight?"

"Sixty-five."

Ryan's chin dropped. He furrowed his brows. "She carried twenty extra pounds? Are you sure?"

"Yeah. Told her she should be on a hotshot crew."

"Thanks, Reed." Ryan's mouth hung open and he clamped it shut. *What the hell?*

"No problem." Reed piled equipment into a golf cart.

Ryan spied Tara sitting on the lawn with Liz and the other trainees and headed in her direction. "Waters, you beat the hotshots. Thirty-eight minutes. Impressive."

She rose to her feet, grinning up at him. "Thanks. I'm pretty pleased. Did you hear what I carried?" She stood to the side, one stunning leg turned out.

"Yeah. About that. Can I talk to you for a second?" He removed his sunglasses and walked a short distance away.

Tara followed and Ryan waited until she caught up to him.

"Why did you carry extra weight? You could have washed yourself out."

She gave him a prideful look. "To prove I could do it. I wanted to see if I could carry sixty-five pounds under forty-five minutes. And I did."

"Why the hell would you risk it? People have suffered cardiac arrest during pack tests carrying the normal weight. That was reckless and you endangered yourself." His words blasted her like the recoil of a gun.

"I'm twenty-eight. I have a healthy heart."

"People younger than you have had heart attacks during pack tests. Age doesn't mean shit."

"I'm in fine shape and I've worked hard at it. I'm fit as any hotshot or any smokejumper, for that matter." Anger crept into her tone and her voice grew louder.

Ryan glanced around and lowered his voice. "I understand you wanting to qualify for a hotshot position, but you didn't need the extra weight."

"Aren't you impressed that I even did this? Why are you shooting down my accomplishment?" She scowled at him.

"Tell me the real reason you added the weight." He pinned his gaze to hers.

She didn't blink. "I told you. For a personal best."

He took off his baseball cap and narrowed his eyes. "No. That isn't it. You're overcompensating. You think you have to outrun and outdo everyone else to make up for not saving that man in Montana. Stop punishing yourself. It leads nowhere, fast. Get counseling instead."

"Why do you keep bugging me about counseling and what does this have to do with my pack test? Since when are you the expert on what makes me tick? You hardly know me."

"I thought yesterday changed that a little."

"Because you kissed me?" She shot it at him like a bullet.

He glanced around making sure no one overheard. "More than that...I wanted to know you better." There was so much more he wanted to say, but pride wouldn't let him.

"But why did you kiss me in the first place, knowing we'd have to work together? With all due respect, Ryan—what the fuck?"

"You're the one who suggested we pretend it never happened, remember?" His fingers combed the top of his head as his frustration level mounted. "Look, you changed the subject."

Tara folded her arms and gave him a defiant look. "No. You're avoiding the subject! You've twisted what I did into—you know what? I can't…" She unfolded her arms and raised her hands in surrender. "I can't talk about this anymore."

She heaved her pack to a shoulder and hurried to the bus, leaving him standing there like a doofus, gaping after her.

Way to go, douche. He'd meant his advice as a good-will gesture, but she took it as him being heavy-handed. He wanted to explain why he'd nagged her about the importance of talking to a therapist about her line of duty death experience—and wanted to tell her how he knew. But there wasn't time. He had a training class to run.

Ryan swung into the front seat of the bus. He glimpsed Tara in the visor mirror, two rows back, scowling at the window. Sadly, he understood all too well why she'd added the weights.

The line of duty deaths five years ago in California still cowed him. He'd battled depression ever since, seeing his helplessness at preventing the deaths as a failure in himself. Had it not been for Gunnar, he would have bailed out of firefighting. The therapy sessions had helped, but he'd stopped going. Instead, he atoned by overcompensating. Hell, that's how he wound up in jump school—to erase the crushing guilt of losing lives on his watch.

Who knew he and Tara would have such a thing in common? When training ends, he'll find the time to tell her before heading out to jump fires.

He glanced at her again in the mirror. She didn't look happy.

Shit. He hadn't meant to ruin her day. Why hadn't he just congratulated her and left it alone? He blew out air and leaned back, flipping through the pack test results. Three washouts, all males. He'll finalize the crew lists and announce them before field exercises this afternoon.

His stomach knotted and his chest felt heavy. He had to make it right with Tara.

If she would let him.

CHAPTER 13

*a*fter lunch, Tara left the mess hall and strolled back to the AFS building. Her heart pounded, but for the wrong reason; Ryan pissed her off big-time.

Her leg and back muscles ached after this morning's fitness test. Ryan's reaction threw her off-kilter. Not what she'd expected. Instead of congratulating her, he thought she needed counseling. *What the hell?*

She called to Angela, walking ahead of her, water bottle in hand. "Divina, how are you feeling?"

Angela stopped and turned around. "Who doesn't feel like a million after a delectable saline drip?" The pink had returned to her cheeks and she'd fixed her hair in a messy ponytail bun, same as Tara's. She still looked tired, but healthier.

Tara scrutinized her. "You look a darn sight better than this morning."

"Why didn't I go be a baby panda bear trainer instead?"

"Maybe because there's no hot-guy baby panda trainers." Tara thought a minute. "Are you sure you didn't put the extra weight in your pack?"

"I swear I didn't and neither did Gunnar. Someone else must have."

"Rego and Hanson had been standing by your pack, you know."

Angela drew back, her mouth open. "You think they did it?"

"I wouldn't put it past them. But we need to find out for sure."

"Ryan told Gunnar to retest me after training tomorrow. What about you?"

"I re-tested after you left." Tara shot her a broad smile. "I broke my record."

"How?"

"I added twenty pounds and came in under forty-five minutes." Tara fiddled with her hardhat.

"I couldn't finish because of extra weight and you added more intentionally?" Angela stopped to look at her. "If you'd failed, you would have been thrown out. What did Ryan say?"

"That I jeopardized myself and did it to punish myself for not saving the man in the Montana fire. He keeps bugging me to get counseling." Tara stared at the ground. She didn't feel like telling her the other reasons she was out of sorts with Ryan, after she'd lectured Angela about getting involved with people on the job.

"Were you punishing yourself?" prodded Angela.

"Yeah, I'm a total masochist. I flog myself before bed every night." Tara laughed.

"For the love of Dixie." Angela pursed her lips. "Judging by your nightmares, I reckon he may be right. You took a dumb risk and could have hurt yourself."

A tinge of regret lanced Tara. She never thought it would be such a big deal.

Angela stared at her a long while. "Remember when I said it wasn't your responsibility to save every person from a fire and how guilt makes us feel useless? Don't hate me, but I'm with Ryan. You should talk to a shrink."

Tara let out a sigh. "There's no time right now. I'll do it after fire season," she mumbled, stopping near the open doors of the training room.

"So, in the meantime eat a pint of cookie dough ice cream or a container of fudge frosting like everyone else. Stop being a steel magnolia. You don't want to melt down on the fireline, okay?"

Tara grimaced. "Don't worry. I won't melt down."

They wandered inside as the room filled with people and fire gear.

Ryan and Gunnar entered and moved to the front. Ryan studied his paperwork, avoiding eye contact with her.

"Hey Tara, impressive job on the pack test!" belted out one of the Chena Hotshots from across the room. He and his buddies gave her air high-fives. "Way to smoke it!"

"Fastest time. Awesome," another guy with a headband chimed in. "We have an open slot on the crew, if you're interested."

Tara noticed Ryan flick his eyes at the guy than back to his paperwork.

"Word travels fast," whispered Tara. It tickled her how others had recognized her accomplishment. She hadn't considered working on an Alaskan hotshot crew...the last thing she wanted was to stay in Alaska.

"A fast woman turns guys on," breathed Angela. "I know whose knickers are in a twist. A certain smokejumper swiveled his radar when you got all that attention just now." Angela tilted her head toward Ryan at the front of the room.

Tara gave her an eyeroll. "You're reading too much into it."

Angela's eyes narrowed. "Okay, then. Stay in denial world. Hope you're happy there."

Ryan interrupted with announcements. "Listen up. Here's your crew assignments. Find the one you're on and get with your crew boss outside. All three crews will have joint field training today and tomorrow."

Gunnar spread the lists across a table in the front of the room as Tara and Angela scrambled forward. "Here we are." Angela pointed. "We're assigned to the Aurora Crew."

Tara scanned for more names. "Liz Harrington, yes!""

"We're on the same crew!" crowed Liz. "We're going to rock this." She high-fived Angela and Tara.

"Good. We have Liz. Are we it for women on Aurora Crew?" Tara scanned the list.

Angela ran her forefinger down the list. "Not unless Robin and Payson are women. The rest must be assigned to other crews."

Tara ambled outside to a long box van, where the driver held a scrawled sign, "Aurora Crew." Hopping inside, the three women sat in the last bench seat of the twenty-person transport vehicle.

Liz glanced around. "Looks like it's just us chickens."

"Howdy, ladies." A fetching, dark-haired guy with 'Silva' printed above his shirt pocket stood grinning down at Tara. His longer hair feathered back from a pronounced widow's peak over brown eyes with thick lashes. He sat a few rows ahead, draping his arm across the top of the seat.

"*He's* on our crew," whispered Angela, staring at the tall, attractive, and obviously ripped firefighter who had just boarded. "I noticed him the first day of training."

"Down, girl," breathed Tara, smirking.

A bulky guy with neck tats and a black bun filled the aisle, with 'Tupa' scrawled on his shirt. He swung into two seats. Tara figured he could lift their van single-handed. Two more guys filed in and Tara did a double take: identical twins. A guy with a long, blonde ponytail followed, and another with round wire-rimmed glasses. Tara chuckled. They should be called Motley Crew instead of Aurora Crew.

Ryan hopped in, claiming his usual shotgun seat. A sharp twinge poked Tara's chest.

"O'Connor is working with Aurora Crew today," remarked Liz.

"Looks that way." Tara crossed her legs, jiggling her foot.

"What do you have against Mr. Gourmet Eye Candy?" asked Liz out the side of her mouth.

"Angela leaned toward Tara. "You're acting like Ryan is a beetle-headed horn beast." To Liz, she whispered, "Ol' Montana here thinks he's a tall drink of water. Just not today."

"He *is*," murmured Liz. "I could lap-dance him all day for free. But that's my other seasonal job."

Tara grimaced. "The problem with stunning guys is, they attract women like honeybees to sunflowers. I learned the hard way when my ex followed several honeybees back to their hives."

Liz nodded. "Sometimes it's hard to land a guy who'll stay faithful."

"All I reckon is, Gunnar is so hot he makes my teeth sweat." Angela waved her hand like a fan.

All three of them laughed. Tara silently thanked her friend for changing up the conversation.

Gunnar climbed into the driver's seat and drove the van out of Fort Wainwright, heading for the surrounding forested hills. Drifting wildfire smoke disappeared. The sun lightened dark, skinny spruce and brightened the pale, peeling bark of birch trees in the boreal forest.

"Liz, what's your other seasonal job?" asked Angela.

"I dance at a gentlemen's club in Reno."

Angela choked, sipping her water. "You're a stripper?"

"Exotic dancer."

"Hence the lap-dance comment," laughed Tara.

"Do you actually dance on a pole?" Angela's face lit up.

"It's a great workout. You should try it sometime," said Liz.

Angela seemed to consider it. "Maybe I will."

Tara snorted. "I'd pay money. Let's find Angie a smooth birch tree to practice on."

Liz laughed. "That could be arranged. Just hook me up with a chainsaw."

The van turned off the highway onto a bumpy, dirt road bisecting a stand of dense, scraggly spruce. Gunnar pulled into the Moose Creek campground and parked.

"Okay, Aurora Crew, let's go." Ryan exited the van.

"Don't forget bug dope." Liz loaded her palms with repellent and rubbed it onto her skin. She offered some to Angela.

Angela waved it away. "Thanks, but I have skeeter spray. Here." Angela passed a miniature spray bottle to Tara. Mosquitoes buzzed their ears as they exited the van.

A pale green AFS truck pulled up, loaded with equipment. Mel hopped out and unloaded tools. He must not be flying helicopters today, thought Tara.

Ryan lowered the tailgate and jumped in the back.

"Here's your tools, folks. Grab a Pulaski. It's yours for the season. Sawyers, grab a chainsaw." Mel dispensed tools to each of the crew, his mullet poking out from under his hardhat.

Angela held up her Pulaski. "I call it Jekyll and Hyde because it has two heads. The grub-hoe side is Hyde, and the axe end is Jekyll." She stroked its long, fiberglass handle.

"Way to fondle your fire tool, Divina," deadpanned Tara, cracking her gum.

"Not touching that one with a ten-foot pole." Liz grinned.

"Not while you're twisted around it," Angela shot back.

Liz cracked her gum and nodded approval. "Carolina, you're fast on the uptake."

"I'm just warmin' up, y'all." Angela winked, thickening her drawl.

"Listen up," said Ryan. "First we'll dig a fireline in that clearing next to the campground." He motioned his head at it and jumped from the truck bed, graceful as a gazelle. "Spread out, ten feet apart. Remove fuel by chopping the vegetation and scraping down to mineral soil. Taiga forests are a bugger to dig with tussocks and thick layers of duff, lichen, and mosses."

Ryan and Gunnar demonstrated, swinging their Pulaskis with the hoe-end out and then downward, to peel back the thick vegetation.

"Practice and then we'll time you." Gunnar strode off along the crew line.

"I'll bet Ryan and Gunnar are good jump partners," commented Angela.

Tara swung her Pulaski. "Of course, they are. Never come between a pair of jump partners. They're connected at the hip."

"Wouldn't it be hard jumping from planes like that?" deadpanned Liz, swinging her tool.

"Jump partners will do anything for each other. My ex wouldn't meet me in person so I could break up with him. Instead, he had his jump partner do it." Tara swung and chopped.

"What a chicken shit." Liz wrinkled her nose.

Tara stopped swinging to scowl at her. "I know, right? My ex jumped from planes to battle raging fires, but he didn't have the guts to face me after I called him out for cheating." She swung with such force that chunks of vegetation sailed through the air and plunked off of Liz's boots.

"He sounds like a nutless weasel." Angela grimaced.

Ryan called out to the crew. "Aurora Crew, you're being timed. Dig a hundred-foot line. Go!" He clicked his stopwatch.

"Wow, what a douche." Liz hacked at her section of line. "Not Ryan. Your ex, the nutless weasel."

Angela chopped the ground. "What did you do when your ex's jump partner showed up to meet with you?"

"I told him to tell Travis I broke off our engagement and threw his ring into the Clark Fork River." Tara swung even harder.

"No way!" Liz shot her a crazed look. "A perfectly good diamond?"

"Actually, I didn't. But I wanted to. Instead, I burned his letters and dumped the ashes in an envelope with the ring and mailed it to him." Tara was winded from swinging so hard.

Angela and Liz exchanged glances as Tara torpedoed grass and weeds in every direction. Her section of fireline was the first to be cleared.

"Hey Liz, we can kick back while Tara digs the whole kit 'n' caboodle while she grouses about her nutless weasel," said Angela.

Liz guffawed and even Tara laughed.

"Time! Not fast enough." Ryan stood at the end of the crew line and pointed his sunglasses toward the women, as a groan emanated from the crew. Everyone looked at the three laughing women.

"Hey, not our fault." Angela wiped away tears and held up a hand at the crew.

The more Tara thought about it, the more her unresolved anger with Travis rolled back on her. Here she was, deep in the heart of Alaska and her hurt and anger were as fresh as ever. *Stop talking and thinking about him.*

"Aurora, take a five-minute break," called out Ryan.

He approached the women. "Ladies, how about splitting up and mixing with other crew? Waters, Harrington, move down the line. Divina, you can stay here."

"Sure, no problem." Liz moved to insert herself between two guys.

Angela stayed put, as Ryan suggested.

Tara sent Ryan a solemn look before stepping down to insert herself between two crew members. *Did he think we were having a sewing circle or something?* Her irritation stuck in her throat, so she held it there rather than smart off with something she'd regret.

Everyone resumed digging fireline until Ryan called another break.

Tara lifted the tip of her neck bandana and wiped her face.

The broad-shouldered guy working next to her dropped to the ground and sat cross-legged. He looked up at her. "Hi, I'm Jon Silva." He rested his Pulaski across his lap and took a sip from his canteen.

"Tara Waters." She plopped down next to him, unscrewing the lid from her canteen.

"I know. Pleased to meet you, Tara." He leaned back and positioned his hardhat on his face for a fast nap. "I'm glad we're on the same crew."

🔥

*R*yan will have Aurora Crew dig fireline all day and night, if necessary. He put the crew through their paces to the point of exhaustion. He understood the women's inclination to work near each other, but he also knew the importance of them blending with the rest of the crew.

He observed Tara working from behind his sunglasses. She tore at the ground as if she were at war with it. Sweat poured down her face and she wiped it away with her sleeve. Every so often she'd touch the orange bandana around her neck. It kind of turned him on. *Knock it off, O'Connor...not the time, not the place.*

That wasn't all he noticed. Silva had been paying close attention to Tara. Ryan knew him well. They'd taken EMT training together, and Silva had been the chief fire medic on several fires. Last season he treated Ryan for a sprained knee and lacerations from a bad jump landing. Silva had also worked fires as a crew boss. He was well-known and had a good reputation. His smooth charisma appealed to everyone, especially women. A pang jabbed Ryan's chest at the thought of Tara succumbing to Silva's' charms.

The sound of grunting and metal clicking against rocks filled the air, interspersed with Gunnar calling out to advance the line. The crew worked steadily, and Ryan stood sentinel with his stopwatch. "Time."

The crew leaned on their tools, wiping sweat and sipping water. The nagging sun beat down.

"Eighty-five feet in six minutes. Again."

Everyone groaned with sighs all around.

"Sorry, people," said Ryan. "Alaska fires burn hot and fast. You don't want to learn this the hard way." He clicked his stopwatch.

"Again!"

CHAPTER 14

*R*yan was a different guy out here in the woods. If Tara wasn't so irritated with him, his incident command mode might have turned her on. Yesterday maybe, but not today.

An eternity passed before he called time and clicked his stopwatch. "Better. Ninety-five feet in six minutes. Good. Now let's cut a saw line." Ryan took off for the vehicles.

Tara pushed off the ground and fell in line to hike back to the trucks.

Once there, Ryan told the certified sawyers to come forward and grab a chainsaw. Silva, Tupa, and a guy named Wolfgang each picked one up. Ryan handed them leather chaps and saw tools. "Your PPE, gentlemen."

Ryan addressed the crew. "You dug a fireline, so you know the difficulty of digging through tundra. In Alaska, we mostly do saw lines. We'll be working with another crew. Sawyers will cut trees and brush, so stay clear when trees fall. Be safety aware, know what's going on around you. Toss the brush outside of the saw line. Capisce?"

"Yeah." A communal response and a bobbing of heads.

"Okay, let's do this." Ryan waved everyone to move on and led off at a fast clip. People worked to keep up.

After a mile or so, they stopped in an area with dead trees from beetle kill. Another crew was already on site. Tara's stomach fell to her boots when she spotted Rego and Hudson.

Ryan pointed to pink flagging tied to dead snags every thirty feet as far as Tara could see. "Here's your line. Sawyers in position."

Silva, Tupa, and Wolfgang moved ahead of the pack, sawing alders and willow bushes.

"Brush clearers, go," ordered Ryan, gesturing the next four people in the line to pick up brush and toss it outside of the saw line.

The rest followed in the same order as before; chopping remaining vegetation, hacking roots, and scraping to mineral soil. Sawyers cut trees and Tara followed a safe distance behind, swamping brush away from the fireline. She respected chainsaws, knowing loggers in Missoula who'd lost body parts due to fatigue or carelessness.

She noticed Ryan talking to some fire bosses, gesturing with his clipboard. Probably talking about crew assignments.

Silva came up behind her. "So, what happened with Angela in the pack test?"

Tara glanced back at him. "She wasn't feeling well and couldn't finish. O'Connor had her taken to the med clinic." No way would she tell Silva the real reason. Not until she found out who'd wanted Angela to fail her fitness test.

"It's handy having two certified EMTs around." Silva chopped at brush.

"Two?"

"O'Connor and myself. He's a certified Smokejumper EMT, and I'm certified as an Alaska Fire Medic. I've run medical units on past fires. But this year I wanted back on the fireline."

"Sounds interesting." Tara heaved the brush outside of the line. "O'Connor's an EMT? Geez, what can't he do?"

"He's not good at relationships." Silva took off his hardhat and brushed back his chestnut brown hair. His rolled-up sleeves revealed forearms with bird tats, covered with hair.

"Well, that's random. How long have you known him?"

"We go back a few years. He's a player and quite the heart-breaker. Never have seen him with the same woman twice."

She raised her brows, looking up at him. He was nearly as tall as Ryan. "Oh, really?"

"Hey, Jon," yelled Tupa. "Need you back here for a minute."

"Nice talking to you." He winked at her and returned to the back of the crew line.

Silva had paid her some attention in class, but more so now that they were working outside. So, Ryan was a player? She tried not to let Silva's comments bother her, but his words stuck to her like glue.

Enough of this, she needed to focus. Saw, toss brush, chop out vegetation, scrape to mineral soil. She liked the cadence of the chainsaws; the sound of work being done. She thought of Dad, how he'd gracefully handled his Stihl as if it were an extension of his arm.

It took a good while for all three crews to reach a rhythm. Occasionally, people fell out of order and Tara somehow found herself behind Hudson. He took his time tossing lightweight brush, annoying those behind him by leaving the heavy logs.

"Heads up, falling timber," hollered Silva, lifting his chainsaw away from a fifteen-foot tree.

Everyone cleared until the tree hit the ground. Tupa limbed it with his chainsaw. "Swamp it."

"I got it. Get clear," hollered Tara, lifting the log and heaving it up onto her right shoulder. She braced to toss it outside of the fireline. Just as she pitched it, Hudson got in the way.

The log struck his hardhat, knocking him to the ground.

"What the *fuck*?" He rolled on the ground, clawing at his hat to tug it off.

Tara stood, stunned. "It was an accident. I didn't mean to—"

"You could have killed me!" Hudson leered. He felt his head then peered at his fingers. No blood, but the log had cracked his hardhat. He held it up. "If this were my head, I'd be dead."

"I'm sorry, but you shouldn't have gotten in the way." She replayed it in her mind. No, she wasn't the one who'd screwed up.

"O'Connor!" yelled Hudson. He stood and glared at her. His otherwise not-bad-looking demeanor turned dark, his face a deep red. Veins bulged in his neck, sending chills through her. She had an urge to flee. Instinctively, she stepped back.

Ryan trotted up. "What happened?"

She breathed relief at his presence. Not that she couldn't handle herself, but the demonic look in Hudson's eyes set off all kinds of alarm.

"Waters threw this log at me." If Hudson could spit poisonous venom she'd be dead.

"It was an accident. He got in the way right as I tossed it." She stared at Ryan.

Ryan examined Hudson's cracked hardhat, then his scalp. "You aren't bleeding, but you might get a lump. Are you dizzy?" He peered at Hudson. "Your eyes aren't dilated, but you should be checked for concussion."

"He got in the way just as I threw the log." She sounded like a recording.

Ryan studied her a long moment, expressionless, making her uncomfortable.

"Everyone take five," he announced to the crew. "Hudson, I'll have someone drive you back to the med clinic. Waters, come with me." He crooked his finger at her and strode off into the woods, radioing for someone to come fetch Hudson.

Her heart sped and not in a good way. Ryan seemed pissed.

He blasted through brush as if it weren't there, his boots snapping twigs. She followed him behind a large clump of alder where no one would hear.

He stopped and faced her. "What's with the attitude?" He removed his sunglasses and let them dangle to his chest, his mouth a straight line.

She stopped short of bumping into him and folded her arms. "I'm not sure what you mean," she said haltingly.

"You've seemed pissed off ever since this morning. You're out of sorts with me. I get it. But heaving a log at a guy? You shouldn't take retribution on an assumption." His all-business voice chopped her like an axe.

"You think I hit Hudson on purpose for sabotaging Angela?" Her voice rose.

"There's no proof Hudson weighted her pack. Or Rego, for that matter," he said evenly.

"Then find out who did. Sabotaging another firefighter is a malicious act and whoever did it should be fired!"

"I'm looking into it. You can't fire people on an assumption."

"You don't believe me when I tell you they did it? Why aren't people held accountable anymore?" Her exasperation bubbled into a boiling froth.

"I can't fire these guys without proof." His calm manner now irritated her.

"So, they'll get away with sabotaging Angela and trying to get me fired?"

The words tumbled out before she could stop them. "When people get away with gender discrimination, it burns out of control like a runaway fire and a guy has sex with people he works with in every town he visits without giving a shit how it hurts others, when all it boils down to is he thinks he's God's gift to women—" She stopped herself and froze, her words wafting in the air like acrid smoke.

Oops. How had this become a rant about Travis McGuire? Her face heated and sweat beaded her forehead. She swiped at it and squeezed her eyes closed, scrunching her face. In what seemed forever, she forced a lid open and peeked at him.

"Are you done?" he asked in a quiet voice.

She took a moment to regroup and cool herself down. "I didn't mean—what I meant to say was, I was talking about Angela's fitness test. Someone wanted her to fail."

"That may be, but we need to stay level-headed." He had a weird expression on his face.

Another Pandora box had sprung open and she knew why. Saying this to a smokejumper gave her immense satisfaction. Problem was, it was the wrong one.

She rubbed the bridge of her nose with thumb and forefinger. "I'm sorry I unloaded like a dump truck…when the smokejumper I should have said this to, is a few thousand miles away." She stretched her arm out in a haphazard direction.

"I got the part about gender discrimination." He scratched his cheek. "But you lost me at sex with coworkers."

"Let me explain…"

"Look, Tara. I don't know what's going on with you. But that's not the issue here. The real issue is you need to focus on your job. Put whatever is bothering you out of your brain. You're a wildland firefighter. Now act like it."

His authoritarian tone pissed her off. "Or what? You'll fire me?" *Keep it together. Don't lose it again.*

He let out a long sigh. "You've brought things up I can't address right now."

"You mean you won't address right now. So, is this the fire instructor talking, or the guy who kissed me? I take it they're two different people." She watched a small spider resting on the toe of her boot, wondering if her anger was hot enough to torch the little bugger.

"We'll talk about that later, but not while we work together. No more screw-ups. You're better than this. It's not good for a new crew to have safety incidents in their first work session. We aren't even on a fire."

She wanted to say *the more I'm around you, the more I screw up.* Instead, she focused on the spider crawling off her boot to cool herself down. She lifted her chin. "For the record, I didn't deliberately hit Hudson, though he may deserve it. He honest to God moved in the way."

"That may be, but I'm still required to write an incident report."

"Tupa and Angela were behind me. They must have seen what happened."

"All right, I'll talk to them." He turned to go.

"Wait." Okay, she'd swallow some pride. She couldn't afford her training instructor thinking she was a raving lunatic. "I wasn't angling for a pat on the back from you this morning," she lied.

He stopped to look at her. "I'm sorry if I offended you, but what you did was reckless. I get that you want on a hotshot crew. You proved you can handle it. Chena Hotshots had an opening, but the slot filled fast. If I'd known you were…" He gestured at her, head to toe. "…this capable, I would have advised you to apply."

"Please put it in writing for Jim Dolan so he can recommend me to the Lolo Hotshots." She put on her sunglasses.

"You're having an off day. Tomorrow will be better and it's the last day of training. Let's get back to it." He walked out of the woods and she followed to join her crew.

All she wanted was to do her time here and go home. She tried to leave her baggage in Montana, but it clung to her like tree sap. She had taken her frustration out on Ryan, because Silva said Ryan changed women like underwear…and because he was a smokejumper. She knew it wasn't fair to him, but she feared a Travis 2.0. *Been there, done that.*

Her heart had split into two halves. One half longed to be loved and the other was an armament of defense. *When you love people, they abandon you.*

Not even Ryan was proving that wrong.

CHAPTER 15

he van rocked along the dirt road leading up to Moose Creek campground, same as yesterday. Sipping his coffee, Ryan looked bleary-eyed at Aurora Crew's worksite up ahead. He hadn't gotten much sleep.

Mel drove. "Glad it's the last day of training?"

"Yep." Hopefully, the day wouldn't be a calamity. He wasn't in the best of spirits after staying up writing Tara's log incident report.

"That good, huh? You'll be back to jumping fire next week, buddy." Mel smiled out the windshield.

Ryan let out a long sigh. "Yep. Back to normal."

Yesterday's discussion with Tara bugged Ryan. Her remark about sex with people at work. What was *that*? Someone had sure pissed her off. Obviously a smokejumper. He was curious to know her story.

Mel lurched the van to a halt at the same clearing as the day before. Aurora Crew piled out.

Ryan adjusted his hardhat and exited the van. "Spread out. We're going to practice fire shelter deployment," he announced, pulling his stopwatch from his pants pocket. "Under twenty seconds. Go!"

🔥

*T*ara yanked the foil shelter from its case below her day pack and fumbled it open. Most of the crew had deployed and hit the dirt by the time she'd managed to shake hers.

"You'll keep deploying until everyone is under twenty seconds." Ryan glanced at her, then back at the crew. "Repack 'em."

Angela stood next to her. "Get with it so he doesn't make us do it again."

"Working on it," she muttered, folding her shelter to stuff it back into its container.

"Today's the last training day. Let's just get through it." Angela closed her shelter case and positioned it under her day pack.

Tara scolded herself for being slow. The harder she tried, the more she screwed up. What was wrong with her? *Come on, Tara, get your act together.*

🔥

*R*yan's patience was at an all-time low. It took four tries for everyone to deploy under twenty seconds. In a real fire situation, they may not have that long. He ordered Aurora Crew to hike the half-mile to resume digging where they left off yesterday. Staying up late last night caught up with him and he let Aurora Crew knock off work early. He instructed everyone to head back to the vehicles and waved everyone ahead.

Halfway to the trucks, someone screamed, followed with laughter. Ryan hurried toward the sounds. When he caught up to the group, Tara and Angela stood in a squirrel cache full of spruce cones, deceptively level with the ground.

"Look at this." Tara laughed, sunk to her thighs, sifting her hands through thousands of cones.

Silva reached in and pulled her out of the ocean of spruce cones. Next, he pulled Angela out and set to work brushing cones off the women.

"Thanks, Jon. I'll get the front," Tara smiled at him, brushing the few remaining cones off herself.

Silva grinned. "I don't mind."

Ryan tensed and his neck hairs raised. He'd seen Silva in action before, charming women on and off the job, skirting the fine line between flirting and friendly assistance.

"That's the biggest cache I've ever seen," laughed Silva, focused on Tara. "Those squirrels worked a ton of overtime."

Ryan stood by, unamused. The crew had worked hard, and he understood their need to release tension. But hadn't he covered ash pit hazards in class? "Let's revisit the hazards of squirrel caches." He picked up a stick and moved slowly around the cache.

"During mop-up at a fire near McGrath, a guy fell in a smoldering squirrel cache. It burst into flame and burned two-thirds of his body. I fished him out and did all I could, but he died later in a hospital." Ryan tossed the stick in the cache. "Stay out of smoldering caches and tree pits."

He rested his gaze on Tara. "Keep your ground radar on when walking through fires."

Once everyone reached their vehicles, they stowed their hand tools, talking and laughing after completing refresher training. People clambered into the crew van.

Silva's attention to Tara bothered Ryan more than he cared to admit. He wanted to talk to her before everyone scattered to go fight fire. Maybe ask her to dinner. He tossed his tools in the back of the van and stuffed his hardhat and sunglasses in his day pack.

"Waters, can we talk a minute?"

"Sure." Tara strolled up to Ryan, smiling, her hair in its usual messy ponytail. Any trace of rancor from before had vanished. She seemed like herself again.

He tried to think of a way to finesse asking her out. *Talk to her about safety.* "Do you remember my talk about squirrel caches in class?"

"Yes. Why?"

"Don't make a habit of playing in them." He worked to keep himself on the level while scanning his brain for a segue to *Want to go out with me?*

"We stumbled into it. Didn't do it on purpose." She gave him a funny look.

He rubbed his forehead. "Don't ever do it on a fire." *Tell her, O'Connor.*

"I won't." Her face softened. "Ryan, I'm so sorry about your friend. It must have been awful. But why do I sense there's more here than pulling a buddy from a squirrel cache?"

Damn it. He'd never had difficulty talking to women, but for some reason his mouth wouldn't form the right words. Images played of Silva plying spruce cones off her. "Safety is priority, you know that."

She bristled. "I know about wildfire safety."

I want you to go out with me. Say it, dumb shit. Instead, he stared at her, vexed. "But I'm not so sure about your decision-making." Where the hell did that come from? *You're making it worse.*

"So, it's my decision-making abilities you're concerned about?" She scowled at him.

This was evolving into something he hadn't intended. "A few days ago, I advised you to get counseling. We think we can handle people dying on our watch. Not always."

"Why do you keep bugging me about it?" A wild look crossed her face.

"Because your boss asked me to—" he blurted. *Oh shit, I blew it.*

Her face looked as though he'd gutted her. "Oh. Now I get it," she said quietly. "The only reason you were nice to me was because Jim Dolan told you to keep your eye on me. That's what he talked to you about on the Copper Peak Fire, wasn't it? Watch out for poor, little Tara. Like I'm some helpless, damaged person." Her face flushed.

"No, that's not it at all—"

She cut him off. "You smokejumpers are no different from the rest of us. I know jumpers. I planned to marry one. You're the demi-gods of firefighting, so you demand perfection from the rest of us."

"Perfection?" He strained for calm and rubbed his forehead. "I've seen what happens when people make bad decisions. You saw how fast the fire devil destroyed life and property on the Copper Peak Fire. Perfection is irrelevant. When I talk safety, yes, you should listen."

"I do listen. I make good decisions. I've got this." She spoke with a firm tone.

"You say that a lot." He folded his arms. "Have you always been this difficult?"

"Yes!" she snapped. "As a woman I'm forever proving myself. So I must work twice as hard. It gets old, always having to prove I can do the job. But you know what?" She pointed a finger at him. "I suck it up because I love firefighting."

He put his hands on his hips. "Not once have I asked you to prove yourself. *You* own that one."

"You keep saying I need counseling. Are you doubting my mental capabilities as a firefighter? Yes, someone died on my watch. It was tough, but I'm dealing."

It was time that he told her.

Now, how to form the words. He spoke slowly. "Several years ago the Santa Ana winds blew up a fire in Southern California. It ran before we could stop it. Our hotshot crew had to listen to the horrific screams of five people trapped in a house. We couldn't get them out." He paused to look away and his brow furrowed.

He turned back to her. "An entire family burned to death—three kids, two parents and—" He looked away to compose himself. "Not a fucking day goes by where that doesn't weigh on me."

His words hung in the air like whale spray.

Tara stood looking stunned. "Did you—did you get counseling?"

"Yes." He hesitated then looked back at her. "But I didn't stick with it. I should have. Most of my crew quit after that." He stopped, staring off into the woods. *Tell her you want her safe. Not for Jim Dolan, but for you. Say it. Say it…*

Her gaze pierced him. "Why didn't you tell me before?"

He shook his head. "Don't like talking about it."

"I'm so sorry, Ryan. I get what you're feeling." She stared down at the ground, then back at him.

She took a step forward. "You're the one who said it was a sign of strength to talk about line of duty deaths. Maybe I do have issues. But my fire safety and my decision-making abilities are not your concern. As of now, you are off the hook with Jim Dolan. Training is over. You no longer have to watch out for poor, damaged Tara." She turned and walked away.

Stopping, she spun around to face him. "Thanks for Denali. It was wonderful. I'll never forget it." She strode toward Mel's truck, climbed inside, and slammed the door.

Mel twisted around in the driver's seat and shrugged a 'what should I do?' at Ryan.

He stood there, undecided. *Should I go after her?* He let out a long breath and he motioned Mel to go. The truck's engine fired up and rambled down the road.

Gunnar exited the crew van. "What was all that about?"

"Tara's riding back with Mel." His chest clenched. He should have come right out and asked her to dinner.

"I see that. Loosen up, jump boy. You're wound up tighter than a skier's ass on a vertical cliff." Gunnar winked at him. "She likes you."

Ryan rubbed his face, his fingertips scraping stubble. "Could have fooled me. She didn't listen to my safety talks about squirrel caches."

"We both know why your nose is out of joint and it has nothing to do with squirrel caches, my friend. You like her, and not just a little." Gunnar grinned. "Don't worry. Your secret's safe with me." He slapped Ryan on the back and headed to the van.

"I'm not a demi-god for chrissakes," he muttered, plopping into the front seat. Okay, so Silva's attention to Tara pissed him off. And what was that bit about marrying a smokejumper? He wondered who; he knew most of them after years of working fire.

Dolan would be pissed for ratting him out, and Ryan had sure messed things up with Tara. The chances of seeing her the rest of the busy fire season were nil. Even so, he couldn't help thinking what it would have been like to hook up with her.

Chinook Fire Station had requested a crew to be on stand-by for Interior fires and Ryan agreed to send the Aurora Crew.

His training obligation was over. True to his word, he had kept an eye on Tara for Jim Dolan…and then some. *I'll return to the Jump Shack to do what I do best.*

Jumping fire.

CHAPTER 16

*T*ara didn't say much in the crew van to Chinook for Aurora Crew's first fire assignment. She didn't sleep much last night. The van cruised the Steese Highway heading to the Chinook Fire Station, ninety miles north of Fairbanks.

Angela sat behind Tara and tapped her shoulder. "Feel like talking about it? You seemed upset last night so didn't want to bug you."

Tara faced forward and shook her head.

"Saw you talking to Ryan yesterday. Color me clueless, but it seemed like you two were arguing."

Liz leaned forward from her seat next to Angela. "Wasn't he impressed with your pack test?"

Tara turned to face her crewmates. "Nope. And it seems he doesn't trust my decision-making. I told him I was tired of proving myself and it went downhill from there." She bit her lower lip and hesitated. "He said when he worked on a hotshot crew in a bad California fire, they couldn't save a family of five. I didn't know what to say."

"Oh, man," breathed Liz. "That's intense."

Angela laid her hand on Tara's shoulder. "Hon, he understands what you've gone through, and my guess is that's why he advised you to get counseling. His advice came from a well-intentioned place. I don't think you should come down on him for it."

Tara turned to face both women. "I wished he would have told me when we talked before." She'd been so preoccupied with keeping Ryan at arm's length, she'd wasted precious time to truly get to know him.

Angela pursed her lips. "Next time you see Ryan, mend your fence and set it right."

"There won't be a next time. I won't see him the rest of the season."

"You don't know that," said Liz. "Fire is a small world."

"Don't give up on him, hon." Angela made a ponytail and fastened it with a hair tie.

Liz gave Tara a thoughtful look. "I'll bet you and Ryan both have fire signs in your horoscopes, by the way you two spark at each other."

Tara grimaced. "I wouldn't doubt it. The thing is, I knew better. You'd think I'd get a clue. Especially with smokejumpers."

The van pulled up to the quaint, log cabin buildings of the Chinook Fire Station, just as the sun danced rays of light and shadow on the mountains. Everyone bailed out and stretched.

As the designated crew boss, Jon Silva checked Aurora Crew in with the Chinook fire management officer. The crew hauled in their gear and settled into their new quarters.

At dinner Silva introduced the Chinook fire boss, Bing Pickel with an offhanded joke. "Never get into a pickle with Pickel." Of course everyone laughed. Silva always used humor when addressing the crew. They seemed to like it in addition to respecting his fire knowledge and crew boss expertise.

Tara noted how competent and confident Silva was in taking charge, along with his charming disposition; the kind of guy who'd tell you to go to hell and you'd enjoy the trip.

The crew were assigned to three, six-person canvas tents on a pine boardwalk behind the fire station. The women shared a tent with another fire employee, who showed them around. As they walked around the compound to acquaint themselves, Tara noted a row of BLM trucks neatly parked in a spacious parking lot, along with four fire engines.

Chinook's population boasted one hundred but doubled in summer with firefighters and miners. After dinner, Tara, Angela, and Liz jogged around town, which took all of twenty minutes. One gravel road ran four blocks, bisecting Chinook, and that was it. A block from the fire station sat the Yukon Roadhouse, a combination bar, restaurant, and hotel.

The crew met for dinner in the cozy dining room of the main building. Tara, Angela, and Liz sat at one end of a long table with the rest of the crew, talking about the upcoming week. Silva came over to join them and took a seat next to Tara.

"What was the deal with you and O'Connor? You two had your fangs out with each other." Silva lifted a water glass and sipped.

Tara shrugged. "We didn't see eye to eye, that's all."

"You and O'Connor had a 'you-make-me-want-to-be-a-worse-person' thing going on at the end of training." Silva glanced at her. "When people go at it like you two, something's going on."

"Nothing going on. I don't hit on firefighters—or smoke-jumpers for that matter."

"What if they hit on you?"

"I don't encourage it." Tara's firm tone hopefully sent him a loud and clear message.

Silva gave her an appealing smile. "It's not a mortal sin to fall for people you work with. Happens all the time. Didn't you ever watch *Grey's Anatomy* or *Parks and Recreation?*"

Tara leaned back. "I'm only here to fight fire."

"So am I." His brown eyes sparkled at her and his head tilted, reminding her of a suave movie star posing for a head shot.

She was curious why Silva always brought up Ryan. "The other day you said O'Connor was a heartbreaker. Why did you say that?"

"Just making conversation. Thought you should know his reputation with women."

"What makes you an expert on relationships?" She reached for a biscuit and buttered it.

Liz and Angela had paused their conversation to listen. Tara noted Liz always stopped to listen to Jon Silva.

"I was married to three women." He stated it so solemnly, Tara stifled a laugh.

"Wow! All at once? How did you meet them?" Liz popped a piece of biscuit in her mouth.

He gave her a reproachful look. "Give me a break. I'm not a polygamist. I found the first two in the traditional way—in a bar. The third was a birder I found on Tinder."

"A birder on Tinder?" laughed Angela. "Do tell."

"I was teaching ornithology at UAF while working on my doctorate," said Silva. "I did a Big Year once with Audubon and came in at tenth place. I chase birds for fun."

"As opposed to chasing women?" chuckled Liz. She leaned forward with interest. "Tell us about Bird Woman."

"I fell in love with her photo on Tinder when she trolled for a birder husband. I wrote her a letter with the suitability statement she asked for. We were both working on doctorates, so it seemed like a perfect match. We married a month later." Silva paused to sip from a glass.

"Then what?" asked Liz.

He continued. "Our research took us in opposite directions. I found out she hooked up with a birder dude in Mexico, tracking a green honeycreeper."

"And?" asked Angela.

She and Liz waited expectantly as Silva milked the dramatic pauses, which amused Tara.

"Well, they never found the green honeycreeper." Silva pursed his lips. "Unless it was in a hotel in Cancun. We divorced."

"What happened to your first two wives?"

"They divorced me. I was always gone." He smiled at Tara. "Every firefighter's curse during fire season, and every birder's curse chasing snowy owls."

Silva knew how to entertain and clearly loved being on center stage with the women on the crew. Knowing this, Tara decided to make it clear to him she had no interest, other than on a professional level.

The next morning after breakfast, Silva rattled off Aurora's crew assignments. Bing Pickel said a quick good morning, handed Silva a to-do list, and scooted out again. He reminded Tara of the always-late white rabbit, in the way he dashed around.

"Also, I'm sure you're aware we're down two people from our crew this morning. One had a death in the family and the other left for personal reasons. AFS is sending two replacements."

"Who?" asked Tupa, chomping one last piece of toast.

"Hudson and Rego."

The women groaned.

Silva shrugged. "Sorry, AFS made those assignments."

Tara's stomach catapulted. *Great.* She still suspected one of them put the extra weight in Angela's pack. She'd find out if it killed her.

"This is an appropriate time to get to know each other and congeal as a crew. We'll split our work details accordingly. Oh, and keep an eye out for snowy owls. It's the last northern bird on my list I haven't seen. They bring good karma." Silva caught Tara's eye and smiled.

Silva divided the crew into three squads, six in each. He announced the squad bosses: Tara, Payson, and Liz, and tossed them each a set of truck keys and told them their work assignments for the day.

Tara led her squad out to a crew-cab pickup, where they grouped around her. "Let's introduce ourselves, even though you might already be acquainted. I'm Tara Waters."

"I'm Robin from Chicken, Alaska," indicated one of the fair-haired twins with matching mustaches. He pointed a thumb at his brother. "He's Bateman."

"Bateman and Robin. That sounds like..." Tara raised her brows and grinned.

"Yeah, we know," they both said at once.

She looked from one to the other. "How do I tell you apart?"

Bateman pointed to a black bat tatted on the side of his neck.

"Okay, I'm good with it." Tara gave everyone a cheerful smile.

She was pleased Tupa was assigned to her squad. She enjoyed his positive vibes. But what a massive torso! She was amazed AFS found a Nomex shirt and pants large enough to fit him. "Tupa, tell us about yourself."

"Born in Samoa and my family moved to Anchorage." He rolled up his sleeves to display his cuff tattoos. His black beard and the ponytail pulled back on the high part of his scalp reminded her of a pirate. "I've fought fire in Australia and California."

Tara smiled. "Fires there are tough to fight. Thanks, Tupa."

He gave her a curt nod.

"I'm Schwartz. He's Wolfgang." A medium-built gangly guy dipped his head toward the hairy guy next to him. Wolfgang wore round wire-rimmed glasses and had a sizeable space between his two front teeth. His eyes bugged out, giving him a forever astonished expression.

Tara sized up the two. Schwartz had a widow's peak like Silva, but with salt and pepper hair. He resembled a vampire.

"Schwartz and Wolfgang, Bateman and Robin. Tupa. Got it." Quirky names. But at least she'd remember them.

"Tara Waters. Good name for a firefighter. Water puts out *afi* —the Samoan word for fire." Tupa nodded and glanced around. Others nodded with him.

"Good point." Tara hadn't thought of her name that way. "Okay, let's head to our brush clearing site."

"Tupa, you have saw certification, right?" Tara asked as they loaded hand tools and saws in the back of the truck.

Tupa nodded. A chainsaw was like a plastic toy to this guy.

Tara started the truck and drove to their work site. She had a good first day getting acquainted with her squad and thankfully everyone got along as they worked.

As part of a fire-fuels reduction project for the Steese-White Mountains, Bing Pickel had asked Silva to assign Aurora Crew to clear brush from certain sites. For the next several days, the crew's three squads felled standing, beetle-killed trees and dragged them to nearby cleared areas to burn when it became safe to do so.

One of the mornings, Rego and Hudson showed up and Silva assigned them to Payson's squad. Tara only saw them at breakfast and dinner meals and breathed relief at not having to work with them.

For the rest of the first week, Aurora Crew stayed divided into the three squads, familiarizing themselves with the station fire engines and practicing with hose reels from nearby lakes and rivers. Silva drilled the squads on fast and efficient engine response to road accessible fires.

The second week, Tara and her squad pulled guard duty at the Tideman Hot Springs airfield, to make sure no one screwed with the aircraft standing by for fire response. One late afternoon as Tara drove back to the Chinook Fire Station, an enormous white bird with a thick neck landed on the truck's windshield. The massive wings stretched across the glass, blocking her view of the road.

She slowed the truck. The bird paused, staring at her with wise, yellow eyes. This must be Silva's snowy owl. She admired its elegance and splendor. The graceful bird lifted off and she watched it soar over the spruce and fade into the sky.

Her squad slept soundly; no one had stirred. She didn't bother to wake anyone. This moment was her private gift to treasure. Not all things must be shared.

She considered the snowy owl as a good omen.

🔥

*M*onday morning, Ryan rose at his usual 4:05 a.m. for his daily workout. He never set his alarm on the hour; always five after, as a reminder of the five people who lost their lives on his watch. Ever since that tragic day, the number five figured prominently in his life, like a corporal punishment.

After working out and showering, he grabbed his jump gear and hauled it to the Ready Room in the Jump Shack. He hung it on his locker. When Zombie finished roll call, Ryan prepared his equipment. He and Gunnar were on the jump list as second load, first stick.

Lightning strikes had kicked up hundreds of fire-starts all over the state. While Ryan waited his turn to go, he packed firefighting tools and food supplies into cargo boxes, then inspected and repaired parachutes. Gunnar worked on harnesses and repaired equipment in the manufacturing room. Ryan's shoulders felt lighter now that he was back on jump status.

The siren sounded and the first load of eight jumpers raced to the Ready Room. Ryan and Gunnar hurried to assist them into their Kevlar suits, then helped them do safety and gear checks.

The eight waddled out to the tarmac in their weighty jump suits. They walked up the metal ramp to the open door of the Twin Otter, props whirring. Fires had sprung up in the Tanana and Galena zones. This jump ship was heading to Galena.

"O'Connor, Alexanderson, second load, front and center. You're flying to Tanana Zone. Hustle, boys," hollered Zombie, clipboard in one hand, radio in the other.

After Ryan and Gunnar helped fellow jumpers into their gear, they suited up themselves. Seth Boone, a third load jumper, helped Ryan into his gear.

Boone yanked Ryan's harness, tightening it. "Too bad you aren't going to Galena where the best food is." He grinned, straightening twisted straps, and securing Ryan's PG bag. Ryan auto-piloted through his checks: Reserve chute, fire shelter, survival gear.

Another Twin Otter pulled up on the tarmac outside the Jump Shack. Ryan, Gunnar, and six other jumpers boarded. He shuffled to the back to claim his usual place on the cargo boxes to take a nap during the quick flight to Tanana. Gunnar claimed the space opposite him.

As the plane began to taxi down the runway, Ryan's thoughts drifted to Aurora Crew and how they were faring at Chinook. Alaska's Interior had the usual high number of lightning strikes, so no doubt they were busy.

He thought of Tara. Both had said things to piss each other off. He pulled out the folded, crinkled Incident Action Plan he had stuck in a pocket of his jump suit a few days ago. He read through it and shook his head.

Should have chosen another option. Like sticking with my rule of no relationships with firefighters. He didn't have time for a girlfriend anyway. No smokejumper did.

Alaska was a big place. Chances were remote he'd even see Tara again. He tore the paper into pieces and shoved them into his pocket. When he hits the ground, he'll toss them in the fire.

And watch them burn.

CHAPTER 17

"*W*ake up, fire call!" Tara startled awake as Silva called to the women outside their tent. "It's go time!"

Tara squinted at her wristwatch. It was 6 a.m. She sprung from her bed along with Liz and Angela. The three women donned yellows, pants, and boots, readied their fire packs, and filled canteens with water.

"Aurora Crew, let's roll!" yelled Silva. "Squad bosses, follow me."

When they reached the parking lot, he tossed keys at Tara, Liz, and Payson. "Squad bosses: Take a truck engine and your groups to our staging area. Maintain radio contact."

Tara hated eating dust, so kept her window rolled up on the gravel road to the fire. She offered Bateman her radio and he turned up the volume to follow fire activity.

A smoke column rose about six miles away and a helicopter circled it. As they closed in on the fire, Tara noted it burning a dense stand of Sitka and white spruce. The three squad vehicles pulled into a clearing and everyone jumped out.

The truck thermometer read ninety degrees, surprisingly hot

for this early in the morning. Tara and the others grabbed their gear while Silva spread the topo map on the hood of his truck and gave the whole crew a quick briefing of their direct attack plan.

"Payson, take your squad to the right flank," instructed Silva. "Waters, your squad will dig fireline on the left flank. Harrington, yours will douse the tail with piss-pumps. Safety first. Know your escape routes. Stay in the black."

Silva pointed east. "I'll be lookout on that rise. Keep each other informed. Let's go, girls and boys."

Aurora Crew scattered to their three squad positions.

"Come on, guys, you heard him. Left flank." Tara grabbed the chainsaw and lowered her goggles over her eyes.

Tupa helped her into the straps that held the water bladder to her upper back. Her squad gathered their firefighting equipment.

"Know your escape route, gentlemen." Tara led off, hiking a steady clip. The others fell in single file behind her.

"Not much wind, thankfully," said Tara over her shoulder to Tupa, her boots crunching tinder-dry ground. Smelling smoke made her adrenalin pump.

"Yep. One less thing," he responded.

Tara had made sure her squad knew their jobs from all their drill practice. They set to work like a well-oiled machine, taking turns sawing and clearing to create a fireline. It took most of the day to get a containment line around most of the fire. By nightfall, the weather brought cooler air, making things easier.

A truck pulled up with water and food. Tara and her squad gobbled fresh sandwiches in between finishing digging the fireline. Around midnight, all three squads had contained the fire. A village crew from Circle arrived to do mop-up.

"Good job, Aurora. Let's demobe this puppy," Silva called out. "Load up the tools, Circle Crew is mopping up."

Tupa fist-bumped Tara. "Our squad name should be Afi Slayers—fire slayers."

"Afi Slayers. I like it." Tara grinned at him.

Tara and her newly dubbed Afi Slayers squad drove back in the twilight. Ryan's safety tip played in her head—keep headlights on during this time of day. She clicked them on, Ryan heavy on her mind. She missed his calm voice and easy manner and wished she could talk to him.

He'd be proud of Aurora Crew for successfully containing their first fire. Too bad he wasn't around to celebrate their first success. Someone would no doubt tell him about it. Fire was a small world.

As she pulled into the parking lot, radio chatter picked up. Overnight lightning strikes had blown up the Interior with fire starts. A Twin Otter pilot's voice squawked. "Dispatch, got a load of jumpers heading to Tanana Zone. Twelve souls on board."

Static, then dispatch response. "Copy that, two-seven-zero."

Were Ryan and Gunnar onboard? They must be if they were first on the jump list. A twinge tweaked her chest, with the sudden urge to tell him she was sorry.

Please don't let anything happen to Ryan. I want the chance to make it right with him.

&

The next three weeks brought hot temperatures and more fire to Alaska's Interior. Chinook's thermometer hit the 90s. Aurora Crew responded to several road-access fires and effectively contained them all. Their days were action-packed, and the crew had grown into a cohesive team.

At breakfast on the 4th of July, the day before they were scheduled to leave Chinook, Silva announced the day's assignments. "Unless we get a fire call, we'll wash the fire vehicles and clean up the fire station equipment. This afternoon we'll participate in Chinook's July 4th celebration. I know it's a holiday, but you're still expected to help. You'll get your holiday pay. Please cooperate and do whatever you're asked."

Silva studied his clipboard. "Waters, Divina, and Harrington, the Colorado fire management officer has requested your presence in the truck parking lot at 1 p.m."

"Why?" asked Tara.

"To help with the July 4th parade. Toss candy to the kids." Silva shot her his signature smile, then motioned to the crew. "The rest of Aurora, come with me. Bing Pickel has things for us to do to get ready for the parade, which will last all of five minutes."

After lunch, Tara, Angela, and Liz sauntered out to the parking lot. A fire engine was positioned behind two pickups, already decorated with red, white, and blue balloons and crepe paper.

An older guy with snow-white hair and mustache stood in the bed of one truck. He reminded Tara of a skinny Colonel Sanders, except he appeared fit as any firefighter. He jumped from the tailgate as if sticking a gymnastics vault at a perfect ten.

"Hello ladies. I'm Samuels, from the Grand Mesa National Forest in Colorado. I'm up here helping out. I have a job for you." He grinned and tossed Smokey the Bear and Woodsy Owl costumes on the ground.

"Put these on."

The women exchanged startled looks. Tara was first to speak. "Excuse me, but it's ninety-eight degrees. It's too hot for these suits." She pointed to a round thermometer with a smiling chipmunk on its face, tacked onto a wall of the main office.

"Seriously? It's hotter than Satan's house cat." Angela waved her hand at her face.

Liz wiped her brow. "Sure is."

"This is our good-will gesture for this community. I understand the Chinook Fire Station firefighters participate in the town's July 4th festivities, so told them I'd help out." Colonel

Sanders picked up Smokey the Bear's head. "Two of you put on the suits and the third will give out candy."

"It really is too warm for this," muttered Liz, lifting Smokey's bottom and peeking inside as if it contained maggots.

Angela stooped to pick up Woodsy Owl. "This is heavier than a bag of boulders."

Colonel Sanders folded his arms. "Are you ladies refusing this assignment? If so, I could have you fired for refusing a directive."

"This old-schooler thinks it's the military," breathed Liz, so only Tara and Angela could hear.

"Are you threatening us if we don't do this?" Angela smiled sweetly, turning on her Southern charm.

Colonel Sanders straightened. "Fire isn't a democracy. When your superiors give you a directive, you do it or else you're gone. A good firefighter isn't intimidated by a little heat."

Tara placed her hands on her hips. "Why didn't you ask some of the guys to do this? You know, in the spirit of equality."

He stared hard at her. "They were assigned other duties." He held out Smokey's head. "Climb in the truck bed and put this on."

Tara considered walking away. She didn't believe AFS would send the three of them home for refusing to wear the bulky costumes in this heat. Then again, she could envision this guy being a stinker about it. She didn't want to risk her job or be considered a bad sport.

"All right." Tara blew out a sigh, wiping sweat from her forehead. "I'll be Smokey."

"That's the spirit," erupted Colonel Sanders like a coach in a Superbowl game.

Colonel Sanders turned to Liz. "Blondie, you can be Woodsy Owl," he said, as if bestowing her with the congressional medal of honor. He winked at Angela. "Alabama can give out the candy."

"North Carolina," Angela corrected. She pressed her lips together and picked up sacks of candy.

"Let's get this over with." A corner of Liz's mouth twitched as she dragged Woodsy over to the truck behind the one Tara was to ride in. Liz put on the Woodsy Owl suit, complete with the Robin Hood cap and oversized feather poking out of it.

Tara laughed as she bent to pick up Smokey's dusty blue jeans, hairy top, and the oversized head. She tossed them in the truck bed, then climbed in. She pulled the heavy suit over her Nomex. The minute she put on Smokey's head a reeking stinky-socks odor smacked her nostrils. Her gag reflex kicked in. She swallowed it back.

Tara peeked through her eye holes and it struck her as funny to see a stripper decked out as Woodsy Owl. Despite her own discomfort she burst out laughing.

It didn't take long for the Smokey sauna to drench Tara. Sweat poured from her, worsening the odor, like an unshowered, overripe hockey team occupied Smokey with her. She had her hair pinned up, but it didn't help. Her scalp oozed sweat along with everything else.

Colonel Sanders hopped up in the truck bed and sat on a folding chair next to her.

"Hot in here," muttered Tara.

"Suck it up, buttercup." Colonel Sanders' voice pierced her suit.

"May I please have some water?" Tara's mouth had become cotton.

Smokey's head lifted, and ice water slapped her face. She inhaled droplets, causing her to have a coughing fit.

"I meant to drink," she choked out.

"Wave to the kids," bellowed Colonel Sanders, oblivious.

She didn't see any kids. Through her costume, she could see their truck had pulled out of the compound and was driving along Chinook's main gravel road.

"Hey Smokey, how about some candy?" Hudson's voice sounded from the side of the road. Tara put her oversized, furry paw into a tub of wrapped candies, unable to grab them. Colonel Sanders yanked her paw and slapped candy on it. She stepped back like a pitcher winding up for the Cubs and flung them hard as she could.

"Ow," whined Hudson.

Good.

It didn't take long for Tara to overheat. She lifted Smokey's head to suck in cooler air. *Oh, sweet relief!*

"No peeking. You'll ruin it for the kids," Colonel Sanders hollered.

The truck with Woodsy Owl followed close behind. Liz had to be as miserable as she was. Tara glimpsed Angela's head bobbing alongside the truck, throwing candy to people on the side of the dusty road.

"Angie," Tara hollered. "Come here a minute."

Angela moved toward her. "How are you doing under there?"

"Get me a bottle of water. I'm dying in here." Her voice sounded muffled inside the stinky head.

"Smokey doesn't talk!" Colonel Sanders barked at her eye holes.

"I'm so done with this." Tara pushed off Smokey's head and let it land on the truck bed. "Smokey may not talk, but I sure do. Stick a fork in me, I'm done." She waddled to the rear of the truck bed to jump out.

"Get back here, Smokey. You are not finished until I say you are."

As Tara prepared to jump out, Smokey's foul-smelling head plunked down over her own, disorienting her. The truck lurched and she fought for balance. Angela ran up with a water bottle, holding it up to her. "Tara, grab it."

She bent to grab the bottle and stumbled.

"Smokey is drunk," someone shouted, followed by waves of laughter.

Still fighting for balance, Tara rocked back to grab the bottle. She became disoriented and stumbled around the bed of the pickup. Her heart sped and her head throbbed. Unable to catch her breath, a tingling sensation swept her. She tipped sideways and had the sensation of falling through the air. She landed hard on her back. *What the hell?*

"Ow!" She lay there motionless, trying to catch her breath.

"Smoky is *down!*" Someone yelled.

"Tara?" Angela's voice and the scales of laughter faded to black.

CHAPTER 18

*R*yan had obtained an updated fire situation report before leaving the AFS Smokejumper Base. A five-acre wildfire burned toward the village of Bettles, on the western edge of the Jack White Mountain Range in Alaska's Interior, threatening multiple structures. Since the fire posed a threat to the town, it called for a full-blown, direct attack.

The CASA 212 pilot reduced airspeed from 170 knots to 110, as he prepared to circle the jump spot below. The plane was well-suited for jumper missions in remote Alaska. Rugged and versatile, the plane carried eight smokejumpers and equipment with supplies for three days.

When the pilot cut airspeed to 100 knots and leveled out at three-thousand feet, Stu Lavin tossed out the crepe-paper streamers to test air movement. The blue, red, and yellow streamers were twenty feet long, ten inches wide and weighted to drift the same speed as a smokejumper under a canopy. Stu had decades of smoke jump experience and was chosen as spotter for his ability and leadership. Ryan trusted Stu's judgment in only allowing jumpers to leave the plane if all conditions were to his satisfaction.

Stu pointed down at a small clearing. "Do you see the jump spot?" His voice streamed into Ryan's helmet intercom.

"Yes." Ryan peered through his heavy-mesh face mask out the open door. The wind howled around the opening and turbulence caused the plane to jump. He kept a wary eye on the wind direction. The last thing a jumper needed was to drift into burning trees.

Stu signaled the pilot to make the final pass into the wind. "On final. She's spotting and spitting firebrands a half mile ahead of the flame front. Did you see the streamers?"

Ryan dipped a nod and adjusted his helmet. He appreciated this process of making sure jumpers were on the same page as the spotter.

"There's 200 yards of drift. She's burning hot, creating her own wind. Don't go downwind of the ridge or you're fucked. Are you ready?"

"Yes." Ryan and Gunnar each responded, competing with the engine roar.

"Get in the door." Stu motioned Ryan forward.

Ryan gripped the bar by the door and knelt on one knee, his toe near the edge. The whistling wind and the plane's motors hummed in his ears, despite his helmet muffling them. He zeroed in on his jump spot. No matter how many times he'd jumped, his heart still pumped, and his blood flowed fast. Tree spires three thousand feet below resembled toothpicks encased in green velvet.

"Get ready!" Stu poised his hand above Ryan's shoulder.

Ryan focused on the stunning horizon, backdrop to the red-orange blaze. This is what he loved about Alaska, spectacular and dangerous at the same time. He awaited Stu's signal to throw himself out of the airplane and fly. This was his favorite moment, when adrenaline rocketed through his system. He loved this job.

Gunnar stood on the ready behind him as second man, first stick.

Take a deep breath, you're only skydiving into lethal, flammable wilderness.

Stu slapped his shoulder and Ryan pitched himself through the opening. Schizophrenic winds spun him as he defaulted to his checklist: Jump, look, reach, wait, pull—he tugged his cord and his square parachute opened. He continued his checklist. *Check my canopy, check my airspace, check my reserve handle, right turn, left turn, stall check, and orient to jump spot.*

He transitioned from chaos to serenity, and silence. Two minutes of peace as the plane engine faded. He toggled toward the jump spot, floating quiet, like a ninja. *Enjoy it while you can, before the crazy.* He positioned his boots together, landed, and rolled. Nailed it.

Gunnar flew in close behind. "Eee-haw!" he yelled, toggling, landing, and rolling behind Ryan. He stood, gathering his chute. "Let's tackle this demon."

The other four jumpers flew in and landed behind them. They gathered their chutes, daisy-chained the lines, and shed their jump suits.

Ryan's radio crackled with Stu's voice. "We're going live on the next pass to drop cargo."

"Copy that, CASA." Ryan looped the parachute lines in a daisy chain to keep them disentangled, before stowing his chute.

The plane circled and dropped two para-cargo boxes, drifting under small, white chutes.

"There's your goodies, boys," Stu's voice streamed.

Ryan keyed his radio and waved at the plane. "Thank you, sir."

The pilot dipped a wing before heading off.

"Let's do this before she gets greedy." Ryan knew the woods the way a moose knew his river. When he hit the ground, he tuned everything out except the tasks at hand. He eyed distant flames as he made his way toward the duct-taped boxes.

"You're IC for this one, so lock and load." Gunnar unclipped the small, white chute from the cargo boxes and produced a Spyderco folding knife. He sliced open a box and distributed gear to the other jumpers.

Lightning in the west drew Ryan's attention. Fast-moving storm, with fierce winds. He chose a nearby river for the anchor point for their saw line. If they worked fast, they'd hold it before it ran uphill.

Ryan readied his gear for the short hike. "I'll light a backfire. You work the west flank and saw fuels to the river. Pace yourself. We'll be here a while."

"Don't let lightning spike your brain. See you in a few." Gunnar slung his chainsaw to his shoulder and hiked downhill into the smoke.

Ryan grabbed his gear and took off. He pulled out his radio. "Boone, do you copy? Gunns is on the west flank. You guys grab the east one." He enjoyed incident commanding fires, controlling the chaos and bending it to his will.

Boone responded. "The winds are fickle in this storm. Not only is the fire less than a quarter of a mile from Bettles, but she's running toward your position."

"I'll check it out," responded Ryan, picking his way through deadfall as he hiked uphill for a clear view. He reached a hilltop to find the smoke had turned dark and dirty and it had changed direction. He and Gunns were now in the path of the running flame front, just as Boone said.

A firebrand came at him and he jumped aside. It hit the ground and ignited, shooting flames upward. His chest tightened. The last thing he needed was to become the flaming skull of *Ghost Rider*.

He keyed his radio. "Gunns, you copy?"

Gunnar's voice came back at him. "Better haul ass. She's running!"

Ryan clicked his radio. "Air attack, what's your position? Hit this runaway head."

"One minute out," responded Max, the retardant ship pilot.

"Gunns, incoming mud drop."

Radio silence.

"Gunns?" Still no response. "Damn it." Ryan headed down the steep slope, where 'Treeminator' shrieked through a towering, white spruce—Gunnar's nickname for his beloved 3-foot Stihl chainsaw.

Gunnar angled Treeminator deep in the base. *Rawwwwrrrr...*the spruce fell with a *whump*. He puffed out his chest with a pleased expression. "Slowing this mother down."

Ryan grinned. "You're crazy. You know that?"

Gunnar killed the saw motor and they dragged themselves uphill in the thick smoke, airborne debris bouncing off their hardhats. Some landed on Ryan's shoulder and he swept them off as they humped uphill.

A plane droned overhead, swooped low, and banked left.

"Spotter plane. Here comes the drop. Up to the ridge, go." Ryan sprinted upward.

The thunderous sound of the DC-10 roared up the draw.

"Where's our helo scoopers, boys? Dip the river and drop some water behind us. Air attack, ground ops, you copy?" Ryan broke into a run, Gunnar alongside.

"Two drinks incoming," snapped his radio.

Max cut loose the red-orange glop, pelting the ground like golf-ball sized hail.

"Get down!" yelled Gunnar.

They hit the ground on their bellies next to a stand of tall spruce. The glops of red gel struck hard, slapping their backs with heavy force. Max flew low and Ryan knew the danger to the air tanker with tall flame heights and heavy smoke. *Did it slow the fire?*

A crackling whoosh above them answered his question.

Gunnar snapped his head up and pushed off the ground. "Ryno, look out!"

Ryan turned to see the top snap from a tall, burning snag, dripping salmon-colored gel. He dove out of the way as it crashed to where he'd been standing. Another close snag *whump*ed to the ground, scattering ash in slow motion. Ryan's heart leapt out of his chest and his breaths came short. "Fuck! Let's get out of here." He sprang to his feet and ran. Nothing like a near miss to motivate a guy up a mountain.

"You lucky shit." Gunnar panted behind him. "That widow-maker would have speared your ass."

They made it to the ridgetop. Breathing hard, they watched the fire slow its advance toward Bettles. Score one for air attack.

"She's finally lying down." Ryan squinted through binoculars.

Gunnar blew out air. "About time. Now we can get in there and cut a line before she kicks up in the morning."

"Dispatch, need a weather update." Ryan spoke into his radio for the latest report.

Good news. Dispatch reported weather would improve. The jumper crew sawed and dug line all night, thanks to the twilight. Around 4 a.m. Ryan and Gunnar staggered to their gear and shook out their sleeping bags on the other side of the ridgetop.

"Screw setting up the tent." Ryan pulled off his boots, grunting, and fell back on his sleeping bag. "I'm coyoting. Let the bears chew on me."

Gunnar zonked out, coyoting on top of his.

As he drifted off, Ryan wondered how Tara and Aurora Crew were doing. He fantasized pulling his fingers through Tara's silky mane and fell asleep, dreaming she rode naked on a horse, hair cascading around her like Lady Godiva.

The last thing he remembered was pulling her off the horse and they fell to the ground together, her hair swaddling him like a blanket.

He slept better than he had in days.

🔥

*R*adio static startled Ryan awake. He sat up and sipped water from his canteen. He opened an MRE and tore open a package of crackers with his teeth, spitting out the foil.

Gunnar woke and moved off to relieve himself. "Love the smell of fire in the morning. Means more money in my wallet."

Ryan keyed his radio. "Boone, do you copy? O'Connor here. You boys ready to end this party?"

"Affirmative. Time for a real party." Boone's voice crackled back.

"Tanana base, do you copy? Place an order with AFS dispatch for two mop-up crews. We need a taxi ride back to base. Pick up Boone and the boys on the east flank first. We're on the west."

"Copy," responded a woman at the base. "We'll have a 212 to you in twenty."

They gathered their gear and humped it to the saddle, where a Bell 212 helicopter would pick them up. Ryan took in what was once stunning Tanana Zone scenery of rolling hills and majestic slopes, now a dark, smoldering landscape.

"Can't wait for a thick juicy steak, a dump truck of mashed potatoes, and some lefse." Gunnar put on his chainsaw bar cover, readying it for transport.

Ryan packed his own equipment. "A hot shower and an amber."

"You left her in California, Bro," grinned Gunnar, taking off his fire shirt and airing his armpits.

"Thanks for the reminder." Ryan pictured shapely dark-eyed

Amber. He still had a hard time with her decision that the porn industry needed her more than he did. She made more money than Ryan without breaking a sweat…or maybe she did under all those lights. *I'd rather jump from airplanes.*

A high-pitched noise pierced the morning air. Ryan scanned the scorched area around them. Nothing but ash and smoke.

"What the hell?" asked Gunnar.

"Shh, listen." Ryan tilted his head toward the sound.

Another high-pitched sound, like whimpering. He crept along the blackened ridge, following the sound to a huge, charred stump. Something grayish-white and dark squirmed in the ash. He leaned in, disbelieving. "Gunns, come here."

Gunnar hoofed over and squatted. Ryan held a dark, gray wolf pup. Gunnar picked up a light gray one. Several more scooted out of the hole under the stump.

"Where's your mama, little guys?" Ryan scoped the area for mama wolf, then lifted the pup, inspecting it. "They can't be more than a couple weeks old."

"Little gray wolf pups." Gunnar checked out his little guy.

"This one's in tough shape."

"Any more in there?"

Ryan raked ash and dirt with his fingers, uncovering another, but it remained still. His fingers explored further, finding another writhing body. "Four. One didn't make it."

"What do we do with them?"

"Can't leave them. They'll die." Ryan glanced around. No sign of mama wolf.

"I'll get my day-pack." Gunnar handed him the pup and strolled to his gear, a short distance away.

"Bring water and a Visine bottle."

The pups were dehydrated and ravenous. They nosed Ryan's glove aggressively for a drink. He removed his gloves. Their fur felt soft, but the tiny teeth and claws were razor-sharp.

Gunnar returned with his daypack and canteen. He

unscrewed the cap and poured water in it. The dark pup licked greedily but couldn't get the hang of lapping it.

"Pour out the Visine, rinse the bottle and put water and sugar in it," instructed Ryan. "We'll give them droplets." He scrutinized their packed equipment. "Stuff these little guys in your pack. We'll take them with us. Fairbanks Wildlife Rescue will make sure they're fed and cared for."

"Fire wolves. Geez, hope the mother doesn't want a piece of us." Gunnar glanced around.

"If she shows up, we leave them here. This is a late litter; they're usually born earlier in spring."

Gunnar scrutinized one. "Mom won't touch them with our scent on them."

"Guess we're committed then." Ryan gently placed each whimpering, wriggling pup in Gunnar's pack, and carried the pack to the helo retrieval point.

As if on cue, the Bell 212 rotors sounded, and the helicopter landed on the open ridge. Gunnar tossed in their gear and pulled himself aboard with the other jumpers. Ryan handed Gunnar the pup pack and hopped aboard. The pilot lifted off, swinging the fourteen-passenger helo toward Tanana. On the way, the jumpers took turns holding and feeding the pups droplets of sugar water from Gunnar's Visine bottle.

"Poor little guys." Ryan worked the dark gray pup's mouth open, noting such sharp teeth for a young pup. Then again, it was a wolf.

The brutality of fire. He'd seen his share of collateral damage; the charred animals, trying to escape, taken down as flames overtook them. He'd jumped out of the way of stampeding deer and elk in Lower Forty-eight fires.

He recalled one story where a bear on fire had charged out of the flames toward a hotshot crew boss. He said it was the most beautiful, terrifying thing he'd ever seen. He and his Granite Mountain Hotshot crew of nineteen later perished in a fire at

Yarnell, near Prescott, Arizona in June 2013, when their escape route was cut off. Stories like that tend to stick with a guy.

Several hours later, the helo landed at the Tanana fire base, where a fixed-wing Twin Otter waited to transport the jump crew back to Fairbanks. Ryan, Gunnar, and the others headed to the plane with their gear. Ryan's pack made a ruckus. The wolf pups turned out to be great entertainment for everyone on the plane.

On the flight back to the smokejumper base, Ryan's thoughts drifted to having the next two days off as part of his work rotation. He figured he'd do some fly fishing for grayling. And maybe after fire season he'd take Boone up on a standing invitation to split a condo in Belize for a month. Do some fishing for mahi-mahi or sailfish.

He looked forward to it.

CHAPTER 19

$\mathcal{T}$ara blinked her eyes open and ran her tongue along dry, cracked lips.

"Hey hon, feeling better?" Angela dabbed a cool, moist washcloth on her face.

"Why am I here? What time is it?"

"You fainted and fell off the truck. Silva carried you here and fussed all over you. It's two in the afternoon."

She thought for a moment. Oh yeah, Smokey the Bear.

Liz appeared behind Angela's shoulder. "Colonel Sanders groused that it served you right. Silva reported him and filed a complaint with Bing Pickel. He felt bad for making us report to that dickhead."

Angela nodded. "He sure did."

"Wow." Tara pressed a hand to her forehead. "Silva filed a complaint?"

"After you took a header out of the pickup, I tore my head off, stripped off my yellows, and beelined for the mess hall in my bra and Nomex pants. Chugged three Gatorades." Liz laughed.

"Would have bought a ticket to see that." Tara pushed to sit, accepting the blue Gatorade Angela offered. She gestured at Liz with it. "You should work it into a dance routine."

"There's an idea." Liz pretended thoughtful consideration.

"Tupa told Colonel Sanders to get the hell out and go back to Colorado," chuckled Angela.

"Yeah, Tupa and your Afi Slayers squad wanted a piece of Colonel Sanders," laughed Liz.

Tara lifted the back of her hand to her cheek, then leaned back on the bed. "Still feel crappy."

"You need to rest. We leave for Fairbanks in the morning. We've completed our rotation and have two days off, remember?" Angela rose to let her sleep.

Tara needed no convincing. She drifted off, dreaming of parachuting from the back of pickup trucks.

*T*ara woke refreshed, but ravenous. After a shower, she felt like a phoenix that had risen from the ashes. She dressed in a clean, red T-shirt and jeans, and sat on her bed to braid her hair.

Angela came into their bunkhouse. "Hey sleepyhead, it's chow time."

"I could eat an entire moose," said Tara. The women walked to the dining hall and took a seat on a long table bench. The rest of the crew straggled in.

"Hey Smokey," Rego yelled from the end of the table. "Heard from your paws lately?"

"Only *you* can prevent wildfires," smirked Tupa.

Everyone laughed and Tara couldn't help smiling. She turned to Silva. "Thanks, Jon. Guess I owe you one."

He smiled. "Waters, you were out of it. When you took a header out of the truck, we thought you were a goner."

She took in their laughing faces. How funny she must have

looked. "Well Jon, we were team players and cooperated like you told us to."

He seemed sheepish. "I'm so sorry. I heard how the lame-o threatened the three of you. Honestly, had I known, I wouldn't have insisted. At any rate, I nailed his balls to the wall and filed a complaint against him."

"You didn't know the guy was a bonehead," said Liz in her matter-of-fact tone.

"Wish you could have seen yourself. A drunk bear laid out on a gravel road like possum roadkill," joked Angela, spiraling her finger downward.

"Where is Colonel Sanders anyway?" asked Tara.

"He went back to Kentucky Fried Chicken for all we know. We should turn him in to PETA for mistreatment of bears and owls," wisecracked Liz.

Everyone laughed, including Tara. A cell phone circulated with a video and stills of Smokey suspended in midair. As miserable as she'd been, the images were comical. She couldn't help laughing at herself.

"This is our last night in Chinook. What's on the agenda?" Tara surveyed the long table.

"Fourth of July party at Yukon Roadhouse," said Silva. "I'll buy the three of you a cold one as a peace offering, to beg your forgiveness."

"Sounds good. Let's go." She grinned and pushed back from the table.

"Me too," Liz chimed in. Everyone stood and filed out the door.

Seemed like the entire town was partying at the Roadhouse by the time Aurora Crew arrived. The party spilled out onto a back-patio deck bordering a generous lawn, where people threw darts and horseshoes.

Tara stayed inside and played pool with her Afi Slayers squad, while Liz enjoyed her reign as queen of the foos-ball table. The rest of the crew scattered outside to play horseshoes. Tara finished her game of pool and joined Silva at an antique juke box in a corner.

He fed quarters into the coin slot. "This must be the last holdout where needles drop onto vinyl. How about some Johnny Cash with *Ring of Fire?*" Silva shot his brows up at her.

"Yeah, play it." Tara lifted her Alaskan Amber and clinked bottles with Silva. "Thanks for helping me today, even though it was partially your fault."

"I feel bad. Tried to be Mr. Cooperative, so Bing Pickel would give our crew a superior performance rating." Silva angled his head. "Had to get you out of the Smokey Bear suit before I could pick you up and get you to your tent."

"Thanks for leaving my Nomex on." A corner of her mouth quirked up.

"That part was *not* my job. I pride myself as a gentleman." Silva took a long pull on his beer. "Glad you're feeling better."

"Thanks to Gatorade." She sipped her own bottle and grinned. "If the situation were reversed, no way could I lift you to my shoulder with or without a Smokey suit."

"But wouldn't it be fun trying?" He pulled on his beer, his dark eyes seriously checking her out.

Heat climbed to her face. She liked and respected Silva, but nothing more. *Change the subject.* "I saw your coveted Snowy Owl, by the way." She may as well share it, knowing how much Silva would appreciate it.

"No way! Where?" He drew back with wide eyes.

"When I drove the crew back to Chinook from Tideman Hot Springs a few days ago."

"And you didn't tell me?" He seemed genuinely offended.

A twinge of guilt twisted her. "I meant to. It landed on the windshield with its wings spread. I slowed and it stayed there. We had a stare down. Did you know it's speckled with black on top and its under wings are solid white?"

"Yeah. I did know that." His face softened. "Snowy Owls are a good omen. You should feel lucky."

"It's one of the most stunning birds I've ever seen. Why do you suppose it landed on my windshield?"

"They seek beauty." He moved closer; his gold-flecked brown eyes boring into her.

Silva was a charming, attractive guy, no getting around it. If she were to break her no-flings-with-co-workers rule, she wished it would be with Ryan; but he wasn't here and she felt like dancing.

Beer in hand, she swayed her hips to the music and Silva joined her, creating their own dance floor. She noted his eyes checking out her lengthy frame, resting on her form-fitting T-shirt. The song changed to *Wildfire*, a slow ballad from the 70s. Silva pulled Tara in close for a slow dance. She hesitated, then placed her hands on his solid shoulders. It was odd seeing him out of his yellows, and hard not to notice how well he filled out his UAF T-shirt.

As they danced, his hand moved slowly around her shoulder blade and it felt good as he lightly massaged it. She almost said, "A little to the right," but caught herself. He nuzzled her, singing in a low, sexy voice.

The song ended but he didn't let go of her. Before she turned her head to ease away from him, his lips nearly brushed hers. She gently pushed him away.

"Oh, don't." He gave her a hurt puppy dog look with those thick lashes. A lot of it was the beer talking.

Tara rested her hand on his forearm. "Jon, we can't...you know that."

He gave her a rueful look. "I know. But I really want to kiss you."

"Thanks for the dance, Jon." She took great care to sound polite.

"Sure." He gave her a disappointed smile. His eyes lingered

on her a moment before he turned away to join a game of foos-ball.

Angela and Liz lined up a round of Jell-O shots on the bar, while Tupa, Bateman, and Robin compared scars like Quint and Hooper in *Jaws*.

"Waters, front and center. Jell-O shots with tequila and rum," Liz called out to her.

Tara ambled across the room to the bar to study the red, blue, and green shots lined up like containers of Easter-egg dye. They'd all have to roust each other out of bed in the morning, but she rationalized they could sleep on the way to Fairbanks. She downed a red shot and Liz and Angela cheered. The warmth spread, tingling her system. She reached for a green one. And a blue one.

"We're gonna have sugar hangovers, y'all." Angela threw back a shot.

Silva swayed toward Tara. "Come on, Waters. *Smoke Gets in Your Eyes*. Don't worry, I won't try to kiss you. I'll be good." He grinned and held out his hand.

At first, she hesitated. But he seemed back to his old self after she'd drawn her line in the sand. She took his hand and rested the other one on his shoulder. Closing her eyes, she imagined he was Ryan; wishing it were so.

"Cutting in, dude," slurred Hudson, as he pried Tara away from Silva. Hudson grabbed her waist and before she could react, he yanked her into him so hard, he stumbled and nearly took both of them to the floor. He reeked of booze and she was surprised at how sloppy drunk he was. Then again, she wasn't.

"Stop it, you jerk." Tara put her hands to his chest and shoved him as hard as she could.

Hudson stumbled back and came at her again with rheumy eyes. "Not until you blow me." He grabbed her around the waist again and squeezed her breast. *That did it.*

Instinct kicked in. Tara thrust her forearms up—breaking his hold on her—and curled her fist to give him a powerful upper cut under his chin, knocking him backward. He sprawled against several chairs, knocking them over.

Everyone in the bar stopped to see what had caused the ruckus. Tara stood, rubbing the knuckles of her right hand, surprised at her strength.

"For the love of all things manly, Mike. You let a woman do this to you?" Rego shook his head in disgust as he dragged Hudson to a chair and plunked him on it. Hudson's head lolled back, and he passed out, drunk.

Rego looked up at an imposing bull moose head with a massive antler rack. "Keep an eye on him, Bullwinkle." He turned to Tara. "Mike damn near polished off a fifth of tequila. He'll be out for a while." He gave her a lopsided smile. "Nice right hook you got there."

"Thanks. My dad taught me." Tara looked over at Hudson's snoring form.

Tupa fist-bumped her upper arm. "*Toa malosi*. Fierce warrior."

"Wow," said Silva with an astonished expression. "Remind me never to piss you off."

Tara shook her head at Hudson's limp frame. "That was too weird."

"He's so drunk he won't even remember it. Don't let it ruin your night." Silva winked at her and wandered to the pool table to join Tupa for a game.

The rest of the bar resumed business as usual, as if this were a common occurrence. Maybe in Alaska, it was. Around midnight the Roadhouse emptied, except for the women, two holdouts at the bar, and the bartender, who urged everyone toward the door. Most of the crew had trickled back to the fire station, including Silva. She headed for the door.

"Whoa, Nellie! Where do you think you're going?" slurred Angela, throwing her arm around Tara. "No, you're staying here,

I have a job for you." She pointed to Hudson passed out in a chair. "Hang 'em high, Clint. On Bullwinkle." Angela grinned, pointing her thumb up at the imposing bull moose head with ubiquitous antlers, mounted high on the wall above.

"You're not serious. We can't reach that." Tara squinted up at the moose head, swaying. She grabbed hold of a table edge and clung to it to steady herself.

"Yes, we can. Help me." Angela tried lifting Hudson, then gave up, letting him slide back on the chair. She snapped one of his red suspenders. "Go hang with Bullwinkle," she slurred.

"Okay, let's all three lift him." Liz moved toward Hudson.

Angela straddled two chairs, then grabbed one of his arms. Liz struggled to push him up to her, but to no avail. Tara tried, but her muscles were liquid. The harder they tried, the harder they laughed. Hudson was dead to the world.

A door slammed. Tupa appeared from the men's john.

"Tupa, we're making a sacrifice to the moose gods." Liz waved him over. "Lift this sorry POS and wrap his suspenders around those antlers."

"Why you want to do that?" asked Tupa, as he stood blinking at the women.

"He groped Tara. Plus, we think he put extra weight in my pack, so I'd flunk my fitness test." Angela proclaimed it as fact.

"That's some bullshit. Anything for you ladies." Tupa picked Hudson up as if he were made of feathers.

"Suspenders," slurred Angela, pointing. "Hang them on the antlers."

Tupa stood on a chair and Liz braced it. Tara and Angela took hold of Hudson under each arm and lifted him high enough that Tupa could grab hold and hoisted him high enough to stretch Hudson's suspenders around a massive antler. He dwarfed the smaller man, making it seem effortless. Tupa jumped off the chair to view his handiwork.

Hudson dangled like a smokejumper hung up in a tree.

"Time to go, y'all," Angela zigzagged toward the door.

Liz and Tara followed, giggling. Tupa brought up the rear, and the four musketeers made their way along the short, gravel road to the fire station in the rosy twilight.

Tupa stopped abruptly and held up his hand. "Ladies. Be like Samoan warriors. Do the Haka so people won't mess with you." He demonstrated. Grunting and thrusting out his tongue, Tupa bulged his eyes. He squatted, beating both hands on his chest, and stomping his feet. "Learn from a master. Do what I do."

Angela, Tara, and Liz did their best, all the while giggling. Angela slapped her hands against her well-endowed chest. "Ow, hurts to pound my girls."

"Slap your thighs instead," instructed Tupa, walloping his so hard it sounded like the crack of a bat on a ball.

"This is how you scare the knickers off your enemies?" Angela drawled, circling Tupa.

Tupa grunted words Tara didn't recognize. She'd seen the New Zealand All Blacks rugby team do the Haka on TV, but she'd never seen someone do it in the flesh. It was quite intimidating.

They gave up trying to follow along with the grunting, slapping, and tongue protrusions, so Tupa gave them each a piggyback ride on the road back to the fire station. Tara knew the price they would pay in the morning. Thank goodness for the next two days off after their twenty-one days of fire duty.

Once they reached the station, Liz and Angela stumbled into their tent and Tupa deposited Tara on her bunk. "Good night, *toa malosi*," he said.

She rolled off his back like a limp noodle. "Good night, Ryan," she mumbled, before rolling over and snoring with the rest.

CHAPTER 20

The wheels touched down and the CASA taxied to the Jump Shack. The weary jumpers tramped down the plane ramp a little before noon. Ryan pressed the pack of whimpering wolf pups to his chest like a sack of groceries.

Gunnar shuffled ahead of him. He stopped and turned, raising his phone. "Ryno, let's get a photo."

Ryan paused to smile and lift a whimpering pup.

"Good one." Gunnar approved the photo and hauled his gear inside.

"Gunns, call the wildlife rescue people. Phone number is tacked to the wall in the Loft."

"Okay."

Ryan carried the pups inside, where several jumpers had sterile eyedroppers already torn from plastic bags. Someone appeared with a cup of warm milk mixed with water.

The guys set to work caring for the baby wolves. Everyone took photos with the pups and posted them online. It wasn't long before the base phone rang. "O'Connor, go make yourself presentable. A TV reporter is on her way," hollered Zombie.

"Great," mumbled Ryan. He wished someone else would talk to her. Leaving the pups to the care of his fellow jumpers, he plodded to the locker room for a hot shower. The soothing spray massaged his aching neck and shoulders and melted away the fire stink. He watched the black water swirl around his sore feet.

He thought of Tara and wondered what Aurora Crew were up to. She and Angela would have loved seeing the wolf pups. Too bad they were still up in Chinook. He wished he had her cell phone number.

He finished up and dressed in a T-shirt and cargo pants, and ran his fingers through damp, outgrown hair. One of these days he'd remember to cut it. As he moved past Zombie's office, he noted the local TV crew had arrived. A woman in a tight red dress and black stilettos chatted with Gunnar. Her face lit up when she spied Ryan.

Gunnar pointed at him. "There's your wolf man."

"Hi Ryan! So, you're the one who found the wolf pups?" gushed the attractive reporter, beaming perfect, white teeth at him. "I'm Seth Boone's sister, Marissa. He introduced us at an end of fire season party last year."

"Oh. Yes, I remember." Ryan smiled, then froze as lights, cameras, and the cute reporter converged on him. Seth had tried hooking him up with his pretty sister. But Ryan never got around to asking her out.

"I'm with Channel 2, KVUU in Fairbanks. Boone texted me photos of you with the wolf pups. I'm here for a quick interview," she said sweetly, brown eyes sparkling.

She hollered at Gunnar, holding two pups. "Please hand me one of those puppies."

Ryan gave her an odd look. *Puppies? Seriously?*

Gunnar raised his brows in a bemused expression and offered her a wriggling, dark gray pup. She promptly handed it to Ryan and scooted in close with her microphone. Gunnar moved out of her vision and made faces at Ryan as the gorgeous reporter flirted.

Ryan relayed the story of finding the wolf pups. The reporter motioned at two women from Fairbanks Wildlife Rescue and introduced them. The camera stayed on Ryan as he rubbed the dark gray pup's ears. He inserted water droplets into the insatiable mouth as he talked about finding them. When the reporter stepped over to the Wildlife Rescue people who would take over care for the baby wolves, the cameraman motioned Ryan over to hand one of them a wolf pup.

The televised display was awkward and annoying, but Ryan knew the importance of this for the public. Wolves were popular, and Alaskans loved their wolves, as did the rest of the country. This was obviously Marissa Boone's golden moment, and Ryan wouldn't deprive her of it.

He also knew it was good PR for the smokejumpers. He flicked his eyes at Zombie in the background, nodding approval. It didn't hurt to score points with the boss.

When Marissa finished the interview, she was in no hurry to leave Ryan. His stomach gurgled protest and he hoped she heard it; he needed a graceful exit. "Excuse me. I have business to attend to. Thanks so much." Before she could protest, he gave her a quick handshake and politely bowed out.

Ryan trotted to the mess hall and hurried inside. After collecting his food, he dropped to a table to inhale a steak, potato, and salad, with four pints of milk.

Gunnar showed up and set his tray on the table across from him. He swung his never-ending legs over the bench. "The ladies liked the wolf pups."

Ryan glanced up. "What ladies?"

Gunnar leaned toward him with a dumb look. "Which ones do you think?"

"Aurora Crew?" Ryan asked hopefully.

"Affirmative. They're here. Arrived from Chinook yesterday.

They have today and tomorrow off before they're dispatched to the Shackelford project fire."

"No kidding." Ryan straightened at this welcome information.

"I texted Angela the wolf pup pics." Gunnar tapped his phone and held it up to Ryan.

"Yeah? What else did she say?" Ryan asked in a casual tone, blood pulsing through his veins. He pushed food around his plate, then chomped a roll, faking a devil-may-care attitude.

"Jon Silva has the hots for Tara. And she likes him." Gunnar speared a piece of steak and pointed his fork at him. "If you like her, you better act on it."

"What do you mean she likes him?" quipped Ryan as he stabbed a piece of his own steak and yanked it off with his teeth. He twirled his fork in the air while masticating his steak. "If I *like* her? Did she text in Algebra class?"

Ryan knew Silva had set his sights on Tara from the beginning. Twinges of jealousy poked him.

"Hot women don't last long. Someone invariably scoops them up. That's why I hooked up with Angela before we jumped fire." Gunnar shot him a playful grin. "So she would anticipate my safe return."

Ryan narrowed his eyes. "Sly dog. You never mentioned you fired your guns, Gunns." He grinned at the cardboard milk pint as he opened it.

"We were busy saving Bettles if you recall. When a guy fights fire he can't be thinking about women." Gunnar stuffed a forkful of potato in his mouth.

"S'pose not." But Ryan had. And afterward, he had the most incredible, erotic dream about Tara, and had awakened with a hard ache in his groin.

Gunnar scowled at him. "You know you want to ask her out. Do it. If you don't, you'll regret it and I'll have to listen to your whiny ass next time we jump fire."

"I'll take it under advisement." Ryan dropped his napkin on his plate. He stood and picked up his tray.

"You planned to go fishing. Or are you going to go...*fishing?*" Gunnar twirled a pretend reel.

"Have to bait the hook first." Ryan winked at his jump partner and headed out the door.

CHAPTER 21

*T*ara relaxed on her bunk, scrolling through her phone, a towel wrapped around her after showering. Even a barracks bed felt good after sleeping on a canvas cot for several weeks. "I love these photos you texted with Ryan and Gunnar and the wolf pups." She stared at Ryan's photo. He was grungy, like the first time she met him, holding a gray pup—the sexiest photo she'd ever seen, except for the one of him posing on the glacier.

Angela turned from the mirror, hairbrush in hand. "Check out the local news sites."

Tara scrolled local news and a headline appeared with Ryan's photo: *FIREFIGHTERS SAVE WOLF PUPS*. "Oh my God, Ryan's on NBC and CNN. Angie, did you see this?" She held the phone out to her.

"Adorable wolf pups, huh? Not to mention the hot cutie holding them. Gunnar texted. He's coming over and we're going out." She wrapped dark tresses around a curling iron.

"Gunnar's here? That means—"

"Good deduction, Sherlock. Yes, Ryan is here. And he'll be alone in his room, hint-hint. You need to talk to him."

"I don't know if he'll want to see me."

Angela gave her an eyeroll. "Remember when I said next time you see him to mend your fences? Well, this is your 'next time'. Get fixed up. Help yourself to whatever I have. And put on your face."

Tara shrugged. "I don't have makeup."

Angela finished applying mascara, stuffed it in her makeup bag and zipped it closed. She tossed the bag at Tara.

"Now you do." Angela looked in the mirror and turned her face to each side. "There. Now I don't look like a wild-assed mountain woman."

A loud knock startled Tara. She sprang from the bed and scurried into the bathroom, clutching the towel around her.

"Hold on a minute, Gunnar!" Angela called out. She stuck her nose in the crack of the bathroom door. "Don't expect me back tonight." She pointed a finger. "And get yourself over to Ryan. If you blow this, I'll throw a dying duck fit as we say back in Duck."

"Quack quack," deadpanned Tara, crossing her eyes at the finger in her face.

"Your duck imitation needs work."

"Divina, you'd make a good drill sergeant."

"I was a lifeguard. Same thing." Angela smirked and withdrew her finger. "Toodle-oo! I'm out of here," she sing-songed, slamming the door behind her.

Tara stepped out from the bathroom. She stood for a long moment, staring at the ever-present mosquitoes flirting with the window glass.

Ryan's here.

The thought of him being nearby sped adrenalin through her. Was he at the Jump Shack or in the barracks? She snatched her wristwatch from the nightstand and her fingers trembled with excitement as she fumbled the clasp.

Tara paced the room, considering the hazard of falling for a guy most women swooned over. Smokejumpers were chick magnets; their sexy allure was irresistible. She'd seen it time and again. Hell, she'd fallen for one herself. Hadn't she learned from that experience?

Do I really want this? Only way to find out is to go see him.

Spotting her camera on the dresser, she picked it up and powered it on. Up popped the photo of her and Ryan kissing on the glacier. Jim Dolan's words played in her mind: *Pay attention to signs when they present themselves.*

Tara slid hangers back and forth in the tiny closet. Sure enough, Angela owned alarmingly sexy threads. She found a form-fitting, low-cut blouse buttoned down the middle; sea green, to match her eyes.

She wriggled into her black tank top, the one edged in lace that she wore the night she bumped into Ryan in the hallway. She put Angela's blouse over it, jacket style.

The irony wasn't lost on her. Her fire world was a balancing act. She worked hard to blend in with her mostly male co-workers on the job, but she refused to surrender her femininity. She had always taken pride in maintaining this tricky balance.

Tara tugged on her jeans and spotted a pair of Angela's sandals. A little tight, but not enough to matter. She moved to the mirror above the bathroom sink and lightly applied mascara, shadow, and lip gloss. Staring at her reflection, doubt crept in. *What if Ryan wants nothing to do with me? What if I knock on his door and he's with someone?* Biting her lip, she deliberated.

The loud, abrupt knock on the door made her jump. After peeling herself from the ceiling, she remembered Liz suggesting they go for pizza.

She swung the door open. "Hey Liz…" She trailed off, staring in disbelief.

Ryan stood smiling at her with his baby blues.

A shock wave swept Tara like a tsunami, in addition to her personal magnitude ten earthquake.

They both talked at once, then stopped, laughing.

"You go first." Ryan's big-hearted smile spared no dimples.

Tara relaxed into a wide smile. "You're back from Bettles."

"How'd you know I was in Bettles?"

"Radio chatter."

"You're back from Chinook."

"How'd you know we were back?"

"Gunnar chatter."

She laughed. "Yeah, he and Angela have been texting. Want to come in?" She swung the door wide, hoping he wouldn't notice her heart smacking her chest like it wanted out.

"I stopped by to see—if I were to ask you to dinner, would you go?"

She pretended to think hard as his heat messed up her equilibrium. "And if I were to respond, I'd say sure, I'll go." She felt like a teen accepting a first hot date.

"Have you been to Pike's Landing?" He leaned against the door sill, scorching it, hands in his pockets.

She needed fifty mud drops to cool *this* fire. "Haven't been anywhere except Chinook."

"It's next to the Chena River. Decent food."

"Hang on. I'll grab my wallet." She walked on clouds to her dresser and caught him in the mirror, seriously checking her out. Her insides shifted.

"You won't need it."

"I prefer to pay my own way." She expected him to argue as she plucked her wallet from the dresser.

He didn't.

"Okay, ready." She said breathlessly, moving toward him.

Ryan wore civilian clothes, a stark contrast to his usual fire garb. A charcoal-gray, rugby shirt clung to his form, long sleeves pushed up on his forearms. Jeans hugged his long legs. Dressy, for a firefighter.

"Wow." His brows lifted. He pushed off the door sill and cleared his throat. "You look great."

"Thanks."

She closed the door behind them, and they ambled down the hallway and stairs to the exit.

Tara caught his fresh pine scent as she rambled about the fires they fought near Chinook. She planned to apologize for what happened before, when the time was right.

He opened the back door to the barracks and held it for her.

She opened her mouth to protest, then clamped it shut. *Dial it back. You don't have to prove you can open your own doors. Not tonight.*

Ryan led her to a shiny, blue Mustang convertible and opened the passenger door.

She gave him a surprised look. "Yours?"

He beckoned her in. "Mostly Melbourne's. He lets me use it on occasion."

"Thought all you Alaskans drive pickups." She sunk into a plush, black seat.

"Not when we want to impress women." He winked and closed the door.

The wink and his dimples together turbo-blasted her. She couldn't take her eyes off him as he rounded the front of the car and sank into the driver's seat. *Wow.* He was...he was...every word she thought of to describe him sounded lame.

He searched for his ignition key and inserted it. "My pickup isn't running. Mel and I rebuilt the 'Stang engine together, so we share it."

"You're a regular Captain America. Smokejumper, EMT, plane pilot, and engine mechanic. Is there anything you can't do?"

"I can't toss up an omelet and catch it in a pan." He flashed a quick grin and accelerated after turning onto the highway.

"Neither can I." She leaned her head back, unconcerned about what Ryan couldn't do.

They stuck to polite conversation, exchanging stories about firefighting the past few weeks. So much to say, but where to begin? She racked her brain for a way to apologize. *Mend your fence with him.*

When they arrived at the restaurant, she loved the rustic Alaskan décor with the antlers, antiques, and snowshoes on the walls.

"Reservations for O'Connor," Ryan said to the hostess.

Tara's chin dropped. "Reservations? You planned this."

"I took a gamble."

The hostess led them to a table in a corner with the closest view of the slow-moving river.

"This is fabulous. We can watch the ducks." Tara loved the intimacy of this setting. It was nature-centric, like him.

Ryan settled in and ignored his menu. "Already know what I'm ordering. They do great king salmon." He leaned back in his chair, so easy on the eyes it ought to be a crime.

When the server arrived, he ordered a bottle of California merlot.

"I'll do the king salmon." Tara noted him studying her with a hint of a smile.

"Ditto," he said.

The server delivered their wine and poured two glasses.

She watched the red liquid swirl into her glass. "Do you miss California?"

"Sometimes. I visit my dad in Pasadena in the off-season and jump fires there on occasion. Otherwise I explore Alaska to squeeze in more hours of flight time." He looked up at the server and thanked her.

"It's a beautiful place."

He lifted his wine. "Here's to showing you more of it."

Tara clinked his glass with hers. "I'd like that." She smiled and sipped.

Gazing at the peaceful river, she loved how the evening glow reflected on the slow-moving water and she welcomed its divergence from fire. She hoped she was on the right path, being here with Ryan.

"You really do look good tonight." His gaze steadied on hers.

"Feels great to be out of Nomex. You clean up nice yourself." She leaned back, drinking him in and noting the broad outline of his chest and shoulders. His sleeves were pushed up on his tanned forearms, and for the first time she saw a number inside a small flame tatted under one of them. The number five.

Ryan poured more wine and she watched it tinkle into her glass. "Heard what an excellent job you all did on the Interior fires." He leaned back, relaxed.

"It was great. Everyone knew their jobs. Silva assigned me as squad boss when we divvied up to work the flanks."

"What else did you do up there?"

Tara sipped her merlot, feeling the warmth course through her. She told him about the fourth of July, Smokey the Bear, and their prank on Hudson.

"Would have paid money to see that. How'd you pull that off?" He flashed her his million-dollar smile with those two sexy divots that made his face light up.

"Tupa helped us. He could lift ten Hudsons with his pinky. I still think Hudson weighted Angela's pack."

"Still no proof."

She didn't want to tell him about Hudson groping her at the Roadhouse and how she'd cold cocked him. Not yet, anyway. They were getting to know each other, and she didn't want him to think she had a habit of decking her crewmates.

Their food arrived and the server placed identical plates of king salmon with garnish, garlic-smashed potatoes, and sautéed green beans in front of them. They ate in between small talk about fire. Ryan talked about the fires he'd jumped and what it took to contain them.

Tara finished the salmon and beans but pushed the potatoes

around her plate. "I can't eat any more." She rested her fork on her plate and leaned back, huffing out air.

Ryan had cleaned his plate in the time it took her just to eat her salmon. "So. How did Silva do as crew chief?"

"Great. He knows the job and knows fire. Everyone likes him."

"You like him?" he asked, sipping his wine.

She took a deep breath and her insides knotted. *Where was he going with this?* "He's a nice guy and treats everyone fairly."

"Heard he has a thing for you."

She choked on her wine. "A thing? Who told you, a fast raven?" *Who's been gossiping about her?*

"Fire is a small world. You know how word gets around." His eyes penetrated hers. "Besides, I noticed his fondness for you in training."

"Maybe you read too much into it. As I recall, the last time we talked, you chewed me out."

"You did the same."

"I know. I'm sorry for what I said." Tara stared at the ducks riding the river current.

Ryan rested his forearms on the table. "I didn't ask you here expecting an apology. I shouldn't have pressured you about counseling."

"I told you. I'd handle it on my own. I know Jim Dolan told you to help me with it and I appreciate that, but I've got this." She looked at the river to steady herself.

"You made that clear the first time." An awkward silence settled between them.

"How about we forget everything and start again?" He lifted his wine in a truce.

She thought a moment. "Not everything. I can't forget Denali. Or the glacier. Or how easy you are to talk to—" She looked away then back at him. "Why did you show up at my door?"

Ryan glanced at the river, then locked his glacial eyes on hers. "I lit a backfire near Bettles—before the crazy. The sun hovered above the mountains, rays coming through the trees. The flames changed from orange to dark red as the fire settled for the night. Same color as your hair…it reminded me of you."

She slid her gaze to him. "That's so poetic."

He had thought about her. She sat in a daze, her face warming at the casual way he'd said it. She lifted a hand to her cheek.

The server appeared and asked if they wanted more wine.

Ryan made a no gesture and set his glass on the table.

His voice quieted. "I don't know how else to explain it. I want to know you better."

"Well, I'd be lying if I said I never thought about you. It's just that…I'm not sure I can get involved again." Her words felt lame and immature, but it was her truth.

He leaned toward her. "Who hurt you? I probably know him, there's only four-hundred-thirty smokejumpers nationwide."

"Travis McGuire." She shot it at him like a bullet.

"Seriously?" He sat back, looking surprised. "I've jumped fires with him. He's a helluva smokejumper. Did a terrific job as IC on the Copper Peak Fire. Nice guy."

She raised a brow. "Not how I would describe him."

"What did he do to you?"

Tara sighed. "We were engaged to be married and he four-timed me."

"Four-timed? How does that even work?" He tilted his head to the side and ticked off four fingers. "Four women at separate times or all at once? Sounds like an orgy."

"Ha, an orgy!" She threw back her head, laughing as she envisioned it.

"Well, was it?" His smile spread to a full-fledged grin, like a dimmer switch gradually turning up.

She was grateful for the lighthearted moment. "No, not an orgy. He hooked up with three women and me at various times."

Ryan shook his head. "I'm sorry he did that to you."

"Don't apologize. You didn't do it."

"You're right. But if he hadn't, you wouldn't be here with me. Do you think I'd do the same?" He reached across the table and placed his hand on hers.

She searched his face, trying to decide whether to parachute off a cliff with someone who did it for a living.

"The answer is no, Tara. I wouldn't."

She wanted desperately to believe Ryan but couldn't help thinking what Silva had said about him.

"You're so…" The words balled up in her throat. She swallowed hard. "Are you a guy who goes from woman to woman?"

"Why would you think that? Don't you trust me?"

"I don't know you well enough to make that call."

"How about we fix that?" He pushed back his chair. "Come on. Let's walk along the river."

"Sounds good." She reached for her wallet.

They each stuffed their cash inside the folder with their dinner bill, leaving it on the table.

When Ryan stood and stretched, she tried not to gape as his shirt lifted, exposing tight skin. She imagined what he looked like bare-chested and drew in a short breath.

They followed a paved walkway next to the wide, serene river, a gentle breeze fluttering birch leaves along its banks. A couple strolled by with a golden retriever puppy on a leash.

"Oh, that reminds me." Tara pulled out her cell and held it up, displaying Ryan's photo with the wolf pups. "Tell me about finding the wolf pups. Ryan, you're a celebrity. You're even on national news."

"While Gunnar and I waited for our ride, I heard whimpering from under a burned-out stump, and there they were. Brought them back and gave them to the Wildlife Rescue people."

"Where was the mama?"

"Nowhere to be seen."

"I'd give anything to hold a wolf pup. What an incredible experience." She envisioned him kneeling on a blackened mountaintop and digging through ash to find the litter.

"Yes, it was. Glad we found them when we did."

Ryan veered off the path to sit on a bench overlooking the river, where the mottled ducks gathered to ride the current.

She sat next to him, fiddling with a dandelion. Every cell in her body tuned into his heat.

He watched the birds for a long moment. "Thanks for having dinner with me. I wanted to see you before fire season ended and we scattered to the wind. I'm sorry I was hard on you the last day of training." He glanced at her. "Didn't mean to be pushy."

"Don't apologize. I'm sorry for my rants. I'm sure you've guessed by now they were about Travis." She watched the swirling water.

"Please know I would never do something like that."

"Like I said, I don't know you well enough."

"I can help you with that." He scooted closer and cupped her cheek, gently turning her face toward his. He angled in, with his lips close to hers. "Can we start with this?"

She nodded and closed her eyes, remembering how his lips felt when he kissed her on the glacier. Her blood rushed to the surface, like the pull of a full moon on a high tide.

He kissed her gently at first, gradually easing his tongue to find hers. He slid his arm around her.

Everything faded as she lost herself in him, tasting merlot and garlic. Tingles shot through her like lightning bolts.

He deepened the kiss. A phone vibrated a notification.

She couldn't get enough and pressed into him.

The phone insisted.

Still kissing her, he let go of her cheek and shoved a hand in his pocket to silence it.

Loud quacking erupted with ducks splashing, causing them to break their kiss. "Duck fight," he spoke against her lips.

She fluttered her eyes open and laughed.

He pulled back to retrieve his phone. "It might be Zombie." He held it up and checked it, then shoved the cell in his pocket. "Boone texted. Everyone's at the Howling Dog. Ever been?"

"No."

"Firefighter watering hole up at Fox. Want to go?" He kissed her again, tingling her neck down to the tips of her toes.

She drew back, smitten. "I'd rather stay and make out with you next to this beautiful river."

"We won't stay long. I want certain people to know we're together now."

"Would one certain person's last name begin with an S?" kidded Tara, cocking a brow. She enjoyed Ryan's desire to show the world they were now together.

He chuckled. "You're a quick study, Waters. But first, I have to do something." He rose from the bench.

She didn't want to let go of him. "What?"

"I need a better angle." Ryan grasped her hands and pulled her up and tight against him. Brushing her hair back with his palm, he kissed the side of her neck, his breath hot on her skin. She tilted her head back and he ran his fingers through her hair.

"O'Connor," she gasped, her knees buckling. Now *that* ricocheted her girl parts. She wanted him. Now. Next to this river. If he said the word, she'd have her clothes off in a DC-10 minute.

Ryan disentangled his fingers from her hair, arranging it as if to cover his tracks of having been there. He stepped back; cerulean eyes fixed on hers. "I've been burning for you since the flight to Fairbanks. Like the Blue Oyster Cult song."

"I love that song." She looked at him a moment. "So, true confessions. When you fell asleep on my shoulder, I thought of hooking up with you in the airplane rest room."

His face lit up and he laughed. "Really? Damn. Wished I'd

known. Ever since you walked into my training class, I've wanted to kiss you. Didn't think a room full of firefighters would have appreciated me laying one on you in class."

He grinned and brushed a curl from her face.

Her breath hitched as he touched her. "They probably would have cheered us on, but we'd have been fired."

"Ya *think*?" He up-talked, making her laugh.

"Angela had her eye on you at first, you know."

"I knew who I wanted." He cradled her face and kissed her. Moaning, he dropped his hands and backed up. "Waters, if we don't go, I'll do things I may be arrested for doing in public. Come on." He brushed his sun-bleached hair back with both hands.

Ryan slipped his arm around her, and they strolled back to the car. He turned the ignition and leaned across the center console to kiss her, taking his time with it. Easing away, he puffed out air.

"Holy shit, Waters." He shifted into gear and pulled out of the parking lot.

"Holy shit, O'Connor," she breathed, head whirling. She pressed it against the head rest to control her want of him.

After a half hour drive on the Steese Highway to the tiny berg of Fox, Alaska, Ryan pulled into the Howling Dog parking lot and cut the engine.

She opened the car door, and the band's pulsating beat quickened her pulse. This was their big reveal: The cat would be out of the bag and swinging from the rafters when she'd sashay in with Ryan O'Connor.

"Everyone will know you're with *me* now. Are you okay with that?" Claiming her as his seemed important to him. He helped her from the car, then pressed her against it, giving her a slow, sumptuous kiss. Pine and soap filled her nostrils. Ending the kiss, he drew back, licking his lips as if enjoying a decadent dessert.

Thank goodness the car propped her up or she'd have

puddled onto the asphalt. For a split-second she wanted back in the car to have more of him. "Yeah. I'm okay with that," she squeaked out.

His eyes reflected the flickering neon light from the bar. Hypnotic and sexy. "Okay, let's go in." He offered his hand.

When she took it, he winked affirmation and she lifted his hand and squeezed it. As apprehensive as she had been about him, this felt right. Better than right. She was foolish for having doubted him.

Ryan led her to the door and swung it open. Once inside, he put his hand on the small of her back.

And she was more than okay with that.

CHAPTER 22

"The Pope and President Reagan stood on this red carpet on a platform when they visited Fairbanks back in the 1980s. Howling Dog installed it on their stage," yelled Ryan, competing with vibrating subwoofers. He pointed to a sign on the wall next to the stage as the band belted out a timeless classic, *We Will Rock You* by Queen.

Ryan guided Tara across the front of the stage as people clapped and stomped to the pounding beat.

Like wolves marking territory, Ryan wanted all males to know that Tara was now his. He chuckled at this as he steered her to the back of the bar. He couldn't remember ever feeling this way about a woman.

She was beautiful tonight.

"Hey, Ryno is here!" Gunnar stood from a large table of smokejumpers, beer held high. Angela sat next to him, holding her own with the rowdy group. Gunnar had commented earlier to Ryan how he'd landed the hottest babe of the season.

Ryan smiled. *Don't think so. I've landed the hottest.* He liked this intelligent, competent woman who could out-do the hotshots.

"Hey Wolf Man, grab a brew and get your puppy ass over here," yelled Boone over the band. "And bring your new friend."

Gunnar shoved two chairs at Ryan, and everyone scooted theirs to make room. Ryan placed them together and motioned Tara to sit.

Angela came over and patted Tara's shoulder. "About time you two got together." She winked at Ryan and sat next to Tara.

"I'll get us a brew. Pick your poison." He leaned sideways, darting a glance down Tara's luscious tank top. *God, she looked good.*

"Alaskan Amber," she said, big green eyes smiling at him. He glimpsed his co-workers, his brothers, nodding subtle approval.

Ryan stood to fetch beers. He moved past a table and someone called his name. He turned to see Silva, Rego, and a few from Aurora Crew, motioning him over.

"Hey, O'Connor, hear how we kicked ass up at Chinook?" yelled Silva.

"Yep, congratulations," Ryan yelled back.

The guys raised beers in reply with hoots and hollers.

"Aurora Crew is heading to the Shackelford Fire tomorrow morning. Hey man, you did a stellar job with refresher training. Pull up a chair. Take a load off." Silva pushed one back with his foot.

"Thanks, but I'm with Tara." Ryan made sure he said it good and loud, while motioning at her across the room.

Tara watched them intently. Ryan shot her a happy smile.

Silva slowly nodded and raised his beer at Tara.

She grinned and waved back at Silva and blew a kiss to Ryan, as if knowing they were discussing her.

Good. Now Silva has the message. *Mission accomplished. Stop hitting on her, pal.*

The band stopped and they no longer had to shout.

"You're with Waters now, huh?"

Ryan gave him a close-mouthed smile and nodded.

"Lucky man. I tried, but she evidently had the hots for you. Gave her a squad boss assignment on the fire. She did great. The crew respects her." Silva took a pull on his beer.

"Good to hear." Ryan was impatient to get back to Tara.

Tupa laid a King-Kong-sized hand on his shoulder. "Helped Waters to her tent one night and she said, 'thanks Ryan'. She missed you, bro. She's a kickass firefighter."

"I know." Ryan glanced across the room at Tara talking to Angela.

Tupa grinned. "Word of warning, bro. She has a mean knockout punch. Don't piss her off."

Before he could ask why, Tupa wandered off. *A knockout punch?* He turned to fetch the beers.

"O'Connor," Silva called after him.

Ryan turned around.

"She's a fine woman. Don't hurt her." Silva pointed his beer bottle at him.

Ryan opened his mouth for a smartass remark but reined himself in. "I don't plan on it."

They stared hard at each other, like two bull moose in a standoff. Ryan was the first to look away and he moved to the bar. He couldn't help liking Silva. He'd been good to work with the past few seasons but Ryan had never competed with him for a woman. He was thankful Tara had resisted Silva's advances.

Ryan returned to the jumpers' table with beers and took his seat next to Tara. Gunnar pushed to his feet and stood next to him, as a hoot went up around the bar. Several flat screens on walls around the bar showed the pretty, stilettoed reporter interviewing Ryan as he cradled a wolf pup in each arm.

"Ryan O'Connor is right here!" hollered Gunnar, pointing at him. "Ladies and gentlemen, this is the guy who saved the wolf pups!"

People in the bar switched their attention from the flat

screens to Ryan. Breathless gasps arose from the females in the crowd. "I want to marry him!" yelled a woman.

"Thanks, Gunns. I so didn't need that." Ryan shot a look at Tara. She laughed and rested a hand on his shoulder, watching the rest of the news broadcast with everyone else.

When it ended, Gunnar stood and raised his beer. "Stand up, O'Connor. To Ryno, saver of fire wolves!"

Ryan stood, like a spooked grizzly trapped by a wolf pack.

The jumpers followed suit and stood in a beer salute. "To Ryno, saver of fire-wolves!"

The whole bar went nuts. People whooping, hollering, and whistling. Several women came over to the jump table.

A blonde tugged his arm. "You saved those cute wolf puppies. So adorable," she purred, with hard-to-miss cleavage he concentrated on not gawking at. Two more women flocked to him, bombarding him with questions. *What was it like? How cute. Where did he find them?* A woman yelled *I love you* from across the room.

He didn't want to be rude, but he didn't need this on his first date with Tara. Uneasy with all the female attention, he sat back down and slid his arm around her, hoping the women would get the hint he wasn't up for grabs. He leaned into Tara and spoke in her ear. "This is crazy."

She nodded, a weird expression on her face.

I shouldn't have brought her here. In his eagerness to show her off as his, he hadn't considered her feelings. He scolded himself for his selfish, narcissistic move. If he'd known this would happen, he wouldn't have talked to the reporter.

Tara leaned in to say she was going to the restroom. She rose and worked her way through the crowd.

The band began playing again and a couple of women pulled Ryan out of his chair to dance. "Thanks ladies, but I'm with someone." He broke away from the women and made his way back to their table. *I don't need this right now.*

He scanned the bar for Tara. She must still be in the restroom.

The band finished a song and people clapped and hollered. The late-evening crowd partied hard, intensified by the firefighters on leave before heading back out to risk lives to protect Alaska's beloved wilderness.

Ryan waited impatiently before asking Angela. "Where's Tara?"

She shrugged. "Still in the ladies' room, I guess."

Silva came toward him and motioned his beer at the door. "She left. I warned you, dude."

Ryan stared at him and bolted out the door. *Have I screwed this up before I even got it off the ground?*

CHAPTER 23

"*T*ara, stop! Where are you going?" Ryan's voice rang out behind Tara in the cool twilight air.

She hurried ahead of her Afi Slayers squad to catch a ride with them back to Fairbanks.

This was all a huge mistake. Residual pain from her ex still lodged deep inside of her, like a tumor. She should have seen this coming with Ryan. Same replay, different state. *How could I be stupid enough to fall for this again?*

"Where's the car, Bateman?" She sped up to a jog, darting eyes around the parking lot.

Bateman pointed to the right.

Ryan came up fast and gripped Tara's elbow. "You're with me. Don't leave with them."

"Let go of me." She yanked away from his grip. "I'll go with whomever I please."

"I'm sorry. It was because I was on TV." He raised and dropped his arms at his sides.

Tara glared at him. "That's not why I left."

"Want us to wait? We'll be in the car," called out Bateman.

Everyone piled into his Subaru, leaving the passenger door open for her.

"Be there in a minute," Tara responded.

She narrowed her eyes at Ryan. "Here's the deal. No matter where we go, you'll always have women chasing you. You're—well, it doesn't hurt to look at you and I'm sure you know that. You're quite charming and every red-blooded woman picks up on that."

"Thanks for the compliment, but I don't want other women."

"Look Ryan, I don't want to be that jealous person who can't stand women flirting with her guy. I did it with Travis and I won't do it again. I know how this goes and I know how it ends."

"You don't know how it ends. No one knows how it ends."

Tara sat in the Subaru with her hand on the door. She scowled, unblinking into Ryan's darkened eyes. "No. I'm ending this now."

"We just got started." His tone rose. "You know what? I *hate* McGuire for what he did to you."

"So do I." She pulled the door closed.

Ryan opened it. "Let me take you home. I have to tell you something."

He stood in the glare of the bar's neon light with a pleading look. His eyes held an urgency that made her curious. And they were hard to resist when he looked at her like that...which pissed her off.

Her better judgment cried out no, and her wild, out-of-control heart screamed yes. Tara sighed, hoping she wouldn't regret this. "Go ahead, you guys, I'm going with O'Connor."

She got out and slammed the door and the Subaru pulled away. She folded her arms. "All right. Tell me."

"Please get in the car, I'll explain on the way."

He led her back to the Mustang and opened the passenger door. She sunk in the seat, wondering how her fabulous evening had gone up in smoke. She wished they would have stayed at the river or gone somewhere private. So much for that.

"Seat belt—please," said Ryan. Ever the safety guru.

Tara grumbled something inaudible and buckled in. She faced the window and let silence bounce around the car.

Ryan broke it by turning on an mp3 mix and pulled out on the Steese Highway. Ed Sheeran sang about finding love and losing it again.

Story of my life.

She watched the midnight sun toy with the mountains and she felt naked and exposed in the twilight. She missed the dark shield of night so Ryan couldn't read her. Right now she hated that he was so good at it.

"Remember during training when you screwed up? I came down on you hard for a reason." Ryan gripped the wheel at ten and two, eyes on the road.

"And what might that be?" she said, her voice clipped.

He stared at the road. "I wanted you safe on fire because I...I cared for you. I didn't want you to get hurt."

"Cared for me?" Her tone wreaked of sarcasm. "You had a funny way of showing it."

She watched white highway dashes appear and disappear.

"As your training instructor, I didn't dare show it. I had to wait until we no longer worked together. You have no idea how hard that was."

"The last day of training, you said my decision-making ability scared you. What did you mean?"

"How you make decisions to keep yourself and others safe— and how easy it is to get injured or lose your life on a fire."

Tara stared out her door window. "It's because of what happened on the Montana fire, isn't it? You think I used poor judgment trying to save the homeowner."

"I want you to assess situations and recognize the dangers, no matter who's in charge. Don't blindly trust people to watch out for you."

"What are you saying? That our crew bosses don't watch out for the safety of firefighters?"

Ryan turned down the music and let up on the accelerator. "Tell me about Smokey the Bear and the fire boss from Colorado. Details."

"I told you what happened," mumbled Tara.

He glanced at her. "Tell me again."

She explained how Colonel Sanders told the women to do what he called 'assigned duty' for the 4th of July parade and if they didn't do it, he'd have them fired.

"Didn't your gut tell you it was a bad idea?" asked Ryan.

"Yeah."

"But you did it anyway." His tone sounded mean.

Tara's hackles raised along with her voice. "Why are you grilling me on this?"

"Why did you do it if your instinct told you not to—"

She cut him off. "Because he threatened to have us fired!"

He gave her a look. "He wasn't your direct supervisor. Didn't it occur to you that the three of you were singled out? You've taken the harassment training, same as I have."

"You blamed me for the log incident with Hudson, when he was the one who got in my way. I know he's the one who over-weighted Angela's pack. He was the harasser, but you singled me out for it."

"You're the one who said when people ignore harassment and gender discrimination it spreads. Yet you didn't call out Colonel Sanders. What the fuck, Tara?"

"Silva filed a complaint against the guy. I was a little out of it at the time," she shot at him, pushing her temper back. Their discord knotted her heart into an aching glob.

"When he ordered only the women to put on the suits in damn near a hundred degrees, the three of you should have pushed back and told him why." He lifted a hand off the wheel to make his point and gripped it again.

"I did when I thought I'd pass out—told him to stuff it, then lost my balance and blacked out. It's a tad difficult to file a complaint when you're lying on a road in an oversized bear head."

He chuckled. "Sorry, but that visual is funny." His brow furrowed and he grunted. "Good old Silva to the rescue."

"What is it with you two? You're jealous of him, aren't you? He's the main reason you took me to the Howling Dog."

"I don't want him hitting on you anymore. He's your crew boss, for chrissakes. He knows better than that."

"You hit on me when you were my training instructor. What's the difference?"

Ryan clammed up and focused on driving. They rode in mutual silence until he pulled into the barracks parking lot and turned off the engine.

She fixated on blinking runway lights in the distance. "He's not my type."

"Who *is* your type?"

She chose no response, only turned toward the side window and stared into the twilight.

Ryan stared out the windshield. "When you're on a fire and she runs at you, you know your escape routes. But what would you do if given an order that endangered your safety?"

"What do you mean?" She rested her head back.

"Weigh decisions and keep safety a priority. I drummed this into all of you during training. All I'm saying is, don't risk your life or the lives of your crew because someone tells you to. It's okay to question decisions if you have good reason. I want you safe."

She snapped her gaze to his. "Okay, I get it. Thank you for the advice." His restless and edgy demeanor threw her.

"I'm sorry I screwed up tonight." He sounded sincere, but

she didn't know whether to believe him. She didn't know what to believe.

"Ryan, I don't think it'll work with us. I'm not ready for another involvement." She tried hard to believe it but knew she was on shaky ground. She opened the door and got out.

"Thanks for dinner. Thanks for everything." She slammed the door and hurried inside the barracks before she would burst into tears.

Ryan caught up to her as she reached the second floor. "Tara."

In the dark hallway, she turned to face him, walking backward. "There's nothing more to say. Good night." Heart speeding, she turned her back to him.

Take the hint and go to your room.

He didn't.

She hated herself for hoping he wouldn't.

She stopped at her door and rested her forehead against it. Ryan came up behind her and rested his hands on her shoulders. She turned to brush his hands away. Inhaling his scent, she tortured herself with what she couldn't have. Fear poked needles in her chest at the idea of taking another gamble with her heart.

"I told you. I can't do this." She twisted from him to fumble her key in the lock. Hands shaking, she turned the handle and pushed the door open. She was holding it together as best she could—but she felt fragile and exposed.

"I don't believe you."

Tara entered the empty room and turned to face him, her eyes brimming with tears. "Listen, O'Connor. I don't like a player. I won't share you or compete for your attention. Been there, done that. Not doing it ever again."

"I'm not a player. I won't cheat on you." He stood framed in the doorway, diminishing it. "What will it take to convince you?"

"I won't be hurt again, dammit!" She pushed the door closed so he wouldn't see her spilled tears.

Ryan caught it and stepped in. He closed the door behind him. "Say the word and I'll go." He reached behind, his hand on the doorknob. "Say it."

Her gaze slid away from his. "If I tell you to stay..." Her voice shook.

She was coming undone and backed into her nightstand. Things clattered to the floor.

She didn't care.

"Say it, Tara."

She couldn't. A bewildering tear rolled down her cheek.

Her thoughts flashed back to the river...when he kissed her on the glacier...his head on her shoulder on the flight to Fairbanks. Hell, she'd fallen for him the second she'd locked onto his magnetic blues in the Montana fire. The undeniable truth rankled her.

If he stays, this will be my point of no return.

Her breathing grew ragged as her mother's words from long ago sounded. *Be resilient with love and you'll have no regrets.*

"Give me another chance. Jump this fire with me?" His voice was husky and seductive.

Her heart beat fast, knowing what he was asking. "Only if you promise me a safe landing."

"I promise." He said it sure and easy, as if taking an oath.

She had made split second decisions before, some good, some bad. He'd laid his cards on the table. It was her call whether to fold or keep playing.

Every reason to resist him dissolved. She thought of rushing to him but wasn't quick enough.

Ryan crossed the room and pulled her to him so fast the breath left her lungs. He kissed her deeply and she returned it. He tightened his arms around her as she hungered for him in a way she'd never known. His kiss energized her and rocked her deep down to her core.

He pressed against her, threading his fingers in her hair. Her blood quickened as his body heat melded with hers. She cocooned herself in his masculine scent; the outdoors mingled with a hint of musky cologne.

She plummeted in a free fall from Denali's peak. Every cell in her body electrified and her pulse pounded in her ears. He tasted sweet and luscious. She closed her eyes and lost herself in him. She moaned, rubbing his muscled back. *Oh God, he felt wonderful.*

He broke the kiss and nuzzled her neck. "I want you, Montana," he breathed in her ear.

"I want you too, Alaska." She found his mouth and pressed her body hard against him. Edging him toward her bed, he backed up willingly. Her hands explored his sculpted chest and rippled abdomen and her breath came fast.

Kicking off her sandals, she pushed him onto her bed. She untied his massive athletic shoes and pulled them off, followed by his socks. She had never undressed a guy before. Her ex had always removed his own clothes.

This was unfamiliar territory. Undressing Ryan turned her on. And she liked it.

He raised his brows at her taking the lead, waiting for her next maneuver. She liked that too.

Removing her blouse, she let it drop, then knelt on the bed, and straddled him. She pulled off her tank top and bent to kiss him, and he stroked her sleek hair as it fell around him. She raised from his lips and looked into his eyes, glinting in the twilight.

"For someone who said you couldn't do this, you're sure doing it," he breathed, lifting his hips.

"Said I wouldn't, not couldn't. Significant difference," she breathed back. "Safety tips?"

"Now that you mention it." He produced several condoms from his pocket. "I took another gamble."

"Why doesn't that surprise me?" She grinned at him, secretly elated he'd planned for this.

He pulled back. "Number five, option C, six and seven."

"What?"

"My Incident Action Plan for dating you. Objective complete."

"You are so the job. I know what an IAP is but haven't a clue what you're talking about—and right now I don't care." She continued undressing him, determined to make this first time memorable. She unbuckled the belt on his cargo pants. "Lift up, O'Connor."

He lifted his hips easily as if she weren't sitting on him.

She grasped the buckle and pulled the belt from his pants. "Let's see what you're made of, Alaska boy. And I'll show you how we Big Sky girls keep our boyfriends warm at night."

Tara twirled his belt like a cowgirl and let it fly. The buckle hit the window and clattered to the floor. She shot her arms in the air like a gymnast. "Tada! That's my ice-breaker."

They both burst out laughing.

Ryan recovered first. "You mean window breaker. You can't aim for shit." He folded his arms behind his head, eyes gleaming. "You're a firefighter. You can do better."

"Are you challenging me?" She ran a seductive tongue along her lips.

He breathed hard. "Oh, yeah. Let's see what you've got."

She leaned forward and kissed the side of his neck. "First, I'll whisper sweet fire nothings, like...fuel loading..." She exhaled the words slow and sensual, as if spewing erotica on a phone-sex call. "...Fire hose...Fuel moisture...Drip torch..." She whispered in his other ear. "Now let's toggle your chute to the jump spot, fly boy."

That did it. She had him writhing.

He moaned and his lids became heavy. "Stand up. I want to unwrap you."

"Quid pro quo, smokejumper."

"Deal."

She lifted herself off him and stood on the floor, waiting.

He pushed off the bed and stood in front of her. Bending his head, he kissed her and reached around to unclasp her bra. He took his time easing the straps from her shoulders, kissing each after tugging them off. He gazed at her breasts like he wanted to devour them.

She raised his shirt up over his head, taking in his sumptuous chest and abdomen. Heaven help her, he should be on the Australian Firefighter's Calendar, holding puppies and kittens.

He unbuttoned and unzipped her jeans, easing his hands inside and worked everything down slowly, sliding kisses down a breast and along her stomach. When he had her pants and undies to her ankles, she lifted her feet one at a time out of them, and he kicked them away. He was so procedural, she wondered how often he may have done this before—but she didn't care. He arranged her hair to one side, so it all hung down the front of her, then drew back to take her in.

"Tara, you're my Lady Godiva."

His words scintillated her. She moved close and tugged down his zipper, the same as he had done to her. She slipped her hands inside of his pants and around the back to his cheeks. Her breath caught. *Solid muscle back there.* A wildland firefighter's derriere. She lowered everything from the waist down and he swept them away with his foot.

In the hazy dusk of midnight, they explored one another. He reminded her of a perfect sculpture with remarkably defined abs. She'd be content to ogle him all night, but she wanted him so badly, she ached. She had never known this depth of want or affection…for anyone.

Ryan picked her up and laid her on the bed, standing over her. "You're stunning, Montana." He laid beside her, pressing close. The flimsy bunk squeaked, making a threatening sound. "This bed's gonna collapse," he said into her lips, then slid his mouth down the line of her throat.

"Let it," she murmured, sliding her palms along his rippled abdomen. His fire-eating body earned every sweaty ounce of muscle: Mountain after mountain, tree after tree, creek after creek, carrying countless pounds of gear, and anything else that floated from the sky. Every ounce of a wildland fire's unforgiving, grueling labor had sculpted this beautiful human being.

Tara was greedy, wanting all of him. She guided him on top of her and he gently slid into her. When he pressed all the way inside, she thought she would shatter. He felt good. It wasn't long before she detonated. Tectonic bursts of color coursed through her brain in a collage of nirvana.

He soon followed and moaned into the side of her neck, taking a while to stop moving.

As they shuddered, she cupped his face and kissed him. She loved how their tongues swirled in a symbiotic rhythm. He lifted his lips from hers and rolled to her side, panting. She propped herself up on an elbow and brushed back his hair with her fingertips. Her finger traced his long lashes.

"I saw colors—blue as your eyes." She kissed him deeply, and he returned it. When they came up for air, she snuggled into him. This is where she'd wanted to be, ever since seeing him for the first time. She admitted that now.

They both dozed for a short while. Tara blinked her eyes open, loving Ryan's warmth. She roused him by kissing him awake. "I want you again, smokejumper. God help me, I want you."

He bit his lip and moaned as she kissed his neck, working her way to his chest. She felt him ready again and she unrolled the condom on him, straddled him and eased him inside of her. Undulating in a gentle cadence, she surrendered to the moment, watching his expression, loving every low moan he uttered. She peaked and he soon followed. She fell to his chest, panting against his neck. "God, Ryan."

"We make a good team," he breathed, his chest rising and falling under her.

"Are you evaluating our performance, Mr. Instructor? FYI, red this time, with a touch of gold."

She felt his heart speed under her. "Do you always hallucinate when you—"

"Never have before." She covered his mouth with a lingering kiss, then rolled off and nestled her head against his shoulder.

He chuckled. "You've never seen red or gold with anyone else?"

"No," she laughed. She loved the feel of him and the intimacy. Her palm caressed his firm skin, memorizing his muscles, like braille. She'd forgotten the feeling of contentment of another's warmth in the night, the sound of serene breathing that soothed her to sleep.

She spooned into him and his warm breath was on her shoulder. "I want you with me on fire. Apply to jump school. Fight fires with me." He kissed her neck.

"We wouldn't get any work done," she murmured. A joyful tear rolled down her cheek. She had sailed off Denali in a free fall. So far, Ryan offered her a smooth descent. She sealed the deal by welcoming him into her heart—and fiercely prayed he wouldn't break it.

Only time would tell if he would guarantee her a safe landing.

CHAPTER 24

*R*yan's wristwatch beeped 4:05 a.m., as it did every morning, waking him to squeeze in his workout before jumper roll call and breakfast. He'd forgotten to turn off the alarm, being a bit preoccupied last night.

Tara slept as he reached to turn it off. She nestled into him; hair wrapped around her like a goddess. He wanted to make love to her again before life elbowed its way into them.

Before he could act on it, his phone vibrated somewhere on the floor. Annoyed, he raised her arm and inched away from her. He sat up and found his pants in a crumpled heap lying in the corner. His belt lay nearby and he chuckled, recalling how sexy she'd looked, twirling it like a wild rodeo queen.

He wanted her again and considered waking her. Instead he lifted the sheet for a last glimpse, admiring her muscled legs and the gentle way her hip curved as she rested on her side. Her elegant form was an artist's rendering. And that hair...he'd better duck out of here before he couldn't get the damn erection zipped up.

Ryan finished dressing and found his phone. He grimaced at the text: *Your day off is canceled. Report to the Jump Shack ASAP.*

He bent to kiss her. She stirred but didn't wake. Spotting a notebook and pen on her dresser, he scribbled: *Be safe on the Shackelford Fire. Remember what we talked about. R.* He picked up her cell phone and tapped her number into his own phone. On impulse he took a selfie and placed her phone on her nightstand.

Letting himself out the door, an uneasiness stirred his insides. He walked briskly toward the Jump Shack, drumming his fingers and thumb on the side of his leg. He didn't welcome the unease, especially after his night with an incredible woman.

The siren sounded as he approached the Jump Shack. He sprinted inside just in time for roll call.

Zombie yelled from the Loft. "Shackelford Fire made a run toward the air force base. Storm blew it up. Let's go, boys."

Ryan bolted for the Ready Room to change his clothes and suit up. First, he helped Gunnar and Boone suit up and adjust their straps and PG bags on their fronts. Boone helped him do the same and told Ryan he was Jumper-in-Charge for this jump operation—all on two hours of sleep.

It was worth it.

❧

The white Chinook helicopter reminded Tara of a beluga whale with two rotor blades on its back. The loader left the door open after instructing them to buckle in tight. He passed a bucket around with rubber ear plugs. She sat between Angela and Liz along the wall of the sizeable helo, keeping one eye on the open door and the other on the pilot. She grabbed earplugs and passed the bucket.

Angela held a plug in each hand, eyeing Tara. "I'm dying to know what happened last night. Ryan tore out of that bar like pirates kidnapped you. Thought the poor guy would dissolve on the spot."

Tara smiled. "We worked through it. Didn't get a chance to talk to him this morning. He'd gone before I woke up."

"Because all jumpers were called. Their time off was canceled and Gunnar tore off like a madman to the Jump Shack."

"Where'd they get dispatched?"

Liz leaned forward. "If you would've attended the fire briefing this morning, you'd know heavy winds blew up the project fire and it's running toward Shackelford Air Force Base."

Tara gave her a sheepish look. "I slept in. Only got a few hours of sleep last night."

The Chinook's engines spun the rotors and the powerful helicopter vibrated with sound.

"Here we go! Let's kick ass, ladies and gents." Tupa fist-bumped Bateman and Robin. "This fire won't know what hit it once Aurora and the Afi Slayers smack it down."

"Sounds like a rock band," Tara hollered back with a thumbs-up. The rest of the crew responded with whoops and hollers.

The massive helicopter rose and flew forward. This was Tara's first time in a helo this large, but thanks to Ryan she wasn't as nervous about flying. While the rest of Aurora Crew chatted excitedly about working their first project fire, Tara leaned back and watched out a window as the Chinook headed southeast from Fairbanks. She soon smelled smoke and burnt resin. Boreal forest passed below, with stands of dark spruce and light birch.

She wished Ryan had wakened her to say goodbye before leaving. Tara closed her eyes, crazy with longing. Reaching in her shirt pocket, she pulled out his note and unfolded it. She read it again and zipped it back in her pocket.

She thought back to last evening and how she lost her resolve when Ryan followed her into her room and kissed her. Travis had never kissed her like that; he'd always rushed to his grand finale and then fallen asleep.

Ryan had been gentle and loving—taking his time making love to her, like a delicious ritual. She closed her eyes and inhaled deeply, reliving every move, recalling every sensation.

"Here we are, Aurora," called out Silva, pointing out a window.

Tara blinked her eyes open, taking in a tent city in the wilderness. The Chinook descended to a large bench on a mountaintop. Timbered slopes stretched as far as she could see. Sizeable columns of black smoke rose in the distance. The helicopter set down on a cleared, makeshift helipad.

"Hold up. Wait for the signal to unload," yelled Silva over the *whop-whop* of the rotors.

The pilot slowed both rotors. A heliport manager, in a white helmet and yellow Nomex, ducked under the rotors to open the door and unfold the aluminum steps. He stood at the bottom, guiding firefighters away from the tail rotor, as they exited.

When the crew was at a safe distance, Silva whistled for attention and the crew gathered around. "Okay, ladies and gents, listen up. I'll check in with Ops at ICC and get info where to set up our camp. We'll deposit our gear there before heading out on the fireline." Silva strode toward the ICC, a group of large tents that made up the nerve center of project fire operations for the Shackelford Fire. The ICC managed twenty-five crews, totaling four hundred-fifty firefighters for this one fire alone.

The base camp may have been in the middle of nowhere, but it pulsated with a hard-edged efficiency, like a well-oiled machine. Firefighters scooted ATVs along worn paths, boxes strapped on the rear with bungies. Aurora Crew followed Silva to their assigned camp site. The faint smell of smoke and constant whop of helicopters permeated the air.

Angela came up behind Tara. "Hudson's here. He came up in another helo. I heard him tell Rego he got a ride with the

Circle Crew to Wainwright. Think he knows we were the ones who pranked him? Tupa wouldn't have spilled, would he?" she whispered.

"No. Tupa wouldn't do that. If Hudson knew, don't you think we'd know by now?"

"Hard to tell. He's a sneaky Pete." Angela shifted the fire pack on her back. "Hudson can't prove anything. A guy I played horseshoes with at the roadhouse told me someone always wound up on those moose antlers at the end of wild parties. Some weird tradition started by the miners. That's where I got the idea." Angela smirked.

Tara turned around with a wicked grin. "You're going to hell, Divina."

"Mm, but I'll enjoy what sends me there." Angela winked.

Silva pointed to a grassy area next to another crew camp. "String your tents near this wall of trees, folks."

Tara scanned the nearby hotshot and Type II crew camps. Hard to say how many; their camp sites were strewn everywhere. Cardboard signs tacked on trees or stuck on sticks in the ground displayed crew names: Chena Hotshots, Midnight Sun, North-Star, and Tanana Chiefs. In training, Ryan had talked about Alaskan village crews as being some of the best in the U.S.

"I know where I'm sticking my tent." Rego marched to the wall of trees and dropped his gear on a grassy area, a good distance from the noisy pathways and ATV trails.

"I know where I'd like you to stick it," snickered Liz.

The women snatched up the spots, leaving a space between their tents and Rego's. Tara had her tent set up in no time. She'd done it so much she could assemble it in her sleep.

"What a perfect spot." Hudson sniggered at the three women and dropped his gear between Rego and Tara's tent spots.

Liz shot Tara a look and grimaced. "Lucky you."

Tara opened her mouth for a smart remark when a radio crackled at a nearby crew camp. Was that Ryan's voice? She followed the sound down a pathway to the next camp. A Bendix King radio hung on a tree branch. She leaned in and listened.

"...Wait for the mud drop. She's running like a speed demon. Keep escape routes a priority. Don't get turned around in this shit." Her breath caught. That was Ryan, all right. His voice sent heat shooting through her, shocking her with sudden desire. Goose bumps lifted.

"Max, do you copy? Need a drop, in front of the head and the right flank to slow her, so we can kill hot spots. Back burning won't work, wind's too strong and blowing toward the base."

"Copy. Right flank first, then I'll hit the head," replied Max. He must be the tanker pilot.

The hair on her neck stood on end.

A group of firefighters stood out front of their camp latrine, talking and laughing, drowning out the radio chatter. She itched to raise the volume but didn't dare mess with someone else's radio. Finally, the people wandered off and she listened.

"...O'Connor, control your boy down there, he's turning me on."

A roaring noise ensued, then Ryan's voice. "Hard to control a reprobate, Max. Jump crew, clear the right flank and move in. Know your escape routes."

Silva interrupted. "Aurora Crew, time to head out."

Tara hurried to her tent to grab her gear. She swore she'd left a handful of granola bars inside to take with her to work. Puzzled, she fell in at the end of the crew line.

Behind Hudson.

As they hiked out of camp, Hudson turned around and walked backward. He snapped a granola bar in half and took a bite. "These are delicious. You should try one." He pulled a handful of green packages from his pocket. "Oh wait, I have to save these for later." He flashed a smile that shot a chill through her.

Her heart thudded at the unnerving reality that Hudson had

taken her granola bars. That meant he'd been in her tent while she'd listened to Ryan on the radio. Her stomach squeezed. She would confront Hudson later. Now wasn't the time as they headed out to the fireline.

Ryan's voice on the radio had mollified her, despite his being on the front lines. She wasn't worried. He knew what he was doing after jumping and incident commanding so many fires. Besides, he was Mister Safety. An image flashed in her mind, of Ryan tearing open a condom in the name of safety. She nearly laughed outright.

Nothing bad would happen to Ryan O'Connor. She was sure of it.

CHAPTER 25

"On final! O'Connor, Alexanderson, first stick," yelled Stu, standing near the open door of the CASA. "Slow the head. Figure strategy for mud drops. Keep the IC informed if he should evacuate the air force base."

Ryan and Gunnar moved into position and waited for Stu's orders.

"Get in the door."

Ryan nodded affirmation and crouched as Stu tossed out streamers. Ryan studied their erratic movement to gauge how he would fly.

"Three hundred yards of drift. Watch your ass." Stu slapped Ryan's shoulder.

Ryan threw himself into the immensity of sky roaring at him. When his chute deployed, he steered his toggles in the erratic winds. The plane noise faded, and the only sounds were the crackle and snap of dry spruce. He smelled resin and observed black smoke. The wind pushed him toward the trees. He checked his blue-and-white nylon canopy and guessed the winds at thirty knots.

The fire ran solid and robust, its right flank charging up a mountainside so fast, it was like a reverse tsunami. One-hundred-foot-tall flames marched across the bottom land toward Shack-elford Air Force Base, spitting fireballs a half mile ahead of the burning front.

He worked hard to toggle away from the trees. Damn squir-relly winds. Gunnar whooped and hollered above him.

"Come on, wind. Knock it the hell off," he muttered, steering right with all his strength as he skirted the tops of towering, white spruce. The leader tips were damnable spears and he wasn't in the mood to impale himself.

He sailed above a wall of trees, barely clearing them, when a sudden gust propelled him to the left. He'll kiss a spruce or worse unless he takes evasive action.

"Shitdamn!" His feet skated down the outsides of branches, sheering off needles and limbs as if he had razor blades on his boots. He skimmed the prickly boughs and toggled hard right, hit the ground and rolled. Something sharp nailed his shoulder blade.

"Damn it." Not his best landing, but at least he didn't skewer himself. Rubbing his shoulder, he cussed the offending rock and pried it from the ground, heaving it away from the jump spot.

Gunnar touched down and rolled. He gathered his chute and daisy-chained the lines.

Ryan squinted up at a tall spruce. "Shit, cargo box is hung up." He lowered his goggles over his eyes and hauled himself up the trunk with a folding saw. His boot snapped a branch and sharp-needled boughs slapped his face as he plunged down. Finally he found a strong enough limb to break his rapid descent. He resumed climbing and reached the two limbs cradling the cargo box. He sawed them and the box plummeted to the ground.

By the time Ryan hit the ground, Gunnar had the box open, pulling out equipment.

"Hand me a piss-pump," ordered Ryan.

Gunnar hung it on Ryan's back and tightened the straps. As Ryan adjusted the bladder weight, his radio sprang to life.

"O'Connor, Boone here. What's our strategy?"

"Starting recon. Stand by." He took off at a brisk clip uphill with forty-five pounds of water undulating on his back. He hiked a quarter of a mile up to a flat area to assess the situation. Multiple smokes from spotting ahead of the fire's headwall scattered a half-mile ahead of the flame front.

"Wait for the mud drop. She's running like a speed demon. Keep escape routes a priority. Don't get turned around in this shit," Ryan machine-gunned into his radio, eyeing the DC-10 retardant ship approaching from Fort Wainwright.

"Max, do you copy? Need a drop at the head and the right flank. Back burning won't work. Wind is too strong and blowing her toward the base."

"Copy," responded the DC-10 pilot. "I'll hit the right flank first."

"Right flank, incoming. Get clear!" panted Ryan into his radio, running and jumping over deadfall and tussock clumps. Pain-in-the-butt things were ankle-turners. He hated them.

Boone radioed. "O'Connor, six jumpers strung along left flank. We'll get the spots and work our way to you up front."

"Stay clear while Max drops his mud. Wait for my go-ahead." Ryan worked his way to the front, swinging his Pulaski, chopping vegetation, and squirting hot spots with his bladder pump.

Gunnar caught up and they scrambled up a slope for a better view. The retardant ship dropped mud on the right flank, then circled to aim for the head of the runaway fire.

While they waited for the drop, Gunnar lowered two chain-saws to the ground, readying them for use. "Here comes Max."

The thunderous DC-10 air tanker aimed for a center drop on the head with dead-on-balls accuracy. Ryan popped in ear plugs as the plane's three McDonnell-Douglas engines delivered forty-five thousand pounds of thrust, the sound vibrating his chest. He loved the raw, roaring power, and the ability required to master it. Air tanker pilots were his heroes.

The doors boomed open, and the graceful red gel cascaded through the air, covering the landscape like a cerise quilt. Ryan thought of retardant drops as works of art the plane painted in the sky—crimson clouds suspended for a brief moment like a jet entrail, before wafting down to smite the orange monster.

"Yeah, baby!"

Ryan turned to catch Gunnar with Treeminator extended from one arm and Ryan's chainsaw, Slasher in the other, posing in a road warrior stance from a Mad Max movie. Gunnar raised both saw blades high into the air, aiming them at the low-flying air tanker. As the DC-10 dumped its load, he threw his head back. "Ohhh, yeaaahhh, sweet release—" Obviously simulating another kind of release.

"Was that good for you?" Ryan smirked, impressed with his jump partner's feat of strength…or insanity, depending on one's viewpoint. At least the saws weren't running.

"O'Connor, control your boy down there. He's turning me on," radioed Max against the fading sound of the DC-10.

Ryan keyed his radio and grinned. "Hard to control a reprobate, Max."

He admired Gunnar's proficiency at turning certain aspects of firefighting into a sexual connotation. Thankfully, Gunnar exercised the good sense not to do it around other firefighters.

"Jump crew, Max laid her down. Contain right flank. Remember your LCES, boys." Ryan appreciated short cuts to fire lingo. It would take him forever to say, *remember your Lookouts, Communications, and Escape.*

Boone's voice crackled back. "We're on it."

"Gunns, time to kick ass." Ryan took off running with Gunnar alongside. The drops bought them a tight window to get a saw line in.

As they neared the nasty blow-up, Ryan noted the fire had jumped Eagleridge River and was charging full speed toward the air force base. He spoke into his radio as he ran. "Air attack. Max, hit the head with more mud."

"Copy," Max responded. "Two minutes out."

Ryan and Gunnar stopped short on a hill overlooking the river. The men stood riveted by the torrid, beautiful scene as orange towers danced and crimson orbs taunted, roiling high above the tree line. Three moose stood motionless in the river, witnesses to the ruin. The tranquil river reflected the spectacle— a silent onlooker to the destruction.

"Wish winds would change so we could back burn." Sweat streamed down Gunnar's face.

"If only. Go on ahead. I need to take a leak." The heat was intense. Ryan swiped his forehead with the back of his hand.

"Okay, see you in a few." Gunnar disappeared and soon Ryan heard the *rawrrrr* of a chainsaw firing up.

Ryan didn't see the wolf sneak up behind him. As he finished relieving himself and zipped, a female with low-hanging teats materialized in front of him, about six feet away. Mud caked her light, gray fur. She might have cooled off in the river, then rolled on the riverbank. Her head lowered and she panted, studying him with gray-flecked eyes.

Don't look her in the eye. He did a quick mental inventory of what he had for a weapon: Pulaski and a pocketknife. He thought of the fusees in his pack, used for lighting backburns. No. It was inconceivable to torch a wolf. Plus it would take too long, and he'd be half-eaten before he could light one. He pictured the headlines: 'Smokejumper lights wolf on fire!'

Ryan remained still as the wolf shook the wet from her fur, flinging droplets of water and mud. She circled, sniffing. The eerie, orange glow of the wildfire reflected in her eyes.

Stay calm. No sudden moves. "Hey there, girl. Did the fire chase you from your pups?"

The wolf cocked her head and perked her ears forward.

He continued his soothing tone. "Good girl. That's right... you'll be okay."

Ryan stood his ground while his mind raced. The sound of Gunnar's chainsaw, the moose, the river—even the wildfire's intensity all faded, as he concentrated on the wolf. Slowly, he lifted his arm to reach behind for the Pulaski attached to his pack, fumbling with the Velcro straps.

Sniffing, the wolf padded within two feet. She circled and came closer, nosing the bottom of his pack, as if searching for something. The wolf pup scent was still on his pack! Could this be the mother? If so, she must have traveled at least two hundred miles from her litter. *Nah, she wouldn't do that. Would she?*

Ryan lowered his Pulaski with one hand and clutched the long handle with the other to maneuver it into position. Holding the tool steady in front of him provided a false sense of security. But it was better than nothing. He let out a shaky breath.

The wolf backed up and growled, baring her teeth.

His chest clenched. Heart pounding, he tightened his grip. *Can I talk my way out of a wolf attack?*

What the hell. "Your pups are safe, Mom. You don't want a piece of me. I wouldn't taste good." Ryan's voice wobbled, anticipating any unpredictable move.

She lifted her snout and flicked her ears forward, studying him. Suddenly, her head pivoted; something spooked her. She darted away as abruptly as she had appeared, leaving Ryan quaking in his boots. He lowered his Pulaski and exhaled; unaware he'd been holding his breath.

His radio crackled. Gunnar. "Ryno, where are you?"

Heart still pounding, he retrieved his radio and keyed it. "On my way."

Ryan hiked downhill to Gunnar and the rest of the jumpers, sawing a line in a wide swath to slow the head. It was the only thing that could prevent the fire from reaching the buildings dotting the air force base. If they couldn't knock the fire back, he would tell Zombie to issue the mandatory evacuation order.

Ducking a red glitter-shower of spruce cones, Ryan positioned his chainsaw at the base of a spruce as swirling ash and burning debris dropped down on him.

Boone on the radio. "O'Connor, you copy?"

Ryan freed a hand from his saw. "Copy. Weather update?"

"Wind's shifting to the east, toward the mountains. No threatened structures."

Ryan peered at the fire wall running toward them. "Are you sure? If not and we back burn, we lose the base."

Intolerable silence on the radio.

He keyed his radio and paced, eyeing the advancing fire wall. "Running out of time."

Boone again. "Weather update said winds have shifted, blowing east, not southeast."

"Copy, thanks." What he wanted to hear. He keyed his radio. "Jump crew, wind shifted, back burn is a go. Move fast." His skin heated as the head charged toward the jump crew. He gauged his escape route outside of the left flank and edged closer to it.

Ryan shoved the radio into the holster clipped to his waist belt. Priming his drip-torch, he stepped briskly across the front of the saw line, igniting parched willow and alder. Gunnar headed in the opposite direction doing the same. It took thirty minutes to light the backfire so the gusts would blow it toward the head. The convective head winds sucked in the back burn, creating a wide, black barrier next to the saw line. Ryan's strategy worked, as intended. The runaway blaze sucked in the back burn and succumbed, like a spent dragon out of fuel.

No evacuation necessary. Ryan sighed relief.

He assessed the black swath between the jumpers and the fire's head. After losing its fuel source, the blaze had quieted like a tamed lion. "Okay sports fans, that's a wrap. Incident Command, she's ready for mop-up."

Dave Doss's voice responded. "Copy, O'Connor. Dispatching Aurora Crew for mop-up."

Ryan smiled into the radio. "Good choice. Appreciate a ride out of here."

"A helo is on the way," responded Doss. "Nice work, O'Connor. Remind me to give you a raise."

He laughed. "You're a stand-up guy. JIC clear."

Exhausted, he set down his drip torch and collapsed to the black ground, staring up at cloud shapes. What did he expect after two hours of sleep last night?

Gunnar flopped next to him. "Wake me when they land."

"That's what I get for spending the night with a hot woman." Ryan watched a peregrine falcon glide overhead, searching for anything the fire may have spared.

"You can say that again," mumbled Gunnar.

"Well, at least I didn't get eaten by a wolf. And...I think I'm in love, Gunns."

"No shit. I was wondering when you'd get around to admitting it."

Ryan dozed for what seemed like two seconds before the *whup-whup* of an incoming helicopter woke him.

CHAPTER 26

*T*t was a five-mile hike from base camp to the left flank of the Shackelford Fire, where the terrain sloped gently down to the forested bottomlands. No helos were available. Aurora Crew had no choice but to hike to their work site after setting up camp. Tara didn't mind. She had energy to burn after last night. The thought made her mouth turn up.

At a high point in a burnt clearing, Silva stopped the crew. Wisps of smoke rose from glowing embers. Tara squinted at the leading edge of the fire, about four miles away, as it chomped its way toward the air force base.

"Okay folks, this is the mop-up site for our twelve-hour shift. We'll work in a grid, so spread out along the edge of the black. Turn the soil over to expose hot spots and squirt them with your piss-pumps. Take your gloves off to feel the ground with bare hands."

Tara and Angela set to work on their piece of charred ground.

"Mm, love the feel of ash in the afternoon," purred Angela, sensuously raking bare fingers through soil and ash. "This does wonders for my complexion." She dabbed a little on her cheek.

Tara laughed. "I heard Ryan on the radio before we left. He's with jumpers down there at the fire's head." Tara straightened and peered downslope.

"Did you hear Gunnar?"

"No, only Ryan and the tanker pilot. Wish I had a radio."

"Silva has one." Angela cocked a brow.

"Wonder if he'd loan it to me."

Angela laughed. "So, you can listen for your honey-bunny? Not likely. You broke Silva's birdie-lovin' heart."

"Not my problem." Tara shrugged a shoulder and pulled small binoculars from her day pack, squinting into them. "Two helos landed in the black down there and lifted off again. Can't see much else." She shoved her binoculars in her pack.

"You've been wearing that silly grin since we left AFS this morning. You're even smiling at these confounded ashes."

Tara was blissfully aware of a sated contentment that permeated every nucleus of every cell in her body. She squirted a hot spot with her water pump.

Silva ambled over. "Waters, where did you go last night? O'Connor looked for you after you left Howling Dog."

"Oh yeah?" This could get interesting.

"Did he find you?"

"Why?" Tara tried not to seem annoyed, but her tone still came out surly.

"Wondered if you got home okay."

"Yes, I did." She paused to sip her water canteen. Two eagles cruised above, capturing her attention. She watched them soar over the spruce and out of sight.

"I've known O'Connor a few years. This is my fourth season with AFS."

"Uh-huh." *Where was he going with this?*

"Watch out, he's a wolf. I've seen him in action. Women won't leave him alone and he won't leave them alone."

She straightened and leaned a hand on her Pulaski. "Jon, why do you keep saying these things?"

"Don't want to see you get hurt, that's all." Silva cold trailed his fingers through ash and soil. "I'd be careful about trusting him."

Tara gave him a slight nod. She swung her tool so hard a cloud of ash dust and dirt swirled up and she coughed.

"Angela, do you have a wipe handy? Got something in my eye." Tara faked it to avoid further conversation with Silva and made her way over to Angela.

Silva kept working and moved some distance ahead.

Angela unzipped her shirt pocket and produced a clean wipe. Tara removed her sunglasses and wiped her eyes.

"Thanks. Much better." She resumed cold trailing the soil.

"Careful, careful," sing-songed Angela in a low voice.

"You catch all that?" Tara pursed her lips.

"Course I did. My hearing is so good I can hear a mosquito sneeze in the woods," lilted Angela, swinging her Pulaski and dragging it through the soil. "I should work for the CIA. Maybe I'll meet a Jack Ryan. Think they're taking job applications?"

"Sure, why not." Tara scowled at the ground. "So why is Silva talking about *my* Ryan?"

"Please tell me you aren't that clueless. Silva is so sweet on you, he'll say anything. Guys are as shrewd as women when competing for one. But to their credit, they aren't as vindictive." Angela smothered a smoke with dirt.

"But Silva saw me with Ryan, so he should have gotten the message."

"And Silva saw you leave without Ryan. Why did you do that?"

"Got cold feet. I didn't want a Travis 2.0...didn't want to get burned again." Tara stood and leaned back, gazing up at a towering, charred spruce. "Like this poor tree."

"Hey." Angela straightened and gave Tara a look of

reproach. "You and the tree may have been torched, but you're both still standing."

Tara gave her a wry smile. "Divina, you have skills. You should be a therapist."

Angela scoffed. "I'll get right on that after I work under cover for the CIA as a panda bear trainer. Seriously, you should give Ryan a chance. He strikes me as good people. Besides, he puts fires out. He wouldn't burn you."

"I hope you're right." Tara appreciated her friend's positivity. *Travis put out fires too, and he burned me.*

Why did Silva care whether Ryan hurt her? Whether Silva's comments were true or not, she knew one thing for sure: She wouldn't let herself become just another line on Ryan's parachute.

Aurora Crew finished their twelve-hour shift. Silva tried finding air transport back to base camp, but all helos were busy slinging water loads and transferring other crews.

"We're hiking back to base camp," he announced.

A groan reverberated through the crew, weary from their long shift.

Tara and Liz fell in at the end of the line, debating what they'd wish for if they found a genie in a bottle. Liz couldn't decide between a bottle of expensive champagne or a massage by Jason Momoa. Tara preferred the massage...but from a certain smokejumper.

Hudson's voice grumbled behind Tara. "Silva can't expect us to work a twelve-hour shift, then make us hike all the way back to camp."

"So, pack up your toys and go home." Tara tossed over her shoulder. She was in too good of a mood to let Hudson's whining annoy her today.

"And don't let a spruce hit your ass on the way out," quipped Liz in front of her.

Hudson appeared next to Tara and slid an arm around her.

"You should be the one to go home," he whispered in her ear. "After what you did to me."

Tara yanked herself away from him. "And what might that be?"

"You assaulted me. Then left me on those damn antlers." He moved in close and brushed a hand across her breast. "I know a way you can make it up to me."

She shoved him back. "I decked you once. By God I'll do it again." Her teeth clenched, along with her chest.

Hudson laughed. "We'll talk later, babe." He smooched his lips at her, then jogged up front to walk with Rego.

Not if I can help it. The first time Hudson groped her she should have reported him. She didn't want the stigma of being a complainer, but if she let him get away with his behavior, she'd be part of the problem. *I don't need this on my first project fire.*

She would take care of the problem.

Once and for all.

CHAPTER 27

*M*elbourne left the rotors spinning as eight smokejumpers hefted in their gear and pulled themselves on board the Bell Super Huey transport.

"Burnin' daylight, folks," said Mel into his hot mic from his left front seat, as Ryan heaved himself in beside him. He pushed back his hair to put on the flight helmet and snapped the strap under his chin.

Ryan spoke into his hot mic. "This one damn near kicked our ass."

"I heard." Mel scanned left and right before lifting off.

"What's the plan, Stan?" Ryan buckled his seat belt.

"My instructions are to return you guys to the Jump Shack." Mel stared ahead, guiding the helicopter to cruise altitude. He glanced at Ryan. "Afraid I have bad news. There's been a smoke-jumper fatality."

Ryan closed his eyes, dread locking his chest. "Which base?"

"Missoula. Jumping a fire in Idaho. Chutes didn't open."

"Have they released the name?"

"McGuire."

A scorching realization. "Not Travis McGuire."

Mel scanned his airspace. "Yeah, he's the one. Know him?"

"Jumped a few fires with him in the Lower Forty-eight. He IC'd the Copper Peak Fire I jumped in Montana a month ago."

The same fire where he met Tara.

Oh no. Tara. She planned to marry the guy at one time. Ryan didn't want her hearing it on random radio chatter or some other way. He should be the one to tell her. Or should he? They were beginning a relationship; one he hoped would have staying power. But McGuire was a fellow jumper, so Ryan thought it was only right he should tell her.

He stared at the birds-eye view of the Richardson Highway leading to Fairbanks. Any firefighter fatality hit hard around the entire wildland fire community. But a smokejumper death hit especially hard. Since the 1940s, less than a handful of jumpers had died in parachute jumps. An impressive record, given several close calls through the years. The blow was a bitter one for anyone who jumped to fight fire.

Mel landed the Super Huey on the tarmac next to the Jump Shack.

As the rotors slowed, Zombie waited to greet the jumpers as they shuffled inside. "You boys hear about the smokejumper down south?"

"Yeah." Ryan leaned his fire pack against his locker. "A Zulie, on an Idaho fire."

"Tough break." Zombie's gruff tone spoke for all of them. "I moved all eight of you to the bottom of the jump list for tomorrow, so you could get some rest."

Everyone mumbled their thanks.

Ryan had an idea. He strode back to the tarmac to talk to Mel, still perched in his pilot seat finishing paperwork. "Hey bro, think you could shuttle me up to Shackelford Fire camp tomorrow?"

Mel flicked his eyes at him while scribbling his pen on a

government aviation form. "Can't in the morning. Afternoon is open unless I'm called elsewhere."

"You're a good man."

"Don't let word get around. I have a reputation to uphold." Mel paused and raised a brow. "Is it the redhead?"

Ryan grinned. "You're a quick study, Kemosabe."

"Stands to reason. McGuire was from Missoula and Tara is from Missoula. Figured there might be a correlation."

"He was her ex-fiancé. Thought I should inform her of his death." Ryan stared out the windshield at the blinking airport lights. *Did Tara still have feelings for McGuire?*

Mel whistled through his teeth. "Wow. There's a tough one. Geez Ryno, you're an upstanding guy. Didn't know you had it in you."

Ryan gave him a wry smile. "Me neither. But thanks."

"Don't get all mushy on me. Now get the hell out of here. I have to put this bird to bed." Mel rested his clipboard between the seats and flicked switches on the instrument panel.

Ryan exited the helo and waved as Mel lifted off, heading for the helicopter hangar.

He hauled his gear into the Jump Shack and arranged it in his locker. Weariness made him hit the wall as he trudged to the barracks, each step a colossal effort. Hard to believe it was just this morning he had wakened next to Tara.

Had his earlier unease been a premonition about McGuire? He dreaded telling Tara the guy she once intended to marry was dead. If she had married him, she'd be a widow now. Ryan shook his head at the randomness of having worked with McGuire, then falling for the woman he didn't marry. If Tara's boss hadn't sent her to Alaska, Ryan wouldn't have seen her again.

Life had a way of orchestrating events as if grandly designing the future. He thought of the feather floating aimlessly in the movie, *Forrest Gump.* How much of his life was pre-determined and how much was chance? He thought back to his being at the right place at the right time in the Montana fire.

Random or not, it's when I saw her for the first time.

He fell into bed, wishing he could talk to Tara, but cell phone service in a fire base camp was not likely. If they were in the real world, in the off season, he could talk to her whenever he wanted. See her whenever he wanted. Make love to her whenever he wanted.

He'll see about working on that.

CHAPTER 28

*T*ara crawled into her tent and zipped it closed. Baring her feet, she fingered two blistered toes. She'll wrap moleskin around them in the morning. Mosquitoes teased with their high-pitched whirs, but she was too tired to care whether they were inside or outside of her tent.

Her thoughts turned to Ryan. She pulled her Nikon from her pack and powered it on, clicking through photos of him on the glacier and of them posing together. She brushed a finger over his image. "Good night, O'Connor," she whispered.

She powered off the camera and tucked it in her pack, then fluffed her travel pillow and snuggled inside her sleeping bag, falling asleep to the chuff-chuff of helicopters overhead. She dreamed Ryan drifted down in his inflated parachute, yelling at her to get out of the way. He landed on her and she became entangled in his parachute, the blue-and-white nylon twisting around her. When she fought her way out of his chute, he was gone.

The dream jarred her awake and she had to relieve herself. She sighed, not relishing the idea of traipsing the long path to the ladies' latrine. Groggy, she put on her camp shoes and

Nomex pants and padded on the path to the women's toilet area. The twilight made it easier to navigate the narrow path through dense stands of spruce and birch.

She finished her business and headed back on the trail to Aurora's camp. A figure strolled toward her. Odd for this time of night—or early morning.

It was Hudson.

Her gut turned sour. She steeled herself and put her chin down to brush past him.

He stopped a few feet in front of her. "Well, well, it's the queen herself. To what do I owe this honor?" His eyes darkened.

She gave him a pained look. "Not now, Mike. It's the middle of the flipping night." Why does it have to be *him*? She took a short breath and tried to brush past him

He lurched forward, blocking her path. "Exactly. I think you and me could have some fun."

"Let me pass." She kept her tone firm and measured as she backed away, her pulse rising.

"I don't think so." His smug expression and steely eyes prickled her skin.

She swallowed hard and clenched her teeth. "Get out of my way."

"You have such a pretty face. What a shame if something were to happen to it." He leered at her, his eyes fixed on her breasts, accentuated by her tank top.

Her heart knocked. She fought to keep the tremor from her voice. "You are officially in deep shit for threatening me."

"Hm. Says who? Let's reassess which of us resides in deep shit at the moment." He gave her a sardonic smile. "You left me hanging at that bar in Chinook. An unwise decision. One you'll regret, I'm thinking."

"Know what's an unwise decision? Groping people against their will. When I report you, you'll be out of here so fast you'll think being hit with a log was fun." She glared and moved swiftly past him.

Not fast enough.

He grasped her wrist, yanked her against him, and wrapped his other arm around her, pressing her close. "You won't report anything. I'll make sure of it. Like I said, it would be a shame to ruin this pretty face."

He gripped the back of her neck and pressed his lips on hers in a sloppy kiss. He was strong, but her adrenaline helped her wrench free.

She shoved him away. "Let go of me, asshole!"

"Mm, you taste good." He reached around her, and she felt something leave her pants pocket.

Hudson backed up, dangling her worn, orange bandana with his thumb and forefinger. "I'll keep this for a souvenir. It'll come in handy."

"Give it back!" She spit the words like bullets, clenching her jaw.

"Come and get it, sweetheart," he taunted.

She lunged for it and nearly lost her balance when he dodged her.

He smirked. "Nice try. You'll regret what you did to me in Chinook." He licked his lips, reminding her of a copperhead snake. Laughing, he turned and continued on his way to the men's latrine, twirling her precious bandana.

"And you'll regret threatening me," she spit at him, heart pounding.

His laugh echoed in the twilight and she hated him.

For a split second she thought of charging after him to get her bandana back. *No. That's what he wanted.* Who knew what he would do?

She'll get it back tomorrow. When she reports him, he'll be demob'ed off this fire in an Anchorage minute, as Ryan would say.

God, I miss him.

Tara hurried back to camp with furtive glances over her shoulder. She ducked inside her tent and zipped it closed, heart thumping. Her watch told her Aurora Crew would be up in two hours. Sitting cross-legged on her sleeping bag, she mulled what to do. She couldn't let Hudson get away with threatening her.

Blech. The guy creeped her out. He was like a Jekyll and Hyde. Two personalities: The nice guy and the jerk. She pawed through her pack for a face wipe and rubbed it over her mouth.

What would Ryan do if he knew what Hudson did? She had miscalculated Hudson; his heart was blacker than she thought. Her pulse quickened at the thought of him following up with his threat.

He won't get the chance. I'll make sure he doesn't.

Tara dressed in her Nomex and tugged on her boots. She'll go to HR first thing when she wakes up before Aurora Crew leaves for the fireline.

I have to get Hudson off this mountain.

CHAPTER 29

"Waters, you in there?" yelled Silva. "Everyone's ready. Let's go."

Tara's eyelids fluttered open. Her muscles ached. Her brain tried willing her muscles, but they weren't listening. She groaned at the prospect of leaving her tent.

"Tara, wake up." Angela tapped her tent wall. "We're all waiting for you. Hurry."

"Working on it," she called out. She unzipped her tent, crawled out, and stood blinking with a killer of a headache.

"Good morning, starshine. You look like putrified death," said Angela, sipping coffee.

"I feel like it," muttered Tara.

Tara ticked through her checklist and readied her day pack with the gear she'd need for the day. She shuddered, recalling last night's encounter with Hudson. Her eyes scanned the crew. Hudson was at the head of the crew line, talking to Rego.

"Aurora, time for fun and games," Silva called out from the front of the single-file crew line. He took off and the crew fell in behind him.

First things first: She must file her complaint with HR. Would anyone be there this early?

Angela was last in the crew line and Tara tapped her on the shoulder. "Angie, tell Silva I'll catch up. Have to go to HR."

"Okay, but why?" Angela's eyes grew big.

"Tell you later." Tara left her gear at camp and sprinted up to the ICC. Not much activity this early. She didn't see movement in the IC tent, let alone HR. She checked the line of large tents and spotted a guy with a clipboard. "I need to talk to someone in HR. Do you know where they are?"

"Both HR staff flew out last night to another fire. They're shorthanded. You'll have to wait until they return this afternoon."

Talk about a letdown. She felt the urgency to report Hudson *now*.

"Where's the IC?" she asked.

"Doss is flying the fire perimeter. He won't be back until this afternoon." The guy was terse and in a hurry. She'd have to wait until the HR staff returned. In the meantime, she'd tell Silva what happened.

"Okay, thanks." She hoofed it back to Aurora's camp, gathered her gear, and hustled to catch her crew.

She'll keep her distance from Hudson and work near Tupa. If Hudson were to try anything, Tupa would flatten him like roadkill. He'd become big-brother protective of Tara since working with her on the Afi Slayers squad in Chinook.

Finally, she saw dots of yellow moving through trees along the worn trail. When they arrived at their work site, Tara jogged up to Silva. "Jon, I need to talk to you."

"Can it wait? We have to get to work."

She let out a sigh. "Sure."

"Catch me at lunch." He patted her shoulder, then backed up to address the crew. "Okay folks. Work in a grid, same as yesterday. Smother and douse smokes." He motioned the crew to spread out.

Tara set to work near Tupa. Angela worked a short distance away and kept glancing at her. Tara knew Angela was dying to find out why she'd gone to HR.

"Okay, people, lunch break," yelled Silva.

Thank God. Tara was ravenous after running to catch up with the crew. She sat on a scorched log next to Angela.

"Okay, spill. Why'd you go to HR?" asked Angela.

Tara glanced at Tupa and Wolfman sitting close by. Working in proximity with eighteen people didn't supply much privacy.

As she leaned in to tell Angela, Silva approached. "You wanted to talk to me."

She nodded and motioned him out of earshot of the others. "Last night I was—"

"Aurora Crew, do you copy?" The IC cut in on Silva's radio. He held up a finger in a wait-a-minute gesture and moved off to talk. When he finished, he shrugged at her. "Wind has picked up and we need to douse these hot spots. We'll talk later, okay?"

Tara hid her frustration at Silva putting her off. It wasn't like him, but then he'd been less friendly after she and Ryan had hooked up. She could wait until later. At least the job kept her from thinking too much about last night.

When Silva called a stop for the day, the crew formed into single file for the hike back to base camp. He ambled back to her. "Waters, can you go up front with Rego to set the pace? You're our best pacesetter."

"Can someone else do it today?" She was exhausted and didn't want to be anywhere near Hudson.

"Come on, Waters. We'll get to base camp faster if you're pacesetting."

She was too weary to argue, so she jogged to the front as the crew hiked an old ATV trail. Despite the hot fire, the ground was spongy, rutted, and unstable, with smoking dead snags.

As Tara hiked up a small trail incline, she heard screaming. "Help! Someone help me!"

She broke into a run. Sprinting uphill she rounded a corner. Hudson was flailing in an ash pit that had combusted. Flames licked at him and his pant legs were on fire.

Despite what he'd done, he didn't deserve to burn to death. Tara leaned in and extended her arm over the hot flames. "Hurry Mike! Grab hold!"

"Get me out of here!" Hudson clawed at her and grasped her hand, his eyes wide with terror.

Tara positioned herself behind him and grabbed hold under his armpits, dragging him from the blazing ash pit that once sheltered tree roots. She laid him on his back and beat the flames on his pants with her gloves.

Rego rushed up as Hudson crumpled on the ground, screaming. Silva knelt on the ground to remove Hudson's charred boots. The laces had burned off.

Hudson writhed in obvious agony. "Oh God oh God, it hurts!"

The stench of burnt flesh hit Tara's nostrils. She pushed her lunch back down.

Silva tore a first aid kit open with his teeth, then ripped apart what was left of Hudson's pants. "Waters, radio for a medevac, stat. Hudson needs a hospital." He dipped his head toward the radio on the ground.

Tara snatched it up and requested a helicopter from dispatch.

"Soak some gauze. Hurry," ordered Silva, holding an open packet up to her.

Hudson pushed up on an elbow and pointed at Tara. "Don't let her near me! That bitch tried to kill me!" He fell back, moaning.

What? Did he really say that? Tara's chest tightened. "I did not! I pulled you out."

"You shoved me in—you tried to kill me!" he spat through clenched teeth.

All heads swiveled in Tara's direction.

She swallowed hard and her heart thumped as she backed up, stunned.

Silva shot her a look as he gave first aid to Hudson. Tupa and Rego helped.

Angela rested a hand on Tara's shoulder. "He's in shock, he doesn't know what he's saying."

"Yes, he does," muttered Tara.

A cruel understanding seeped through her. He accused her, despite her having helped him. Who *does* that? She remembered an abnormal psych class in college, about sociopaths and psychopaths. This guy sure fit the bill. A shiver shot up her spine.

Tupa used his pocketknife to open gauze packs. He knelt to help Silva, who was snapping on nitrile gloves. The rest of the crew stood watching.

"Someone quick! Pour water on this." Silva held out a square of gauze.

Rego splashed it with his canteen and Silva applied the wet gauze to Hudson's stinking mass of black, pink, and red flesh.

Hudson stopped screaming.

"He's going into shock," gritted Silva. "Rego, water."

Tara looked on with a different kind of shock.

Rego saturated more gauze and Silva continued placing it on Hudson's legs. "Get him some Tylenol or whatever we have," Silva directed. "We need to prepare him for an air evac."

Liz pawed through the box and retrieved a packet. She ripped it open and snapped her finger at Rego. "Canteen."

Rego gave his canteen to Liz and she knelt next to Silva. "Hudson, can you hear me? Take these and a swig of water."

Hudson's eyes dulled as he slipped into shock.

Liz knelt and supported his head. She placed tablets on his

tongue and held a canteen to his lips. "Drink this and swallow, Mike," she ordered.

Hudson choked back pills and water, then his head fell back as he lost consciousness. Liz took a jacket out of her pack, rolled it up and placed it under his head.

Silva glanced at Rego. "How far is the helo?"

Rego keyed the radio. "Twelve Tango Charlie, what's your ETA?"

Whop-whop rotor noise on the radio. "Five minutes. When you hear us, guide us in."

"Copy," said Rego.

"Liz, please keep an eye on Hudson." Silva rose and pulled Tara aside. "Why would he say you pushed him?"

"That's why I've been trying to talk to you. But in confidence." Her head spun with the craziness of the situation. Who will believe her now?

Silva stared at her with sincere concern. "All right, later. Got my hands full right now."

Tara had screwed up royally. She should have told Silva right away what happened last night. And she shouldn't have told Hudson she would report him. The crafty little dickhead had beat her to the punch with his own accusation.

"Anyone see what happened?" Silva called out to the crew.

No one spoke, except Rego. "I ran up and he was lying on his back on the trail. Waters was beating flames on his pants with her gloves."

"Did you see anyone push him or pull him out?"

Rego fixed on Tara, then Silva. "No."

Tara stared at Rego as the sound of whirring rotors filled the air. He said she'd helped Hudson, not hurt him. Chalk one up for Rego. Maybe he wasn't a loser after all.

Everyone put on their goggles as the helo prepared to land in the adjacent blackened area. The pilot hovered while Silva guided him with arm gestures to a level landing spot in the field. Rotor wash whipped ash around them.

"Okay, folks, hold up a minute." Silva took off his yellow shirt to shield Hudson's burn wounds the best he could from blowing ash and dirt. He looked oddly out of place in his white tee.

The pilot powered down and two paramedics jumped out, ducking below the spinning rotors. They unloaded a canvas stretcher and went to Hudson, lying on the ground.

"I'm the ICC fire medic. Who's in charge?" asked the woman paramedic with a purple ponytail.

Silva spoke up. "Me. Both his legs are badly burned." He explained what happened.

The other paramedic knelt next to Hudson. "We'll get him onboard first and stabilize him on the flight to Fairbanks. Decent job with the first aid." He nodded at Silva.

Purple ponytail dipped a chin at Tupa and Silva. "We'd appreciate your help."

Silva and Tupa each took a shoulder and lifted Hudson, while the two paramedics slid the stretcher under him. The four carried Hudson to the helicopter and loaded him. The paramedics climbed onboard. As the air ambulance lifted away, Silva's radio crackled with the pilot informing Fairbanks Memorial Hospital their ETA was forty minutes.

As Tara watched the helicopter disappear over a ridge, she sensed the shitstorm ahead when she would report Hudson. Great. *He'll get a pity party while I'm labeled a hack.*

"Aurora Crew, get this ash pit fire out. Rego, set up a pump and hose lay to that small stream over there." Silva motioned to the other side of the field where the chopper had landed. "Watch out for other ash pits, people."

"Don't have to tell me twice," muttered Rego, unspooling the hose he'd tied to his fire pack.

Tupa and the Afi Slayers helped Rego, and soon they'd extinguished all coals in the ashpit.

The exhausted crew resumed hiking, more wary, but eager to get back to food and rest.

Hudson's accusation unnerved Tara. Was he sick and twisted enough to deliberately jump into a burning ash pit so he could accuse her of pushing him in? Even if he fell in by accident how could he have the presence of mind to accuse her?

She wished HR would have been there this morning.

What a flipping hot mess.

CHAPTER 30

*R*yan helped the first load of eight jumpers suit up and gear up, then he and Gunnar loaded the para-cargo boxes on the plane.

Once the jumpers were on board, Ryan closed the door and signaled an all clear to the twin-engine, C-23 Sherpa. The pilot acknowledged and the plane taxied to the runway for takeoff.

His duties done for now, Mel could fly Ryan up to fire base camp to tell Tara about McGuire. He opened his locker and donned a clean yellow Nomex shirt, hardhat and gloves, then strolled to the helicopter hangar.

Mel rubbed the windshield of N74 Juliet, one of the busiest helicopters for shuttling fire managers. He raised his head in greeting. "Hey buddy."

"Decent weather today, at least." Ryan opened the passenger door and lifted himself into the seat. He buckled in and eased on the white helmet with a built-in headset, snapped his chin strap, and centered the hot mic in front of his lips.

"Winds are behaving for now but a large front moves in tomorrow." Mel opened the pilot door and climbed in. He tucked his cleaning cloth in a pocket on the side of his seat. He slipped on his helmet, buckled in, and fired up the engine. As rotors turned, Ryan waited for Mel to finish his pre-flight check.

"You're my eyes on starboard." Mel's voice fed into his ears.

"Aren't I always?"

"I don't know now that you're all moosey-eyed these days. Gunns says you're in love." Mel powered the engine and smiled at the windshield. "But then I already knew that."

"Ha, so Gunns ratted me out. Next time we jump, I'm pushing his ass out first." Though Ryan joked, he had a tremendous longing to take Tara in his arms, to fill the aching emptiness that only she could fill. *I've never felt this way about a woman.*

Mel flipped switches on the instrument panel and lifted Juliet, heading southeast to the base camp, thirty-five air miles.

Ryan checked his watch. ETA in twenty minutes. He scanned airspace out of habit, as if he were piloting.

Earlier that morning, he'd called the Missoula Smokejumper base for an update on Travis McGuire. Since the Forest Service was still investigating, their spokesperson could only say his chutes hadn't opened correctly. Ryan had also contacted the Shackelford Fire Incident Commander, Dave Doss, to find out when Aurora Crew would return to base camp for the evening. He told Dave he had an urgent message for a firefighter concerning a death notification.

"How long will this take? I can wait at the helispot until someone needs to land." Mel flicked his finger at a stubborn compass needle and frowned. "Got to fix this damn thing."

"Half hour, tops."

"If they kick me out, I'll let you know. Got your B.K.?" Mel glanced at him.

"Yup." Ryan tapped fingers and thumb on his radio as he eyed the base camp helispot up ahead on a low-elevation bench.

Mel skirted the treetops for the last mile and lowered Juliet to the helispot, slowing the rotors.

"You're a good man." Mel reached for a clipboard and

glanced up. "Gunns was right. Either you're in love or you've turned into a regular gentleman."

Ryan gave him a close-mouthed grin. "See you in a few." He got out and moved below the twirling rotors. First, he'd check in with the IC. He hurried to the Incident Command Center, consisting of five sizeable tents clustered in an open meadow. He spotted Doss in the middle, talking on an iridium satellite phone, and surrounded by people with clipboards. Ryan waited for him to finish.

Doss noticed him and waved. "O'Connor, good to see you."

"How goes the battle, Dave?" Ryan shook his hand.

"Aw, you know, just when you think you have the sonofabitch, she blows up again. Thanks for kicking ass on the head yesterday. Prevented evacuation of the air force base."

"We were lucky the wind changed."

"Luck is a lot of this game, isn't it? Who's the firefighter you need to see on Aurora Crew?"

"Tara Waters. She was the fiancée of Travis McGuire, the Zulie jumper killed in Idaho. She's a friend, so figured I'd tell her in person, rather than her hearing it elsewhere." Ryan conveniently left off the "ex" connotation to make it seem urgent.

"Bad blow to the fire community when that shit happens." Dave examined his watch. "Aurora should be back by now. Crew camps are down that way." Doss pointed and rubbed his eyes with thumb and forefinger. "Been a long day."

"Always are. Thanks."

"Don't envy you, delivering news like that." Dave shook his head and ducked into the IC tent.

Ryan strode downhill to Aurora's camp. Three firefighters came toward him, holding their hardhats. A blonde, a brunette, and a redhead. *His redhead.*

Liz and Angela were engrossed in an animated discussion. Tara lagged a little behind, her head down.

Angela saw him first. "Lord, love a duck—if it isn't Ryan O'Connor!"

Tara snapped her head up and a big smile lit her face.

He continued toward her, grinning.

"It's really you." She threw her arms around him, nearly knocking him over. She hugged him hard and he liked it.

"It's really me." He was delighted with her happiness to see him. *Good call, making the decision to come up here.*

Tara drew back to look at him. "Why are you here?"

"I had to see you."

Her expression changed to sheer joy. Unabashed, she planted a kiss on his mouth.

God, he loved it. He pulled back, not because he didn't welcome her luscious lips, but they were out here in front of God and everyone else.

"Geez, guys, get a room," purred Liz, grinning.

Tara's emerald eyes sparkled. "I can't believe you're here. I heard you on the radio yesterday when you jumped the fire. Are you working at Shackelford base camp now?"

"Not exactly." He didn't have much time. "I need to talk to you—alone."

Tara glanced at Angela and Liz. "See you later, guys."

"Buh-bye." Angela winked at him, and she and Liz continued their way.

He scoped for a private place amid the flurry of activity with crews coming and going and people hauling equipment. "Come on." He threaded his fingers through Tara's, leading her through a dense stand of sun-dappled spruce.

Alder brushed Nomex and their boots crunched twigs as he practically pulled her along. Most of their serious talks had been in the woods except for their red-hot night together.

When he was satisfied with enough privacy, he stopped and pulled off his Ray Bans, letting them dangle to his chest. It took every ounce of will power not to ease her to the forest floor and make love to her, but his ride was waiting, and he had the unwelcome news to deliver.

Tara wasted no time. She reached around his neck and kissed him, forcing his lips open with her tongue. She tasted minty and he inhaled the smoke in her hair.

He returned the kiss, his tongue seeking hers. Her lips were warm and welcoming. Backing her into a birch, he pressed hard against her. Clearly aroused, he slid his hand between the buttons on her shirt. She untucked it and guided his hand under her shirt and tank top to give him access to a breast.

Tara explored his mouth with her tongue and whimpered. She slipped her hand down below his belt, massaging him.

He tensed and moaned, then ended the kiss, withdrawing his hand from under her shirt. "We'd better stop." His voice was husky.

"Mmm, don't want to," she whispered, cradling his face, and kissing him again.

He didn't want her to stop but the clock was ticking. "God, what you do to me." He rested his hands on her shoulders and slid his palms down her yellow-shirted arms to hold her hands.

"I've missed you." She seemed tired but she was still a beauty. That hadn't changed.

"It's only been one day," he chuckled, stroking her hair. "But I can't stay. I came to tell you something."

"I'm glad you're here. I so need to be with you right now." She smiled up at him.

"I want to be with you, too, but don't have much time. Mel is waiting with Juliet." He brushed back strands from her messy ponytail and kissed the side of her neck. "And I'm expected back at the Jump Shack."

"So good to see you. You have no idea." She buried her face in his fire shirt and squeezed her arms around him.

He sensed something wrong. Something was off. Maybe she

already knew about Travis. He moved back and cupped her cheeks. "Everything okay?"

She nodded, but her expression said otherwise. "What is it you have to tell me?"

He hungered to kiss her again but had to get on with it. He tenderly rubbed her shoulders. "There's been an accident. Travis McGuire. He jumped the Lochsa Fire in Idaho...his chutes didn't open..."

She took a step back and gave him an odd look. "Why are you talking about Travis?"

"I wanted to be the one to tell you. Didn't want you hearing it in some random way." He reached for her hand and stroked it with his thumb.

"Travis—is he dead?" Tara fixed on him, wide-eyed.

He squeezed her hand, nodding. "I'm sorry."

"Oh, God." She stumbled back against the birch and wiped a shaking hand across her mouth.

He moved close to comfort her. "No one knows why his reserve didn't open after his primary chute didn't work. It was a malfunction."

"Travis had jumped at least a hundred fires. How could this happen?"

"No one knows yet. The investigation is ongoing." Ryan was uneasy about parachute malfunctions same as anyone else. But he'd never let on to Tara.

"Ryan, what if—" she choked off and her breath caught. "What if the same thing were to happen to you?"

"Don't think like that," he erupted. He didn't have an answer for her. They both understood the dangers of his job.

"You know how I always say I've got this? I don't have a grip on anything right now. It's like losing Travis all over again. People in my life either leave or die."

Ryan lifted her chin. "You're the strongest woman I know.

You'll get through this. I'll help you." He pulled her to him and wrapped his arms around her.

She stiffened and he sensed her tensing, holding back what she couldn't suppress any longer.

"Let it out," he said softly. "No one is judging you. Let it all out."

She squeezed him hard and the sobs came. Her shoulders wracked with such force, he wasn't sure how to respond. He held her, rocked her. *Contain her...contain her like a fire. This I know how to do.*

Ryan felt McGuire's loss as a fellow smokejumper, but as far as he was concerned, Tara was his now. He liked Travis, but if he would have been faithful to her, she wouldn't be in Ryan's arms now. Life can turn on a dime. Or, he thought glumly, a fire.

He had jumped into different territory now.

CHAPTER 31

*T*ara's senses narrowed and the woods wheeled around her. Travis? Dead? The words fell on her like boulders crashing down a mountain. A piece of her stripped away. She had been a dam holding back a swollen lake. Her tears had cut loose in a flood out of her control.

Ryan held her tight until her sobs subsided. She didn't want him to let go and rested her head on his chest. His heartbeat comforted her.

He reached in his pocket for a hanky and offered it.

She took it and dried her tears. "Dad always said there's no crying in firefighting."

"Not true. Not always." His eyes mirrored empathy, preventing her from freefall.

"I appreciate your coming here to tell me."

"You'd planned to marry him at one time. Figured his death might be hard for you."

"I tried hard to get over him after breaking our engagement. I kept thinking something was wrong with me." What she didn't say was, breaking off the engagement nearly destroyed her after losing her father.

"Nothing's wrong with you. Trust me." His voice was low and rough. He kissed her palm. "Do you still love him?"

The tender touch of his lips had rippled through her, but his question tipped her off balance. "I thought I did. But that was before."

"Before what?"

She looked straight at him. "Before you."

Radio static. Melbourne talking. "O'Connor, this is seven four Juliet. Lift off in ten, incoming traffic."

"Copy. On my way," he replied to his radio, his gaze steady on Tara.

Forcing a smile, she lightly tugged his shirt collar. "You better go."

He tugged her to him for a long, tender kiss, then separated from her. "Sorry to deliver this shocking news and then rush off. Next time we'll meet on a happier occasion."

She tucked her head against his neck, wanting to stay like this forever. "I don't want you to go. I know you have to, but I don't want you to," she whispered.

"I'd stay if I could. Hang in there with me until fire season ends. I'll take you to places you've only dreamed of. But for now, we earn the bucks to do it. Deal?"

"Deal." She pressed against him, wanting his reassurance to envelop and comfort her like a cozy quilt—and calm her in this insane world of death and accusation.

Ryan pulled back. "Stay safe on this fire. You know the drill. Make good choices."

She chuckled. "You're the one who jumps out of perfectly good airplanes."

He leaned in and kissed her, sending a want all the way to her core. When he tried to pull back, she wouldn't stop kissing him. Finally, he backed away, rubbing his mouth with the back of his hand.

He glanced down at himself. "Cripes, Waters. Now look what you've done."

She grinned, reaching for him, knowing their kiss made him feel the same way she did.

He held up his hands. "Stop. If I don't leave now, I'll tear off your Nomex and have my way with you right here." He motioned to the forest floor.

"I can think of worse places." She gave him a coy look and pushed pine needles with her boot as if clearing a place to lie down. "Promise me you'll stay safe."

"Always."

"Where will you take me that I've only dreamed of?" She was thrilled that his after-season plans included her.

"Ever ride the Pacific Coast Highway on a Husqvarna 701?"

She scrunched her face. "On a chainsaw?"

A squirrel chattered at them and Ryan laughed.

"You're such a fire chick. Husqvarna doesn't only make chainsaws. They've cranked out a motorcycle or two. Or if you prefer, we'll sip glacieritas on a Kenai Fjords cruise, watching whales breach."

"Both. I want to do both." She fought for strength. "This must have been awkward for you, coming up here to tell me about Travis. Thank you."

"I don't do things like this for just anyone." Ryan cocked a brow and turned to go.

She wanted desperately to tell him about Hudson. "Wait." Her heart thumped—should she?

By the way, Mike Hudson threatened your girlfriend, then accused her of trying to kill him by shoving him in an ash pit.

No time for that right now. She'll deal with it.

"Waters, if I don't get out of here…" Slivers of sun streamed between spruce boughs, backlighting his broad shoulders, and glinting his hair gold.

He was the most beautiful thing on this mountain.

She lifted her chin. "Check your chutes, O'Connor."

He nodded, smiling. "If I have to promise to be safe, so do you." He hesitated, then put on his sunglasses, and strode off.

"I promise," she called after him.

He waved before disappearing from the woods.

Aching for him in a way she'd never known, she watched his yellow shirt disappear into the spruce. She leaned back on the birch, slid to the ground, and drew her knees to her chest. She wept...tears for not saving Dad. Tears for the old man she couldn't save. Tears for Travis abandoning her and now he was dead. Yes, she had loved him, or thought she did.

But Ryan was in her life now and she missed his reassuring presence. He had tossed her a lifeline by making plans with her after fire season. Now she had something to look forward to. His going to the trouble to fly up here just to deliver the news about her ex only proved that he did care about her.

But what hit home were the perils of smokejumping. The fears Tara had whenever Travis had jumped a fire. When she broke off the engagement, she remembered feeling relieved at not having to bury those closet fears anymore. Fears that no one dared talk about in fire.

And now, those fears had wormed their way back. She'd have to learn how to force them down to the basement of her psyche all over again. If something happened to Ryan...she couldn't go there.

They each promised the other to stay safe.

After all...a promise was a promise.

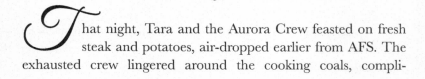

That night, Tara and the Aurora Crew feasted on fresh steak and potatoes, air-dropped earlier from AFS. The exhausted crew lingered around the cooking coals, complimenting Silva on their fantastic steaks. Jon took pride in his gourmet cooking skills.

"Thanks folks. Glad you enjoyed your bad-ass steaks. Later, boys and girls, I'm beat." He started for his tent, then stopped next to Tara. "You've been wanting to talk to me. Sorry to put you off again, but can you stop by later? Got to clean up and do some paperwork first."

"Sure." Tara looked up at him. She couldn't help but notice Jon's flattering profile in the twilight. If not for Ryan, she may have been tempted to respond to his friendly flirtations.

The Afi Slayers squad and the women sat on logs around the cooking circle. Tara enjoyed their company after bonding as a squad in Chinook. They approved of her leadership and she'd earned their respect. That meant the world to her.

"Too bad about Hudson. Goes to show, you gotta be careful in the black. People assume everything in the black is safe." Tupa munched a leftover steak, his massive hand holding it like a cookie.

"Why did Hudson say you pushed him in? That's a helluva thing." Bateman spit on his glasses and rubbed the lenses with his kerchief.

"No idea. He was in shock, I guess." Tara rose, giving Liz and Angela an urgent look. "Ladies, time to head to the latrine. Good night, everyone."

"Good night, ladies," said Tupa.

The others said good night as they rose and retired to their tents for the night.

"Okay, spill," ordered Angela, as the three women hurried up the path toward the women's latrine.

"Is Ryan working this fire?" asked Liz.

"No. He made a special trip here to tell me Travis was killed jumping a fire in Idaho. Ryan knew him and thought he should tell me in person."

"I'm so sorry," gasped Angela. "I wouldn't have called him a nutless weasel if I'd known he'd be kicking the bucket."

Tara forced a smile. "Just because a person dies doesn't make them a saint."

"It's still a bitter blow. If you'd married him, you'd be a widow now. Either way, you would have lost him."

"True." Tara watched a helicopter hovering to land.

"Ryan came all the way up here to tell you about Travis?" Liz put a hand to her heart. "How romantic. No guy has ever done anything like that for me."

"Romantic?" Tara raised her brows.

"Your new heart throb travels miles to tell you in person—on a fire no less, that the man you once intended to marry died on a fire. And the weird thing is, they knew each other. This reminds me of the Spielberg movie about firefighting and the air tanker pilot in love with Audrey Hepburn." Angela pulled a wipe from her pocket to dab her eyes.

"*Always*," Tara smiled at her crew mate.

"Always what?" sniffled Angela.

"That's the name of the movie. *Always*."

"Except the tanker pilot isn't in love with Audrey Hepburn. He's in love with Holly Hunter," said Liz.

"And they danced to *Smoke Gets in Your Eyes*," purred Angela.

Liz continued. "He's dead, but loves her so much he saves her life, so she can fall in love with the hot air-tanker pilot."

"Brad Johnson," sighed Tara. "*Always* was Mom and Dad's cult film. Believe me, I was amazed that Ryan came all the way up here to tell me about Travis."

"I knew from the git-go he was into you," said Angela.

"It was meant to happen," Liz said matter-of-factly.

Angela gave Tara a coy look. "Is it too soon for the "L" word?"

Tara's cheeks heated. "Way too soon." *Or was it?*

They reached the ladies' tarped shower area and ducked

inside. Tara made sure they were alone. The women grouped in a circle while Angela pawed through her toiletry bag for a brush.

"Okay, why did you go to HR this morning? I've been in suspense all day." Angela bent to brush her hair.

"Hudson threatened me last night." The words sounded foreign, even as she said them.

Angela tossed her head up, wide-eyed. "When? What did he do?"

"Last night on my way to the latrine, he wouldn't let me pass. He said we could have some fun and said what a shame if my face were to be messed up. Then he stole Dad's bandana from my pocket."

"Holy shit!" Liz threw her arms up. "Why couldn't he stay in his tent and jerk off in his sleeping bag like a normal guy?"

Angela stared at Tara with fire in her eyes. "That's a bona fide threat! If he were here, I would dangle his puny, little dick on a spruce tree for the bears."

"I tried to report it this morning, but no one was at HR. When our crew got back, Ryan was here. I wanted to talk to both of you before I go to HR."

"So that's why Hudson accused you of pushing him in the ash pit." Angela waved her brush. "How could he even think to say it when he was in pain?"

"Because he's a sociopath," said Tara dryly.

"Don't you love it when karma kicks someone's ass who deserves it?" Liz smiled.

"I don't wish horrible things for people. But when the universe does kick their ass, makes me all warm and fuzzy inside." Angela straightened, tossing her dark tresses.

Tara stared at her two friends. "I don't want the crew to find out."

"Stop worrying what they'd think. They respect you, especially your squad. And they liked how you thwacked Hudson in the bar. That's the crazy stuff that fills our heads when these things happen." Liz grimaced.

Angela looked at her. "Have you ever been threatened with physical harm?"

"You think it never happens in my line of work? What rock do you two live under?"

"Sorry, Liz. This is just all so weird." Tara gave her a sheepish look.

Liz waved away the apology. "You can't let Hudson get away with it, burn injuries or not."

Angela had her fighting face on. "From the beginning I felt he was slithery, like a water snake. You have us for witnesses. We know you didn't push him in and Rego knows you didn't."

"Did you tell Ryan?" asked Angela.

"There wasn't time. Plus, I want to handle it myself."

"But Ryan could help you with this." Angela looked at Liz, who nodded agreement.

Tara paced. "I know. He saved my ass the first time I met him. I don't want him thinking he has to rescue me every time I have a tricky situation."

"But if you want a close relationship with Ryan, you need to be honest. Don't forget, fire is a small world. He's bound to hear it anyway."

"Not only that, if Ryan finds out you told Silva and not him, he won't like it," Angela pointed out.

"You're right." She should have told Ryan. *Too late now.*

"Well, you have to tell Silva because he's your crew boss. Plus, report it to HR. And you should file a police report for threats of physical harm." Liz put her hand on her hip.

The thought of filing a police report sickened Tara. "I've already played it out. I don't want to demobe. I'm here to fight fire and I need a good referral for the Lolo Hotshots. I won't get one if I leave this fire."

Angela pulled out a toothbrush and waved it. "Get a restraining order."

"Hudson's gone. Doubt if I'll see him again," said Tara.

"I'd get one anyway." Liz leaned into her. "Oh, I have other juicy news. After Hudson medevacked out, Rego told Tupa that Hudson bragged about adding weights to Angela's pack before her fitness test."

Angela stopped brushing and pointed her toothbrush at Tara. "I knew that rat bastard did it!"

Liz chuckled. "Rego said Hudson was giddy with pleasure for trashing Angela's fitness test. Aren't you glad we strung him up on the moose?"

"We should have run him up a flagpole instead." Tara glanced at her watch. "It's half past eight, I've got to go."

"First tell Silva. Then go to HR." Angela finished brushing, sipped water, and turned to spit a fast stream.

"Angela, you have to come with me to tell them Hudson sabotaged your fitness test." Tara strode out of the shower area.

The women hurried back to Aurora Camp.

"Good luck. Let me know what happens." Liz unzipped her tent and crawled inside.

"Okay," whispered Tara as she and Angela approached Silva's tent. A flashlight was on inside, so he was awake. "Hey, Jon?"

"Yeah," Silva responded.

"Got a minute?" Tara waited.

Silva unzipped his tent and poked his head out. "Sorry, I've been so busy. I've been working on the incident report about Hudson." He lifted a clipboard.

Tara squatted next to him. "I won't take up much time. Thought you should know I went to HR this morning to report a crew behavior violation, but no one was there. Hudson threatened me last night."

Silva stared at her, then looked at Angela, who nodded.

"Shit, Waters. You mean with physical harm? That prick! Why didn't you tell me?"

"It happened right before everyone got up. I didn't want to wake you. That's where I went this morning, but HR wasn't there. And then Hudson had his accident and blamed me."

Silva's mouth fell open. "I'm sorry I kept putting you off. You know how it is when the IC wants something done. Do you want me to go with you to HR?"

"No, I can handle it. Angela's coming with me because we found out Hudson was the one who sabotaged her pack test back in training."

"Seriously? Oh man." Silva rubbed his eyes. "I'll talk to HR and provide a statement of what I observed today before Hudson got medevacked."

"I'd appreciate it." Tara rose to her feet.

"Thanks for telling me. I'll get with HR after you talk to them." Silva put his hand on her knee. "Are you all right?"

She nodded. "Just tired."

Silva shook his head. "Everyone knows Hudson's a loser, so don't fret about it. People respect you. No one will believe him. I'll see to it the dickhead gets fired." His eyes lingered on her with concern.

"Thanks, Jon." As Tara stood to go, she smiled, remembering the real reason for Ryan's agitation the last day of training. He never liked Silva hitting on her. She knew that now. She also knew Silva had said those things about Ryan to win her heart. But Silva was a smart guy. He knew his boundaries and had backed off when Ryan made it clear he had won Tara's heart. She respected Silva for that.

Tara and Angela hiked up to the Incident Command Center in the twilight and entered the tent with the Human Resources sign. A guy and a woman sat at a table working on a spreadsheet.

"Excuse me, can we talk to someone about a private matter?" Tara asked the woman.

"Concerning?"

"A crew behavior violation," said Tara.

"And I'm here to report one too, about the same person." Angela's drawl kicked into overdrive.

The man and woman exchanged glances. He pushed back from the table and looked at Tara. "Come with me and my co-worker will help your friend." He looked at Angela.

Angela lifted her chin. "I'm Angela Divina."

"Have a seat, Angela," said the woman, motioning her to a chair across from her.

The man led Tara to a private corner at the rear of the tent. He gestured to two folding chairs. "Have a seat. My name is Marc Stevens."

"Tara Waters." She folded her hands. "A member of my crew harassed and threatened me, then accused me of pushing him into a burning ash pit."

Stevens regarded her for a long moment before picking up a pen and clipboard. "I'm so sorry. Tell me what happened."

She explained the entire sordid mess, starting with Hudson's comments the first day of training and ending with his threatening her and accusing her of trying to kill him.

"You're sure it was Mike Hudson?"

"Yes. The one medevacked this afternoon."

Stevens nodded. "The burn injury. What happened?" He sat cross-legged, hands on his clipboard.

"He fell into a burning ash pit on our hike back to base camp." She blew out a heavy sigh. "I came here to report him this morning, but no one was here."

"We had business on other fires." Stevens raised his brows, scribbling on his notepad.

"Hudson accused me of shoving him into the pit. He said I tried to kill him."

Stevens leaned back, scrutinizing her. "Did he say this in front of others?"

"Yes, the entire crew."

He scrawled on his clipboard. "Anyone see it happen?"

"No. The guy is a sociopath. He sabotaged Angela Divina's fitness test by adding extra weight to her pack."

Stevens eyed her over his glasses. "Who's your crew boss? Does he or she know about all this?"

"Jon Silva is my crew boss. Yes, he does."

"I'll need to talk to him." He sat back and let out a sigh. "And you're sure the person who did all this was Mike Hudson?"

She gave him a funny look. "Yes, why do you keep asking that?"

"Are you aware his stepfather, Duncan Martelle, is the director of the Alaska Fire Service?"

She felt like a Mack truck just flattened her. "No, I didn't know." Her body went numb.

"Not that it makes a difference. But it could make this situation difficult for you."

"Are you saying Hudson will get a pass because his stepdad runs the show?" Heat spread in her face.

"No, that's not what I'm saying. But it would behoove you to have witnesses."

Her anger rose to the forefront. "For which infraction? His harassment, threats to physically harm me, or his sabotage of a firefighter's fitness test?"

"Each allegation." He dropped his gaze to the clipboard, poised to write.

"I better tell you we hung him on a moose antler—and I punched him for groping me." She cleared her throat.

He gave her an odd look. "On or off duty?"

"Off. At the Yukon Roadhouse the night before we left Chinook."

He gave her a plaintive expression. "Didn't help that you escalated the situation."

"And it didn't help that he physically assaulted me before

that, but here we are. The moose antlers were meant as a prank. But it still doesn't justify his threats to hurt me or accuse me of trying to kill him."

Stevens sighed. "You'll need to get witness statements. Otherwise, it'll be your word against his. We'd like you to submit a written statement and you may have to demobe once the agency investigates."

She fought to control her temper. "I don't want to demobe. I want to stay and work. I shouldn't have to leave because some jerk on my crew has it out for women firefighters. And he should not be excused from what he's done because he was injured. Or that he's the stepson of a VIP."

"Understandable. Other than that, do you feel safe here? Anyone else you're concerned about?"

She stood to go. "No. The guys on my crew are fantastic."

Stevens stood with her. "I'm sorry this happened."

"So am I. I've worked lots of fires and never had problems. I hope you take care of this one." She turned to leave.

"I'll keep you posted once the agency investigation is underway. Could take a while since Hudson was injured." Stevens pointed to a blank space on the complaint form. "Jot down your email address."

She scribbled it. "Thanks."

When she walked out to the main tent area, Angela had gone. She was beat and her body let her know it.

Tara strolled back to camp, stupefied. Hudson's stepdad was an agency muckety-muck? Would he be held accountable? She wanted to talk to Ryan before he found out from someone else. *I should have told him when he was here.*

She powered on her cell. No service. Fifteen per cent power left. All this technology and she couldn't even text Ryan. To save what little juice was left, she powered off her phone.

Reaching Aurora's camp, she whispered next to Angela's tent. "Angie, you awake?"

Angela unzipped and Tara crawled in. "Alaska's a flipping wasteland when it comes to cell reception," grumbled Tara. "And my phone's dying. I can't plug into a tree."

"Bateman and Robin have portable chargers. Hit them up tomorrow," whispered Angela. "How'd it go with HR?"

Tara slapped a mosquito on her cheek. "Told Stevens everything. How did your talk go?"

"I told her what Rego said. Hope they fire Hudson." Angela sat cross-legged and offered her a moisture wipe. "She wants to talk to Rego."

Tara rubbed her eyes. "Hudson's stepfather, Duncan Martelle, is the director of the AFS."

"Get out of here. Are you serious?" Angela wiped her face.

"This should be an interesting process."

Angela finished cleaning her face. "There's more shitty news."

"What could be worse?"

"Liz talked to some hotshots who arrived from base a bit ago. When she said she was on Aurora Crew, they asked if she knew Tara Waters. They said social media has been exploding with you bedding down guys on Aurora Crew. Specifically, Silva and Hudson."

Tara spluttered. "What? Jon shouldn't be dragged into this. Who's posting it?"

"Who do you think? Hudson posted on Facebook and Twitter, smearing your name from here to the North Pole and back. Without cell service or internet here, we can't put a stop to it."

"Why am I not surprised?" Tara pinched the bridge of her nose with thumb and forefinger.

"Hudson has trashed your reputation, thanks to the wonder of social media. I can picture that snake-weasel in his hospital bed, working his thumbs like a chimp on speed."

"You'd think he'd be in too much pain."

"He's a masochist. They thrive on pain." Angela said it with such authority a roomful of people would have been convinced.

"Shit, what should I do?" Tara's temples pounded.

"Hon, it gets worse."

"What could be worse than the last thing?" Tara put her hands on her head.

"He posted on social media you tried to kill him."

"Oh, God," Tara yelled it. "Online?"

"Shh, hold it down," cautioned Angela.

"Ryan is bound to hear this. Oh no, I should have told him when he was here."

"Hon, he knows you. He won't believe it. Ryan's not the sort to believe vicious lies. The way he looked at you today melted my sweet little heart. I've had guys look at me...but never like that." Angela wore her dreamy look.

"We're still getting to know each other. He'll be scared off with all this drama."

"Ryan doesn't scare easily. He's a smokejumper, remember? You reported Hudson to HR. Now let the agency work through its process."

"What a freaking mess." Tara's head ached.

"We're moving out at the usual 4 a.m. Better get some sleep."

"Thanks. You're a good friend."

Angela hugged her. "We'll get this figured out, don't worry. I've got your back."

"And I have yours. 'Night." Tara crawled out to her own tent.

She powered on her phone to text Ryan. She was desperate to get a message to him. Thank goodness he'd put his number in her phone the morning after their night together. She texted.

Need to talk to you. Whatever you hear about me, don't believe it.

She pressed 'send' and read the note saying her text will send when there's service. It was all she could do for now.

She tapped her photo icon and up popped Ryan's luscious

peepers, smiling at her. She pressed the image to her heart before powering it off.

Everything was a hellacious inferno. Her heart burned for Ryan. Her reputation was in flames, and her job was in jeopardy. And there was always the physical fire to fight. So much had happened since she arrived in Alaska. If she would have saved the guy in the Copper Peak Fire, would she still have wound up here? If not, she wouldn't have seen Ryan again.

She couldn't sort her confusion, so she prayed. *Please God, let Ryan's chutes open. Don't let anything bad happen to him...or me. Amen.*

Tara hoped it was enough.

CHAPTER 32

*A*fter seeing Tara, Ryan had gone to bed early. He rose at 5:05 a.m. for his usual workout of running the track and lifting weights. He was still low on the jump list.

"Zombie wants us rigging and repairing in the loft," called out Boone.

"After I shower." Ryan took a quick one, pausing long enough to let the hot water massage his back and shoulders. When he finished, Stu came in.

"O'Connor. Zombie said you were in here."

"What's up?" He toweled himself off.

"They medevacked an Aurora Crew member yesterday afternoon from the Shackelford Fire. Since you trained them, figured you'd be interested."

Ryan dressed and towel-dried his hair. "Who'd they medevac?"

"Hudson. The director's stepson." Stu leaned against the wall.

"Seriously? I'll be damned. Didn't see that one coming." He glided an electric shaver around his face. "Wow, the director's stepson?"

"Yep. He's at Fairbanks Memorial."

Ryan raked fingers through his hair. "What happened?"

"Fell in a smoldering ash pit." Stu shook his head.

Didn't any of his trainees listen to his hazard talks? "Thanks Stu. Suppose I'd better pay him a quick visit." Why hadn't Tara mentioned it yesterday when he told her about McGuire? Then again, there hadn't been time for much else. He'd been too busy kissing and consoling her.

"Make it quick, bro. Fires are ramping up." Stu ambled back out.

"Gotcha." Ryan finished up and stopped by Zombie's office to check the jump list. He and Gunnar were third load, first stick. He'd make it quick. As Aurora Crew's training instructor, he felt a certain responsibility, even though Hudson was a douche. And the director's stepson? *How did I not know that?*

Ryan shivered in the morning chill as he stepped outside, remembering Melbourne saying severe storms were forecasted. He tugged on his denim jacket, unlocked the Mustang, and sped toward the hospital.

At the reception desk, he asked the nurse to see Hudson. She called to obtain permission and gave Ryan the okay to enter Hudson's room. He strolled down the hall and knocked on the partially open door. "Hudson? Mike? You awake?"

"O'Connor. Come in." Hudson responded in a dull voice.

Ryan pushed open the door and stepped into the room. Hudson seemed okay, except for his discolored legs. The darkened skin presented a stark contrast to the immaculate sheets.

"Heard you were injured. What happened to your safety plan?" Ryan forced a cheerful tone.

"Tara Waters pushed me into a burning ash pit."

"She what?" Ryan scrunched his face, wondering if he heard right.

"She tried to kill me!" Hudson leered, gesturing at his blackened legs on top of the covers. "Look at this shit."

"Kill you?" Ryan had come to expect Hudson's whiny melodramas. Par for the course with this dickwad.

"Waters and her bitches have been out to get me from day one. You saw when she tried to kill me with the log. They hung me on moose antlers up at Chinook and I ended up missing the van to Fairbanks. Then she pushed me into that burning ash pit. If that's not attempted murder, I don't know what is."

Ryan tried to keep a straight face at 'Waters and her bitches'. Sounded like a rock band. The rest of his ludicrous allegations sounded even funnier. "Hey Mike, ever think you had this coming? I warned you about shooting your mouth off the first day of refresher training."

"Never said anything that wasn't true." Hudson reminded him of a fangless rattlesnake coiled on his bed. All rattle and no bite.

Ryan thought a moment. "Tara strung you up on the moose all by herself? She's strong, but..." He pursed his lips amused, visualizing his ripped girlfriend bench-pressing Hudson. He couldn't keep a grin from forming.

"Woke the fuck up and couldn't get the fuck down. Ow." Hudson winced, moving his leg. "Had to get a ride to AFS with a village crew from Circle."

"Is that right?" Ryan folded his arms. Humor the douchebag. "Maybe they did it, thinking you might have put extra weight in Angela's pack before her fitness test." He stood at the end of Hudson's bed. "So, did you, Mike?"

Hudson's demeanor changed to unconcern. "Doesn't matter. My stepdad runs the whole shit-show. I'm not worried, but your slutty girlfriend should be. I'll make sure she's fired." Hudson shrugged. "And I'm pressing charges."

Ryan stared at Hudson as if he'd sprouted devil horns, which wasn't hard to imagine. "You're what?"

"You heard me," sneered Hudson.

"Dude, that's fucked up, even for you." Tara wouldn't deliberately harm anyone—it didn't fit her. He moved closer. "What happened up there? Truth."

"God's honest truth? I nailed her." Hudson's lipless grin reminded Ryan of a serial killer boasting of his latest conquest. "Your slutty girlfriend slept with me. She's a tiger." He growled like one.

"Tell me you didn't just say that." Ryan's blood boiled as he squeezed the bridge of his nose with thumb and forefinger. He fantasized torturing Hudson with a drip torch, then dousing him with salt and acid. Since he didn't have his drip torch handy, he'd settle for smothering him with a pillow instead.

"Truth bites, doesn't it?" Hudson popped some pills in his mouth and gulped them down.

Ryan glared at him. "You're lying. Tara can't stand your sorry ass." His neck vein pulsated while debating whether to beat the shit out of Hudson or just slug him.

"Don't believe me? Check the pocket of my shirt." Hudson pointed to a chair in the corner with his dirty yellow Nomex draped over it.

Ryan walked over to the sooty shirt. He shoved his fingers inside the pocket and retrieved a dirty orange bandana smelling of smoke and eucalyptus. He studied it, incredulous.

"My souvenir for screwing her. She's a good lay."

Ryan knew Hudson was baiting him, but he couldn't stop himself. Like a shot, he lunged and grasped Hudson's hospital gown with both hands, yanking him close. "She wouldn't give this to you. How'd you get it?" He knew this bandana held special significance for Tara. She was never without it.

Hudson smirked, cocky as hell. "Told you. I fucked her."

The walls rushed in at Ryan and back out again. He twisted Hudson's gown around his putrid throat. "That burning ash pit was nothing compared to what I'll do to you," he gritted, tightening his grip.

Hudson narrowed his eyes. "You can't touch me. My stepfather will fire your ass, pussy boy." He lifted his cell phone. "I can make it happen right now."

"Told you before, don't fuck with me." Ryan let go with one hand to snatch Hudson's phone and jam it into his back pocket.

A siren notification sounded on Ryan's phone in the other pocket. He knew what the text was without having to read it: *Fire call! Report to Jump Shack ASAP.*

He ignored it, still locked on Hudson, fighting the urge to kick his ass into next week.

"Hey tough boy, answer your phone," gurgled Hudson.

Ryan let go, shoving Hudson hard against the headboard.

"Ow!" hollered Hudson. "You assaulted me!"

The tendons in Ryan's neck and shoulders were so taut he thought they might snap. He stretched his neck and reset his shoulders. "You lucked out. I was getting ready to throw your pathetic ass through the window."

"You don't have the guts." Hudson flashed him an overconfident grin.

"We'll see." Ryan slid on his Ray Bans and headed for the door, gripping the edge for control. If not for the fire call, he would have gone to work on the bastard.

"Gimme my phone," snarled Hudson.

"Oh, I forgot. Here!" Ryan faked reaching into his back pocket, then tossing it at him.

Hudson flinched, grabbing at thin air.

"Aw gee, sorry. No phone for you." Ryan aimed a phony, toothy grin at the asshole.

A nurse peeked around the door. "Time to change your dressings, Mr. Hudson."

Ryan pointed his Ray Bans at him. "Shame about your mishap, Mr. Hudson. Too bad you won't be back on fire anytime soon—if ever."

"I said gimme my phone," Hudson shot back, wincing as the nurse applied an antiseptic.

Ryan shrugged, smiling. "You must have misplaced it."

He left the room, his boots pounding the linoleum to the exit. He shoved the front hospital door open with such force, people turned and gaped. He sprinted to his car, peeled out of the parking lot, and sped through an intersection, unconcerned what color the traffic light was. Flicking eyes at the speedometer, he gunned it all the way back to Fort Wainwright, topping ninety.

He pulled out his cell and danced his thumb on Tara's number. The call wouldn't connect. Spotty cell service could be a pain in the ass at a fire base camp. He blew out a heavy sigh.

Hudson said some damning things. Ryan couldn't for the life of him figure out why, other than he was an evil lunatic.

I'll get to the bottom of things after I jump this fire.

🔥

hankful for not being pulled over during his NASCAR sprint to Fort Wainwright, Ryan bolted from his Mustang into the Jump Shack. He beelined for his locker in the Ready Room. Gunnar was already suited up and helped Boone and the rest into their jump suits. Ryan shoved Hudson's phone into a zippered pocket. He'll sift through it when he gets some down time.

"Our chariot awaits. Get your ass in gear." Gunns helped Ryan into his Kevlar jump suit and they waddled out to the Dornier 228 fixed wing, propellers spinning.

"Where to?" Ryan clipped his PG bag onto his harness and secured it.

"Delta Junction. Storm blew in, lightning and sixty mile per hour winds blew it in all directions. Over a thousand residents at Fort Greely are standing by to evacuate the Army post. Four hundred fifty-three residents of Delta Junction have already evack'ed their homes. It's burning hot toward the Trans-Alaska Pipeline."

"How close?"

"Two miles and closing. We're jumping that portion, and the two CASA loads behind us will jump the Fort Greeley and Delta blowups. This fire's nasty. They even had to evac bison from the Delta Junction bison range."

Ryan's brows came together. "Hope Alyeska Pipeline Company shuts down their pumps to slow oil flow. Fire and crude oil don't exactly mix."

The loadmaster heaved cargo boxes into the back of the plane while Zombie barked orders. "O'Connor, you're jumper-in-charge for third load. Boone, you're JIC for second load."

Gunnar lobbed a sandwich and some energy bars at Ryan as they boarded the jump ship, helmets tucked under their arms.

He settled into the aft of the plane and consulted his watch. ETA was thirty minutes. Fairbanks skies again full of smoke.

The Dornier lifted off. "Lots of tongues wagging down there." Gunnar gestured with his head. "You should know what's being said."

"What tongues, who's wagging?" Ryan rubbed his eyes, still agitated from his confrontation with Hudson.

"Guys at Wainwright are saying Tara's sleeping around at fire camp."

Ryan narrowed eyes at Gunnar. "What the hell are you talking about?"

"Hudson's on social media posting all kinds of crap about her."

"I visited the dickhead in the hospital, thinking it was the 'right' thing to do." He shook his head. "What a waste of time." He unzipped his pocked and retrieved Hudson's phone. Not much juice left. He tapped the Facebook icon and up popped Hudson's page. He scrolled, and sure enough, what Gunnar told him was true. He took screenshots of Hudson's defamatory posts.

"What did Hudson say when you saw him?"

"That he slept with Tara and accused her of trying to kill

him." Ryan held up Hudson's phone. "Same shit he posted here. The guy is messed up."

"Scroll deeper, bro. He posted she did her fire instructor to pass training. And even screwed Jon Silva." Gunnar shook his head.

Ryan scrolled with his thumb and saw the comments. "Evil prick. Why the hell would he do that?" He ran his fingers through his hair, peering out the windows. How had things spiraled down so fast?

He powered off the phone and shoved it in his pocket, zipping it closed. He pulled out Tara's orange bandana from the sleeve he'd tucked it in. "Hudson said she gave this to him, but she wouldn't do that. She's never without it."

"Sorry you had to hear about all the scuttle-butt about Tara." Gunns leaned back, squinting out the window at the smoke.

"So you decided to tell me before we jump a blow-up near the biggest fucking oil pipeline on the continent." Ryan shook his head, drumming his fingers and thumb on his thigh. "Your timing sucks."

Gunnar shrugged and adjusted his helmet and face mask. "Thought you should know."

"Nothing I can do until after this fire, Gunns." Ryan put on his helmet and took deep breaths. "Time to focus. See you on the ground." He peered out the oval windows at the tall flame towers eating toward the Trans-Alaska Pipeline like it hungered for crude. They didn't have much time.

Stu motioned to Ryan after removing the door, smoke and heat blowing inside. "High winds aloft, the jump spot is that large clearing. Two hundred yards of drift—don't fly into the burn." Stu pointed and tossed streamers out the door.

Ryan studied the conditions, watching erratic streamers toss like feathers. He nodded at Stu. "Yeah, got it." *Steady. Horizon. Focus.* He gaped at the enormous swirling smoke columns.

The Dornier circled, jumping, and bucking from unstable air pushed by large thunderheads.

"Your objective is to protect the pipeline and you need to do it yesterday. Careful down there." Stu waited for eye contact.

Ryan glanced at Stu and nodded. Stu slapped his shoulder and he leaned back and pitched himself out as he'd done countless times, disliking the whooshing sound of air whipping him like a piece of paper. He toggled hard for the clearing, but winds pushed him toward burning trees. He yanked hard to the left, forcing his stubborn chute toward the jump spot.

"Dammit!" He pulled hard to stay on target as a gust rushed him toward a tall spruce. Skewering himself was a greater concern than jumping from the plane. He'd heard the horror stories and didn't want to become one.

He missed the spruce, but hit the taller, dead snag next to it. He drew his feet together to kick the spear of the leader tip aside. Thankful for the metallic mask protecting his face, his body became a human chainsaw, shaving off brittle limbs and branches as he slid down the dead tree stem. One sharp branch tip threatened to harpoon his right leg. He prayed his Kevlar jumpsuit would do its job. His boots snapped branch after branch until he jerked to a halt. His chute caught the top of the snag and he dangled high above the ground.

He squinted up at the gaping hole in his chute. The nylon had torn. When it tore further, he dropped down a few feet. It ripped and he dropped again. *Please hit a seam and hold. That's why we sew reinforcements on the chute seams.* He reached inside the pocket of the lower right leg of his jump suit for his let-down rope. Another rip dropped him further.

"Get the lead out. There's this thing called a fire about to crisp our asses!" yelled Gunnar from the ground below.

"Think I don't know that, dicklick?" The fast-advancing flame front rushed heat at Ryan's face. He had to work fast.

"You're fifty feet up. Want daddy to come rescue you?"

Concern replaced Gunnar's usual, carefree manner. "Make tracks, dude, or we'll incinerate."

Ryan eyed the flame towers racing toward them. "The top of this mother better not snap off," he muttered, working at lightning speed to tie one end of the rope on the trunk so he could lower himself a little at a time until he could stand on the ground.

A decisive crack shattered the air above him. The top third of the towering snag broke, sending the chute, let-down rope, and Ryan pitching to the ground.

"Ryno, roll fast!" yelled Gunnar, as the treetop aimed its spear at Ryan.

Shit, which way? He rolled left and the tip lanced the ground where he'd landed a few seconds before. His heart skipped a thousand beats as his chest clamped down.

"You lucky shit. You're like a cat. Is this your fourth or fifth life? I've lost count."

"Tenth, I think. Let's get the hell out of here."

"Look at the bright side. You didn't become a shish kabob." Gunnar helped Ryan to his feet and untangled him from the rope and chute lines.

A thunderous rumble snapped Ryan's head up. Two colossal fire whirls swirled around an enormous smoke column as fire exploded in all directions, like an incendiary bomb. "Screw the chutes. It's a fucking double firenado!"

"Twice the fun. Make tracks!" Gunnar grabbed his gear and he and Ryan hauled ass, running as fast as they could.

Ryan's hang-up in the tree had cost them valuable time. He yanked his radio from his holster as he ran. His lips tightened and a current accelerated through him.

"Dornier—Stu, do you copy?" he panted, legs still pumping. "Our jump spot burned over. Drop the others near the pipeline."

Stu's voice crackled. "Copy. Winds are worse. Head east

toward the Trans Alaska Pipeline and meet the jump crew there. Keep it together down there, Ryno."

Ryan was too out of breath to speak. He keyed two response clicks on the B.K. instead. The jumpers on board must be getting a show, cruising above them while they raced the flames on the ground. They were undoubtedly betting bucks whether Ryan and Gunnar could outrun it. They must look like scurrying ants from three thousand feet.

"She's moving faster than us. What's the plan?" Gunnar panted.

"Run like hell," yelled Ryan against the freight-train sound of the fire. He pointed left. "There! Safety zone." At this point, he'd welcome anything devoid of fire. Even the sixty-four-foot-wide TAPS gravel strip.

The men veered left out of the direct path of the massive flame front. They put some distance between themselves and the fire, but they still couldn't let down their guard. Ryan eyed the pipeline zig-zagging uphill, then peered up at the plane traversing the smoke.

He slowed to a jog as they reached the gravel pad supporting TAPS. "How far——" he took several hard breaths. "——have we run?" He bent, hands on thighs, panting.

"Ten miles," puffed Gunnar. "Felt like ten."

"Two or three, easy." Ryan drank greedily from his canteen, water dribbling down his chin. Sweat covered his neck and he swiped at it, wiping it on his pants. He was thankful their cross-country sprint coursed level ground. He doubted he could have covered the same distance on a slope.

The rest of the jumper load floated to the ground, shed their jumpsuits, and gathered their gear. The flame front marched across the bottomlands toward the pipeline, consuming all in its path.

As jumper-in-charge, Ryan formed a swift plan to protect TAPS. He wasn't interested in finding out what would happen when a humungous pipe full of crude overheated. He was in no mood to be James Bond in *The World Is Not Enough*.

"Listen up, boys. This TAPS gravel pad is our anchor point. We'll back burn from here to the flame front," instructed Ryan. "First, we go get our cargo boxes." He keyed his radio. "Boone, do you copy? What's the fire doing where you are?"

Boone responded. "The CASA deposited the last two jumper loads in Delta and Fort Greely. We're on the right flank with the hotshot crews. Can't get in front of it. Winds are too strong. We're protecting homes in Delta and Fort Greely. Two retardant ships are on their way from Canada."

"Copy that." Ryan eyed the airborne cargo boxes drifting to the other side of the mammoth forty-eight-inch diameter oil pipeline, carrying crude from Alaska's North Slope eight hundred miles to the Port of Valdez.

The eight jumpers hiked on the gravel pad alongside the above-ground pipeline and scattered to reach their dropped cargo. The smokejumpers grabbed their fire equipment and hustled to space themselves at intervals along the massive pipe-line to back burn between it and the flame front.

Ryan sliced through silver duct tape with a boxcutter and pulled two drip torches from a cargo box. He passed one to Gunnar. "Here you go."

Gunnar accepted the torch. "What I told you up there. Sorry, but thought you should know."

Ryan raised his brows. "Appreciate the thought, but your timing sucked."

"You don't think any of that's true about Tara, do you?"

Ryan ignited his torch. "Of course not. Why would you say that? Hudson's a sick, twisted jerk." His anger had bubbled on medium-high ever since leaving the hospital.

"You sure she isn't a slut like Amber?"

Comparing Tara to Amber was inconceivable. Ryan didn't

think, just did it—dropped his drip torch and swung at Gunnar, catching him square in the jaw.

Gunnar staggered back, his unlit drip torch in his hand. He shot forward and charged Ryan, pushing him to the ground. "Knock it off, mother-fucker. We have a fire to fight."

"Then keep your damn mouth shut," said Ryan through gritted teeth, eyeing ominous columns of black smoke rolling toward them.

"Get a grip and stop being a candy-ass," grumbled Gunnar, rubbing his jaw. "Hudson threatened her."

Ryan went numb and his fingertips tingled. "Huh?"

"A friend of mine in HR said Tara filed a harassment complaint against Hudson for threatening to hurt her after he accused her of trying to kill him. Apparently, he did it the night before he medevacked out." Gunnar pushed to his feet.

"Well hell, this gets better and better." Ryan revved up his drip torch. Hudson had threatened Tara. What a load of shit. He wanted to set the world on fire.

"Thought you should know. Don't slug me again." Gunnar rubbed his jaw. He fired up his drip torch.

Ryan shook his head. "Told you, your timing sucks." He aimed his drip torch. Drip, poof, the sweet sound of igniting willow and alder, and the velvety sound as thirsty brush accepted flame.

"You have a good right hook. Shit, bro." Gunnar moved his lower jaw back and forth.

"Had I known Hudson threatened Tara when I saw him today, I would have put him through plate glass." Ryan moved sideways, working his drip torch. "Got all your teeth, Norske?"

"Near as I can tell." Gunnar ran a finger over his teeth.

"Then man up and quit your bitching." Ryan grinned at his jump partner. Satisfied with his backfire, he put out his drip torch and picked up a chainsaw.

Lion-eyed and determined, Ryan sprinted along the pipeline

gravel pad to chainsaw nearby trees. He eyed the approaching flame towers, tossing embers and airborne debris, gunning for the pipeline like a terrorist hellbent on destruction.

His body worked on autopilot while his mind raced. Why hadn't Tara told him about Hudson? Did he threaten her before or after Ryan saw her up at base camp? When she'd said she didn't have a grip on anything, he assumed she meant McGuire's death. He didn't know whether to be angrier with Hudson or with Tara for not saying anything.

Never had Ryan fought a fire with such fury. Thorny nettles and thistle jabbed his legs as he wielded his chainsaw like Conan the Barbarian; sword upon the enemy, slaying his ruthless foe. Intense, sweltering heat assaulted him, and sweat ran down the furrow in his back. Ash and dirt swirled while a crazed, irrational energy fueled him as he knocked down flames with a vengeance.

Several hours passed by the time Boone radioed. They'd contained their part of the fire. Ryan staggered back to take stock of the trees and foliage he'd destroyed to save a pipeline. He plodded up a small rise to assess. His back-burn strategy worked. Now out of fuel, the fire slowed, and smoke morphed from black to white. Good. Mission accomplished.

"O'Connor, you copy?" radioed the IC. "We're sending crews to hold the line and mop-up. And a bird to extract your jump squad at TAPS Pipeline Milepost 562."

"Copy." Ryan gathered his jumpers and ordered them to pack up and haul equipment to their extraction point. Feeling spent, he fell in at the end of the line. He did his damnedest to compartmentalize and shove aside the disturbing events that had vaulted front and center into his world.

So, this was what passion for a woman was like—made him so savage he'd assaulted his best friend and leveled everything in sight to contain a fire. His anger had percolated into a full-blown conflagration.

After his night with Tara, Ryan found what he'd been

searching for. A woman like her. She understood his world and knew what made him tick, more than he did. She was a smart, competent firefighter, and a beautiful woman with a terrific sense of humor and a heart of gold. And he admired her. She'd lit a fire in him. He couldn't extinguish this flame—it burned too fierce. He'd do whatever it took to protect her, whether she wanted him to or not. Probably not. And that was a chance he was willing to take.

But what he loathed more than anything, were liars and vermin like Hudson screwing with his world. He'd underestimated the evil in the guy.

He resolved to find out the truth.

Even if it killed him.

CHAPTER 33

$\mathcal{W}$hen Tara woke the next morning, she hastily dressed and readied herself for another day on the fireline. Making sure her fire shelter was secured in place below her pack, she slung her pack over her shoulders, wriggled into her harness, and buckled it.

Silva addressed the crew. "Listen up. More storm cells are moving in." He paused to cough and clear his throat. "Both flanks have flared, and the fire's made a sizeable run. We'll work the left flank and back burn the green between the Richardson Highway and the flame front. We'll have to hike to our assigned area. Aviation's too busy to transport us."

Aurora Crew grabbed their gear and filed out of base camp. Silva led the way with his GPS tracker in hand. The ICC computers had stopped talking to his tracker, so he'd entered their destination latitude and longitude manually.

Angela fell in line behind Tara. "Good, no more mop-up."

"We'll see real action today." Tara couldn't shake her unease eyeing the ominous rows of lofty cumulus clouds with charcoal bottoms, brooding over the mountains, waiting to wreak havoc on their world. Forked lightning zig-zagged across a purple sky and wind gusts swayed the trees. Her chest tightened.

"Not sure I like the looks of those clouds," called out Liz, behind Angela.

"Me neither." Angela scoped the sky. "But rain ought to help."

"We're crazy. We run toward danger when most run from it." Liz chuckled. "At least there's no snakes here. Not like in Nevada."

"Only ravenous bears and wolves with a dash of charging moose and B-52 bomber mosquitoes." Tara scanned the foreboding edge of the large front moving in. Dark plumes of fire smoke drew closer as they approached the left flank. The fire had ravaged several ridges and continued to spread.

"Okay folks, here's where we start back burning." Silva stopped walking and the crew gathered around him. "The IC wants us to stop the fire two miles from the highway, so they can keep it open. We'll construct a new line and back burn toward the flame front. Know your escape routes and where everyone is at all times. Let's go, kids."

Silva's radio announced a forecast of 60-mile-an-hour winds for the afternoon. Tara recalled the last time she'd experienced such a forecast; the day of the Copper Peak Fire.

Tara lit her fusee and torched alder and willow. She worked methodically, the morning breeze carrying the back burn toward the flame front. She watched the sky and kept track of her crewmates—Tupa, who moved uphill ahead of her, and Wolfgang a short distance to her right. The crew back burned a steady pace up a gradual incline.

She paused momentarily to wipe sweat from her forehead.

"Tara!" The voice was sharp and insistent.

"What?" Thinking it was Tupa, she moved in the direction where she'd last seen him. An enormous, burning stump bounced down the steep embankment, vibrating the ground. She spun around as it rocketed past where she'd been standing. It would have hit her had she not stepped out of the way.

One hand flew to the razor-sharp pain piercing her chest, caused by her thundering heart. The other hand cupped her mouth. "Tupa, thanks for the heads-up!" she called out.

No response.

She yelled louder. "Tupa!"

"Waters, he's way up there," Wolfgang peered over a boulder on her right, pointing.

She looked where he pointed. Tupa was quite a distance from her up the hill, back burning.

"Tupa, thanks for the heads-up on the stump," she yelled again.

"What stump?"

"The one you just warned me about," she shouted.

He shrugged. "Wasn't me."

"Wolfgang, did you call my name?"

"Nope," he hollered back. "Good thing someone warned you though."

Baffled, she shook her head and checked around her. *Did she imagine it?* She couldn't have. Someone had called her name, so she'd get out of the way. But who?

Silva whistled and motioned the crew to group around him. "Weather's deteriorating. Winds gusting from the northwest." He stopped for a coughing spasm, then continued. "The ICC reassigned us to the right flank since we've prevented the fire from gumming up the highway. We'll hike across the black and take our position on the right flank, before winds blow the fire in the opposite direction."

He huddled with a topo map and his GPS tracker, then radioed for coordinates to manually input their new target position. The ICC computer still wasn't feeding them into his tracker. GPS technology was great, and Tara thought how some people had a tough time letting go of their precious maps. She smiled.

Jim Dolan was that way. He always said his map was right and the GPS was wrong.

Tara approached Schwartz, Wolfgang, Tupa and the women. "Did any of you call my name a bit ago?"

They shook their heads. "Hearing things?" teased Angela. "The wind out here plays tricks on your ears."

Who had warned her?

She eyed the menacing sky. "Dad, if that was you...thanks." She reached up with a shaky hand to rub her father's lucky bandana and remembered Hudson had it. Her chest hollowed at her sudden vulnerability.

The radio squawked with latitude and longitude coordinates. Silva pulled out his small, weather-proof notebook and jotted down the numbers. He entered the data into his GPS tracker. "Okay, sports fans, we have our target location. Let's go." Another coughing spasm swallowed the last of his words.

Tara didn't like the sound of that. Silva had been coughing steadily since lighting the back burns this morning. She figured he was just sensitive to smoke.

Aurora Crew filed out with Silva in the lead. Rego slipped to caboose position with the other radio. Tara positioned herself in front of Rego to listen to radio traffic, hoping to hear Ryan.

A flash of lightning and a sudden thunderclap made every head turn to the sky, as the crew humped up the mountain to cross several miles of black toward the right flank of the Shackelford Fire.

More than ever, Tara wished she had Dad's good luck bandana.

CHAPTER 34

*R*yan sprawled in a booth at Smokin' Joe's Alaskan Barbecue, while he and the other jumpers waited for a ride back to the Smokejumper Base in Fairbanks. Mel had flown the jump crew in the Bell 212 helo from the TAPS fire to the town of Delta Junction, where they now enjoyed a leisurely lunch in a cozy restaurant. An AFS bus was due to arrive soon.

Gunnar sat opposite him, gnawing on ribs and fries while watching a flat-screen, wall TV. "Hey, wolf boy, you're on TV again." He pointed his French fry at the screen.

Ryan chomped the last of his bison burger as he watched himself holding wolf pups on a Channel 2, Anchorage news broadcast, while Boone's sister, the pretty Fairbanks reporter, interviewed him. The reporter ended with footage of herself and the frisky wolf pups enjoying their new home at the Wildlife Rescue facility.

"Look, you're famous, bro." Gunnar grinned at Ryan and looked around at the other jumpers in the restaurant, whistling and clapping after the wolf story ended.

"Ha, right." Even though Ryan slept on the helo and on the

short van ride to the restaurant, he dozed off when the broadcast ended.

Gunnar snapped his fingers. "Hey sleepyhead, your cell is charged."

Ryan blinked his eyes open to Gunnar pointing at his phone. He'd plugged it into an outlet before they sat down. He yanked out the power cord and shoved it in his pack, then powered on his cell. A text message from Tara popped up and he tapped it.

Need to talk to you. Whatever you might hear about me, don't believe it.

He texted her back:

No worries. We'll talk after you demobe. Stay safe.

He tapped a fire emoji with a happy face and hit send. Who knew when she'd read it.

She obviously knew about Hudson's rumors. Ryan tapped her number, then remembered Aurora Crew would be on the fireline now. Her voice mailbox was full. He made a mental note to tell her.

"Did Tara's phone get your bat signal?" Gunnar munched a fry.

Ryan chuckled at the superhero reference. "Yeah. She texted not to believe what I hear."

"Any idiot can get on social media and trash people with lies."

"Especially when none of it is true. Hudson's a demented, pathological liar. He wouldn't know truth if it bit him in the ass." Ryan swirled his coffee, frowning into his cup.

"I hope for both your sakes, none of it is." Gunner balled up a napkin and dropped it on his plate.

Ryan gestured with his phone. "Not much I can do until I talk to her."

"I beg to differ. We both know where one certain cockroach is, don't we?" Gunnar gave him a wicked look.

"What's that cunning Norske mind of yours conjuring?"

Gunnar grinned. "Remember the guys at your thirtieth birthday bash at Boone's house, jumping off the roof when the cops showed up?"

"How could I forget?"

"Boone's former Navy SEAL buddies. What do you suppose is their going rate to coerce a confession?" Gunnar worked a straw in his monster-sized coke.

Ryan stared blankly at him, then broke into an understanding smile. "Would they want money or favors?" He reached across and stole a fry from Gunnar's plate.

"If it's money, I'll pitch in for the cause. You may be ugly, but you have a good right hook and you don't suck fighting fire. And I like Tara." Gunnar helped himself to an abandoned French fry on Ryan's plate.

"Keep talking." Ryan tapped his phone screen off and set it on the table.

"We'll need a helo with heli-rappelle gear, a recording device, and a laptop. And lots of duct tape."

"Are you suggesting what I think you are?" Ryan pursed his lips and flicked his eyes at Gunnar. "Not too shabby for a pretty-boy, Olympic jock. You aren't just another shallow sycophant after all."

"I have my moments of genius. You're just not always privy to them." Gunnar tossed a fry at him.

Ryan held up his hands. "I've underestimated your badass self. Correct me if I'm wrong, but won't we go to jail if we're caught? Not to mention losing our jobs."

"No fire people or equipment would be involved. If anyone can get a recorded confession out of Hudson, Boone's former SEAL buddies can. What do you care how they get it? Hudson would be held accountable and not even Stepdaddy Martelle will be able to save him. And we'd be rid of him for good."

Ryan studied the ceiling, then leveled his eyes at Gunns. "Talk to Boone. But no one else can know."

Gunnar leaned in. "Don't worry. They'll stealth the shit out of this."

"Boone used to pilot aircraft on covert ops out of Elmendorf Air Force Base." Ryan scratched his stubble. "He lives for this Tom Clancy shit."

"That's why we need an A-Team. I'm no James Greer, and you're not Jack Ryan," chuckled Gunnar.

"Nah. Just Ryan." He grinned, his wheels spinning.

Gunnar gave him a thumbs-up. "Leave it to me. I'll take care of it."

"Our ride is here," Boone called out from the restaurant doorway.

"Speak of the devil." Ryan spotted the green AFS bus idling outside the open door.

Reeking of smoke, greasy fried food, and unspeakable body odors, Gunnar and Ryan gathered their gear. Grinning ear-to-ear, they ambled out the door with the rest of the jumpers.

How did that song go by Justin Timberlake? *What Goes Around Comes Around.* Ryan hummed a few notes and smiled.

Some days ended a helluva lot better than others.

*A*urora Crew traversed the smoking and blackened boreal forest on their way to the right flank. They ascended a steep, mountain slope, working their way up to a ridge through dense fuels of spindly, black spruce.

Tara noted Silva knitting his brows whenever he glanced at his GPS. He studied it often, along with fits of coughing.

One of the eighteen firefighting rules Ryan had emphasized in training: *Know what the fire is doing at all times.* The rule Tara had ignored in Montana when she nearly lost her life. And here she was, breaking the rule again.

The crew lost track of the fire when they had dipped in

elevation. The smoke became dense. The situation reports on the radio said storm cells had blown up the Shackelford Fire and it was running west.

If Tara wasn't mistaken, they were west of the main fire, side-hilling a slope. She tried to quell her nervousness by focusing on other things. Like pain.

"Does anyone have moleskin? My blisters have blisters." Tara's voice wobbled as her boots trampled roots and she side-stepped fallen trees.

Silva coughed and stopped in front of Tara. "Waters, I have some. I'll get you fixed up."

"Thanks, Jon." If she hadn't fallen for Ryan, she might have for Jon. He was a kind, generous person. And because he knew fire and his way around the woods, she felt reassured with him leading the crew. But the frequency of his coughing alarmed her. "Jon, are you okay?"

"Yeah, Silva, why are you coughing so much?" Rego chimed in, walking behind Tara.

"I do this sometimes. No big deal." He shook his head, poo-pooing it.

Besides herself, Rego and Silva were the most woods savvy. Since Hudson was gone, she had come to know Rego. He wasn't the jerk she first judged him to be. As the oldest crew member, he was old-school in his views about women working in fire. He had explained to Tara how hard it was to resist his instinct to protect the opposite gender on and off the job, because his mom had drilled it into him. Tara no longer faulted him for thinking that way. Instead, she demonstrated that she could handle any aspect of the job, and he seemed to respect her for it.

The crew stopped walking while Silva checked his GPS and topo map. His coughing sounded bad. Thick smoke saturated the air.

Tara approached him. "Jon, what does the GPS say?"

Silva squinted at the tracker screen and scrutinized his topographic map. "We hiked up and down these two finger ridges, so we must be on this third one, here. Deadman's Ravine." He pointed his pinky finger at a wide area between the left and right fire flanks.

Tara winced at the name 'Deadman's Ravine,' and peered at the map. "Are you sure? This mountain has five finger ridges." The terrain was tricky, even for expert map readers.

"According to the GPS, we're on track to our target location," said Silva. "Pick up the pace. Let's go." He took off and everyone followed.

Air quality worsened, as they progressed along the ravine. Tara inhaled smoke and coughed. Angela had loaned her a faded, red neckerchief that she fished from her pocket and tied around her head to cover her mouth and nose.

Her head pounded, pulsating her temples. Each inhale increased the pain. The smoke was so thick she thought her head would explode. She unsnapped her canteen from her harness and swigged some water. Her gut churned, noticing everyone else doing the same.

Angela came up behind her. "I have a splitting headache."

Tara called over her shoulder. "Jon, what are they saying on the radio? Where's the head of the fire?"

"Wait a minute." Silva bent and wheezed. He coughed so hard she thought his lung might fall out. She didn't like the sound of it. "Jon, are you okay?"

He pulled out an inhaler and took a few puffs. He exhaled, coughing. "Don't worry. I'm fine," he choked out.

"You don't sound like it." She knew he wasn't if he carried an inhaler.

Tara fought for calm. She'd become accustomed to Silva taking charge, but his breathing was deteriorating. The smoke was bad and the entire crew had trouble breathing. They must be near the fire's runaway head—and weren't supposed to be here.

Her eyes burned and she lowered her goggles. She took the map from Silva's gloved hand. "Let me see your GPS."

He handed her the tracker. She squinted at the screen, then the topo map. The latitude and longitude numbers were not lining up.

Tara's heart thudded. "Jon, are you sure we have the correct lat and long?"

"I wrote it down." He showed her his small note pad with the numbers scratched on it.

She compared what he'd written with the GPS screen and her chest clenched. "These numbers don't match." She showed him. "We're on the wrong ridge."

"Impossible," Silva choked out, erupting into a coughing fit.

"I need your radio." Tara pulled his radio from his waist belt and keyed it. "Rego, hold up, we need to regroup." The crew line stopped moving.

She ran ahead to Rego and showed him the map. "The GPS put us on the wrong ridge. There must be a miscommunication of the numbers somehow. Silva's coughing so bad he can hardly talk."

Rego pointed to a ridge on the map. "Shouldn't we be on this fifth finger ridge to reach the right flank?"

"Yes. But we can't see where the fire is from the bottom of this ravine. We should have reached the right flank by now." Tara took the map from Rego and studied it, trying to recall how many smaller ridges they'd traversed. She pointed with her little finger. "We must be here, on this middle ridge."

Rego held up his hand. "Wait, listen."

The crew gathered around Rego and Tara as a plane's engine whine grew louder and zoomed directly over them. A low, deep rumble followed.

"Spotter plane for an air tanker." Tara peered up into smoke.

"What are they doing here?" asked Tupa. "Retardant ships hit the hottest parts of the fire."

"We must be...oh shit," said Rego, wide-eyed. Everyone exchanged bewildered looks as the low rumble increased to a deafening one.

The familiar engine sound told Tara it was a DC-10 on final for a drop. "Incoming retardant ship."

"But what's it doing *here?*" yelled Tupa, squinting upwards in a futile attempt to see through the smoke.

The unmistakable squeal of metal doors opening clued Tara in. "Everyone, down!"

The crew hit the ground like balled-up hedgehogs braced for danger, hands clasped behind necks. The thunderous roar sounded like a NASA rocket launch, vibrating Tara's insides.

"Not good, people!" yelled Tupa, as metal gates squeaked open, raining thousands of pounds of scarlet gel on Aurora Crew.

Thick glop slapped their backs with the force of an ocean wave. Tara's backpack broke some of the force, but the wind still whooshed from her lungs. The mighty DC-10 thundered past, the sound of its jet engines fading. The entire landscape became the color of sockeye salmon meat, including Aurora Crew.

"What the fuck!" Rego jumped up in battle-ready mode. He and Tara exchanged crazed looks.

"Doesn't matter what the map or GPS says, we have to get out of here." Tara struggled for composure. She didn't want to panic anyone. *How would Ryan handle this? He'd stay calm and get them the hell out.*

Silva doubled over coughing and stumbled back. Liz appeared at his side to help. His coughing prevented him from speaking and all eyes fixed on Tara and Rego.

Tara took a confidence-building breath and worked to keep her voice from wobbling. "You guys all realize we're in the path of the head." She squatted to wipe away gel to inspect the vegetation. It was green, not black. Somehow, they'd wandered from the black to the unsafe, flammable green.

Her heart nearly stopped as a freight train sound thundered in the distance. The sound grew louder by the second. Alarm flashed through the crew. *The runaway head of the fire!*

Tara wondered how close it was. A convective heat wave answered her question.

"We need to get out of here *fast!*" She locked stares with Rego, and he gave her a quick nod.

She turned to Silva. "Jon?"

He nodded at her, coughing.

"He's having trouble breathing, you'd better take charge." Liz had her arm around Jon's waist, helping him walk.

Silva pointed at Tara. "Yes. You're in charge," he croaked, hacking out another lung. He yanked his radio from his belt and held it out to her.

She froze. The image of the doomed homeowner in Montana flashed. She'd be damned if that would happen again. Only this time it would be seventeen times over.

Tara keyed Silva's radio. "Air support, this is Aurora Crew. We seem to be in front of the head. Can you drop another load?"

No response.

"Air attack, this is Aurora Crew, do you copy?" Tara peered at the energy bars on the radio screen. Zero, zilch. She looked up at Rego. "I need a fresh battery. Find Silva's battery bag."

Rego darted over to Silva and searched his pack. Silva stuck his hands in his pockets and shook his head at Rego.

"He must have dropped his battery pouch," reported Rego.

"Please don't say that." Tara felt nauseous and her head pounded. *They were on their own.*

Schwartz vomited. People were sick from lack of oxygen.

Tara shoved the GPS tracker into her back pocket and held out the dog-eared topo map to Rego. "Screw the GPS. Where do you think we are according to this?"

"Here, Deadman's Ravine." He pointed to the same spot on the map both Silva and Tara had pointed out.

"We have to climb this damn-near vertical mountain." Tara squinted at an area on the topo map where the lines squeezed together. "This is our only way out."

Rego glanced at the barely visible base of the mountain. "We sure as hell can't stay here." Debris and firebrands now rained down on them.

Tara returned the dead radio into Silva's waist holster. "I'll get everyone out, okay?"

"Thanks." Silva nodded with bloodshot eyes. A racking cough consumed him, and he doubled over.

"Listen up, everyone," shouted Tara, pointing to the slope. "I'm taking over for Silva. We've got to run for it up that steep mountain. Rego, help me get everyone up. Haul ass!" Tara knew this escape route was a gamble. Fire ran fastest uphill, but they'd die if they stayed in the ravine.

"Don't have to tell me twice," Tupa intoned in his deep voice.

"Tupa, help Liz with Silva. Go!" Tara dodged airborne debris as she broke into a run to the base of the hellacious mountain.

Rego herded the crew like a border collie as they followed Tara up the mountain like frightened, lost children. Tupa grabbed Silva on one side and Liz took the other, sliding her arm around Silva's waist. He towered over her, but she was strong. If anyone could get Jon up the mountain, Liz could.

Tara brought up the rear to make sure everyone got out before the ravine lived up to its name. She scrambled up, clawing at rocks and clutching alder to hoist herself up the near-vertical incline. Sometimes she clambered on all fours. She tripped on a dropped Pulaski and nearly lost her footing. Moving fast proved treacherous, but they had no choice.

It was then she thought of her good friend. She called out. "Angela, are you up there?"

"Behind you," called out Liz. She barely made out the figures of Liz and Silva up ahead in the heavy smoke.

Tara peered behind to see a figure climbing. "Angela?"

"I'm here," panted Angela.

"Come on, Angie, hurry!" Tara thought everyone was ahead of her. In her near-panic state she hadn't noticed Angela lagging behind.

An alder branch slapped Tara's face as she continued scaling upslope. Needle-sharp spruce boughs spiked her skin. Thank God for goggles.

Another low rumble grew louder.

"Retardant ship is back!" shouted Tara. The DC-10 was a sure indicator they'd die if they couldn't outrun the flames. Tara prayed the drop would buy them time enough to escape. Her head throbbed.

"Everyone down!"

Metal gates opened, hurling another ocean of gel at them as the DC-10 passed over, leaving only the petrifying rumble and the snap of flames powered by high winds.

"Go, go, go!" Tara's terror spurred her to climb faster.

A blood-curdling scream sounded behind her and faded. Tara stopped, coughing under her neckerchief. She peered down into smoke. "Angela?"

No answer.

"Angie, answer me!" Tara peered through the smoke. Couldn't see a damn thing. *Did Angela fall?*

"Liz, help Jon and keep going. I'm going back for Angela," Tara called up to her.

"Okay, but hurry." Liz tugged Silva upward and they vanished into the smoke.

Tara debated. She was alone, but she couldn't leave her crewmate. She picked her way back down, her boots seeking purchase on treacherous ground.

"Answer me, Angela!" she screamed, her boots sliding on loose rocks and dirt.

No response.

"Angela!" She dug her heels into the rock shale. Each downward progression meant death if she didn't get her ass in gear. Her next step avalanched her down a rockslide. Arms flailing, she clasped an alder, held on, and stopped herself from sliding to the bottom.

Her boot thudded against something. Coughing, she made out a figure, face down on the precipitous incline, unmoving.

"Talk to me, Angela." Tara knelt next to her. Still no response.

Oh God, is she dead?

Tara slapped her cheeks. "Angie, *please*, say something," she choked, tears rolling. She saw Angela's chest move. Breathing, but unconscious. She must have hit her head. No time for first aid. No time for anything. "Oh God, Angie, how do I get you up this stinking mountain?"

Think. Dad slung me over his shoulder when I was little. Fireman's carry.

Tara steadied herself and dug her boots in. She removed Angela's pack. She couldn't carry both and had no choice but to leave it. Grabbing Angela's arm, Tara tugged her friend to a sitting position, her head flopping like a rag doll. She bent to position Angela across her shoulder and struggled to stand. Her boot slid and she teetered, fighting to keep her balance.

She gripped Angela with her left arm and kept her right hand free to grasp brush and tree limbs to pull herself up. Her friend grew heavier with each uphill push. Tara clung to the side of the mountain, her head down. She lifted her left leg and dug her boot in for stability, then pushed off with her right foot. It was slow going with the extra weight.

The flame front closed in roaring like a pissed-off Godzilla, snapping and exploding trees. Smoke billowed, choking her. *Where's the damn ridgetop?*

Step up, dig in, step up, dig in.

Angela's too heavy. I won't make it.

She stopped, panting hard. Teetering, she lost her footing. As she fought to keep from skidding, Angela slid off her shoulder and rolled downhill.

"No-o-o--!" screamed Tara as her dear friend disappeared into heavy smoke.

CHAPTER 35

ombie met the jumper's bus when it stopped at the Jump Shack. He flagged down Ryan and Gunnar.

"A crew is in trouble on the Shackelford Fire. Need to send a couple of jumpers with current heli-rappel certification. Looks like it's you two." He peered over skinny eyeglasses at Ryan. "More hazard pay and overtime will put you one step closer to your Cessna."

The jumpers exchanged impassive looks.

Ryan marveled at Zombie knowing which carrot to dangle. It was no secret how badly Ryan wanted the Cessna. "Sure, why not? We'll need to unload and repack our gear."

"Make it quick," Zombie called after them as they headed toward the Jump Shack.

Ryan knew his boss had zero sympathy for jumpers. He continually reminded them they had all winter to rest, but they were *his* twenty-four seven, May through September.

"You're a Cessna whore," Gunnar muttered as they tramped inside to their lockers.

Ryan shoulder-bumped him. "Don't see you turning down hazard and oats."

"What do you take me for, a dumb ski jock?" Gunnar grinned, heaving his pack onto the long bench in the middle of the locker room.

Ryan chuckled that his jump partner was anything but. "Not when I'm a Cessna whore." He sank to the bench for a moment to regroup, thankful he'd slept on the bus from Delta. His radio squawked. He pulled it from his holster and turned it up.

Max, the DC-10 pilot, was talking. "...saw a crew that shouldn't have been near the head. Made two drops to buy them some time. Hope they got out."

Engine noise as another pilot responded. "Why were they there?"

"No idea. I turned them pink."

"Hotshot crew?"

"Don't know. All I know is they shouldn't have been there."

Ryan and Gunnar moved fast to ready their gear for round two. He hoped this would be a smooth and quick operation, with nothing too terribly dire.

Zombie poked his head into the locker room. "Your ride's here."

Ryan shoved his radio in his holster and finished helping Gunnar into his jump suit. "If it's a hotshot crew, we'll embarrass the shit out of them."

"For sure," chuckled Gunnar, helping Ryan with his suit and gear.

They grabbed their day packs and first aid kits and clambered aboard the Dornier, ready to go. The props were already spinning.

Stu greeted them as they came onboard. "Here's the deal. We'll circle to see if you can fly. Max says smoke is dense and it's hard to see the ground, even with infrared. He was lucky to spot the crew. If we can't get close, you'll have to rappel in with Juliet. Zombie says you're both still certified, right?"

Ryan nodded. He and Gunnar had obtained their helicopter

rappelling certification at the Forest Service National Rappel Academy in Salmon, Idaho, when they crewed in California. Before the beginning of every fire season, Mel took them up in Juliet for refresher training to stay current with their certification.

The plane rolled and abruptly powered down. Stu emerged from the cockpit. "Change of plans. Max says too smoky for fixed wing. Mel's on his way with Juliet. You'll have to rappel in."

"Okay." The sudden change of plans didn't faze Ryan. It was part of the fire game. He and Gunnar picked up their gear and exited the plane as Melbourne lowered Juliet to the tarmac.

Zombie stood outside the door holding two Army green Nomex flight suits.

"Guess we won't need these." Ryan peeled off his Kevlar suit from over his yellow and green Nomex.

Zombie shoved a flight suit at him. "Boone's your rappel spotter."

Ryan took the suit and quickly stepped into it. He stuck his arms in and pulled it over his shoulders. "What do we know about the crew?"

"We don't know their status, other than they escaped the blow-up and made it to a ridgetop. What the hell they were doing at the head of the fire is anyone's guess. Radio communication is down, so their batteries must have died. Here take this," grumbled Zombie, handing Ryan a radio. "This one has a fresh battery. Give me yours."

Ryan swapped radios. "Thanks, Zombie." The nickname slipped out, but Ryan was too weary to give a shit.

Zombie ignored it. "Make sure everyone comes back safely. Including yourselves," he mumbled and headed into the Jump Shack.

Ryan and Gunnar waited for Boone to exit the helo so he could do his required spot checks of their gear. He tapped their leather gloves, PG packs, and rappel harnesses and gave them a thumbs-up. The three men ducked under the rotors to hoist themselves inside Juliet's rear crew door.

Once onboard, Boone clipped each man to a sturdy web line connected to a "Y" static line, anchoring them to the inside of the helicopter. Ryan in turn hooked Boone to an anchor system, since Boone would be leaning out the door to ensure the men rappelled safely to the ground, while Mel hovered in place.

All wore white helmets with built-in headphones and hot mics. Ryan and Gunnar buckled into stiff canvas seats facing backward. Boone sat in the spotter's seat, facing forward. He'd been an Air Force flight engineer, and Ryan placed full faith and confidence in his spotter capabilities, same as he did with Stu.

Rappelling from helicopters was much easier on his knees, back and other joints, but Ryan preferred smokejumping. To him, it was easier than perching on helo skids in midair and inverting to dangle and rappel to the ground.

Boone leaned toward them. "Did Zombie brief you?"

"Somewhat."

"You'll be dropping into dense timber on a ridgetop where the crew is trapped. When you hit the ground, assess the situation, and relay their status. Stabilize the injured and make a helispot to land Juliet for transport."

"Copy that." Ryan peered out the window. The smoke worsened the closer they came to their destination. More acreage had burned since he'd jumped the other end of the Shackelford Fire to save the air force base. As they neared the fire, gusts swung Juliet like a loose pendulum.

He glimpsed wide smoke columns rolling skyward. The fire had regained control, whirling flame in all directions, increasing his pucker factor. Fire conditions like these electrified his neck hairs enough to light up Fairbanks.

Tara, I hope you're nowhere near this shit.

Through holes in the smoke, he spotted pink and yellow shirts, strung out along a blackened, smoking ridgetop. The crew must have escaped up that near-vertical slope to the ridge. A narrow escape, for sure. Ryan shook his head at how lucky they were.

Boone's voice boomed in his ears. "Do you spot the crew? We'll drop you five hundred feet to the west of them. Rappelers, stand by. Will be tricky to hold Juliet still in these winds."

Both men nodded.

Boone spoke to Mel. "This is the closest we can get. Establish hover over this small clearing."

Smoke drifted, allowing glimpses of timber sticking up like furry toothpicks on the ridge. Mel slowed Juliet's forward momentum and held his bird stationary, as Boone instructed.

"Hover established. I'll set you up at two hundred feet and move you up from there. Get ready," Mel instructed in their headsets.

Boone responded. "Ready. Opening doors. Starboard door open."

Mel's voice streamed into his ears. "Master caution."

"Master caution reset. Position to the left—three, two, one, hold. Bring her thirty feet lower."

"Opening doors. Port and starboard doors open," reported Boone. "Good for altitude. How's your power?"

"Good." Mel scanned his airspace.

"We're still high. Bring her down some. Dropping ropes." Boone peered below the helo, then turned to Ryan and Gunnar.

"Heli-rappelers, hook up." Boone extended his arms, pointing out both sides like a flight attendant doing a safety demo. "Rappelers to the skids."

Ryan hooked himself up and Boone inspected his connections and checked hover conditions.

"Rappel the shit out of this, boys. Get into position."

Ryan exited the port door. Gunnar out the starboard. They poised on the skids, feet spread, ready to rappel the ropes. They leaned back as the rocking helicopter hovered, Mel holding Juliet steady as she goes. A strong gust swung them, and Mel revved the rotors to counter the offset. *Don't look at the bouncing landscape. Don't want to lose my bison burger.*

"Rapellers, go!"

Both men hit the release on their ropes, leaned back to an almost upside-down position, then eased themselves to the ground below. Despite Mel's best efforts, Juliet swung wildly, causing Ryan and Gunnar to sway like puppets on a string.

"Damn!" yelled Ryan. Gunnar cussed the equivalent in Norwegian from the other side.

Ryan gauged the distance to the ground from the skids. "This is why I switched to smokejumping," he muttered as the ropes lowered him, swinging under rotor wash and the deafening *whup-whup* of Juliet's blades.

His feet hit the ground in time for him to see a wall of fire race across a gully and up the next ridge. The hovering helo kicked up ash, soot, and loose debris. Ryan adjusted his goggles and tugged his neckerchief over his nose and mouth.

Boone dropped the ropes and two water cubie-containers. Juliet swung away, vanishing into smoke.

Ryan removed his helmet and stuffed it in his day pack, along with his EMT kit. He and Gunns hustled along the ridgetop to reach the crew.

He held his breath, hoping for no injuries.

CHAPTER 36

*T*ara slid fast down the rock shale on her butt, digging her heels in to control her speed. She sighed relief to find that a tree had stopped Angela from rolling further down the steep incline. She moaned as Tara grabbed hold of her arm and hoisted her once more over her right shoulder, digging one boot in at a time, resuming her climb. *I have to get up this sorry-assed mountain.*

She continued up, squinting into smoke at a dark shape. Angela moaned. As Tara moved closer, the shape became a gray, rocky ledge, with rocks piled above and around it. Wild-eyed and legs trembling with fresh panic, she knew they were trapped. She desperately searched for an escape.

"No, God no!"

Sweat poured out of Tara as she lowered Angela to the rocky ground. She glanced back at the smoky abyss for a glimpse of fire, but only heard its snapping, deadly approach. Too smoky to see or breathe. She coughed hard.

They were out of time. Her chest clenched at the cruel, unthinkable truth that she couldn't outrun this. Sorrow pushed up, ripping her insides.

The sound of the fire petrified her, along with the horror of what it would feel like to burn alive. Disappearing, as the old man had in the Montana fire, bored a hole in her soul. She didn't want to simply disappear. No one would find their bodies. Angela's daddy would have no body to bury.

"Angie, wake up." Tara shook her friend.

Angela lolled her head, but only moaned.

Tara rolled her pack off her shoulders and fumbled for her fire shelter. Their only chance for survival was to deploy their shelters on this rocky outcrop. Her eyes darted around, surveying their situation. She hoped the rocks would prevent flames from reaching them as the fire burned upslope.

A horrifying thought struck. *I left Angela's pack behind with her fire shelter!*

"Oh, God." The breath left her lungs. She swallowed hard.

She would have to fit them both inside a fire shelter designed for one person. Could two people survive entrapment in the same one? She racked her brain. Three people had survived a shelter deployment in a burnover on the Kincade Fire in California, in October of 2019. She knew of situations where two firefighters had survived in one entrapment.

But this was a last resort, not a fail-safe measure. Shelters had limitations. They weren't designed to withstand more than five hundred degrees Fahrenheit before disintegrating. *Please God. Don't let this fire burn hotter than that.*

Sweat ran under her shirt and pooled at the small of her back. "Angie, we have to get in my shelter. Now!"

Angela didn't move.

Tara clawed at apple-sized rocks, tossing them aside, burrowing down to soil so they'd have pockets of precious oxygen. Ryan's voice played in her brain. *Toss all fusees away from a deployed shelter. They could ignite.* She groped for her fusees and heaved them downhill.

Ryan will chew her out after his repeated safety lectures and her assuring him she'd be safe. Here she was again, caught in another situation. She felt cursed without Dad's bandana. She imagined Jim Dolan shaking his head if she died. Like father, like daughter.

She needed to set the GPS tracker to help/rescue mode so people could find her. She tapped her back pocket. Nothing there. The pockets were torn out. The GPS must have fallen out when she slid down the mountain on her ass. *Dammit.*

As she had done a gazillion times in training, she unzipped the rectangular carry case, yanked the thick red tape, and pulled the ring tab. She pulled the tightly packed shelter out and shook it. Ryan's countless drills with this familiar routine offered her an illusion of control—until the wind whipped the silver shelter like a sail on a boat, determined to wrench it from her grasp.

"Stop it, dammit!" she sobbed, squeezing her fists tight as she tussled with it. The stupid thing wouldn't cooperate. "I'm putting my shelter over both of us. Roll onto your stomach." Tara couldn't let go of the shelter to position Angela's face to the ground.

Her crewmate remained still.

Tara kicked her in frustration. "Roll over!"

"Ow!" Angela cried out, struggling to roll over. "My knee's out of joint."

"We don't have time, Angie." She panted.

The fire galloped up the slope, radiant heat cooking her skin. Her Nomex felt like tissue paper as she struggled to position the wind-blown shelter to insert her foot inside a corner strap. Instead, it wrenched free, whipping frenetically with a mind of its own. She watched, horrified, as it flew from her hand and blew against a tall rock wall behind the outcrop.

"No-o-o-o!"

Tara stumbled over Angela, frantic in her haste to catch it before it flew away. She cried out as the winds slid it up the craggy, gray wall. One end flapped to break free. She heaved herself at it, her shoulder slamming into granite.

"Aagghh!" she cried out in pain.

Winding a corner of the shelter around her fist, she folded it into her body so the winds couldn't snatch it again. She choked back sobs and stumbled back to Angela, face down on the rocks. With one hand clutching the shelter, she bent to grab hold of Angie's shirt collar, dragging her to where she'd cleared the rocks. She straddled her friend, kicking one foot inside a corner strap and inserted the other in the opposite corner. Making sure the end would cover Angela's boots, her eye caught something scurrying toward them. A squirrel. *Welcome to our nightmare.*

She fell on top of Angela while gripping the handles of each top corner, and wriggled them under the shelter, like a cocoon. The wind jerked the shelter like a kinetic force. With all her strength, she pressed the four corners to the rocks. *Dear God, please give me the strength to hold this down.*

"Press your mouth and nose to the ground," Tara ordered against the din of crackle, snap, and roar.

Angela wriggled, making it difficult for Tara to hold the corners down.

"Stop moving. I can't hold it!" yelled Tara.

"I want out. I can't stay here." Angela continued squirming.

"If you do, we die!" Tara pressed her taller body against her friend with sheer force of will. Despite Angela's frenetic, yet weak attempts to wiggle free, Tara struggled to hold the four corners in place. "Lie still, Angie, please," she pleaded, burying her face in her friend's shoulder.

Relentless, tornadic winds whipped their only shield between life and death: A thin piece of aluminum foil laminated to a thin sheet of silica, Kevlar and Nomex. The winds were at least seventy miles per hour.

Please God, let it be enough, prayed Tara as the obdurate sides of the shelter pulled away and flapped. If hot gases were to leak in, their lungs would sear. Sure death.

Tara strained every muscle to press all four corners of the obstinate shelter to the ground.

"Angie, help me hold this. Tuck the sides under your elbows and knees." Tara's voice competed with the inferno's roar sounding like a rocket lifting off.

Angela tucked the side under her right knee, then pressed her elbows to the ground to anchor the sides. Tara couldn't tuck anything, her arms and legs splayed like Da Vinci's Vitruvian Man, pressing the four corners to the earth with such force she'd surely push through to Antarctica. A polar ice cap would be a godsend after this holy hell.

Armageddon rained embers and burning debris on the shelter. Tara prayed they wouldn't burn holes in it. She knocked stubborn debris off by shifting her weight, while holding down the edges. Trees snapped and broke, becoming airborne missiles, vibrating the earth when they crashed. *Please don't let a burning tree fall on us.*

"I'm scared. I can't stay here," cried Angela.

Tara pressed her mouth to Angie's ear. "It'll be over soon… it'll be okay, it'll be okay…okay…okay…" She rambled, saying anything to soothe her friend.

The inferno's main push surged like a tsunami, thundering like a thousand DC-10s. The momentum lifted Tara's boots as if someone yanked them with a rope. She fought to keep the shelter from flipping over.

Here it comes. *The Burnover.* "Hail Mary full of grace—oh God, oh Ryan…"

She forced her boots to the ground as the flame wave hit their shelter like a tornado. Her flesh felt as it were broiling on a high oven setting. *This is what cremation feels like. Hail Mary Our Father I don't want to die…*

The sound of flames disemboweling timber terrified her.

Branches crashed, resin snapped, rocks cracked. A leviathan intent on obliteration.

The end of their world.

She squeezed her eyes closed. Foil rippled and snapped as wind bent flames close. Fear replaced oxygen, consuming every cell in her body. The gloves weren't enough. Her hands trembled from relentless tension and she couldn't hold the shelter down any longer. But she'd be damned to let hell's fury have it.

"No way, bitch! You'll have to come and get us!" she raged, defiance bleeding out her veins. She wouldn't go down without a fight. But she was losing the battle.

I'm going to die.

At least she wouldn't die alone. Part of her cried *don't give up* and the other half shrieked, *get it over with*. Her heart foundered as pieces of life flickered a steady stream of people, places, and the love she'd take with her; Mom, Dad, Travis, her friends, her crew, Angela...and Ryan. Next to Jim Dolan, Ryan was the closest thing she had to family. She'd known it from the beginning but wasted precious time denying it.

She loved Ryan more than anything. You don't know what you've got...

Till it's gone.

"Tell Ryan I love him," she choked out into Angela's ear. "If you live and I don't...promise me you'll tell him."

"Don't. God, don't say that!" Angela's voice muffled with heaving sobs.

"Promise me. Do it or he'll never know!" wheezed Tara. Her face contorted, muscles trembling from the effort of her arms and legs pressing incessantly to the ground. Toxic gases had seeped in. What little moisture remained inside her, rolled out as tears.

"No, no, please don't," sobbed Angela, her words barely audible as the fire storm intensified.

"Promise, dammit!" Tara felt herself cough but couldn't hear it against the inferno's jet engine roar.

She felt, rather than heard Angela's whimper. "I promise…"

Every word hurt Tara's ravaged lungs. "Don't open…till the fire's gone. Stay here—promise me," she gasped as heavy debris hurtled onto the foil, threatening to collapse it.

So, so hot. Moisture oozed from every pore. Tara's back baked. Her breath came short and fast, pounding her temples.

"I promise," coughed out Angela between sobs.

Tara's one supreme wish was to take another breath. Without much oxygen, she could only suck in tiny hiccups. If God were merciful, they would die quick from toxic gases before burning to death. Her poor, shredded lungs were failing her.

"Love you, Angie…love you," she rasped. Weak and light-headed, she tried to resist passing out. Her breaths grew short and less frequent. A weird euphoria waved through her and a peaceful detachment took hold as she waited for the wildfire to rob her of life.

She stopped fighting and resigned to the force hellbent on destroying her.

The mighty leviathan had won.

As Tara's universe faded, a thunderous roar vibrated through her and a heavy weight pressed down. The crashing, snapping, the heat, Angela's sobbing—all ebbed from consciousness as she spiraled down…down…down…

Into the black.

CHAPTER 37

"We're so glad to see you," Liz cried out as Ryan and Gunnar approached the crew.

"We didn't know it was Aurora Crew in trouble." Ryan peered around Liz, scanning for red hair under a yellow hardhat.

"O'Connor." Rego strode to greet them. "Hey man, glad you're here. We have minor injuries, nothing major. Smoke inhalation, mostly. Scrapes and cuts." He gestured to the group, sitting on the ground. "And Silva's asthma."

Ryan did a double take. "Is Silva okay? What's wrong with your radios?"

"Liz calmed Jon down and he's breathing easier. Somewhere he lost his battery bag." Rego shrugged. "This whole thing is a clusterfuck of magnanimous proportion."

"We'll deal with that later. For now, let's get everyone out of here."

Gunnar lugged a cubie to Rego. "Get these people some water, then grab some guys and clear a spot for Juliet to land."

"I'm on it." Rego took the container and set to work pouring water into cups and canteens for the crew.

Ryan made a superhuman scan of every crew member. *Where was Tara?*

"Tara and Angela—" Liz's voice caught. "—they didn't make it, Ryan. I'm so sorry," she sobbed.

"What do you mean, they didn't make it?" The unease in his stomach shot through his chest up to his throat. *Not Tara.*

He'd hit the ground without a chute. "Where…how?"

"Jon had a bad asthma attack and needed help to get up the freaking mountain. Tara was behind me and said she was going back down for Angela. Everyone made it to the top, but them—" Liz choked up again.

Silva came over and put an arm around Liz. Holding an inhaler, he stared at Ryan. "Find Tara. We'd all be dead if it weren't for her. It's my fault. I screwed up the coordinates," he said with a hoarse voice.

Ryan only stared. Words weren't coming at all right now.

"Jon, it's not your fault," Liz chided him. "Everyone got confused in this terrain."

Ryan braced himself. "Talk to me, Liz."

She turned to him. "Angela must have fallen. No one could see in the smoke. I couldn't help Tara look for her. I had to help Jon. The fire chased us uphill." She put a hand to her mouth.

Silva squeezed her shoulder and she composed herself. "Jon has asthma. Tupa and the rest inhaled smoke and have minor cuts, but they seem okay."

Ryan and Gunnar exchanged uneasy glances, then Ryan took charge. "We'll take it from here. Gunnar, triage. Figure out who's injured, then organize groups for transport. Coordinate with Mel. Hopefully, it'll clear enough to set Juliet down on this ridge. Keep your radio handy. I have to get down the mountain." Every second counted. *I should already be down there.*

He backed up to talk to the crew. Many coughed as they sat on the ground. "Aurora, listen up. We'll get everyone out. Mel is standing by with Juliet. I'm heading down to search for Tara and Angela." Ryan keyed his radio. "Seven four Juliet, do you copy?"

"Copy. Seven four Juliet," Mel responded.

Ryan rapid-fired into his radio. "Status update. Minor injuries. Three trips, six per load. Two firefighters—" He hesitated, words catching his throat. "—two firefighters unaccounted for. I'm on a search and rescue. Gunnar will coordinate with you."

"Copy. Want me to fly a grid, see if I can spot them?"

"Affirmative. Do it and keep me posted. Heading downslope now. O'Connor clear." He holstered his radio and stared at Liz.

"Tell me where you last saw Tara and Angela. Show me your escape route." He studied the blackened slope, hoping the women would appear. His insides turned over.

Liz pointed along the ridgetop. "Go two hundred feet along the ridge, then head down from that crooked snag."

Silva spoke up. "I'll help."

"No Jon, stay here. Your asthma will worsen," cautioned Liz.

"I need to help search. I love her too, you know." Silva's coughing sounded painful.

Silva's words jarred Ryan, but he maintained a neutral expression. "Don't worry. We'll find her. We'll find them both."

Ryan pulled Rego aside. "Help Liz keep Jon still. The more he moves around, the worse his cough will be. Are you willing to take charge of the crew?"

"Yeah." Rego jerked his head at the charred slope. "You'd better get your ass down there. Tara would be here if she weren't in serious trouble."

Tara's squad approached, led by Tupa. "O'Connor, me and Afi Slayers will help search." He gestured at the guys who'd gathered around them.

"I need everyone to stay here. I don't want people spread out in case this fire changes its mind." Ryan scrutinized the smoking, devastated slope he was about to traverse. Some stumps were still burning. He took off sprinting along the ridge.

"Ryno, wait!" Gunnar caught up to him. "I should go with you. You'll need me in case—when you find them. You can't get both out by yourself."

He stared hard at his jump partner. "Good point. Put Rego in charge. Silva's in no condition to coordinate crew retrieval."

Gunnar went back to Rego, briefed him, and gave him his radio and extra batteries.

Ryan resumed jogging along the ridge and pulled out his radio. "Seven four Juliet, Nick Rego is heading up crew retrieval. Gunnar's coming with me."

"Got it," replied Melbourne, Juliet's rotors sounding in the background.

Silva's declaration of love for Tara knocked Ryan back. He knew Silva had tried to win her affection, but he hadn't expect him to be in love with her. But right now, Ryan cared more about finding Tara than worrying about which of them had won her heart.

He wasted no time plunging downhill into the apocalyptic terrain. Nothing but smoking black interspersed with gray and still-burning snags. The fire storm had moved on, leaving devastation in its wake.

As he tore down the scorched slope at breakneck speed, Ryan slapped his first aid kit, making sure he'd remembered to strap it to his waist. He'd also strapped two water canteens to his other side. He charged through the black, Gunnar working to keep up, ash and smoke kicking up behind them.

This afternoon when lifting off from Fort Wainwright, the furthest thing from Ryan's mind was that he'd be searching for Tara. The premonition and unease he'd had since leaving her bed had been about her, not Travis McGuire's death.

Ryan's worst fear had always been that something terrible would happen to Tara on a fire. And now he knew why.

He loved her.

Smoke spiraled up and around still-standing trees, all in danger of toppling to the ground without warning. The mountain was so steep he slid on his ass in places, skidding in ash and soot. He put his neckerchief over his nose and mouth.

Radio static. "O'Connor, this is Max. Do you copy?"

He lifted his radio and keyed it. "Copy. Go ahead."

"Heard you talking to Juliet. I'm the one who notified AFS to assist the crew in trouble."

"Yeah, Aurora Crew. What can you tell me?"

"When I made the drops, I saw them in the path of the runaway head, so dropped two loads to buy them time to get out. Didn't understand what they were doing there."

"Uh-huh." He dug his boot heels into ash mixed with soil, rapidly traversing around still-burning stumps.

"Another thing. On final for a third drop, I saw a deployed shelter, so dropped mud on it."

"Where?"

"Halfway up from Deadman's Ravine, in a rocky area."

Ryan paused to peer downslope, spotting the burned-out, smoking ravine. "One shelter or two?" He wasn't sure he wanted to know.

"One. Didn't see a second."

A bomb hit his chest. *Fuck.*

Radio silence as this sunk in. Gunnar cast an uneasy glance at him as they thundered down the slope, sixty feet apart.

"Okay Max, thanks."

Ryan yelled at Gunnar. "We need to split up. They're somewhere along here." He pointed across the ruin.

"Gave Rego my radio. I'll whistle if I see anything." Gunnar split off, side-hilling the slope.

Whirring rotors. Melbourne must have heard Max's transmission and zeroed in on the location. "O'Connor, seven four

Juliet. I've ordered another helo to help transport crew. Thought I'd give you a hand first."

"Seven four Juliet, thanks for the help." Ryan waved up at his friend.

"I'll fly a back-and-forth grid to see if I can locate the shelters."

"Copy that, Juliet. O'Connor clear." Ryan would make a point to thank Mel. Time was of the essence.

"Come on, Melbourne, find them," muttered Ryan. *Alive.*

As if in response, Mel's voice came on the radio. "O'Connor."

"Go ahead."

"I see one shelter. Did you say there were two missing fire-fighters?"

"Yes."

"Only one shelter. In a stony area, next to a rock face."

Ryan's heart jumped. One shelter, one person. *Where was the other?* Dread made a ruthless assault on his chest. He skidded to a halt. Keyed his radio but couldn't speak, fixated on the barren black.

Endless trails of smoke drifted where the breeze slanted them. A crackle and snap of splintering wood, then a *whump* behind him. A burned-out tree succumbed to gravity. Unphased, he didn't look back.

One shelter. Fuck.

Glancing down, he spotted what used to be a Pulaski, buried in ash, it's handle burned off. He bent to pick up the hot metal with his gloved hand. Gritting his teeth, he emitted a primitive sound and hurled it as far as he could. He watched it spin through the air and fall back to the ashes.

Mel's voice. "O'Connor, you copy?"

He swallowed hard, dreading the inevitable. "Yeah. Lead me in."

"Give me a mirror signal. I'll guide you to the site."

"Okay." Ryan pulled his signal mirror from his day pack and flashed it at the circling helo.

"I see you. You're not far. Sidehill east, then south to the rocky area. You'll see it."

"Any signs of life?" Ryan wasn't sure he had the courage to face who—or what he may find. He jammed the mirror back in his pack.

"Negative. Leaving you to it. I'll standby." Mel circled in a wide berth above the area.

"Thanks, Juliet. Clear." Ryan scrambled downhill as fast as his feet could carry him. Gray shale led to the outcrop Mel had spotted. Sliding to a stop, he spotted the rocky ledge through gutted trees. Trepidation took hold of him. He yanked off his glove and put two fingers in his mouth, whistling for Gunnar.

Gunnar whistled back.

Ryan lit a fusee and tossed it high as he could to let his partner know his location. No need to worry about torching anything. There was nothing left to burn.

Gunnar appeared next to him. "Found this." He held out a black, melted object that looked to be a GPS tracking device at one time. It turned Ryan's blood to ice.

Ryan took it from him, staring at the mutilated screen. Shoved it in his pocket.

"Look. There." Gunnar pointed through seared trees at an orange, charcoaled lump on the ground.

Ryan blinked. "Not sure I can do this." He spoke so low Gunnar leaned in.

Gunnar nudged Ryan's arm with the back of his hand. "I'll do it. Wait here."

You must suck it up and do this. "We'll both go." Ryan set his jaw and broke into a run.

"Tara! Are you there? Answer me!" hollered Ryan in his incident commander voice, tripping on rocks with Gunnar on his heels. A snap sounded behind them as another snag thudded to the ground.

Ryan slid on pink, charred rocks, and stopped. Bright coral-colored globules covered rocks, dirt, trees—and the shelter. Max's mud drop. The shelter was barely intact, a mottled pink and black, the color of barbecued, red salmon. Phos-Check retardant had transformed the landscape into a distorted red and black checkerboard.

Smokejumpers knew not to remove firefighters in burned over shelters, but to let the fire investigators do it. This was different—a unique situation. *Tara may be in there. I don't want strangers doing this. I need to do it.*

Every human being has a breaking point. Ryan never thought his would be something like this. He hesitated while Gunnar moved to the burned-over shelter. Tendrils of smoke rose from ash as Gunnar knelt next to it.

"Angela? Are you there? It's Gunnar."

Ryan's heart machine-gunned. To his amazement, a faint response came from inside.

"Gunnar! Oh God, you found us," responded a raspy, muffled voice.

Gunnar yanked up the side of the charred foil. It crumbled in his fingers.

Ryan sank to his knees in disbelief. There was Tara, draped over Angela. She looked asleep, her head resting on Angela's shoulder. Her Nomex had partially burned away. The back of her yellow shirt had burn holes, exposing a green tank top. The backs of her green Nomex trousers had burn holes as well. He pushed closer and removed his gloves. "Tara, it's Ryan." He gently shook her shoulder.

"Oh Ryan," cried out Angela, from underneath Tara. "Is she alive? She won't talk to me."

"It's okay. We'll take care of her." Ryan tore at his green, one-piece flight suit, ripping each leg over his boots as he yanked it off. He spread his torn suit on the ground and something chirped. A squirrel with an obviously broken leg huddled next to Angela on the floor of the seared shelter.

"Gunns, help me." Ryan lifted Tara's shoulders, while Gunnar grabbed her long legs. Her fingers curled into both palms. Ryan undid the chin strap of her yellow hardhat and eased it off. "Turn her over."

Tara was unconscious and her skin had turned blue. Ryan eased her onto his makeshift ground cover. He popped the buttons of her yellow shirt, adrenaline powering him. He pressed an ear to her chest. No heartbeat. He placed two fingers on her carotid. No pulse. Checked her breathing. Nothing.

"No, goddammit!" Ryan checked his watch to note the time, then started CPR compressions. "Gunnar, radio Mel to get over here, ASAP," he ordered his friend.

"Seven four Juliet, medevac emergency, retrieval of two fire-fighters," Gunnar rapid-fired into his radio. He helped Angela to a sitting position. She cried and coughed but otherwise seemed okay.

"Copy. On my way," replied Mel.

"Gunns, you do compression. I'll blow air," ordered Ryan.

Gunnar knelt next to him and interlocked his fingers, pumping Tara's chest with the heels of his hands. Ryan bent, tipped her head back, and covered her mouth with his, blowing air into her lungs.

"Tara came back for me after I fell. She saved my life. Don't let her die. Please, Ryan, don't let her die…" Angela was inconsolable.

"Switch," ordered Ryan, straining not to let worry of losing Tara overwhelm him. He and Gunnar exchanged places. Ryan interlocked his fingers and pressed the heels of his hands sharply on Tara's heart. *She can't die. I refuse to lose her.* "How long has she been like this?"

"I don't know, a couple minutes before you got here," rasped Angela.

Ryan checked his watch. *Ten minutes.* He bent to blow air into Tara's lungs. His brain zoomed at warp speed with the sole focus of reviving her.

"Tara made me promise..." sniffled Angela, clutching her injured knee. "If she died and I lived, she made me promise...to tell you she loved you. Or you'd never know. She loves you so much, Ryan." She choked off with heavy sobs.

He'd been so intent to restart Tara's lungs, Angela's words slid off him.

Fifteen minutes. Chrissakes, breathe, breathe!

Gunnar blew air into her lungs while Angela prayed.

Ryan kept the compressions steady, watching Tara for signs of life. He was vaguely aware of Juliet landing. He would give anything for a defibrillator. Time check. *Twenty. Fuck!*

"Switch." Ryan blew air into Tara's lungs and Gunnar pumped her heart.

Rotor wash swirled ash and soot, but Ryan couldn't stop. Even the time it took to load Tara on board the helo could cost her life if he didn't keep working to revive her.

Mel slowed the rotors as Stu and Silva appeared from Juliet. Silva wore goggles and an N-95 mask as he strode toward them.

Gunnar squatted next to Ryan. "We need to load her now."

"Not yet," Ryan snapped between breaths. Time check. *Twenty-five fucking minutes.* Any longer without oxygen and her brain cells would begin to die.

Ryan blew air into Tara's mouth. Her mouth twitched. He leaned back to assess when her eyelids fluttered.

"She's breathing!" Ryan placed fingers on the side of her neck. Hopeful as hell, he found a pulse. Faint, but a pulse.

Tara coughed.

"She's alive! Oh God, she's alive..." Angela trailed off, a hand over her mouth.

"Thank God," said Silva.

Ryan sighed relief. Every muscle in his body loosened. "Time to go." *Thank you, God.*

"Get Angela onboard first," instructed Ryan, cradling Tara's head in his lap.

He eased her upright to clear her lungs. She coughed so hard he felt the pain. She blinked her eyes partway open.

"Tara, can you hear me? Do you know who I am?" Ryan cupped her chin. He turned his ear to her mouth to listen for response, since whirring rotors drowned all other sound.

"Ry—Ryan," she whispered in his ear. She closed her eyes and her head rotated to the side.

"Tara, honey, stay awake. Stay with me, baby, stay with me." He checked her pulse. Heart still beating.

He would give anything for a saline drip. Ryan unsnapped his canteen from his belt and poured water in the cap. Dipping his finger in the water, he moistened Tara's lips, then tilted the cap to dribble it in her mouth. Her tongue ventured out to lick her bottom lip.

Ryan bent to kiss her. "Good girl. Breathe, honey breathe." He dribbled in more water.

Gunnar returned and squatted next to Ryan. He placed a hand on Ryan's shoulder. "Angela's on board. Time to load Tara. You okay, buddy?"

He nodded. "Be careful with her," he said gruffly as he pushed to stand.

Gunnar, Silva, and Stu carried Tara to Juliet, ducking under spinning rotors. Ryan climbed on board and cleared space on the floor between the front and rear-facing seats. He pulled out a space blanket and knelt to ease Tara into the helo head-first, with Silva and Gunnar holding her legs. Ryan pulled her inside and laid her on the blanket. Unconscious, but she still had a heart-beat. She'd stabilized. He kept a close eye on the rise and fall of her chest as he sat on the floor with her head in his lap.

Gunnar hopped in to help Angela into a back-facing seat and sat next to her. Stu rode shotgun and Silva climbed in back and sat on the other side of Angela. Gunnar knelt on the floor to wrap the knee she'd dislocated and somehow managed to pop back in place.

"All souls on board and buckled in!" Ryan called out to Mel.

"Ryno, oxygen in left compartment. Get the mask on her," shouted Mel, ramping up Juliet's rotors.

Ryan reached behind him to open the compartment. He pulled out a small tank and applied the mask to Tara's nose and mouth. He turned on the flow and closely monitored it, keeping an eye on the rise and fall of Tara's chest.

"Go like hell!" he shouted to his pilot buddy, relieved someone else was in charge for the moment.

He tried to uncurl Tara's fingers, but she'd gripped the shelter so hard her muscles had seized in that position.

Ryan sat and contemplated the woman of his dreams, who not only saved her crew but her own life and Angela's. He admired her. Sudden unworthiness washed over him. *She's a better person than I am. If she makes it, I have some apologizing to do.*

Did he imagine Angela saying that Tara loved him? Possibly. The entire time he worked to revive her was a blur. He kissed her forehead and whispered in her ear, willing her to respond.

Glancing up, Ryan caught Silva studying him with sad eyes. For a split-second he almost felt sorry for him—almost. He gave Silva a nod of thanks.

A tear crossed Angela's cheek and she blew Ryan a soft-hearted kiss.

Melbourne lifted Juliet, swung her sharp to the northwest, and flew maximum speed to Fairbanks Memorial Hospital.

CHAPTER 38

*T*ara walked away from the flames. A vibrant rainbow beckoned with all colors of the spectrum. It was the most beautiful thing she had ever seen.

"Punkin." A figure came toward her.

"Dad? Oh Dad, I've missed you so much!" Tara ran to his arms. Her father was as handsome as she'd remembered. "You've come back. I thought you were dead. It was awful. I was so lonely."

Her father put his knuckle under her chin, as he always did. "I'm sorry. It was my time to go."

"No, it wasn't. I love you. I want to stay with you."

"I want to be with you too, but you must go back."

"But I was prepared to die. I must have because you and I are together now. Please let me stay." Tara stood with him in tall, lazy grass mixed with a dazzling array of purplish, magenta flowers waving in a soft breeze.

"Oh, sweetie. How do I explain this?" He bent to pluck two of the bright flower stems and held up the fully blossomed one. "This is fireweed. My bloom reached the top because summer has ended for me. This one's mine."

He offered her the other. "This one is yours. It's partially bloomed because your summer hasn't ended yet."

Tara took the stem and looked up at him. "Dad, please don't leave me again. I have so much to tell you. If not for you, I wouldn't have been able to get my crew out—or get Angie up that mountain."

"You were determined to be a firefighter and I couldn't talk you out of it. I helped you that day with the rolling stump. Called your name so you'd get out of the way."

"I knew it! I knew it was you. But I still failed. I couldn't save Mom. Or you. Or the man in Montana. Not even Angela…or myself."

He cupped her face. "My precious girl. You've always thought you must prove yourself. But you don't. Not to me, not to anyone." He kissed her forehead. "You haven't failed…you've always put others first with your generous heart."

Tara looked away at the bright field of magenta. "But I have failed, especially you. And I've failed Ryan."

"You'll certainly fail him if you don't go back. Go to him. He loves you. Almost as much as I do."

Tara looked back at her father, but he was gone. "No… please, come back, come back…" *Why does everyone leave me?*

"Tara." A familiar voice called out to her.

She turned toward a brawny figure strutting toward her. "Travis?"

"Hi, gorgeous." Travis swaggered to her with his classic, dazzling smile and wavy dark hair. He took her in his arms. "I've missed you, babe."

"Travis, I'm sorry your chutes didn't open."

Travis cradled her face. "And I'm sorry for what I did to you. You didn't deserve it. But you can't stay here. Go back to O'Connor. He's the one who loves you. Go." Travis released her and she fell backward, plummeting in free fall. The rainbow faded and the fireweed flew from her grasp. She'd lost them all—

Dad, Travis, Angela...and now Ryan. She'd never see him again.

She had lost everything.

🔥

*T*ara coughed. *Where am I?*

Voices. "She's breathing...load her on Juliet...get Angela onboard..."

She couldn't open her eyes. A heaviness pushed down on her. *Who is it? Who's there?*

A familiar, deep voice. "Tara, can you hear me? Do you know who I am?" Someone had hold of her.

She forced a lid open, but her sight blurred. She blinked to focus on the love of her life.

The sky lived in his eyes.

"Ryan," she whispered, closing her eyes to dream about the one she'd come back for.

🔥

*R*yan couldn't remember the last time he'd prayed. But he was sure doing it now. He must keep Tara alive. Every minute he checked her pulse and breath. Pulse still faint and shallow, quick breaths. Every so often he whispered in her ear to see if she'd respond.

No one spoke during the fast flight to Fairbanks. Silva and Angela's coughs were the only human sounds. All eyes were on Ryan and Tara.

He glanced at Angela, who put her fingertips to her lips and held them out to him. He nodded thanks and held tight to the woman he loved and wasn't willing to live without.

Mel landed Juliet on the helipad in back of the main hospital building. Ryan peered out the window. Medical staff waited with gurneys. Everyone unbuckled, waiting for Mel to shut down the helo.

When the rotors slowed, Gunnar swung the door open. Ryan carefully laid Tara's head down and jumped out, waving in medical staff. "We have several injured firefighters, but this first one needs immediate attention. I'm an EMT. I'll fill you in."

Three paramedics hefted Tara onto a gurney along with her oxygen, and Ryan stepped briskly beside it as they wheeled her toward the open double doors. She was still unconscious.

Ryan briefed the hospital staff what he'd done to revive her. "She has burns on her back side and she inhaled a shitload of smoke." He reached out to brush tendrils from Tara's face, noting much of her long hair had burned off.

Two nurses followed, wheeling Angela on a gurney with Gunnar walking alongside. Two more paramedics loaded Silva into a wheelchair and a nurse pushed him behind the gurneys.

The nurses and paramedics listened wide-eyed, as Ryan explained how both women had survived the burnover in a fire shelter. He stayed alongside Tara as they rolled her into the emergency corridor.

A staff member held up a hand. "You must wait in the lobby, sir."

"Okay. Thanks." He watched Tara disappear behind double doors. Worry and exhaustion mashed his gut.

Gunnar came up behind him. "Come on, bro, take a load off." He gestured to a row of chairs against a wall.

Ryan shuffled over and sank into a chair. Elbows on knees, he rested his head in his hands. Then it hit him like a toppling tree. He could have lost her. What would he have done if he couldn't have revived her?

"You done good, fly-boy." Gunnar grinned. "Those two are damn lucky. Don't think you and me could survive in one shelter. You're too much of a pussy. You'd scream to get out."

"Thanks, Norske." Ryan raised his weary head. "But I'd

rather chew off my arm than cuddle your limp dick in a fire shelter." He leaned his head back on the wall and rolled it to the side, looking out the windows. It was getting darker now that the subarctic summer was half over.

A nurse pushed Silva's wheelchair near the double doors to the ER and stepped away to the main desk. Silva sat with an inhaler, waiting to go inside.

Ryan pushed from his seat and approached him. "Hey Jon, how are you doing?"

Silva looked up at him. "You look how I feel. Like recycled bear shit," he croaked. "Any word on Tara?"

"Not yet. Glad you're okay." He squatted next to the wheelchair. "Got to ask you, Jon. What the hell was Aurora Crew doing in front of a fucking blow-up?" He'd never known Silva to screw up like this.

Silva stared at his lap. "Somehow the lat and longs got messed up. Not sure whether it was ICC's end or my end." He took a draw from his inhaler, paused, then blew out air, shaking his head. "I couldn't breathe, so lost focus on what I was doing."

Ryan waited. He didn't want to press, but he had to write the incident report for Dave Doss. He needed to know how trained, experienced firefighters wound up in such a perilous situation.

"We contained the left flank near the Richardson Highway, then hiked across the black to the right flank. There are five finger ridges on that fucking mountain. The map and the GPS tracker didn't match and we wound up on the wrong ridge. When my asthma kicked in, I told Tara to take charge. She led Aurora Crew out of the ravine."

Ryan pulled the melted, black piece of plastic from his pocket. "You mean this GPS?"

Silva gawked at it. "Tara had that. How did you get it?"

"Found it while looking for her." Ryan sighed and shook his head. "Jon, how the fuck did you pass the pulmonary function test with asthma?" Ryan had tested along with everyone else before fire season. He knew Silva wouldn't have been rehired with an asthmatic condition.

"An ex-girlfriend at the clinic signed off on my paperwork." He gave Ryan a sheepish look. "I guess I'll be in trouble for noncompliance with the IC firefighting directive."

"You're in bigger trouble for falsifying a medical exam. Shit, Jon." He shook his head. "No one was insubordinate in lieu of the situation. But I have to write up what happened for the After-Action Review that Dave Doss will be conducting."

Silva was the last person Ryan would have expected to screw up location coordinates. If it *was* his fault, no one will know until after the AAR. Ryan liked Silva, but he had almost lost Tara. "I won't rat you out for falsifying your medical. That ball is in your court. But when you feel up to it, I'll need your written statement of what happened for my incident report."

Silva winced and gave a small nod. "Thanks to you and Gunnar for your help."

"Glad it worked out. And thanks for helping us transport Tara and Angela."

Silva looked up at him with bloodshot eyes. "I love her, O'Connor. But she chose you." He gave Ryan a desolate look. "Since I had to lose her to someone, it may as well have been your sorry ass."

Ryan gave him a partial smile and patted him on the shoulder. "Get well, dude."

The nurse took hold of the wheelchair and rolled Silva through the double doors.

Ryan peeked in after him to see what he could before the doors swung together. He shuffled over and sank into a seat next to Gunnar. Leaning forward, he rested his elbows on his knees and rubbed the bridge of his nose with thumb and forefinger.

"What a clusterfuck."

Gunnar patted his back and yawned. "It's over, buddy. Get some shut-eye."

"Gunns, go on back to AFS. I'm staying here." Ryan sat upright. "But do me a favor. Tomorrow morning, please talk to Aurora Crew. I'll need a statement from each crew member for my incident report. I'll text you about Angela when I get the skinny."

"Sounds good." Gunnar pulled out his radio to request a shuttle.

"Thanks for today, Gunns. Later, buddy."

Too restless to sit, Ryan pushed off the chair and ambled outside. The red sun no longer hovered on the mountaintops. Now it hid behind them as the days grew shorter. He puttered along a sidewalk and eyed two salmon-pink fireweed stems that had pushed up through a crack in the concrete. The stems still had a few tiers of blossoms left on their final countdown to the end of summer.

He fished out his pocketknife and flicked the blade open with his thumb. He cut the long stems, folded the knife closed, and wandered back inside.

Ryan stuffed the fireweed stems inside his shirt and slid down in his seat. He fetched Tara's bandana from his shirt pocket and spread it over his face to dim the harsh, fluorescent light. Her scent filled his nostrils as he hoped upon hope she'd make it through the night.

He laid his head back and inhaled deeply, letting the bustling activity around him fade into dreamy sleep.

CHAPTER 39

a familiar melody of a decades-old soap opera streamed into Tara's ears and a guy talked about the scrubbing bubbles of Rainspell dish soap. Was she dead? Not unless soap operas were on the other side. She struggled to break the sticky seal of sleep on her eyelids.

Pain erupted everywhere throughout her body. It hurt to breathe and it hurt to move. Her head throbbed, and her entire backside felt like a bad sunburn. Her throat was so dry she couldn't swallow. She tasted burnt charcoal, as if she'd been chewing charred campfire coals.

Her arms rested at her sides and she tried wiggling her fingers. Pain shot through them and up her arms. Forcing heavy lids open, she could make out a TV high on a wall and tried to fix on the moving images. Her head rolled to the side and a plastic tube tugged at her nose. An IV tube inserted in one gauze-wrapped hand led to a saline drip. She opened her mouth to speak and coughed.

"Tara, you're awake," Angela's voice rasped next to her bed. She tossed her magazine and pushed from her chair to stand with crutches.

"Where am I?" Tara croaked out, forcing her lids to open wider.

"Fairbanks Memorial. Thank God you woke up." Angela stood looking down at her, eyes full of tears.

"Am I dead?" Her brain wouldn't work. She couldn't make sense of the bright room and Angela standing there with tears running down her cheeks.

"You *were* dead, and then you weren't and then we worried you would die again." Angela dabbed her eyes with a tissue.

"You're not making sense. Why are you crying?" Tara whispered hoarsely, looking around.

Angela's eyes roamed her face. "You don't remember?"

Tara's mind was a blank. She coughed and lifted a hand to finger strands of stinking, singed hair. The smell shot memory into her like a rocket. Her useless muscles trembled her arms when she lifted them.

"Can you help me lift my sheet? I want to see my legs." She coughed. "Geez, I sound like a DC-10 with asthma."

"Okay." Angela lowered the sheet and pulled Tara's hospital gown above her knees.

Tara scanned her lower body. Gauze wrapped each foot. Scrapes and bruises covered her legs like a camouflage pattern. The backs of her legs stung like mad. "Everything hurts. I'm so thirsty."

Angela offered her a tall plastic glass with ice and a bent straw and the cool water on her throat felt miraculous. She gulped hungrily.

"Whoa, little at a time." Angela winced as she held the straw to Tara's lips.

"What happened to your leg?" rasped Tara, licking her lips. She strained to peek over the side of the bed.

"Dislocated knee. I popped the sucker back in." Angela smiled, motioning to a pair of crutches leaning next to her chair. "I have a knee brace."

"Oh, God." Tara leaned back and closed her eyes, trying to remember. The ravine. The mountain. Angela falling. Her dislocated knee. Carrying her uphill. In the shelter. Fire. Smoke. Then...nothing. Perspiration beaded her forehead as she recalled the sensation of not being able to breathe. Her stomach churned and breaths came short and fast.

"Hon, you're hyperventilating. Slow your breath." Angela waited, then tugged the lid from Tara's glass and held it to her lips. "Chew on ice and hold it in your throat. You'll feel better."

Tara breathed easier and gingerly took small chunks into her mouth. It felt heavenly on her parched throat. Inwardly, she heard Ryan's voice telling her to slow her breathing.

"I begged them to put you and I in the same room when they brought us in. Ryan wanted to stay in here with you, but they wouldn't let him—" Angela choked up.

"Ryan?"

"I did what you said. I stayed in the shelter. You wouldn't answer me, so I stayed still, praying for what seemed like forever. Then I heard Ryan calling your name." Angela's eyes watered.

Tara blinked. She didn't remember Ryan calling her name. Why would he be there? They had been on a rocky ledge in the middle of nowhere.

"Gunnar and Ryan found us in the shelter. We all thought you were dead. The look on Ryan's face...They pulled you off me and laid you on the ground. Ryan pushed on your heart, while Gunnar blew air into you. Ryan wouldn't stop. He wouldn't give up. Took forever to get you breathing..." Angela choked up and glanced out the window.

She looked back at Tara. "Ryan never left your side. He rode in the helicopter with your head in his lap, whispering to you and kissing you. I've never seen anything like it." Angela shook her head, swiping at tears. "Gunnar said he'd never seen Ryan do anything like that."

Tara closed her eyes to remember. The sound of a helicopter...someone with her. Dad and Travis. Wait, she talked to them. Didn't she? Was it real or did she dream it?

"Did the crew make it out okay?"

"Yes, thanks to you." Angela raised her chin to look at her. "Hon, you were sent to Alaska to save the Aurora Crew. And Ryan was destined to fall in love with you. That's why you're here."

Angela's words enveloped Tara like a warm blanket. Gratitude cascaded over her. Ryan and Gunnar had saved her life. Ryan breathed life into her and started her heart. Without him, she wouldn't be here. The reality of what happened slammed her like a brick.

Oh. God.

Tara could not speak. She simply stared at Angela like some divine messenger.

"Here, let's raise the top part of your bed," said Angela, pressing a button. The bed brought Tara to an upright position.

"I need to hug you." Angela gently slid her arms around her. They held each other a long moment before Angela let go. "The nurse said Ryan stayed in the lobby all night. They wouldn't let him in because he wasn't family."

Tara's head spun. She wanted to see Ryan more than anything she had ever wanted in her life. But not like this. God, not like this. She was beat to shit and riddled with white gauze and red skin. Her hair reeked from an experience no human should ever have to endure.

Someone tapped the door and a nurse with a long, black ponytail entered the room. "Good morning, missy! Good to see you awake. Let's check those dressings."

She gave Tara a wide smile and rolled her to her side. "In addition to smoke inhalation, you have multiple burns all along your backside. From what I understand they dropped fire retardant on you just in time or your burns would have been far worse." The nurse smiled and checked Tara's saline drip.

"Is there a firefighter in the lobby?" croaked Tara. "He's—he's family." It was her truth and she was delighted to say it.

"He waited all night to see you. I'll send him in." The nurse left, leaving the door partly open.

"Oh Angie, I must look like that raggedy chick who crawled out of the TV in that horror movie," Tara rasped, smoothing her ratty hair. She pulled off the oxygen tube. When she lifted it from around her neck it became tangled in her hair. She gave up trying to disentangle it.

"I stink like I slept in a fire."

"You did. Trust me, Ryan doesn't give a hoot what you look like. Not after what you've been through." Angela limped over and set a brush in Tara's lap. "Here you go."

Tara tried tugging the brush through her hair when a soft knock on the door made her freeze.

"Everyone decent?" Ryan's voice made her heart jump. The anticipation of seeing him rocketed her over the moon.

"Yes, unfortunately," quipped Angela, tugging her gown higher on her chest.

He poked his head around the door. "Hey, Angela, how's the knee?"

"Better, thanks to you. You're my forever hero, along with Tara and Gunnar."

Ryan smiled and entered the room. "Just doing my job."

"Don't give me that 'aw shucks' business. What you and Gunnar did was miraculous." Angela glanced at Tara, still holding the brush near her hair.

"You and Tara need some privacy. And I need some exercise." Angela hobbled on her crutches to the door. "I'll be back later." She disappeared into the hallway.

Ryan stood in the center of the room looking at her. His blonde-tinged hair stuck out in all directions, and stubble covered his jaw. His sooty shirt was no longer yellow, a striking contrast to the sterile hospital room.

"Waters, you're awake." He came toward her.

"O'Connor, it's really you," she whispered. Her brush clattered to the floor.

He stooped to pick it up. "It's really me."

Every feeling she had for him sped to the surface. He was a magnificent sight and seeing him pooled tears. But she didn't care—she had nothing to prove anymore.

"Thought I'd lost you, Waters."

"You can't get rid of me that easy." She fastened her gaze to his. "You have a habit of saving my life."

He grinned. "Don't take it personally." He moved next to her bed and set the brush on the nightstand.

Tara smiled at him through her tears. "Thought I'd never see you again."

He bent to her, holding her gently, caressing the back of her head as she buried her face in his smoke-drenched Nomex. "To hell with no crying in firefighting," he said softly in her ear.

"Thank you, thank you, thank you…" She sobbed into his shoulder.

Neither would let go. She wished he'd crawl into bed with her so she could hold him closer. She sensed he was as emotional as she was by how tightly he held her…her big, tough smokejumper.

He eased back from her. "You're killing my back, Waters. I need to sit."

"You must be exhausted." She let go and reached for a tissue. "How did you find us?"

"Max radioed AFS about a crew in trouble after he dropped mud on you. Gunnar and I deployed. We didn't know it was Aurora Crew until we got there. Then you and Angela weren't —" he stopped and sat in the chair next to Tara's bed.

Her head spun. "I feel dizzy."

"Why is your oxygen tube hung up in your hair? It's supposed to be in your nose." He worked it from her hair and repositioned it. "Breathe deeply through your nose," ordered Ryan, his gentle bedside manner as professional as any doctor.

"You've given me breathing lessons before," she rasped, her gaze on his face. "My lungs hurt when I breathe."

"After what you've been through, you need to take it easy and mend those lungs."

Tara inhaled the oxygen and her lightheadedness subsided. "Thank you, doctor."

She wanted to touch him. To kiss him. She yanked off her oxygen tube. "Come closer."

"You're as difficult a patient as you are a firefighter," he teased.

"Damn straight," she whispered, reaching for him. "And I have fire breath."

"The best kind." He leaned in and kissed her, his tongue gently parting her lips in a soft, shallow kiss. When he pulled back, something different lived in his eyes. Something gentle.

"You taste good. Minty." She brushed his cheek. "Nice scruff you have going on."

He sat back. "Haven't seen a shaver in a while. I was a little busy rescuing someone who told me she didn't need rescuing." He picked up her brush. "You were about to brush your hair. I'm no hair guy, but I can manage."

"No. Just sit there so I can look at you." She cleared her throat.

Ryan positioned the straw in her water bottle. "Take a drink. You inhaled shitloads of smoke. How your lungs didn't sear is a miracle."

She accepted the bottle and sipped the cool water that soothed her ragged throat.

He tucked a hand inside his shirt and pulled out wilted fire-weed. "*Chamaenerion angustifolium.*" He offered them to her.

She accepted the bright pink flowers, propping up the wilted blossoms. "You picked them before they bloomed."

He laughed. "Fireweed blooms from the bottom up all summer. When the blooms reach the top, it means summer is over."

"What?" A familiar déjà vu waved through her. She looked at him as if he'd sprouted fairy wings.

"I forget. You don't have fireweed in Montana. It's an Alaskan thing."

Her pulse picked up. "Ryan, I talked to my dad. He told me to return to you. He gave me a fireweed and said his summer was over, but mine wasn't. He was as real as you are right now." She stared at the spent flowers. How did Dad know Ryan would give her fireweed? *Did I really die and come back?*

"I thought you said he was deceased. Enjoying those painkillers?" he teased, leaning back to check out the prescriptions on her nightstand.

"Ryan, how long was I—not breathing?"

"I'm guessing at least half an hour, maybe longer. Why?"

"Not only did I see my dad, I talked to Travis and he hugged me."

Ryan sat upright. "You talked to McGuire? What do you mean he hugged you?"

She smiled at the jealous edge to his voice. "Travis told me to come back to you."

Ryan raised his brows. "Oh yeah? Nice of him."

"You don't believe me."

"You've had a traumatic experience. Post-trauma stress is normal after an entrapment in a burnover. It was probably an intense dream."

"I don't think so. It was too real." She *did* experience it. "I was prepared to die in that fire shelter. When I couldn't breathe, this strange peaceful feeling came over me and I wasn't scared anymore. I really do think I crossed to the other side."

"A near-death experience?" Ryan's voice grew quiet.

"I think so." She shuddered at how close she'd come to a fire-fighter's worst nightmare.

"Who am I to say you didn't? I've heard it happens."

"How did Dad know to give me fireweed?"

"Was he ever in Alaska?"

"He fought fires here years ago."

"You said your Dad was a wildland firefighter. But you've never told me about him."

"When have we ever had time to talk? Dad died in our house fire. I wasn't there to save him." She dropped her gaze to her hands. "What's ironic is, he switched to structural firefighting and saved so many people in house fires. The world will never see the next hundred million wonderful things Dad could have done. When I talked to him, he gave me the fireweed and told me to return to you."

She fingered the wilting fireweed in her hand. *No, this wasn't a coincidence…it was a miracle. And a sign. Thank you, Jim Dolan.*

Ryan laid a hand over her bandaged one. "I'm sorry about your Dad. Told you before, don't beat yourself up for those you couldn't save. Tara, you saved your crew. And Angela. Not to mention your own life."

Things seemed clearer to her now. The fears that once controlled her had vanished with the fire.

He lifted her hand and kissed it. "I can't imagine what you went through out there. You're one helluva firefighter."

His words warmed her, but it wasn't something she ever wanted to go through again. They shared silence for a long moment, her bandaged hands resting in his.

She broke it first. "Don't they need you at the Jump Shack?"

"Zombie put me at the bottom of the jump list to give me a breather. But I do have an incident report to write up for Dave Doss's After-Action Review."

"Guess I'm in trouble for leading Aurora Crew away from the right flank."

Ryan shook his head. "Far from it. You made the right decision and saved seventeen people. And a squirrel. If you hadn't, we wouldn't be having this conversation."

"The squirrel made it? Where is he?" Tara loved this bit of news.

"Gunnar put it in his pocket and gave it to the wildlife rescue people."

"With the wolf pups? You jumpers are softies."

Ryan sipped the straw in her water bottle and leaned back in the chair. "I'm proud of you, Montana." He handed her the water bottle.

She sipped. "Right back atcha, California."

"Nope, I'm Alaskan now. And you're on your way to being one."

"Guess we'll have to talk about that."

"Don't worry. We will." He stood to go. "Do you remember what I said to you in the helicopter?"

She smiled. "Is this a trick question? I was slightly out of it."

"You're going to have to remember."

"Did you tell me when I was dead or alive?"

Ryan chuckled. "You do realize not many people can say that."

"Ha, right." She looked into his eyes. "Okay, so—tell me now."

He looked around the room. "Not the time and definitely not the place." He lightly kissed her. "Mm, you taste crispy. But it's time I got back to the salt mine."

"Text me a selfie." She thought a minute. "Oh wait, my phone burned with my pack."

"I'll get you another phone. And I'll ask Rosie to let me in your room so I can bring you some clothes when they release you. Behave yourself. No wild parties." Ryan grinned at Angela as she hobbled into the room on her crutches.

Tara imitated Cameron Frye in *Ferris Bueller.* "Ryan O'Connor, you're my hero."

"Don't let word get around. I don't want wild women all over me. One is enough." He pointed at her and disappeared out the door.

"Later, Captain America," she croaked after him.

"Did you tell him?" Angela looked at her, intent on an answer.

"Tell him what?"

Angela leaned her crutches on her bed and climbed in. "What you made me promise to tell him."

She smiled, remembering her plea to Angela when she thought she would die. "Right. I'll get around to it."

Miraculously, she could now deliver the message herself.

But rather than tell him, she'd prefer to *show* him.

CHAPTER 40

*R*yan strolled into the Jump Shack and spotted his boss. "Hey Zombie, what's up?"

Zombie scowled, clipboard in hand. "How's Aurora Crew? I understand you know one of them a little better than the others." He cleared his throat.

Ryan wouldn't take the bait. "We got everyone out okay."

"Good. Finish your incident report. Doss wants it before his After-Action Review. Use my office." Zombie growled at him. "You and Alexanderson can take a couple of days off. Paid leave, on the house. And get a shower. You stink." He wandered off to the Ready Room.

"Right." Ryan moved to his locker and peeled off his clothes. After one of the best hot showers he'd had in his life, he towel-dried his hair and dressed in his usual cargo pants and T-shirt.

Sitting in Zombie's office, he clicked the government laptop to life and pulled up an Incident Report form. He sat back in the rickety chair and exhaled. He was thankful Tara made it through the night. Her integrity and courage dazzled him. Had he been in her place, he wasn't sure he could have done what she did.

As Ryan typed, Gunnar sauntered in with his digital tablet. "Here you go, bro. Emailed the Aurora Crew info to you."

"Hey, you don't suck so bad." Ryan opened his email and found Gunnar's document. "Zombie gave us a few days off."

"Nice of him." Gunnar sucked on a Dum-Dum, the short white stick poking out of his mouth.

"What's the status on what we talked about in Delta?"

"I talked to Boone. Operation Badass is ready to go. Boone's former SEAL buddies will do it. You'll owe them a Denali flight, a fly-in moose hunting trip, plus a stay at your cabin stocked with fish bait and Alaskan Amber." Gunnar finished his Dum-Dum and licked the stick.

"Oh, is that all? Can't wait to hear the details."

Gunnar grinned. "Like I said, if anyone can get a confession out of Hudson, Boone's buddies will."

🔥

*T*en days later, Tara felt ninety percent better. Her coughing had lessened and although her lungs were still sensitive, she no longer breathed like Darth Vader.

On the morning of her release from the hospital, Tara sat on her bed waiting for Ryan to show with fresh clothes. She glanced at the charred remains of her fire shirt and pants, neatly folded on a table. Thankfully, the Nomex had done its level best to protect her as designed. And God bless Max for dropping mud on their shelter. She intended to thank him sometime.

Someone lightly tapped on the door. "Waters? You decent?" Ryan peeked around it and Tara thought she would faint on the spot. His hair was styled back from his shaved face. Sexy, like a gentle wind had blown every hair in place.

"Whoa, you look a thousand times better. It's a new you." He entered the room, holding a daypack.

"I slept most of the past week." She smiled at him, trying not to gape at his gorgeous transformation.

"Good. I see you got your beauty sleep." Ryan nodded approvingly and held the daypack out to her. "Here's some loose-fitting clothes Liz picked out. If you need help changing…"

"Thanks, but I've got this." She took it with a beguiling smile and headed into the tiny bathroom, closing the door.

"You always say that," he called through the door.

"Because I'm always in control," she hollered back. She couldn't remember when she'd been happier. Standing in front of the mirror, she sized herself up. She was anything but sexy. At least she'd showered and washed her hair.

Before Angela left the hospital she'd given Tara a layered cut, hacking off most of her singed hair. What remained hung just below her shoulders, layered and full. Her waist-long hair was history.

"Nice job, Angie," she breathed. The rest of her was a different story. The gauze no longer covered her hands and feet, but they were red and sore. Ryan said Max's retardant drop had prevented far worse burns on her backside.

She held up a mid-length, denim skirt and a navy-blue tank top, which flared out and away from her sore back. She moved slow putting them on. Her burns still stung, but not as bad as before. She found a new cell phone at the bottom of the pack. She opened the door and held up the phone.

"Is this for me?"

Ryan stood in the middle of the room, staring out the window, his statuesque frame enhanced by the sunlight streaming into the room. Hands in pockets, he turned to look at her.

"A disposable. Has your same cell number."

"Thank you." Her breath caught, thinking she could stand there and watch him all day. "I'll pay you back."

"Yeah, I'm really worried about it."

She'd looked forward to being with him for so long, she

needed her hands on him. Tossing the daypack on the bed, she went to him and wrapped her arms around his waist, touching her lips to his in a soft, light kiss.

He ran his fingers through her much shorter hair. "I like it. It's sexy."

"Most of it burned off, so Angela cut it." She shyly rubbed his chest, under his denim jacket. "No Nomex. Aren't you working today?"

"No. Well kind of."

"I thought Zombie gifted you with a few days of paid annual leave." She leaned her weight on one foot, then the other. The bottoms were still tender.

"He has. I'm taking you somewhere special. But first we have to make a pit stop."

"How mysterious. Then let's go." She couldn't take her eyes off him.

"Dave Doss placed you on admin leave for a few weeks. Longer, if you need it."

Tara opened her mouth to protest, but Ryan interrupted and put a hand up to her. "He didn't give you a choice. You need time to mend." He picked up the daypack from the bed and looked at her. "And make some decisions."

All she wanted was to spend time with him. Right now, he was the only thing that mattered. She was standing here because of him. Her mind whirled with what he had done for her.

Tara took the offer to ride in a wheelchair to the car. The nurse pushed her, and Ryan walked alongside to the blue Mustang he'd parked close to the entrance. He helped her into the passenger seat, taking care with her. Her arm and leg muscles felt better, but were still tender.

Ryan seemed in a hurry as he pointed the Mustang toward Fort Wainwright. He stopped in the AFS parking lot and shut off the ignition.

"Come on. I'll help you."

"Why are we here? Aren't we on leave?"

"You'll see." He stopped and helped her out. She didn't mind leaning on him as he led her into the AFS building and the main conference room full of people. As he escorted her inside, people clapped and cheered.

Ryan squeezed her shoulder, then steered her to one of four chairs at the front of the room next to a podium. Gunnar and Rego occupied two of them.

Tara sat next to Rego and Ryan sat on her other side.

Ryan leaned in. "If I would have told you about this, you wouldn't have come," he said in a deep voice.

She looked at him with a caribou-in-the-headlights expression, then took in the roomful of people. Melbourne waved as he leaned on the back wall, next to Silva. The rest of Aurora Crew stood at the back of the room. Bateman and Robin gave her a thumbs-up.

Dave Doss stepped to the front podium. "Good afternoon, ladies and gentlemen. We're here to honor several firefighters. Their brave actions saved lives."

Cheers resounded from Aurora Crew. Tara grinned at Tupa, who led the whistles and applause.

"First I'd like to recognize an extraordinary woman who performed her duties the way she was trained," said Doss. "Seventeen people returned alive because Tara Waters took decisive action in a dire situation."

"Seventeen people and a squirrel!" yelled Tupa from the back and everyone laughed. Tara made eye contact with him and he dipped his head in a fast nod.

First, Doss read a brief account that Ryan had prepared for him. He finished up and said, "Wildland firefighting remains a dangerous profession. Tara Waters, Nick Rego, Ryan O'Connor, and Gunnar Alexanderson, please stand."

Tara whispered to Ryan. "I want to sit—I can't stand for very long."

"Don't worry. I've got this. And I've got you."

Ryan's sentiment along with his sexy wink galloped a sudden heat through her that she couldn't afford right now in a roomful of people. Unconsciously, she lifted a hand to fan herself, then caught it and folded her hands in her lap.

Ryan stood from his chair with his hand on Tara's shoulder. Gunnar and Rego rose as well.

Doss read off a brief account of what each firefighter did, though most in the room already knew. When he finished, he leaned around the men and motioned at Tara. "Would you like to say a few words?"

She gave him a blank look. "My voice is still shot," she rasped. But not really. The last thing she wanted was to talk about her experience. She wasn't ready—she still grappled with the harsh reality of what'd happened and what'd almost happened.

Ryan patted her shoulder. "No worries. I'll do it for you." He stepped to the podium, commanding the room as he always did. Still a charmer. But now he was *her* charmer.

"This is a story of courage and integrity..." Ryan related the story of how Tara led Aurora Crew out of the ravine, with the help of Rego. How she had gone back for Angela and deployed one shelter, saving them both. When he finished, everyone clapped and cheered.

Tara loved how Ryan could hold a roomful of people in the palm of his hand.

Silva called out from the back of the room. "O'Connor didn't tell you all of it."

Doss motioned Silva to come forward, and he strode to the front, winking at Tara as he came to the podium. An inhaler poked out of his pocket. His secret was obviously out.

"I want to start by saying I owe Aurora Crew and everyone else here an apology. Somehow I screwed up and it nearly cost people their lives."

Tara could have heard a pin drop in the room. She knew how difficult this was for Jon.

"When our helo landed at the burnover entrapment, Ryan and Gunnar were working to revive Tara. O'Connor worked twenty-five minutes to restart her heart and get her lungs going. He stabilized her enough to load her onboard Juliet."

Silva paused to draw from his inhaler. "On behalf of Aurora Crew, I'd like to thank these men for saving the woman who saved our crew. I gave my statement to the After-Action Review team before I resigned from AFS. It's been an honor working with each of you."

"Hey man, anyone could have made that mistake." Rego said it loud for everyone to hear.

"Think they'll let me come back as an arson investigator?" joked Silva, with his charming signature smile. He bent to kiss Tara's cheek and she squeezed his arm.

Ryan spoke up. "And a shout-out to Melbourne Faraday, our revered helo pilot for assisting in the search and rescue for Tara Waters and Angela Divina." Ryan pointed to his introverted friend, still leaning against the back wall.

Mel smiled and tipped his baseball cap. Doss motioned him forward and everyone in the room stood to applaud. Doss gave Tara, Rego, Ryan, and Gunnar a framed certificate and shook each of their hands.

"Tara Waters, it's my understanding you want to be a hotshot. We're offering you the position of crew chief of the AFS White Mountain Hotshots," announced Doss. "But it's also my understanding Aurora Crew has unanimously voted you as their new crew chief. The choice is yours."

Doss's words seemed surreal. Tara's chin dropped as Liz pulled her to her feet and Angela joined them on her crutches for a three-way hug. The rest of Aurora Crew came forward, thanking Tara and shaking her hand.

Tupa solemnly took off his abalone shell, fishhook necklace

and fastened it around Tara's neck. "For *puipuiga*, protection. We are family. Here's our ceremonial tribute to you."

Tupa and the rest of the Afi Slayers Squad formed a line and did an abbreviated version of the Haka. They slapped and stomped, their grunts and cries solid as any New Zealand All Blacks' pre-game chant. People loved it and when they finished, more cheering ensued.

"Now that's team-work. You guys should take it on the road," laughed Tara, impressed her Afi Slayers Squad had perfected their moves in complete unison. Warmth flowed through her as Tupa's words echoed in her brain.

We are family.

🔥

*A*fter the formalities, Ryan drove Tara to downtown Fairbanks and pulled into the crowded parking lot of Snowcastle Bar & Restaurant. He hopped out and opened her door. He took her hand to help her out. He couldn't wait to be alone with her. "Aurora has been given the day off and wanted to surprise you with a party. How could I say no?"

"You couldn't. Or Tupa and Rego would pummel you. But I don't want to stay long."

"We won't," promised Ryan. "But you need to make an appearance." He opened a rear door to the party room entrance, then slid his arm around her waist, taking care with her burns.

His eyes slowly adjusted to the dark interior of the backroom of the bar. Cheers went up as they walked in, beer bottles and pint draughts raised in homage.

"Let's hear it for Ryan and Tara. Woot, woot!" It occurred to Ryan they sounded like a flock of inebriated owls.

"About time you two showed up," croaked Silva from his seat at a large round table.

Pizza dotted the tables along with pitchers of Alaskan Amber.

Ryan spotted Gunnar and Angela curled around each other in a dark corner and doing what Ryan wished he were doing with Tara about now. Liz rested her forearms on an old-fashioned juke box, feeding it coins. She chose a song, then pointed at Ryan and Tara.

"You two. Front and center." Liz snapped her fingers and motioned them to the dance floor as *Burnin' For You* played, by the Blue Oyster Cult. One of Aurora Crew's favorite songs.

"Hey, the more cowbell guys," someone yelled, and everyone laughed.

When the song ended, Liz selected *Smoke Gets in Your Eyes.* Ryan drew Tara to him in a tight, slow dance. He loved the feel of her and slipped an arm around her waist.

She spoke in his ear. "Have you ever seen the movie, *Always?*"

"Yeah, Richard Dreyfuss and Audrey Hepburn. Spielberg movie."

"Get out. You've seen it?"

He chuckled. "Well yeah. It's about wildland firefighting. As I recall, the tanker pilot survived, like you did. It was a miracle."

"Only because of you." She gazed at him like he was the only person in the world.

"I did what I was trained to do, just as you did." He pulled her close and she rested her head on his shoulder.

Silva pulled Liz out for a slow dance. He repeatedly placed his hands on her ass and she repeatedly brushed them off. Silva caught Ryan's eye and lifted his brows in a can't-blame-me-for-trying look.

After Jon resigned from AFS, he applied for an EMT job at the hospital. He told Ryan he planned to finish his certification for arson investigation. But first he had to go to California to help with the family winery. Ryan noted Jon was back to his charming self, putting his signature moves on Liz.

The song ended and Tara's phone sounded. Ryan let go of

her and she tapped to answer. "Jim? How are you?" She gestured a wait-a-minute, then went outside to talk.

After a while Tara came back in and grasped Ryan's hand, grinning from ear to ear. "That was Jim Dolan in Missoula. The Forest Service offered me the crew boss position for the Lolo Interagency Hotshot Crew. Can you believe it? It's what I've always wanted. I have to tell Angie." She crossed the room to find her.

Ryan wouldn't ruin Tara's joyful moment by asking her to give up her dream job to stay in Alaska. Half of the fire season remained. What a disappointment it would be if she were to return to Montana. Ryan pulled up a chair to the round poker table as a pang zinged his chest.

Silva, Liz, Rego, and Boone sat around the table playing strip poker. Rego was shitfaced. He held a cigar stump between his teeth, oblivious to cards now and then dropping from his poker hand. He had stripped down to his boxers, with only his furry chest visible above the table.

Liz sat next to him and reached over to rub her hand on his hairy chest. She looked up at Ryan and winked, her hands full of cards. "I do this for good luck."

Rego protested. "Hey! Get out of my goodies. O'Connor, she's harassing me." He pointed at Liz, pretending to be offended.

Ryan couldn't help laughing. Rego had turned out to be an okay guy.

Tara returned and seated herself next to Ryan at the poker table. She reached under it and squeezed his leg. Ryan put his arm around her.

Rego abruptly stood and another card fell from his hand. "Let's toast Tara Waters! The best woman in fire." He raised his beer. "You can be my crew boss anytime."

Everyone clapped and cheered. Ryan liked how people

respected and admired Tara. And she was his. *I must convince her to stay.*

Rego dipped into his meager coin pile and flicked one at Ryan. "O'Connor, play *North to Alaska*, by Johnny Horton."

Ryan grinned at him and went to the antique jukebox. He marveled at how all the old jukeboxes with vinyl seemed to wind up in Alaska. When he returned to the table, Liz was down to jeans and a lacy bra, not the least inhibited. He chuckled, considering what else she did for a living.

Silva was also feeling no pain and employed his full arsenal to win her affection. "Liz, you're my new superhero. I love you."

"Well, sweetie, I guess it's okay since we don't work together anymore." Liz gave Silva a peck on the cheek, then caught Ryan's eye. "What's a girl to do?"

Yes, thought Ryan, gazing at Tara.

What *was* a girl to do?

CHAPTER 41

*W*hen Tupa and the rest of the Afi Slayers squad began the Haka, Ryan suggested that he and Tara should make their getaway. They edged their way out the door into the much quieter afternoon.

Angela hobbled after them on her crutches. "Tara, hold up. Go on ahead, Ryan honey. I want to talk to Tara." She waved him ahead to his Mustang, then handed Tara a small, gift-wrapped box with a blue bow.

"You won't have this on long, but that's the whole idea."

Tara took the box and hugged her friend. "Angie, thanks. I don't know what to say."

"You risked your life for me. I'll never forget it. Can't wait for you to be our crew boss." Angela pressed a couple of flat packets into Tara's palm and folded her fingers over them. "Be safe." She winked and hobbled inside, working her crutches like she'd been on them all her life.

Angela's words meant everything to Tara, yet twisted her heart, knowing the looming decision she had to make. But not now. All she could think of was spending alone time with Ryan.

Ryan had her door open and he stood next to his. "What did she give you?"

"This box." Tara could hardly keep a straight face that Angela carried condoms. When Ryan fished for his keys, Tara jammed the packets into her skirt pocket.

Gunnar abruptly appeared as Tara was about to get in the car. "Ryno, before you go. I have an Operation Badass report."

"What's that?" Tara looked from Gunnar to Ryan.

Ryan shrugged and gave her an innocent look. He wandered over to Tara's side of the car.

"I'll explain. No, that'll take too long." Gunnar held up a thumb drive. "Instead I'll tell you. This is a recorded confession of Mike Hudson. How did I get this, you may ask?"

Ryan slid on his Ray Bans and smiled.

Gunnar grinned back. "Operation Badass was a howling success. Shortly after Hudson got out of the hospital, Those-Who-Shall-Not-Be-Named dangled him below an unidentified rotor aircraft, flew over a fire and threatened to toast him like a marshmallow. When they reeled him in, Those-Who-Shall-Not-Be-Named made him confess. Made him retract his lies about Tara and post apologies on social media. He admitted to sabotaging Angela's pack test and harassing women firefighters. Best of all, no fire personnel or aircraft were involved in the making of this recording." Gunnar seemed proud of his disclaimer.

Tara stood still, her mouth hanging open.

"Nice work, Gunns." Ryan grinned.

"Let's put it this way," crowed Gunnar. "That little dick won't be on a fire ever again. Hudson's Stepdaddy, AFS Director, Duncan Martelle, received a copy of the recording in snail mail." Gunnar straightened, like a noble warrior. "Am I a good bro or what?"

"You've gone above and beyond." Ryan glanced at Tara.

She widened her eyes at him in a what-the-hell-did-you-do look.

"Miz Waters, thou shalt not speak a word of this, but thought you should be privy," hiccupped Gunnar.

"But won't Hudson tell HR what they did?" Tara was incredulous. *Do I really want to know the whole story?*

"Hard to identify people when you're blindfolded. No one would believe that perverted little dick anyway."

"Gunns, you've outdone yourself," laughed Ryan.

"You owe me a Denali flight, bro. And a stay at your cabin. With beer."

"Here." Ryan reached in his pocket and tossed keys to his buddy. "The place is yours for a few days. We'll fly after season ends." He winked at Tara. "With another seasoned passenger along."

"You kids behave." Gunnar pointed at them. "On second thought, don't do that. What the hell am I saying?" Gunnar gave them an un-military salute and headed into Snowcastle.

Tara always thought Gunnar's ego had its own zip code, but she liked him. He would do anything for his jump partner. She smiled that some things never changed.

Ryan gazed at her provocatively across the roof of his car. "Ready to blow this pop-stand?"

She lowered her sunglasses. "I was born ready. Can't wait to show you how much I lov—" She stopped herself. "Um...how much I love—riding in your Mustang." She opened the door and eased herself into the passenger seat.

This isn't the time or place.

He climbed in beside her. "So, you love riding in this car. When you feel up to it, you should drive it." His eyes stayed on her.

She looked at him. "Why are you looking at me like that?"

"For a minute there I thought you were going to say something else."

"Did you now." She smiled out the side window as he started the car and pulled out of the parking lot.

Soon they were on the highway heading northeast of Fairbanks. Tara leaned her head back, enjoying the sun's warmth through the windshield. She needed time to think: Crew chief of the AFS White Mountain Hotshots, crew chief of her coveted Lolo Hotshot Crew, and crew chief of Aurora were all wonderful options. But she was too overwhelmed to make decisions right now. She was happy to finally spend time with Ryan, away from planes and fires.

"What's in the box?" he asked, nodding at her lap.

She snapped from her thoughts. "Should I wait or open it now?"

"Why wait? Open it."

Tara pulled off the bow and tore at the wrapping. She opened the box and lifted out a dark green piece of silky lingerie, holding it up by the spaghetti straps. "Victoria's Secret."

Ryan gave it a once over. "Nice. Too bad you won't have it on long."

She shot him a look. "That's what Angela said."

"Great minds think alike." He adjusted his Ray Bans, smiling at the windshield. "I've always wondered what Victoria's secret was."

Ryan slowed the car and turned right at a mile-marker sign. He drove a quarter of a mile and parked in front of a rectangular building, surrounded by a tall, chain-link fence, a 'Wildlife Rescue' sign on the gate.

"Wait here a minute." He got out and disappeared into the building.

Tara opened her door and inhaled the cool breeze of the sunny Alaska afternoon. Fireweed abounded everywhere. The flowers held significance for her now.

He returned and took her hand. "Come on."

A woman led them to a gate to a fenced compound next to the building. Tara heard animal noises. Most notably, howling. "Good thing you called ahead for an appointment. We close early today." The woman led them through the gate. She entered an enclosed pen and came back out, cradling a wolf pup under each arm. "Your boyfriend thought you'd like to hold one of the wolf pups he saved."

My boyfriend. Tara smiled and shot Ryan a happy look. "Oh yes, I would love to hold one."

The woman held out a wriggling pup, the same gray one Ryan held on TV. He stood back, enjoying the moment, while Tara snuggled the furry male, busy licking her hand.

"They've almost doubled in size in just a few weeks," said Ryan.

"This little guy consumes as much as he weighs every day. Careful, they have sharp claws. We clip them, but they grow fast." The woman gave Ryan the other wolf pup to hold. "A fire-fighter from a village crew found mama wolf near the Bettles fire. She was near death when he brought her to us. We nursed her back to health and have been re-introducing her litter."

Ryan's head snapped up. "I think I met that same wolf. She chose not to eat me and ran off."

The woman smiled. "She's not ready for visitors yet. She's still getting used to us. Come back in a few weeks and you can see her."

"You never mentioned mama wolf." Tara grinned up at him.

"I'll save that story for later." Ryan scratched the wolf pup behind the ears and the contented pup wiggled his hind foot.

Tara lowered herself to the grass, taking care with her sore back and legs. She let the male pup ramble around her, sniffing. He pounced on her shoelace, snagging it with sharp teeth, and made a puppy growl. She picked him up, stroking his fur. "You'll be back in the wild someday, you know."

Ryan took photos and videos of Tara with his cell phone, while she played with the baby wolf. She held him next to her face, posing. The pup squirmed and bit her nose. "Ow, you little devil. Your teeth are sharp."

"It's dinnertime," laughed the woman, offering to take the pup. "This one gets feisty if he isn't fed on time."

"Thank you for letting us spend time with them." Tara smiled. Then she remembered. "Oh, how's the squirrel from the fire?"

The woman crooked her finger. "Follow me."

Tara followed her into a room. The squirrel was recuperating in a cage, its tail singed and a rear leg in a tiny splint. "Hey, it's me. Remember, in the fire shelter?" Tara said to the squirrel.

Ryan stood behind her. "He hasn't a clue what you're saying."

The squirrel nibbled a nut and whipped his singed tail. "I'm glad he made it without you having to give him CPR." Tara glanced back at the gorgeous man standing behind her and noticed the woman gaping at him. Ryan was indeed a remarkable sight, all cleaned up, wearing jeans and a form-fitting shirt, accentuating his wide shoulders and muscled body.

"Thanks so much," she said to the woman.

"You're welcome, Miss. You were lucky from what I understand." She turned to Ryan. "And thanks to both of you for risking your lives to protect our wildlands and for bringing us the animals," she gushed at him.

"Here's something to help feed the critters." He pulled some bills from his wallet. "Thanks for staying open for us."

Ryan deeply touched Tara by arranging this. Once in the car, she squeezed his arm. "Thank you. That was incredible."

"I remembered you saying you wished you could hold one." He handed her his phone.

"How on earth did you remember that?" She swiped through the photos.

"I pay attention." He glanced at her and pulled the car onto the highway.

"That woman was crushing on you, O'Connor. Must be nice

to have every woman worship at your feet." She lifted her sunglasses at him.

"Only want one. No one else holds a candle to her." He squeezed her thigh and a rush zoomed through her.

She had much to tell him and now was as good a time as any. "I haven't had a chance to explain what happened with Hudson."

"It's a done deal now. He's been dealt with." Ryan's gaze stayed on the road.

"But I want you to know what happened." She filled him in with details of how Hudson threatened her.

"If I'd known..." He gripped the steering wheel and blew out air like a prizefighter. "Maybe it's a good thing you didn't tell me. I threatened the lying scum in the hospital. That's how I got this." He fished her faded orange bandana from his shirt pocket and offered it to her.

"You got it back! You did that for me?" She took the grimy, worn cloth from him and clutched it with both hands. "I wanted to tell you what Hudson did when you came up to fire camp. There wasn't time, and then hearing about Travis..." She turned toward her window. "Well, he may have cheated on me, but he didn't deserve to die."

"I know." Ryan rested his hand on her thigh. "But I'm proud of you for reporting Hudson. He'll never work another fire."

She folded the orange bandana. "I don't need this now. Don't have to rely on luck anymore. I've faced down the red monster and lived to tell the tale. Keep it for me." She handed it back to him.

"You sure?"

She nodded.

He stuffed it back in his pocket.

"I was afraid you'd believe those awful rumors Hudson spread around," said Tara.

"Like I have time to go on social media. Besides, you said not to believe them. So, I didn't."

"Does that mean you'll always do what I say?"

He gave her a mischievous grin. "Depends. But I do have one question. What did Tupa mean when he said you have a mean knockout punch?"

Tara gave him a look of surprise. "Oh, you heard about that. That night at the Yukon Roadhouse, Hudson groped me, so I decked him. Didn't know I had the strength to knock him across the room."

Ryan laughed. "Oh man, I would have given anything to see that one. Waters, you continue to amaze." He smiled out the windshield.

A half hour later, Ryan pulled into Chena Hot Springs Resort. They got out and gathered their gear. "You're going to like this."

"It's beautiful." She took in the dense birch and spruce surrounding the hotel and pool, along with hanging flower baskets of fuchsia, geranium, and purple lobelia.

"The hot springs are over there." He dipped his chin toward an area lined with huge boulders and steam rising on the other side of the main building. "We'll explore later."

She took in the gently sloping mountains lush with Alpine fir and aspen trees. And no smell of fire.

Once they checked in, Ryan led her to a grand suite, a corner room he'd reserved for the next few days. When he flung open the door, she went back in time.

She loved the Alaskana décor: knotty cedar ceilings, moose silhouette lamp shades, and a glass coffee table supported with antlers. French doors opened onto a deck laden with flower baskets filled with marigolds and purple lobelia, trailing in a soft breeze. A small glass table with two chairs sat on one side of the deck. Thick, cozy throw rugs graced every room. A colorful quilt depicting sub-arctic landscapes rested on a king-size poster bed.

Felt like home.

"Nothing but the best." Ryan moved to a round, oak table by a picture window and uncorked a bottle of Merlot. He poured two glasses.

"I had no idea Alaskan smokejumpers were so classy," she said out the side of her mouth, grinning.

"We're not animals. Well, except maybe on fire and...on other occasions." He gave her a seductive look. "You may be a kickass firefighter, but you're still a woman who deserves classy treatment."

"I should be doing all of this for you, after what you've done for me."

"Don't go thinking you owe me for saving your life...twice now. But who's counting?" he teased, offering her a glass of wine. "What were you about to tell me when we left Snowcastle?"

"You're putting me on the spot."

He gave her a wry smile. "You're a quick study, Waters."

"Did Angela say anything to you when...did she mention something I made her promise to tell you?" Her eyes roamed his face.

He swirled his glass and stared into it. "She did."

Tara's heart ticked up and she turned to the window, taking in the velvet mountains. "Word travels fast. Can't believe Dolan offered me crew boss of the Lolo Hotshots. It's what I've always wanted and now it's been dumped in my lap." A cluster of fireweed caught her eye, waving in the breeze. She stared at it. *Another sign?*

"You've been offered the same or better here in Alaska."

She turned away from the window and faced him. "I miss my crew back home."

He took her glass and set it on the table, along with his own. "Look, I can make this decision easier." He took her in his arms and kissed her deep, sending an aching need down low. When he finished, he nibbled his way down the side of her neck.

"Oh God. Not fair," she whispered, her fingers in his hair. Her mind reeled. He felt so good. She wanted more.

Instead he pulled back and lifted her chin. "What's your gut telling you? Just say it. What's it telling you?"

She shook her head. "I need time to think."

"No. You don't. I'll lay it out for you. When I found you not breathing and your heart stopped, the thought of losing you was unthinkable. I couldn't let you die on me. I refused to leave that damn mountain without you. I prayed you'd come back to me— and I don't pray." He dropped his hands and narrowed his gaze.

"I've been offered my dream job," she said simply.

He shook his head. "Is being a Lolo Hotshot more important than where you have family? Here's how we roll in Alaska. Most of us are apart from our Lower Forty-eight families. Friends and co-workers become our family. Tupa gave you his necklace for a reason. Family doesn't have to be blood, Tara."

She looked away, fingering the necklace Tupa had placed around her neck.

He stepped back, raised his arms, and dropped them. "What is it you really fucking want?"

She squeezed her eyes closed. Ryan deserved honesty. *Tell him now.*

"You." She opened her eyes. "It's always been you. At first, I was afraid you'd hurt me the same way Travis did. But after damn near dying, when I thought I'd never see you again—" her voice caught, and she struggled for composure. "You're the closest thing to family that I have, and I've only known you a short while."

He grasped her hands. "You need to see yourself through my eyes. I see a strong, capable, smart woman. You don't have to be a Lolo Hotshot to be your father's legacy. You already are. And you don't have to prove yourself to anyone, especially your dad. He's gone. Let him go. You were no more responsible for his death than you were the man in the Copper Peak Fire."

Funny, Dad had said the same thing. "And you were no more responsible for the family in California," she said quietly. "I'd say you've evened that score. You saved me twice. In two different states. God, what does that say about me?"

"That you care about others more than yourself." He seemed to see into her very soul. "You know, both of us need to get over our fucking guilt. We can't be prisoners of the past. The past teaches us lessons, but it's not intended as a life sentence. If we allow ourselves to be affected by every death, we'll have a tough time moving forward." He let go of her hands and picked up his wine glass. "I'll make you a deal. How about we both get professional counseling, then we can be each other's shrinks?"

Tara locked onto the sincerity in his eyes. "You mean like, together?"

"Why not? We're both struggling with the same thing, only on a different scale."

"Okay, deal. Let's do it soon. Together."

"I'll arrange it. Mel knows a good one." He emptied his glass and set it down.

"Just so you know, I said goodbye to my dad. I *have* let him go." She watched Rufous hummingbirds circle a feeder outside the picture window, then looked up at him. "In the helicopter. Did you say you loved me? Or did I dream it?"

"You *do* remember." He pulled her into his arms. "You didn't dream it. When you opened your eyes and said my name, I told you I loved you."

She drew back to look at him. "In the fire shelter, the thought of never seeing you again was excruciating. But the hope of seeing you again made me fight for every blessed breath. You're the miracle." She paused a moment. "I've loved you from the minute your head plopped onto my shoulder on that bumpy flight to Fairbanks."

He laughed. "Why didn't you say so? We could have joined the Mile-High Club."

She raised a brow. "We still can. It'd be fun to see how two tall people navigate a tiny restroom on a 737."

"Who needs a restroom? That's why God invented beds." He dipped his chin toward the California king, his hands on her shoulders.

"Ryan...I don't want what happened to Travis to happen to you."

"Don't think like that. It will drive you crazy. What we do is dangerous and we're both adrenaline junkies. If we move forward together, we'd better be damn good at our jobs, right? No more close calls."

Tara reached for the bottle of wine and refilled their wine glasses. She brushed her finger over an antlered moose etched on the glass and stepped to the window, watching the humming-birds. "Move forward together?"

"You're a born leader. I'd work on a fire with you as the crew boss any day. Stay in Alaska for the rest of fire season. Because after that..."

"After that, what?" She turned to him expectantly, prepared for unwelcome news.

He sipped his wine. "I'm taking you to the American Riviera."

She watched him empty the bottle into his glass. "Something tells me I should know where that is."

"You'll know when you see it." He raked his eyes up and down her frame, his gaze searing her like blue fire. "Come here."

"No."

Her turn for an up and down assessment. Holding her wine glass, she assumed an appraisal stance and pursed her lips. She twirled a forefinger. "First, give us a spin."

He spread his arms and turned in a slow circle. "Do I measure up to your standards?"

"We'll see." She regarded him thoughtfully. It took every ounce of control to keep from launching herself at him.

I love Ryan O'Connor. He's worth the risk. And I love Aurora Crew, my new family.

There it was. Her simple, undeniable truth. "All right, O'Connor." She plunked her glass on the table and pulled off her tank top. She hadn't worn a bra since the fire. Standing there topless, she smiled.

Ryan choked on his wine. "Damn, get to the point, Waters." He slammed his wine glass on the table so hard, the stem broke —obviously stunned by her sudden release of clothes.

She laughed, tossing her hair back. "Ready to make love to an Alaskan firefighter?" Eyes latching onto his, she moved close and kissed him tenderly, her love flowing to him like the Chena River.

"Knew you'd see it my way," he said against her lips. He had her out of the rest of her clothes in record time.

Watching him shed his own clothes made her weak in the knees. Aroused at seeing him naked in broad daylight, she backed up and sat on the edge of the bed. Her back smarted a little and she furrowed her brow. "My burns—I can't lie on my back."

"I'm a smokejumper, remember? We're known for hitting our jump spots without causing injury." He gently picked her up, taking exceptional care to ease her down onto her side. He positioned himself on his side, facing her.

"The first time we made love, you said you had an Incident Action Plan for dating me. From now on when I attend an IAP fire briefing, I'll think of you." She gave him a heavy-lidded look.

His hand slid down her side, dipping at her waist and rising to her hip. "I have an IAP for everything. Even now. I have one to carry out our objective and complete our mission without hurting you," he breathed, pressing into her and kissing her neck. "I'm very procedural."

"*Our* mission?"

"Takes teamwork." He kissed her ear and licked below her

365

lobe, sending her to the moon. "Standard operating procedures..." He kissed his way to her neck. "Knowing our priorities, having adequate resources..." He kissed one breast, then the other. "To coordinate our activity, while ensuring safety." He produced a condom, twirling the packet between his fingers.

She burst out laughing at his safety moment.

"Let's jump this fire, baby." He rolled onto his back. "You're on top."

"You may be incident commander of this mission. But when these burns heal, watch out, when I'm the I.C." She straddled him and maneuvered him inside of her.

He moaned and his breathing became ragged. "Copy that."

God, she loved looking at him. *She loved loving him.*

She trusted Ryan to forever guarantee her safe landings. For the rest of their time off, he aimed for new colors to add to her rainbow of ecstasy each time she careened over the edge. He liked keeping track of her colors, so he could aim for a personal best to generate new ones the next time. She loved his careful attention to detail.

When they woke on the last day of their stay, Tara eased herself on top of his morning erection and rocked gently back and forth. After flying over their rainbows, she fell forward to Ryan's chest, breathing hard.

"I could get used to this," he murmured, his heartbeat pulsing under her. His skin glistened and damp hair matted his forehead.

The bed shook steadily for a few seconds.

Tara sat up at attention. "Oh my God, the earth moved."

He folded his arms behind his head and grinned. "Wow, so I have that effect, huh? What colors that time?"

"No, Ryan, the earth really did move. Didn't you feel it?"

"I was slightly occupied. Must have been an earthquake. Get used to them, my cheechako. Meanwhile, I'll do everything I can to shake the earth for you. Every. Single. Time." He pulled her down to kiss her.

She loved going the distance with him. As firefighters. Co-workers. Friends. Lovers. *Family*. He was right; family didn't always have to be blood.

After round three, she rolled off him and snuggled into his side. Dragging her fingers across his chest, she noted goose-bumps. "Where's the American Riviera?"

"Any place warm, where there's no fire."

She trailed her fingertips down his rippled abdomen. "Ryan."

He shivered and his breath caught. "Uh-huh."

She had him where she wanted him. "I love you. I know Angela told you, but I want you to hear it from me." She kissed his chest and his stomach, working her way south. "Copy?"

"Yeah…oh yeah, copy. You make me happy. And not only because of what you're doing right now." Ryan let out a long, low moan, making her heart cartwheel.

It had been a long while since she had made someone genuinely happy. And ironically, another smokejumper. But this one was a keeper. Her Alaska spark had erupted into a full-blown conflagration that could not and would not be contained. It would flame on, forever uncontrolled.

And she was more than okay with that.

I hope you enjoyed reading *ALASKA SPARK*!

Please take a moment to post a review of this book on Amazon, Goodreads, or Bookbub! Reviews make a difference for an author's success as a writer and they help readers discover the story. I would very much appreciate it. Thank you!
https://amzn.to/3beo8rv

You can join LoLo Paige's spam-free mailing list to find out about the releases and giveaways for the rest of the *Blazing Hearts Wildfire Series* at:
www.lolopaige.com

You can visit LoLo Paige on Facebook here:
www.facebook.com/LoLoPaigewildlandfire

Don't forget to listen to the **ALASKA SPARK** playlist on Spotify, where the songs follow the storyline. I had fun putting this together at:
https://spoti.fi/2Y53gim

Thank You! ~ LoLo Paige

ACKNOWLEDGMENTS

Grateful to all who helped make this book happen by reviewing early drafts, beta reading, or by moral support: Katy Nerlfi, Margie Faraday, Lasairiona McMaster, April Maye, Ginny Rollman, Dot Tideman, Paulette Scherr, Judy Winslow, Marla Murphy, Kathleen Means, Sheila Hall, Sally Freytag, Kay Schaefer, Russ Lawrence, Boone Brux, and Christiane Allison.

Alaska Chapter of Romance Writers of America (AKRWA) critique groups, for support and encouragement: Karen Kiely, Neva Post, Elizabeth Grover, Lynn Lovegreen, Katie Martin, and Emma Butler.

Bruce "Buck" Nelson, retired Alaskan smokejumper, for smokejumper perspective and expertise; and for the use of his photos for promotion at www.bucktrack.com.

Bobbi Doss, my active firefighter consultant with the Hellsgate Fire Dept., Star Valley, Arizona, and many thanks for the use of her photos for book promotion.

S. R. Cyres of Anchorage, for his insightful poem at the beginning of the book.

Debra Eckerling, for encouraging me to set goals to finish this novel.

Angela Ackerman and Becca Puglisi at *One Stop for Writers*, for help, support, and encouragement.

Kevin Potter for promotional help with blurbs and Jessyca Barney with photos.

The U.S. Bureau of Land Management, Alaska Fire Service, the National Interagency Fire Center, and the U.S. Forest Service websites.

Thanks to my fellow Alaskan authors for help, support and encouragement: Tamsin Ley, E.M. Shue, Erin McLellan, Maxine Mansfield, Keenan Powell, Craig Martelle, and Marc Cameron; and Lower 48 authors, Sandra Woffington and Karen Stillwagon.

Legacy Dental Arts, Eagle River, AK for listening to my story ideas and making suggestions while my mouth was full of lidocaine: Dr. Penfield, Cari, Bri, and the rest of the staff.

20Booksto50K and the SPF Facebook Community authors for education on all things writing.

ABOUT THE AUTHOR

In 2015, *The Anchorage Press* published a nonfiction story about a narrow escape while fighting a fire in Alaska's wild Interior. The following year, *Embers of Memories* won an Alaska Press Club award for the best historical piece in all media and suggested turning it into a novel. Four years later, the suggestion became reality.

 In 2019, Book One of the *Blazing Hearts Wildfire Series*, ALASKA SPARK won the honor as a finalist in the Romance Writers of America, Wisconsin Chapter, Fab Five novel contest, competing with writers from around the country. While this is a work of fiction, it is loosely based on true life events. The author has lived in Alaska most of her life. Early in her federal career, she worked as a wildland firefighter for the U.S. Forest Service and the U.S. Bureau of Land Management, having fought fires in Montana, California, and Alaska.

ALSO BY LOLO PAIGE

ALASKA INFERNO
Book Two of the Blazing Hearts Wildfire Series

When *ALASKA SPARKS* Jon Silva left firefighting, that didn't mean he left fire! He's back as a fire investigator, along with the Aurora Crew in Book Two, *ALASKA INFERNO*.

Liz Harrington has a longstanding attraction to Jon Silva after helping him narrowly escape a runaway fire last season. The feeling is mutual, only Jon isn't sure he wants serious involvement with a stripper. Besides, they have nothing in common—and can't seem to agree on anything. But a no-strings-attached fling with the charming Jon Silva might not be out of the question...provided there's no emotional entanglements. Nothing will stand in Liz's way to earn money fighting fires to start up her new business.

Someone is setting a series of fires on the Kenai Peninsula and Jon is summoned to investigate. He reluctantly encounters his ex-wife, who decides she wants him back—and she'll stop at nothing to have him. But when Jon discovers some explosive secrets, his world blows apart. And while Liz and the Aurora Crew fight the largest, most dangerous fire in Alaska's history, Liz learns her business partners are swindling her.

As the firestorm rages on, Liz and Jon are forced to make crucial decisions that could prove disastrous for both of them. Can Liz and Jon overcome the lethal forces determined to keep them apart?

Romance, fire, and arson...another deadly mix!